Melisande looked at him with delight, taking in every detail: the elegant clothes, the hair slightly graying at the temples, the rather cold gray eyes, the stern mouth; she decided he was somewhat formidable, but everything a guardian ought to be.

"So, Monsieur," she said, "you are my guardian."

"I . . . I knew your father."

"Oh, please tell me. I have so often wondered. What was my father like? Where is he now? Why was I left at the convent? Is he still alive?"

"Your father was a gentleman," he said.

"And my mother?"

"Your mother died very soon after you were born."

"And it was you who sent me to the Convent?"

"The education which has been given you here is as good as any you could get. . . . I was persuaded."

She laughed and, because he looked surprised, she said: "I am only laughing because I am pleased. No one has been really interested in me before."

Also by Jean Plaidy
Published by Fawcett Books:

LILITH

The Queens of England Series:
QUEEN OF THIS REALM
VICTORIA VICTORIOUS
THE LADY IN THE TOWER
THE QUEEN'S SECRET
THE RELUCTANT QUEEN

The Georgian Saga:
THE PRINCESS OF CELLE
QUEEN IN WAITING
CAROLINE, THE QUEEN
THE PRINCE AND THE QUAKERESS
THE THIRD GEORGE
SWEET LASS OF RICHMOND HILL
INDISCRETIONS OF THE QUEEN
THE REGENT'S DAUGHTER
GODDESS OF THE GREEN ROOM
VICTORIA IN THE WINGS

MELISANDE

Jean Plaidy

Formerly titled: IT BEGAN IN VAUXHALL GARDENS

FAWCETT CREST • NEW YORK

A Fawcett Crest Book
Published by Ballantine Books
Copyright © 1955, 1968 by Jean Plaidy

All rights reserved under International and Pan-American Copyright Conventions. Published in the United States by Ballantine Books, a division of Random House, Inc., New York. First American edition published by G. P. Putnam's Sons under the title *It Began in Vauxhall Gardens* in 1991.

Library of Congress Catalog Card Number: 90-15551

ISBN 0-449-22191-1

This edition published by arrangement with G. P. Putnam's Sons

Manufactured in the United States of America

First Ballantine Books Edition: October 1993

CONTENTS

PART ONE

The Convent

One

The Convent Notre Dame Marie stood on an incline above the town—of it and yet apart from it. Like a guardian fortress, it commanded views of the winding river. Its hard granite walls seemed to stand in defiance of intruders and in contemptuous scorn of the ruined château which occupied a similar position on the opposite side of the river.

It was said that both Convent and château had been built long before the days of gay King François, and that when that King had passed along the river, he had lingered. Beautiful buildings attracted him as did beautiful women, and he had taken a fancy to the château and the town's girls. He had extended the château and dallied with the women of the town until, tiring of them both, he passed on.

As the Mother Superior was fond of pointing out, the residents of the château had been Revelry and Sin; and now it was nothing but a ruin—a pile of stones here, the remains of a wall there, a spot to which people might climb in order to enjoy a picnic. Last year an Englishman had broken his leg scrambling over the ruins and had had to spend many weeks at the *Auberge Lefevre*, to his great discomfort but to the considerable profit of the Lefevres. Yes, the château represented Sin and the Convent Virtue. This, said the Mother Superior to the little ones in her charge, was a significant lesson to all who looked from the ruins to the solid walls of the Convent Notre Dame Marie. One was the house which had been built on a rock; the other the house which had been built on sand.

The peasants lived by the Convent bells. There were bells to arouse them from their sleep, and bells by which to go to bed. The black-clad figures of those nuns who had not taken the veil were continually seen in the market square, where they offered for sale the products of their gardens and the sewing room. Sister Thérèse was as well known as any of the old men who sat outside the *auberge* talking of days gone by when there had been revolution in France and the streets of Paris had run with blood.

"Bonjour, Sœur Thérèse!" even the children who could scarcely toddle would call after her; and she would turn and peer at them with her gentle, myopic eyes. She was not very beautiful; her back was bent from long work in the gardens, and her dry skin wrinkled and an unhappy shade of brown from the same labours. In the town the people said that she peered at them so searchingly because, in the years which saw the end of her youth and the beginning of her middle age, she had hoped to discover her lover, come to the town in search of her. She would not take her vows, they said, in case he came. And though it was hardly likely that her Jean-Pierre would come looking for her now, the peering had become a habit; but still she would not take her final vows.

She led the novices—the fresh-faced ones, so serious, so conscious of vocation—about the town like a benign shepherd. Leading her sheep to the slaughter which should never be for herself! So said Armand Lefevre; but he was a profane man, a lazy good-for-little, who sat outside the *auberge*, day in, day out, drinking with any who could spare the time for him, and leaving to Madame the business of keeping a roof over their heads.

Just before midday the children would walk in a little crocodile down the steep incline to the town, along by the river, and back again led by Sister Eugenie or Marie or old Thérèse, never loitering, never taking off their *sabots* to dip their toes in the river, for such was forbidden. The town mothers sorrowed for them and referred to them as *les pauvres petites*.

The Englishman who was staying at the *auberge*, and who was invariably sitting outside it with Armand beside him drinking a glass of wine, would follow them with his eyes.

He was tall and distinguished, this Englishman—a real lord, it was said, although he called himself plain Charles Adam. Madame and Monsieur Lefevre shook their heads over that plain name. It was a masquerade, a little secret, they were sure. They had found a kerchief of his with a different pair of initials. C.T. instead of C.A. He was a lord, they were sure; he was an aristocrat of the sort whom they had known before the days of the Terror and had rarely seen since, even though France had once more a King in Louis-Philippe. Madame declared that she knew an aristocrat when she saw one. And, she said to Marie her cook, if Monsieur Milord had a secret, then he was more charming than ever, for it was a romantic secret—Marie could depend on that.

Madame looked down from an upper window on her husband and the Englishman. Armand does not love work, she thought; but he is good for business. It was true; few could resist his talk; he was an inquisitive old man who knew, almost before their conception, when new babies were to be expected; he would watch over town matters with such knowledgeable delight that it was impossible not to enjoy sharing his knowledge and with it his delight.

The Convent bell was ringing and here came *les pauvres petites*. Thérèse was leading them, and with her walked Sister Eugenie, their black garments swinging away from them like broken wings—two black crows, and the fledglings behind them.

Madame looked wistfully at the children who might have been so pretty but for their black clothes. The nuns might be industrious and clever with their needles, but alas! the dear saints were oblivious of the fashion for young children.

Madame sighed, thinking of her own two sons and daughter—all married and far away.

At the end of the crocodile was the naughty little one—the charming little one, whose small oval face with the flashing green eyes always warmed Madame's heart. How old was the little Melisande? Thirteen, it was said; though in some ways she seemed older, in some ways younger; sometimes almost a young woman, at others a charming child.

Melisande loitered at the end of the crocodile. Once she had stopped to talk to a young boy in a boat, and Sister Marie had been angry with her. Had the child suffered? Madame hoped the children were not beaten for wanting to stay in the sunshine, for wanting to play like other children. Nuns were

inclined to suspect sin in what a less holy woman would call
childish naughtiness.

Now they were passing close to the inn and as they came
level with the table at which Armand sat with the Englishman, something clattered to the ground. Madame stared. She
saw that the little Melisande had been carrying her *sabots*
and one had fallen from her hands and alighted right at the
feet of the Englishman.

He picked it up. Melisande had broken from the ranks and
turned back to retrieve her *sabot*. The Englishman rose,
picked up the *sabot* and handed it to the child.

Madame could not resist the temptation to lean out of the
window and listen.

Melisande had lifted her charming face and was looking
at the Englishman with bold pleasure. "It was hot," she
said. "I took off my *sabots*."

Madame thought that Melisande's eyes were like cool clear
water with summer leaves reflected in it.

"Thank you, Monsieur," said Melisande. "I am sorry to
have given you the trouble of picking it up."

He said stiffly in his English-French: "It is no trouble,
Mademoiselle."

"You are English!" cried Melisande. "I speak English.
The nuns teach me." Then she continued in his own
tongue: "How do you do? It is hot to-day. Have you seen
my book? Here is a picture of my grandmother." Then
she laughed in that clear, joyous way which Madame was
sure would be frowned on in the Convent.

The Englishman was smiling. It was the first time Madame had seen him smile.

Melisande stood, her bare feet apart, delighting in what
must, to her, be an adventure. But she looked over her shoulder suddenly, for the inevitable had happened; it would have
been whispered through the crocodile, from tail to head; and
at the head were the Sisters Eugenie and Thérèse. Now they
had stopped; they had seen. At least Eugenie had; Thérèse
was peering about her in anxious concern.

Melisande gave up English and let out a flow of French.
"I have seen you before, Monsieur. You always sit at this
table. I smiled at you as I passed yesterday, but you did not

smile at me. I live at the Convent. I wish I lived at the *auberge*. At the Convent it is lessons all the time." She wrinkled her short nose. "And prayers . . . prayers . . . prayers . . . They hurt my knees."

Eugenie called: "Melisande!"

"Yes, *ma sœur*." She was demure now; she had lowered her lids fringed with the blackest of lashes which helped to make the eyes such a startling green. Now she had composed her features and the eyes showed themselves. They were limpid with innocence. They seemed to ask, "But what have I done, *ma sœur*?"

"Put on your shoes at once."

"Yes, *ma sœur*."

"And join the others."

"It was so hot. I had a blister on my foot. See. I could no longer keep up, so . . ."

"Pray join the others," said Sister Eugenie. "At once."

Melisande lingered long enough to throw a charming glance at the Englishman in which she included Armand. Armand, Madame knew well, had always been susceptible to feminine charm in old or young.

"Monsieur," said Eugenie, "I hope you will forgive this display of bad manners."

The Englishman began to explain in his laborious French. He did not think it was bad manners. The little girl had dropped her shoe and he had picked it up. She had thanked him quite charmingly. No, it was certainly not bad manners; it was the best of manners.

"We regret that Monsieur was disturbed," said Eugenie. She kept her eyes lowered; although she had not taken her final vows and did not live the sheltered life of some of her sisters, although she came out into the world, she would not look into the faces of men.

She led Melisande away, and watching, Madame saw the child marched to the head of the crocodile. Now she must walk between Eugenie and old Thérèse.

Madame offered a prayer to the saints for the children of the Convent, as she drew in her head. Such good people could mistake high spirits for sin so easily.

* * *

Armand, taking in every detail of the little incident, felt wise.
He knew that the Englishman had been startled out of his
calm. It had happened so suddenly. The child had deliberately dropped her *sabot* that he might pick it up and she have
a close look at him and enchant him with her merry tongue.
Well, why should she not? This stately Englishman had a set
of initials on some of his garments which did not tally with
the name he gave; he had a habit of staring at Melisande
every time she passed. Melisande was made to charm and
she knew it; though she had few to try her charm on at the
Convent! It was clear that Thérèse and Eugenie were im-
mune; and it was certain that the Mother Superior was also.
Yet such charm as that possessed by the child should not be
hidden. It should flourish; it was, in Armand's opinion, worth
a fortune.

Now here was the Englishman, so interested in her. That
was why he was always at hand when the children passed;
that was why his eyes lingered on the small figure of Melisande. Melisande was English, Armand had heard. She had
been brought over to France when she was a baby and money
had been paid to the nuns for her food and education. She
was taught to speak English.

How did Armand know such things? He garnered information as a jackdaw does bright stones and bits of glass; he
picked a thread here, a thread there; and threads were made
to be woven together, and in the weaving a pattern was
formed. What should he do as he sat outside the *auberge* if
it were not weaving the exciting patterns which made up
other people's lives?

He and his wife discussed the Englishman's interest in
Melisande as they lay in the big bed together, being careful
to keep their voices low, for the Englishman was sleeping
with only a thin wall between him and them.

"An indiscretion!" Armand had declared. "Depend upon
that."

"That Englishman was never indiscreet."

"All men are indiscreet, Marie."

"That may be so. But he is so . . . English."

"There are indiscretions even in the lives of Englishmen.
Every country has to be populated, my little cabbage. Even

the English, I believe, have found no other means of performing this necessary duty.''

Then the bed would creak with Armand's laughter. Much as he loved all wit, he found his own especially amusing.

"How otherwise would you explain his interest in the little Melisande?'' he had demanded.

"He might be interested in all children.''

"You suggest that they are all his children!'' Armand would be off again. He was so fat that one day, Madame had often warned him, his laughter would do him an injury.

"I must not die of laughing,'' he had whispered; "not until I have uncovered the mystery of the Englishman and little Melisande.''

He was determined to do this, so the encounter between Melisande and the Englishman seemed heaven-sent. Armand had been beside himself with excitement, trying to turn his eyes from the lovely young face, trying not to be overcome by the charm of the child, that he might give all his attention to the Englishman; for through him the secret would be discovered. Young Melisande would have no notion of it.

"Ah!'' he said now as he sat opposite the Englishman. "Monsieur amuses himself with our little town. Monsieur likes our everyday happenings. Is it not so? Our bells . . . our wine . . . our nuns . . . our poor little orphans. . . . And that little one! Very pretty, eh, Monsieur?''

"I find the place restful,'' said the Englishman. His speech delighted Armand almost as much as the mystery which surrounded him; correct as it was, it remained stubbornly English; and he spoke it almost as though it were rather a foolish joke in which he was forced to indulge.

"It is sad . . . sad . . . the little unwanted ones,'' said Armand, slyly.

The Englishman's expression betrayed nothing; but it seemed to Armand that he sat too still, that his fingers had tightened about his glass.

"Yet,'' went on Armand, in the slow careful speech he kept for the Englishman, "perhaps they are lucky, those little ones. A worse fate might have been theirs. The nuns are good.''

The Englishman nodded. "Yes, the nuns are good.''

"And," went on Armand, "it may be good for such little ones to live under a strict rule."

"For such?" asked the Englishman.

Armand leaned forward and let his mischievous eyes rest on the Englishman's face. "These children, Monsieur . . . some have lost their parents; and some . . . they should never have been in this world at all. The result of an indiscretion, you understand? The love between two who could not marry."

The Englishman returned Armand's gaze without a trace of concern.

"That would be so," he said. "Yes, I daresay that would be so."

"And for such, a little strictness might be necessary."

There was silence while Armand refilled their glasses.

"Monsieur," he said artfully, "I wonder sometimes . . . do the parents of these little ones ever think of them? I wonder—for I am a fanciful man—whether the parents come to our little town. We have visitors . . . many visitors. Our town has its beauties. The river . . . the old ruins . . . and many love ruins. It is not without beauty, they tell me. But I wonder, do those parents of the little ones ever come here to see their children? How would you feel Monsieur, if you had a little son—or a little daughter—whom it had been necessary—and the good God knows how easily that can come about—whom it was necessary, Monsieur, to give to the worthy nuns to bring up? I think, of course, of myself. Ah, I should come here. I should come here often to look at the little ones . . . and my own among them."

"That might be so," said the Englishman, flicking a fly from his beautiful blue coat. He was fastidious in the extreme. A perfect aristocrat! thought Armand. And have I gone too far?

The Englishman gave no sign that he resented Armand's not-very-clever insinuations. He went on nodding, drinking his wine, now and then adding a word in his schoolroom French.

Melisande now walked at the head of the procession with the sisters; the other children were watching her, so she must pretend not to be afraid. She was not afraid of anything, she insisted to herself; she was only afraid of being afraid.

She would not think now of the punishment which would surely be hers; she would continue to enjoy the adventure a little longer. There was at least five minutes of sunshine left to her before they went through the gates. She remembered the story of the girl who, it was said, had been walled in when the Convent was built. That was in the chapel and, at dusk, Melisande believed that her ghost haunted the place. She had never seen the ghost; but she fancied she had sensed its presence. She believed that the ghost said to her: "Be happy. Enjoy everything as I did before they walled me in." But that may have been because Melisande was inclined to believe what she wanted to believe. She wanted to be happy; she intended to enjoy as much of life as she could; it was pleasant therefore to believe that the supernatural presence advised her to do exactly what she wanted to do.

She thought of the nun who had had a lover. One of the elder children had told her the story long ago. The nun and her lover had been discovered. The lover was killed; but she, her judges said, had been more wicked because she was a nun and the bride of Christ. She had been unfaithful to Christ. That was a terrible sin, and to punish her, a wall had been built round her and above her, shutting out the light and air; and there she had been left to die.

Melisande had been thinking of the nun when she had dropped her *sabot*. She had known it was wrong to take off her *sabots*, just as the nun had known it was wrong to have a lover. But sometimes sins were irresistible. She had wanted so much to speak to the Englishman. She was fully aware that he watched her. People did look at her. When she passed the bakery the baker used to come out and give her a cake until Sister Emilie had seen and forbidden it. "I am so sorry if I have offended," the baker had said. "Such a pretty child . . . such a charming girl." Others smiled at her, so she was not surprised by the Englishman's attention. She herself was very interested in him, because he was tall and handsome and wore such beautiful clothes. Such a contrast had been that blue coat, that embroidered waistcoat, that wonderful

frothy cravat compared with the clothes of Monsieur Lefevre—slovenly, torn and spotted with food and wine.

Melisande smoothed down her own black garments with
distaste. They were too big for her. "Leave room for growing," said old Thérèse. "It is better to have your gown too
big than too small. It is better to have too much than too little
of the good things of life." Melisande had answered: "But
it is better to have a little of the bad things of life than too
much, and perhaps this black gown is not one of the good
things but one of the bad." Sister Thérèse had clicked her
tongue at that. "Ungrateful child!" she had cried. "Why?"
Melisande had asked, for she could never, as Sister Emilie
had pointed out, leave well alone. "The stuff of my gown is
rough. It scratches me. Should I be grateful for a hair-shirt
. . . which is what my gown resembles?"

Her clothes were ugly and she longed to wear clothes made
of beautiful cloth such as those worn by the Englishman. He
had smiled and seemed pleased because she had dropped her
sabot. His eyes were of a grey-brown shade as the river was
after a great deal of rain when parts of the banks had been
washed away; he looked as though he rarely smiled; yet he
had smiled for her. She would remember that when she was
being punished.

They had turned in through the gates and were crossing
the path between the well-kept lawns. How cold it was inside
the Convent! The bell was ringing. It was time for *déjeuner*.
Melisande's heart beat very fast, for it had occurred to her
that the punishment might result in her missing *déjeuner*,
and she was very hungry. She was often hungry, but hungrier
at this time of day than at any other. *Petit déjeuner*—bitter
coffee and a twist of bread—was scarcely adequate, and it
seemed hours since she had had it. But whatever the punishment is, she told herself, I shall think of the way he smiled
at me and that he does not smile for everyone. She wondered
what the young nun had thought when she was in the darkness with wall all about her—her cold dark tomb.

Sister Eugenie was beside her. "After *déjeuner* you will
go to the sewing room and there Sister Emilie will tell you
what your punishment will be."

After *déjeuner*! Melisande was almost rapturously happy.

There was plenty of time before she need think of punishment; now she could remember the smile of the Englishman while she drank her cabbage soup and ate her piece of bread. She stood at the table, palms pressed together while Sister Thérèse said grace, and her eyes and thoughts were now on the steaming bowl before her. As they all took their seats she glanced quickly at Sister Thérèse at the top of the table and Sister Eugenie at the foot, and quickly looked away for fear they should see the triumph in her flashing green eyes.

The meal was over all too soon. Dumplings, which she loved, followed the cabbage soup; and it was only when she was eating her last mouthful that her fears returned.

Sister Thérèse was watching her. "Do not forget. To the sewing room."

She hated the sewing room and, as she went, she thought of the tedious hours, of fingers sore through sewing rough garments for children like herself, and shirts to be sold in the market square. On a dais was a large table where was laid out that altar cloth on which only the best needlewomen were allowed to work. It was an honour to sit at the table and work in gold and scarlet thread, instead of at the benches stitching ugly garments.

Sister Emilie said that to work on the dais was to work for God and the saints, but to work at the table was to work for mankind.

Melisande had shocked her once by saying that she would rather work for neither; although she loved the bright colours on the altar cloth she would like to wear dresses embroidered with them rather than have to sew for God and the saints.

"Sometimes," Sister Emilie had said, "I think you must be a very foolish or a very wicked girl."

"Perhaps I am both," was Melisande's ready answer, "for *la Mère* says that we are all wicked and all foolish . . . all miserable sinners . . . even the sisters and *la Mère* herself. . . ."

Sister Emilie had been at a loss for words, as her fellow sisters often were with Melisande. "Don't you want to sit on the dais and work on the beautiful altar cloth?" she had asked.

"The needles prick my fingers just the same," Melisande had replied.

But now there would be no question of working on the altar cloth. There would be some hideous task; and she would have to sit at the table and work and work until her back ached and her fingers were sore, to make up for breaking away from the crocodile and speaking to the Englishman.

"Come here," said Sister Emilie.

Melisande obeyed. Her eyes were lowered. It was no use smiling at Sister Emilie.

"You have misbehaved once more, I am sad to hear," she said. "Now you will sit at that table. Take the top shirt from the pile. You will remain there till you have finished it."

Melisande took the shirt. It was of the stiff stuff that she hated. She sat sewing; her stitches were big and uneven. There was blood on the shirt, for she had, of course, pricked her fingers. She carried out her plan and went over the delicious episode again and again.

Soon she was speaking her thoughts aloud. "At least it is not as bad as being walled up in the chapel."

"What was that?" asked Sister Emilie.

"I am sorry, *ma sœur*. I was thinking of the nun who had a lover and was walled up in the chapel."

Emilie was disturbed.

She said: "That is not the way to show your penitence. You must not speak of such things here . . . in a holy convent."

"No, *ma sœur*."

There was silence. Melisande went on stitching, still thinking of the nun and her lover. It was worth while to stitch this hateful shirt for the sake of the day's adventure. Perhaps having a lover—since it must not be spoken of, and it was the exciting things of life which were forbidden—was so much more wonderful that it was even worth while being walled up in a chapel afterwards in the cold and dark, there to stay through the centuries.

In the cold bare room Thérèse and Eugenie stood before the table at which sat the Mother.

The Mother's hands were folded on her breast. It was a

characteristic attitude when disturbed. She was sixty-three but she looked older; her face was wrinkled and almost colourless; her serenity was not easily disturbed over any matter other than that which concerned those whom she called her children . . . the little ones who had been given into her care.

Eugenie spoke. She said: "*Ma Mère*, it is most alarming. The child purposefully did this thing. To take off her *sabots*— that was wickedness to start with, but to let one fall at the feet of this man . . . deliberately! We do not know how to deal with such a matter."

"He is staying at the inn," said the Mother, shaking her head. "It is unwise."

"Mother, you think it is he?"

"I think, Sister Thérèse, it must be."

"But it was the child who made the encounter possible."

"Yes, yes, but he must have shown his interest in her in some way."

"There is something about the child," said Thérèse. "Yes, there is something."

"A wantonness," put in Eugenie.

"She is essentially of the world," said the Mother, and although she was silent for a while, her lips moved. She was talking to saints, the sisters knew; she would be seen gliding about the Convent, while her lips moved thus. All knew that she was praying to the saints. To whom did she pray now? wondered Thérèse. To Saint Christopher? Like the Christbearer, the Mother was seeking to carry a child across the bridgeless river, and like the saint she was finding the burden too much for her.

She looked up suddenly and said: "Be seated."

The Sisters sat and there was again silence, while all three continued to think of Melisande. She was thirteen. An impressionable age, thought Sister Thérèse, looking back over her life, an age when it was possible for the feet to be led along those paths which opened out to voluptuousness, to revelry and sin, winding on and on away from virtue and piety. Sister Eugenie, who had lived all her life in the Convent, was thinking that the simple solution was to whip the child and put her into solitary confinement until the Englishman left the town.

Thirteen! thought the Mother. I was thirteen fifty years ago. Then there had seemed to be security and peace. She saw herself in her parents' mansion near St. Germain; she saw the schoolroom and the governess; she saw the servants when they had begun to show fear in their eyes. They had locked up the house with great care at night. They had whispered together. "Did you hear shouting last night? What if they should come. . . . Hush, the little one listens." She recalled the gardens—the trees in bloom, the fountains playing; she remembered the day when her father and mother had come riding there in great haste. "Jeanne . . . upstairs . . . get your cloak. . . . There is no time to lose." The whispering of the servants, the anxious looks, the haste of her parents . . . they were all like the ominous beating of drums that warned of death and danger. She had not understood then; she had run upstairs knowing only that that which they feared was about to come to pass. We are going to run away from it, she thought. We shall be safe now. But she was wrong. They did not run away. Before she was able to return to them there were shouts in the hall and those whom she thought of for years afterwards as the 'ugly people' were in the hall. She had peered through the banisters and had seen them take her father and mother; they were all over the house; nowhere was safe; nowhere was sacred. She heard the smashing of glass, the shouts, the screams, the drunken voices singing the song which she would never forget.

"Allons, enfants de la patrie,
Le jour de gloire est arrivé.
Contre nous, de la tyrannie
Le couteau sanglant est levé. . . ."

And they had taken her beloved parents away to the Place de Grève where many heads were falling to that *couteau*. She had escaped with her governess who had taken her across the gardens to the copse; and the ugly shrieking people had not come that way. Little Jeanne and her governess had ridden through the darkness to the Convent Notre Dame Marie; and there she had stayed and lived ever since, shut away from horror, shut away from fear. That had happened nearly fifty years ago; and at the time she had been the same age as the little Melisande.

At such an age a child must be carefully protected. The Mother knew what it was even now to wake in the night and see the ugly faces, the blood on a beloved face, the tearing of a woman's silk dress, to hear the screams for mercy. Through her dreams—like drum beats—she heard the notes of the Marseillaise. She hated the world because she was afraid of the world; she wanted to take all little children and bring them into the security of the Convent; she wished their lives—as hers was—to be given to prayer and the service of others. She would like to gather them to her like a mother-angel protecting them from the dangers of the world outside.

But she was wise enough to know that there were some who did not wish to be protected. Melisande was one of these, and she believed they needed special care.

Thérèse was thinking of labouring in the fields, of the ripple of Jean-Pierre's muscles. He had shown her his arms and said: "See how strong I am, little Thérèse! I could lift you up. I could carry you off . . . and you'd not be able to stop me." She had been thirteen then. Life could be dangerous at thirteen.

The Mother had come to a decision. "It must be explained to him," she said. "To-morrow you, Sister Thérèse and you, Sister Eugenie, shall go to the inn and ask to speak to him. You must speak to him with the utmost frankness. Ask him if he has any special interest in the child. If he is the man, he will know what we mean. Tell him that it is unwise of him to come here. The child is quick-witted. If he shows interest in her she may guess something near the truth. He must be asked not to come here, disturbing her, unless he has some proposition to lay before us."

The Sisters bowed their heads.

"It is to be hoped he has not," continued the Mother. "The child needs security, a life of serenity. I had hoped she might become one of us."

Sister Eugenie looked dubious and Thérèse shook her head.

"No, I fear not," went on the Mother. "But she must be

guarded well until she is older. To put ideas into a head such
as that one, might be to put sin there too.''

"You are as usual right, *ma Mère*," said Thérèse.

"So . . . see that she does not go out whilst he is here;
and, to-morrow, go to him and say what I have told you. It
is the best way.''

The Sisters went out, leaving the Mother to hear again the
shouts of the revolutionaries with the strains of the Marseillaise coming back to her over the years.

The clock ticked on. The seams were long. Melisande divided them up in her thoughts so that the material was the
town and the needle herself walking through it. Here was the
church, here the boat yard, here the baker's shop, the cottages, the inn, the river and the ruins of the château. She
pictured the baker at the door as she passed. "A *gâteau* for
the little one?'' It was delicious. She could taste the spices
which the baker knew so well how to mingle in his delightful
confections. Sister Thérèse and Sister Eugenie had not noticed. The baker winced. "We will deceive them," said that
wink. "You shall have cakes because you are the prettiest,
the most charming of the children, and it pleases me to give.''

She could laugh to herself; she was far away from the
sewing room. She went on past the cottages to the *auberge*,
where he sat, smiling at her, without waiting for her to drop
her *sabot*. He said: "You speak English so beautifully. I
should have thought you were English. You shall leave the
Convent and come away with me.'' Melisande was remembering that last year a woman had come to the Convent and
taken Anne-Marie away; the children had watched her leave
in a beautiful carriage. "That is her aunt,'' said the children.
"She is going to live with her rich aunt and have a satin dress
trimmed with fur.'' Ever since, Melisande had waited for a
rich woman to come and take her away, but a man would do
very well instead.

The door opened and Sister Eugenie came in. She went to
the table and whispered a few words to Sister Emilie. Then
Sister Emilie went out and left Melisande with Sister Eugenie.

Sister Eugenie looked at the shirt which Melisande had

been stitching. She pointed with a thin finger to the stitches which were too long and too crooked.

"Take this book and read it aloud," she said. "Give me the shirt. I will finish it whilst you read."

Melisande took the book. It was *Pilgrim's Progress* in English. She read slowly, enjoying the story of the man with his burden; but she would rather have heard the story of Melisande, of how she came to the Convent when she was a baby, and how a rich woman—or a man—came one day to take her away to a beautiful house where she spent the rest of her life eating sweetmeats and wearing a blue dress trimmed with fur.

Madame Lefevre saw the two Sisters coming towards the *auberge*. She paused to look through the window. Armand, sitting at the table, rose to greet the Sisters. Madame heard his loud *Bonjour* and the quiet ones of the Sisters. Armand was flattering and gallant as he was to all women. "I am happy to see you here. Our little inn is at your service."

Madame did not wait for their reply; she went downstairs to see them for herself. She greeted them with warmth as Armand had done.

"They come to see the English gentleman," said Armand.

"Alas!" said Madame.

"I have told the Sisters that he left this morning."

Madame nodded. It was sad indeed; she was filled with melancholy at the thought. "He decided last night," she explained. "He came to me and he said: 'Madame, I must depart to-morrow.' He went off early in the coach."

The Sisters nodded. They were secretly pleased; that much was clear. They thanked the Lefevres and went slowly away.

Armand lifted his shoulders; he was afraid to meet Madame's eyes, for he feared he was responsible for the Englishman's departure. He would not tell Madame of their little conversation.

But he would be back, Armand soothed himself. He would sit here and watch the children, and his eyes would linger on the little Melisande. She was English; he was English; that was good enough for Armand.

Madame stood for a while conjecturing why the nuns had

called; then she turned and went into the inn, for she had her business to attend to.

Armand returned to his seat and his wine. One of the stall-keepers on his way to the market came by with a basket of produce to sell in the square; he called *Holà* to Armand and sat down for a while to drink a glass of wine.

The Convent bell began to ring. It would soon be midday. He heard the children's *sabots* on the cobbles. Sister Thérèse came in sight with the crocodile. Thérèse peered about, calling a greeting. *"Bonjour, Madame." "Bonjour, Monsieur." "Bonjour, mes enfants."*

The children wound their way along by the river, their feet noisy in protest because the day was hot, and perhaps some of them remembered that yesterday the little Melisande had taken off her *sabots* and walked barefoot.

And there she was, eagerly looking towards the *auberge*. Looking for the bird who had flown, thought Armand. Ah, he has gone, my little one. You and I have driven him away.

The children passed on. Armand talked with his companion of the affairs of the town.

Life flowed on, as it had yesterday.

Two

As the coach trundled along to Paris, the Englishman was thinking the same uneasy thoughts which always disturbed him when he made this journey. Each time he made it, he assured himself it would be the last. Yet again and again he came. He was drawn there by the quaint figure of a girl in ill-fitting black clothes with marvellous green eyes which brought him memories.

What use was there in making these journeys? None. What did he get from them but the anguish of memories, the reminder of an episode which was best forgotten and which he could have shelved with an easy conscience? He was rich, and wise enough to know that the most reliable salve for an uneasy conscience which the world could provide was money. He need never have concerned himself with Melisande again. He should have resisted the impulse to see her in the first place. If he had, there would have been none of these pointless journeys. And he had betrayed himself. That was disquieting. An inquisitive old innkeeper, on whom he had looked as a useful source of information, had probed his secret; and it was not what a man did that could bring trouble; it was what others discovered of his doings which chilled the stomach.

Sir Charles Trevenning was a man who rarely betrayed himself. He led a satisfactory life, missed nothing that he wished for, and if what he wished for happened to be something which it would be unwise for the world to know of, the world did not know. Yet he had betrayed himself to a humble innkeeper.

Such made uneasy thinking. Once before he had been caught off his guard, and what had followed? Pleasure, yes;

delight, he might say if he were given to such fantastic expression; but surely such pleasure, such delight, had to be paid for. He had suffered some anguish, some misgiving, a moment of panic; but Sir Charles was not a man to pay more for a thing than that thing was worth.

When he had sat very straight, very controlled, at the table outside the Lefevres' inn, his outward appearance had given no indication of his inner turmoil which had been aroused by the little girl from the convent. When her green eyes had looked into his he had felt his calm expression cracking, as though it had been a shell. It was alarming. A moment outside a humble inn linked itself with another moment under the trees in Vauxhall Gardens; a humble child looked at him as a young woman had looked at him; and Sir Charles was aware of the weakness within him.

He, squire and landowner from Cornwall, magistrate and one of the most highly respected gentlemen of the Duchy, a man of wide financial interests in the City of London, whose friends in the country and town were of high social standing, had no right to be sitting outside an inn in a quiet French town, talking to an innkeeper. He should never have sat beneath the trees of Vauxhall. Had he wished to visit a pleasure garden, it should have been Ranelagh, to which he might have gone in his carriage with a party of friends. Looking back it seemed as though some unaccountable impulse had led him to Vauxhall, where persons of high degree did not go; where, it was said, one did not meet a creature above the station of cheesemonger. And had he not gone to Vauxhall he would never have sat outside a mean little *auberge*, talking to a bibulous, garrulous innkeeper.

So here he was now riding in a coach among humble people, people who gabbled, gesticulated and sweated. He, the fastidious one, forced to that which offended his fastidiousness and yet was somehow irresistible. It was disturbing in the extreme, for it was as though he did not know himself.

He closed his eyes to shut out the sight of the vulgar woman in the corner seat of the coach. Her sprigged muslin gown with the vulgar leg-of-mutton sleeves was none too clean; her bodice was laced to bring her bosom into prominence;

her monstrously large hat took up too much room in the coach; and he disliked the glances she threw at him.

But he had forgotten her in a second, for his thoughts were back to this position in which, because of an evening in Vauxhall, he found himself.

He was there at Vauxhall that summer's day sixteen years before. He saw himself a younger man, proud then as now, but with no knowledge of that weakness within him. He had crossed the river to Lambeth. Why? On what mad impulse?

Vauxhall in early summer! He saw it as though he were there: the avenues of trees, the tables set under the trees, the gravel paths, the pavilions, the grottoes and lawns, the ostentatious little temples which aroused the admiration of the vulgar; the porticoes, the rotundas, the colonnades, the music; the lamps which would scintillate as soon as it was dark; the fireworks, frothed syllabub and sliced ham, scraped beer and burned champagne; and the people on holiday aping their betters.

In the twilight the girls tripped past him in their watered tabbies and bombazines which rustled like the silk of ladies. There were girls in cardinal capes and gay bonnets, swirling skirts and cosy tippets; there were young men—apprentices in flowing cravats, brilliantly waist-coated, gaudy copies of Beau Brummel and the Count D'Orsay . . . in that dim light.

That was how he had first seen Millie; but she was young and sweet enough to bear the light of day.

How had he come to be there? It had begun with his periodic desire to escape from Maud and the quiet of the country to the pleasures of the town, to see old friends, to visit the incomparable Fenella's salon, to hope that their friendship might briefly burst into something more exciting, more amusing, as it had done once and could so easily do again.

Perhaps old Wenna had something to do with it. Odd to be driven from his house by one of his own servants. He had never liked Wenna and he would have dismissed her if he had had his way. But Maud—pliable in most things—would never agree to that. Old Morwenna Pengelly had been Maud's nurserymaid when Maud was a girl of five (how many times had he heard that story?) and Wenna no more than fourteen; Maud was Wenna's 'Miss Maud' and would be so until they died. Why did he call her old? She was nine years older than Maud and five years older than himself. That was not old. But there was an air of age about Wenna. It was impossible to imagine that she had ever been young. At fifteen she must have been a small wizened creature, watching over her Miss Maud and never giving a thought to those things which occupied the minds of other girls of that age. He should be glad. She was a good servant. But he did not like her hostility. There was no other word for it. And ever since her dear Miss Maud had first become pregnant, Wenna's hostility had increased. Foolish woman! But a good servant. No, certainly Wenna had had no part in his leaving home at that time. He had been stifled by the atmosphere of the house. Maud, who would bear a child in three months' time, had become the most important person in it; and he, the master, had been forced to take second place. He could escape to his life outside the house, of course, to his friends for a little gambling, a few dinner parties, supervising his estates, sitting on the bench, hunting; but he had had need of a complete change. Then, there had been the christening of Bruce Holland's boy.

He had said to Maud: "My dear, I think I shall have to go to London, confound it! Business threatens to make the trip necessary."

Then she had tried to hide the pleasure his words had given her, but she could never hide anything.

She had said: "Oh, Charles, how tiresome!" And, hardly able to keep the eagerness out of her voice: "When do you leave?"

She would be thinking: I shall have my meals with Wenna. We shall be comfortable. I shall no longer have to wonder what he is going to say next and how to answer him.

He had said airily: "Oh, in a week or two." And he had watched her settle cosily into her cushions.

He went to her and kissed her lightly on the forehead; he was well pleased with her. There were no irritating wifely questions from Maud. Did it occur to her that something besides business might detain him in London? Such thoughts would not occur to Maud. She was too pure. Her dear Mamma had never taught her to consider her husband's possible lack of morals; the only cause for alarm would have been any lack of fortune.

So, with Maud absorbed in the approach of motherhood, he needed the stimulation which London could give him.

He said: ''Bruce expects me to put in an appearance at the christening.''

''You must, of course.''

He smiled at her calmly. He thought: If the child she is carrying is a girl we'll betroth him to this boy of Bruce's. He almost wished he would be cheated of the son he hoped for; it would be so neat if it were a girl and could be paired off with Bruce's son; and he liked neat arrangements. No! He did not hope for that. He and Maud had been married for five years; and this was the first sign of fruitfulness. His first-born must be a son. There had always been a son and heir at Trevenning. He had feared that Maud was not fertile, and he believed the fault was hers. She was completely without passion; she had dreaded their intercourse in the beginning, and the happiest state she had arrived at was indifference and absentmindedness. Was such a state conducive to procreation? He believed not. Fenella, in whose salon conversation was advanced, declared that it was not so.

Wenna, coming in saw him and, excusing herself, was about to hurry out, but he waved her excuses aside and declared he was about to depart.

A week later he left by post-chaise for London. The journey proved less eventful than usual. There was only one uneasy moment when, crossing Bagshot Heath, the postilions decided that a gallop was advisable; but they had come safely to the inn where Bruce Holland was waiting to greet him, and there he had enjoyed a meal of freshwater fish, roast fowl, cheese and salad such as could be enjoyed only at the posting inn and was not for humbler coach travellers.

He had stayed with Bruce, but his friend had not been such good company as usual; he was absorbed in Fermor Danby, his new son. It might have been that Bruce's absorption had contributed towards that fatal visit to Vauxhall.

He had called on Fenella at the earliest possible moment. Fenella was as magnificent as ever. It was hard to believe there could be such a person until one saw her, heard her, and was part of that community of strange and brilliant people whom she gathered about her. Nothing could have been in greater contrast with the drawing-room at Trevenning than Fenella's salon in the London square. Her husband had squandered her large fortune before he died, and in her early twenties Fenella had found herself with neither husband nor fortune. She had thereupon set about retrieving the fortune; and she made it clear that no husband was going to take it from her. Lovers, declared Fenella, characteristically, were more satisfactory; a woman must look after herself and she needed lovers to protect her from would-be husbands. She was outrageously amusing and her friends and admirers said that she was in advance of her times. Tall, Junoesque, she had a taste for bizarre clothes. Clothes delighted her; she had defied all conventions by establishing her own dress salon for the service of ladies in high society. Fenella's dress salon was as no other; for everything Fenella did was as it had never been done before.

She had her delightful house in the London square; she had her girls to show her gowns. They mingled with the guests—noblemen and statesmen and their wives and friends, both Whigs and Tories. The politics of her guests mattered little to Fenella; she was a woman, she said, who liked to hear both sides of a question. The beautiful Caroline Norton was her friend, and among the guests who came to her drawing-room were Wellington, Melbourne and Peel.

It was said that many of her young ladies found wealthy protectors. There were some people who hinted that Fenella's was a rendezvous for the disposal of feminine wares other than tippets, gowns and pelisses, and that she derived great benefits from gentlemen of wealth and power by the services her young ladies helped her to render. There was bound to be idle gossip about a woman like Fenella.

She accepted the gossip concerning herself as though she enjoyed it equally with the scandalmongers. She grew richer in her elaborately feathered nest. Her morals were elastic. She was warmly generous and good natured, but a shrewd and hard driver of bargains. All those who worked for her were fond of her. She had a surfeit of friends and lovers. She was Queen in her half-world. Many could not understand how a woman—little more than a tradeswoman—could wield such influence and be accepted as the friend of so many men and women of standing. It was true that she was not received in the houses of the great; but Fenella did not wish to be received; she wished to receive.

Bruce Holland, hard-living man about town, typical of his generation, untouched by the new customs, was as much at home at Almacks as he was at a low cock-fight in the East End of London. He introduced Charles to London night life, to bear-baiting and dog-fights, to boxing matches between men of their own class or those frequenters of the water-front sluceries.

He it was who had taken Charles to Fenella's salon.

Once Charles had stayed behind to advise her about some investment of which he had particular knowledge, and he had spent the night in Fenella's company in that magnificent bedroom of soft carpets and thick curtains, of beautiful furniture and ornaments which Fenella had collected from her many admirers.

It had been an exciting experience, repeated on another occasion.

He would have been delighted if it had happened more frequently, but Fenella had many lovers and would not allow herself to become deeply involved with one. A comforting thought, he had believed; and the best possible sort of mistress with an outlook on life which could be called masculine. There would never be unpleasant complications with Fenella; no tears on parting; no regrets. Love for her was a passing joy, as delightful as champagne, to be sipped and enjoyed, not stored and wept over. And in love she was never calculating, never mercenary. What pleasure it was to love and be loved by Fenella, especially after experiencing those dubiously enjoyable practices indulged in with an indifferent and absentminded though legal partner!

But Fenella had failed him on that last occasion. She had assured him that she was delighted to see him, that he was her very good friend; her sparkling eyes recalled with pleasure their last encounter in her perfumed bedroom; but there was a certain vagueness in her smile, for Fenella's interest was absorbed by a young man, a protégé of Melbourne's.

Consequently Charles, deeply disappointed, had left the house in the square and wandered aimlessly towards the river.

He had not realized how far he had walked when he heard the pipe of a cockney voice. "A boat, sir? Cross the river, sir? Vauxhall'll be pretty to-night, sir."

And so to Vauxhall.

As he had strolled through the avenues he had not seen the vulgarity of the place; he had not heard the shouts of the people. It was twilight and the crowds were impatiently awaiting the fireworks display. Somewhere in the distance a band was playing Handel's "Water Music."

Millie was sitting on a seat under a tree, her hands folded in her lap, and he would have passed her by but for the ruffian. This lout had sat down on the seat beside her. Charles stood still, arrested in his walk, because the girl was shrinking to one end of the seat, was trying to rise, but the man had her by the arm. Millie looked desperately about her, and her eyes fell upon Charles, who could do nothing but stride towards her and her unwanted companion.

"What are you doing to this young lady?" he demanded. It was the unmistakable voice of authority, and it startled the ruffian, who released his hold on the girl and shuffled uneasily to his feet as he took in the elegance, the fine cut of that magnificent coat, the cold arrogance of the man who is accustomed to being obeyed.

"I never done nothing . . ." he began.

Charles raised his eyebrows and looked at the young woman whose eyes appealed to him not to leave her.

"Be off with you," said Charles, raising his cane. "And if I catch you molesting young ladies again, it will be the worse for you."

The ruffian first backed away, then he ran. Charles stood looking after him. That should have been the end. But Millie had risen. She was small—not much more than five feet in height; he was immediately impressed by her gentle timidity and a little moved by it.

"I . . . thank you . . . sir," she stammered.

He was about to acknowledge her thanks and move on but, noticing afresh the helplessness and the melancholy in her pretty face, he said somewhat brusquely: "What are you doing here . . . alone?"

"I shouldn't be here by rights, sir," she said. "I came . . . because . . . I had to come." Her eyes filled with tears. They looked bigger and greener thus. He saw that it was the contrast of dark lashes that made them so noticeable. "It was the last place we came to together, sir."

"It is no place for a young woman to be in at such an hour alone," he said, cutting short any confidence he feared she might be trying to make.

"No, sir."

He felt embarrassed. "My good woman," he said to emphasize the difference in their social standing, "no gentleman could pass a young person in such distress as you obviously were. Come, tell me why you linger here."

"It reminds me of him . . . of Jim . . . my husband."

"And he is no longer with you?"

She shook her head and brought out a handkerchief from the pocket of her linen gown.

He looked at her intently and asked: "Are you hungry?"

She shook her head.

"Come, come, tell the truth," he said. "When did you last eat?"

"I . . . I don't know."

"That's nonsense."

"It was yesterday."

"So you have no money."

She twisted the handkerchief in her hands and looked at it helplessly.

"If you will not talk to me there is nothing I can do to help you," he said impatiently. "Perhaps you would prefer me to go away and not bother you."

She gave him another of those deprecating glances. "You are so kind," she said, and he noticed that her mouth was soft and trembling. Her smallness aroused both his pity and excited interest. "I . . . I feel better here, sir," she went on. "That is when I'm not being bothered."

He smiled faintly. "If you sit here alone you will continue to be bothered."

She smiled. "Yes, sir."

"Go home. That's the remedy." Her lips began to tremble again and he went on: "You're in some trouble." It was the worst thing he could have said, for she sat down on the seat and covered her face with her hands. He saw the gloves—black and neatly darned; he noticed how thin she was. He felt that if he left her now he would never forgive himself nor would he forget her. It would be as though he had heard a call for help and refused to listen, as though he had passed by on the other side of the road. He felt in his pocket for money. No, he could not offer her money, not without ascertaining the cause of her distress.

He sat down on the seat beside her. It was getting darker every minute, so it was not likely he would be seen by anyone he knew. He was safe enough. He was discovering that he was interested so deeply that he was ready to take a risk.

"You are in deep trouble," he said, "and I am a stranger. But I might be able to help."

"You're so kind," she said again. "I knew that as soon as you stopped." Her awe of him was obvious, her recognition of his status flattering.

"The first thing is to have something to eat and drink," he said. "I believe that is what you need more than anything."

She rose obediently.

In the eating-house with its evergreen plants in ornamental pots, and its music, he took her to a secluded table, and there, with his back to the crowd, he gave her his full attention. He watched her devour a leg of roast chicken and sip the burned champagne, which put some colour in her cheeks and made her eyes look like translucent jade. Watching her, he felt benign. He thought of Cophetua and the beggar maid or a small boy dipping his toes into a deliciously cool stream. He was savouring a pleasure knowing that he could withdraw whenever he wished to. Though why he should find pleasure in the society of an uneducated girl he was not sure.

It was after she had eaten and when they sat back listening to the music that she told him her sad story. He could hear her voice now— a little hoarse and tremulous with that queer sibilance which he would have thought ill-bred a short while before.

"It fell out like this, sir," she said. "I came up to London from the country—Hertfordshire, that's where my home was. There was a lot of us, you see, sir, and they was glad to get rid of us elder ones, Mother and Father was. . . . I had a chance to work in the mantua-maker's and learn a trade. A girl from our village had gone to her, and when she come home for a little stay, she said she'd take me back with her because there was a vacancy where she was, you see. So I left home. . . ."

She made him see it—the woman with her young girls working in the great room, rising early in the morning, stitching through the long hours, living simply, having no pleasures but each other's company. Mistress Rickards, the mantua-maker, was strict. She would never allow the girls to go out alone. They were never allowed to go to any entertainments—not even a hanging outside Newgate Jail. Mistress Rickards was stern; she beat her girls with a stick when she thought they needed it; and she fed them on skimmed milk and texts from the Bible. They were with her to work, she told them continually; not to frivol away their time. If they worked hard they would one day be good at their trade, at which they could earn a living; then they would not starve in the gutter as some did. On the rare occasions when she took them out she would point at the beggars sitting on the street corners with their hired children, exposing their afflictions, their blindness, their ragged state, their sores. "Pity the beggars," the poor things would chant miserably; and Mistress Rickards would threaten: "You'll come to that, Agnes, you lazy slut. You too, Rosie, you sluggard. Don't think you'll escape, Millie, you awkward girl. That's what you'll come to unless you learn your trade."

They had worked hard and they had been happy within their narrow lives. They used to sit at a bench by the window and the apprentices who passed by would look in and wave; each girl had had her apprentice to be teased about as she stitched and stitched to avoid the harsh prophecies of Mistress Rickards, the mantua-maker.

"And one day," said Millie, in her hoarse yet childish voice, "I had to go to Mr. Latter, the mercer, for a piece of silk a lady wanted making into a mantle. Mistress Rickards

went as a rule, but she'd eaten oysters the night before and
they hadn't agreed with her. She sent me, and Jim was in the
shop.''

She softened when she talked of Jim. He was no longer an
apprentice, she proudly explained, but the mercer found him
too useful to let him go. So he paid him a wage to stay on,
and Jim used to say that he was the one who really managed
the shop.

Their courtship had lasted ten months. Jim was a man with
money. He wasn't afraid of Mistress Rickards. He said he
was going to look after her and she needn't bother any more
about learning a trade. He was going to see that she made
mantles and pelisses for herself, not for others. She was going to be Mrs. Sand, she was.

She almost sparkled as she told him of the night they went
to Vauxhall.

''There was fireworks, and we danced. I kept thinking of
what Mistress Rickards would say when I got back. And
when we did get back, there she was waiting, her hair in
curlpapers and her cane propped up by the door. But Jim
didn't care. He came in with me. He said: 'I'm going to
marry Millie and don't you dare lay a finger on her.' ''

And so they had married, and she had left Mistress Rickards's and they lived in the room which Jim had found for
them in St. Martin's Lane. There they were happy for the
whole of one year.

Her face darkened. ''We'd been married a year . . . exact
to the day. Jim said: 'Let's go to Vauxhall.' So we did. We
danced and watched the fireworks. Jim said let's have a drink.
That was when we was just going to cross the river. So we
went into one of the taverns and we hadn't been in that tavern
before. If only we'd have known we'd never have gone inside
the place. I didn't want the drink. Nor did Jim . . . much. It
was just to round off the day like. That makes it all the
worse.'' She was silent for a moment before she went on:
''We sat there laughing . . . as happy as you like. It had been
a lovely day. Then these men came in. I didn't know who
they were. We didn't know what sort of a tavern it was.
But they were bad . . . them men. First they started to drink;
then they put jewels and things on the table. Jim looked at

me: 'Come on,' he said, 'we'll get out of here.' But as we went to the door one of them . . . a big man in a red coat . . . got up. He was swaying with the drink. He caught me. . . . It was dreadful. I can't bear to think of it.''

He filled her glass and told her to drink. She obeyed. He knew that she had been obeying someone all her life—her parents, Mistress Rickards, Jim.

"Tell me the rest quickly," he said. "Don't dwell on it, because it makes you unhappy."

She nodded. "There was a fight. I remember the glass breaking . . . and the screams. . . . One of them had a gun. They was highwaymen and they'd killed men before. One more didn't make no difference to them . . . and that one was my Jim."

A deep silence had settled on them both. He knew that she was going over it all again, and he was angry with himself for being the means of reviving her melancholy memories. But silence would not help her now.

"Surely the law . . ." he began.

"The law?" she said sadly. "That's for you and your sort. They couldn't find those men, and it wasn't worth much trouble . . . not for a poor man."

He felt humiliated; eagerly he sought for some means of comforting her. He could think of nothing he could do; he found himself ineffectually patting the hand which lay on the table.

The rest of her story was pitiably inevitable. What could she do? The rent had been paid in advance and there was still a little money left. But that had not lasted long. She had spent her last pennies on a trip to Vauxhall. After that? She did not know. She simply did not know. She thought she would go back to the tavern where he had died. Perhaps those men would be there. Perhaps they would kill her as she wished they had on that night.

"I don't know why I came here to-night," she said. "I truly don't know."

He said, to her surprise: "I don't know why I came."

After that he took her to her room and gave her money for food and rent. Perhaps, he told himself again and again, she is a clever beggar. There were many such in London. Some hired babies—the more deformed the better; some even mutilated the children and themselves to make them more almsworthy. Why should not a girl with appealing green eyes concoct a tragic story for a simple man from the country? Who knew—the lout in the gardens might have been an accomplice.

It would have been better to have believed this, to have paid the money that would appease his conscience, and then forget the incident. It could so easily have ended there. The money he had given her would take care of her needs for some weeks. What more could anyone expect of a chance encounter?

But she had continued to haunt his thoughts; there had been many meetings and much heart-searching before the inevitable had happened.

Soon after that first meeting he had been called back to Cornwall where his daughter Caroline was prematurely born. He found Wenna distracted, the household already almost in mourning. Wenna's dark eyes had seemed to flash threats of vengeance on him. But both the child and Maud had lived.

Before very long he returned to London. He could not forget the girl whom he had met in Vauxhall. He told himself that he would try to find some work for her, but in the meantime he would induce her to accept a little money from him.

She was reluctant at first. "How can I take it?" she asked.

His answer was: "Because life is unfair to some and gracious to others. Think of me as an uncle who has come into your life at an important moment."

"You are too young for an uncle!" was her reply. She could be merry and sad, changing quickly from mood to mood. He had glimpsed her capacity for happiness.

In his shrewd and businesslike way he had quickly made arrangements. Millie's landlady was a motherly woman with a fondness for lovers, which she had decided Millie and her benefactor were. She prided herself on her knowledge of the gentry and she recognized in Charles a true gentleman who could be trusted to pay his way. For such she was prepared to make concessions. So concessions were made; and one evening, after a visit to Vauxhall, he stayed with her, for she was as lonely as he was.

How long had it lasted? Was it only three years? Sometimes it seemed longer, sometimes far less. During that time he had found new feelings, new emotions within himself. How many times had they revisited Roubillac's statues of Handel and Orpheus with his lyre? He found enjoyment in the gardens; happiness was contagious. They took the short stage out to the pretty village of Hampstead and wandered over the heath; she picked heather which she said, as a memory of happy days, she would press in the Bible she had brought with her from Hertfordshire. The pleasure gardens were a source of great delight to them both; there they could spend long days away from the streets. They went to Marylebone, Bagnigge Wells; they walked gaily through the Florida Gardens.

It was a new life for him; during his visits to her he tried to look like a successful tradesman as he enjoyed the tradesman's pleasures. It astonished him that there was so much to enjoy in the humble life; it astonished her that there could be happiness in a life from which Jim was absent. He was happy in what seemed to him a gaudy squalor; she was enchanted by what seemed to her luxury. It was the never-ending surprise of the other which delighted them both.

But it had to end. There was to be a child.

She trusted him completely, for she had laid bare the softness in his nature. To her he was not the same man whom Maud had known. He lived two lives; never before had he understood the true meaning of the double life. The gay young man, the reveller at the pleasure gardens, the tender lover of Millie Sand, Charles Adam—he seemed to have little connection with Sir Charles Trevenning.

Once at Hampstead during the first months of pregnancy she had talked of the child. A little girl, she wanted, a dear little girl. "I'd like her to be a lady," she said.

Then she began to enumerate the things which she would like for the child. "I'd like her to have a gown made of *gros de Naples*, and a pelisse of the same stuff and a large pelerine all of silk and a big Leghorn hat trimmed with ribbons and flowers. We had to make a dress of *gros de Naples* when I was at Mistress Rickards's. It took us the whole of the week with the six of us working. We had to get it done so fast that we hardly had any sleep at all.''

"You are thinking of the child grown up," he told her.

"Yes. That's how I think of her . . . as a lady."

"Are you afraid?" he asked.

"Afraid?"

"So many girls would be."

"Oh, that's when they're alone. I've got you."

She was so trusting, so sure of him. Had he wanted to he could easily have deserted her. But he did not want to. Did one desert pleasure? Did one desert happiness and all the real joys of life?

He had changed a good deal since he had known her. It was ironical that the change should be for the better. He was gentler with Maud; he no longer allowed her to irritate him. He was thoughtful, wanting to make up for his previous indifference. How strange that contentment should come through sin; and stranger still that a word like sin could be attached to his love for Millie Sand.

She had died, little Millie Sand, two days after the child was born. How desolate he had been! How sad and lonely! He could not imagine now what he would have done without Fenella, for it was to her he had gone with his tragic tale.

Fenella had taken charge. The landlady was a motherly woman. Let her look after the child until she was two years old; then she could be sent to a convent of which Fenella knew.

It was Fenella who had named the child.

"When Millie talked of her," he said, "she called her Millie. She called her little Millie Sand. . . . That was Millie's own name."

Fenella grimaced. "Millie Sand. It sounds exactly like a mantua-maker's apprentice. Don't forget this child is your daughter, Charles. Millicent. We might call her Millicent. I never greatly cared for Millicent. It sounds a little prim to me and I cannot endure primness. Millicent. Melisande. Why, that's charming. We must call her Melisande. And we'll call her after the street in which she was born. Melisande St. Martin. That's beautiful. That will fit her. She must be Melisande St. Martin."

And that was all, for Melisande eventually crossed the Channel and went to live with the nuns of Notre Dame Marie. There she would be well educated and he need not think of her for years; and it might well be that she—like so many in such circumstances—would never wish to leave the convent. Then his responsibilities to Millie Sand would cease.

But he had not been able to resist the impulse. He had to see his daughter; he had to find out what sort of child he and Millie had created.

So he saw her, the enchanting Melisande; and again and again he had gone back to see her.

Of one thing he was certain. She would not stay in the Convent.

So as the coach carried him to Paris, once more he wondered what the future had in store for him and for Melisande.

Three

Excitement filled the house, and the servants were hard at work polishing and cleaning; everything that could go into the wash-tubs went. The gardeners were keeping the hothouse flowers in perfect condition that they might be brought into the ballroom for the great night. The villagers were full of the pending event; on the night of the ball they would wander up the long drive, part of which was a right of way from the road to Trevenning woods, and get as near the house as they could in the hope of catching a glimpse of the fine ladies and gentlemen who would dance in the ballroom to celebrate the birthday and betrothal of Miss Caroline.

Miss Pennifield, who did all the dressmaking, had gossiped about the beautiful materials of which she was making a ball dress for Lady Trevenning and another for Miss Caroline. Lavender silk for my lady and white satin for Miss Caroline—the white satin to be embroidered with pink roses. "Oh, my eyes!" cried Miss Pennifield when she talked of those roses—and she did this twenty times a day. "I never *saw* such dresses in all my natural."

In Lady Trevenning's sitting-room Miss Pennifield was busily fitting Miss Caroline's dress. Her fingers were trembling a little because this very day the guests from London would arrive, and the dress should be finished by now. Lady Trevenning had declared herself delighted with the lavender silk; but Miss Caroline was always a problem, and she would keep changing her mind about the fullness of the skirt or the set of the sleeves.

Caroline was like her father in appearance, but in place of his aloofness she had an uncertain temper. She seemed to be continually brooding and she was never satisfied. That came of having so many of the good things of life, thought Miss Pennifield, who herself had very little.

"The set on the shoulders is not right," cried Caroline, shaking back the ringlets which she wore in the fashion set by the young Queen. "It makes the sleeves too short."

"But it seems right to me, dear," said Lady Trevenning. "Do you not think so, Pennifield?"

"Yes, I do, my lady." Miss Pennifield, in the presence of her employer, was a different person from the perky little woman the village knew.

"But it does not!" snapped Caroline. "It is too bunchy here, I tell you. That is not according to the London fashion."

Miss Pennifield, with the tears smarting behind her eyes and the pins pricking through her bodice into which in her agitation she had carelessly stuck them, changed the set of the sleeves.

Wenna, who was hovering about Lady Trevenning to make sure she had her wrap about her shoulders, looked at Caroline and understood all the fears and apprehensions which beset the girl.

Caroline was extra touchy this morning. No amount of resetting the sleeve would satisfy her. Wenna knew it. Her dissatisfaction with the dress was the outward sign of her fear that she would not please Mr. Fermor when he came. My poor little queen! thought Wenna. You be all right. You'm pretty enough. You'm the prettiest creature in the world . . . in Wenna's world leastways; and if you're not like the smart ladies to London, well, that be no loss, and I've heard young men be very partial to a change.

Wenna went over to Miss Pennifield.

"Here," she said in her authoritative way, "let me see it, do. Well, what's wrong with that, my precious? It do look beautiful to me. Why, you won't want the sleeves so long they hide your pretty hands."

Wenna remembered. She remembered everything about her Miss Caroline as she did about her Miss Maud. They were her life; they were her passion. Caroline had come back excited from the trip to London. She was fourteen then and had gone to see the wedding celebrations of the Queen. She

had come back full of excitement—not because she had seen
the Queen and her Consort but because she had seen Fermor;
and she had known then that one day she was to marry Fermor.

Caroline had unburdened herself to Wenna, just as she
always had during the days of her childhood. "Come, tell
Wenna." That had been their cry at all times—when she was
happy or afraid. When she was a little girl and had had bad
dreams she would present herself at Wenna's bedside and
whisper: "Tell Wenna." Wenna treasured such memories.
And during that trip to London Caroline had been captivated
by the handsome domineering boy who was only a few
months older than herself. He had finally approved of Caroline, but in a patronizing way. He had even told her she had
pretty hands.

So now Wenna was reminding her of this, and she saw the
soothing effect her words produced.

"That be right, b'ain't it?" she asked the dressmaker.

"It is indeed," said poor Miss Pennifield.

"Now slip it off and let Miss Pennifield stitch it. And I
shouldn't try it on again. My dear life, it'll be spoilt before
you wear it. There . . . that's right. Now you're looking a
little flushed. I'm going to make you lie down and have a rest
before the guests arrive."

"They won't be here for ages, Wenna."

"You never know. Master Fermor will be that eager.
Nothing would surprise me."

That pleased her again. The dear sweet creature, thought
Wenna. She'm so pretty when she do smile.

Purposefully Wenna helped her to put on her dress.

"I'm not going to lie down," said Caroline. "You foolish
woman, do you think I'm an invalid?"

"Very well then. But you'll stop fretting, my handsome,
and you'll go and change into your watered silk . . . just in
case the visitors arrive early. Then take a book and go to the
hammock and wait there."

"Wenna, don't order me," said Caroline.

But she went all the same.

Miss Pennifield took the white satin away to the sewing-room with obvious relief, and Wenna was left alone with Lady Trevenning.

"Wenna, I don't know what we should do without you," said Maud, a little tearfully.

She was tearful on all occasions now, it seemed to Wenna; tearful when she was happy, tearful when she was sad, tearful when she was grateful. It was a sign of weakness, Wenna believed; and she knew that it irritated Sir Charles. Wenna disliked all men, but she hated Sir Charles. He had failed to make her mistress happy; Wenna did not know why; he was always courteous and gentle. He spent much time in London, and Wenna believed she knew the purpose of those visits. "Another woman!" she would say to herself. "Nothing would surprise me. He may be deceiving that poor woman as well, for all we know. I vow he's got a regular little love nest tucked away somewhere." The supposed secret woman qualified for her pity when she thought thus; at other times Wenna hated her with a scorn almost as great as that which she had for the master.

"Poor Miss Caroline!" said Wenna tenderly. "She's a little upset. What girl wouldn't be! With her betrothal about to be celebrated and a handsome young man coming all the way from London and all!"

"A handsome young man whom she has only seen a few times, Wenna. I do hope she'll be happy."

"She seems fond of him, Miss Maud, my queen."

"But what does she know of marriage? It reminds me . . ."

Wenna nodded. It reminded her too. Her innocent Miss Maud twenty-two years ago entering into marriage with the man her parents had chosen for her.

"There," said Wenna, "you lie back and close your eyes. Here's your hartshorn. I'll sit beside you and finish off your new white petticoat. Then if you do want anything I'll be here."

Maud nodded. She was very docile; and Wenna knew how to manage both her precious ones—Maud and Caroline.

Now she looked into her mistress's face and thought of the young girl of twenty-two years ago—young, like Caroline, flattered, delighted, yet frightened.

If only they knew! thought Wenna angrily.

No man had spoken for her, and she rejoiced in that fact. They had sense enough to know when they met one who was too sharp for them.

She thought of Sir Charles who was in one of his absent-minded moods to-day. Wenna guessed something was afoot. She did not quite know what, except that it had something to do with the secret wicked life he led. This morning she had seen a letter lying on his table. It was in a spidery foreign hand. It had come with papers from his solicitors in London. He had said nothing to Miss Maud about it; she would have told Wenna if he had. As if Wenna did not know how to prise their secrets from Maud and Caroline!

Maud was lying back with her eyes shut, the hartshorn held lightly in her delicate fingers. She looked very small and pale. Sir Charles had said: "Maud, if you would only take a little exercise it would do you the world of good." And poor Miss Maud had ridden to hounds and come back exhausted, so that Wenna had had to nurse her with her possets and her remedies.

Wenna, knitting the thick woollen stockings she made for herself or stitching at the undergarments which she made for her mistress—she would not allow Miss Pennifield to make her ladyship's undergarments—would jab her sewing needle into fine linen as though it were a rapier with which to attack the master, or click her knitting needles as though they were clashing swords.

She imagined the shameful things he must be doing with his secret woman in London. Her mental disparagement of Sir Charles grew in proportion to her love for Miss Maud.

When she had been young—one of many children living in one of the cottages by the quay—and they had been glad to get her into one of the big houses, her parents had said: "We'd like to see Wenna settled, for she'll never find a husband." And wouldn't want one! thought Wenna fiercely. I get on like a barn afire without.

Maud opened her eyes and Wenna said: "The master do seem put out this morning. I do hope nothing's wrong."

"What do you mean?" asked Maud.

"There was a letter came with his papers. It looked like foreign writing and he seemed worried after getting it."

"A foreign letter," said Maud. "It would be some business, I daresay. I believe Sir Charles has interests in foreign lands."

She spoke lightly. Business in her mind was something men were concerned with, necessary and to be tolerated, but far beyond the understanding of ladies. Wenna smiled sardonically; she had no such flattering opinions of the business of men.

Caroline was swinging to and fro in the hammock, thinking of Fermor. She saw herself in the white satin dress. It was beautiful, but would it look beautiful to him? When she had stayed in London she had felt very smart in her green striped dress and matching pelerine—until she had seen the London girls.

She and her father had visited Fermor's parents; her mother had been too ill to accompany them. She remembered now the first time she had seen Fermor. It was in his mother's drawing-room. He had been a little resentful, knowing that their parents intended they should marry one day. He had shown this resentment by taking as little notice of her as he need. He did talk to her about his father's country house as though he thought the country was all she could possibly know anything about. The parents whispered about them. "How charming young people are," his mother had said. "Love's young awakening is so affecting!" That had embarrassed Caroline and rendered Fermor gruffer than ever.

When they rode together in the Row he seemed to like her better, for she was a good horsewoman, and she fancied that he would always want people who belonged to him to be perfect.

He tried to pretend that he was much older than she was, but she reminded him that it was only a few months. "But you have never been away from the country before," he retorted. "That makes all the difference." "A few months can only be a few months wherever you live," she answered with spirit. He pretended to be very shocked. "What! Contradicting a gentleman! That is very bad manners." "What about contradicting a lady? In the country gentlemen are supposed to be polite to ladies." "Is that why they are supposed to be such bumpkins?'' he had asked; and he had the last word on that subject. She believed he always would have the last word.

But during the ball which was held at his parents' house he had changed a little. She and he were considered too young to attend and had sat in a gallery with his grandparents and some elderly aunts to watch the dancers. She believed she had looked rather pretty in her blue silk party dress. Then he had said: ''You have pretty hands. They don't look as if they could manage a horse as they do.'' It was a sign of approval. He was becoming reconciled to the fact that one day he would have to marry her.

After that he had become boastful; he had told her of incredible adventures in the streets of London; how he had been a highwayman at one time robbing the rich for the sake of the poor. In some stories he was a terror, in others a hero. She liked his stories though she did not believe them, but it was comforting to think that he took the trouble to make them up for her amusement. They had been allowed to drive in the carriage through the streets of London. He pointed out the Peelers in their top hats and blue tail-coats and white trousers. He asked her to take particular note of their truncheons. He told her that the streets of London were full of dangerous criminals; and he had taken a great delight in pointing out people in the crowd. ''There is a murderer!'' ''Oh look, there's a pickpocket.'' And to please him she had cried out in assumed fear.

He had been ready to like her during those days. They had been taken to Hyde Park to see the Fair which had been erected there to celebrate the wedding. She had been thrilled by the fluttering flags, the bands and dancing, the boats on the Serpentine; the fireworks had especially enchanted her. A servant had been in charge of them and they had been allowed to eat ices which were sold in one of the tents, for everyone was saying that ices were a refined luxury.

On the way back, she remembered, he had told her of an execution he had seen outside Newgate Jail: he had also seen pickpockets ducked.

London had seemed to her a delightful and charming place, and Fermor the most delightful person in it.

She wished she had not seen him kiss the parlourmaid on that last night. Neither of them knew that she saw. He was not yet fifteen but big enough for twenty; and the parlourmaid was a fluffy, giggling sixteen. She had slapped him, as Caroline would not have dared to do. "You . . . Master Fermor . . . up to tricks again!" Caroline had gone shivering to her room and had been rather glad that her father would take her home next day.

She had not seen him since. That was three years ago. The journey between London and Cornwall was a tedious one, particularly on the Cornish side of the Tamar where there was no railway. Wheels were continually stuck in the ruts, carriages overturned, and isolated travellers were a prey to weather and worse. It was not a journey to be undertaken except on serious business.

And now she was nearly eighteen and her betrothal was to take place on her birthday. She wanted to be married; she believed she wanted to marry Fermor; but into her pleasantest thoughts of him would come a Fermor she had met only by accident, Fermor whom a parlourmaid had slapped and accused of being up to his tricks . . . again. Again!

So . . . she was afraid.

He came to find her in the hammock. She had heard the arrival and was expecting him.

"Caroline . . . Caroline!" he called.

She studied him with excitement and pleasure. He was very tall and blue-eyed. He was bronzed, the same braggart whom she had met in London, yet more than three and a half years older than he had been then, and it seemed, far, far, wiser, completely sure of himself, already seeming to be a man of wide experience.

Smiling he took her hand and kissed it; she watched him solemnly. Suddenly, laughing aloud, he tipped her out of the hammock.

"Unceremonious," he said, in the short clipped speech which had not been his before, "but necessary. How tall are you, Caroline? Why, scarcely up to my shoulder. Let me look at you. You're prettier than you were." He kissed her swiftly on the cheek. "Well, haven't you something to say to me? Some greeting? How does a young lady greet her affianced husband?''

She tried to think of something to say and could not.

"I was told I'd find you here," he said helpfully.

She said shyly: "Do you remember when we last met? It was just over three years ago, wasn't it? They made us talk together and they whispered about us."

"Why yes, I remember."

"And we hated each other because they were going to make us marry."

"Nonsense! I was enchanted from the minute I set eyes on you."

"That is not a true thing to say."

"Well, it's a very nice thing," he said.

She laughed and he put his arm through hers.

"I'll show you the gardens," she said.

As they walked he told her how he had spent the time during the waiting. He spoke as though he had scarcely been able to endure the dreary days between their last meeting and this one. They had despaired of educating him, he told her. So he had made do with the Grand Tour. He was just back. The sun had been hot in Italy—hence his sun-baked appearance.

"I like it," she said shyly.

They were determined to be pleased with each other. Everybody was pleased, except Wenna. She, thought Caroline, would like me to hate him so that she could comfort me.

She led him into the house for she knew she must not be too long alone with him unchaperoned. She sat next to him during dinner; after dinner she talked with him. And that night she could scarcely sleep for thinking of him, but she kept remembering that occasion when she had seen him on the stairs with the servant.

She reminded herself that she had nothing to fear. Her parents had arranged the marriage; it was a convenient marriage. Of course love matches were supposed to happen without the aid of parents. But theirs should be a love match which had been arranged for them. Caroline could not bear that it should be otherwise.

* * *

It had all happened so suddenly, so unexpectedly. The day of the great ball had come and everyone had been well and happy then. Caroline had worn her white satin and Fermor had said she looked like an angel or a fairy. They had danced together; and the gentry from the surrounding country had drunk their health in champagne. They were truly affianced; and she wore a diamond ring on her finger to prove it.

The villagers had looked in at the great windows. Some, very daring, had come quite close, and had had to be turned away by Meaker the butler.

It was a hot night. Who was it who had suggested they should go out and dance on the lawn? Why not? There was a moon and it was so romantic. The young people had begged for permission to do so. Their elders had demurred, yet with that hesitancy which means consent. Mammas and Papas had sat on the terraces to watch.

The dew was falling and Lady Trevenning, sensitive to cold, was the first to notice it. She looked for a servant whom she might order to bring her a wrap. Sir Charles was standing near her.

"What is it, Maud?" he asked.

She adjusted the lace scarf about her shoulders. "It's a little chilly. I need a wrap."

"I'll go and get one," he said.

He came into the porch. There was a young girl sitting on the seat there—a young man beside her. Her dress was black and she was very small. He saw her green eyes as she lifted her head to smile at him.

She was quite different, of course. He recognized her at once as Jane Collings, the daughter of his old friend James, the M.F.H. But for the moment she had made his heart beat faster. He thought of the letter which he kept in his pocket, and as he went into the house he forgot why he had come in; he went to the quiet of the library and taking out the letter read it through once more. It was from the Mother Superior of the Convent Notre Dame Marie. She was anxious on account of Melisande. The child was now nearly fifteen and had learned all that the nuns could teach her. She was bright but not *sérieuse*. The Mother had had a long talk with the child and with the nuns who had taught her, and none of them thought that the Convent was any longer the ideal place for Melisande. The girl was restless; she had been caught slipping out of the Convent without permission. She liked to visit the *auberge* and if possible talk to strangers who stayed there. It was disquieting and the Mother was perturbed. Would Monsieur let them know his wishes? It was the advice of herself and those nuns who knew Melisande so well that the child should be taken from the Convent—much as they would miss her and the money Monsieur had paid them so regularly. It was their considered opinion that Melisande should be put to some useful work. She was educated well enough to become a governess. She might be good with her needle if she would apply herself more diligently. The Mother sent her felicitations and assured him that she was his sincere friend Jeanne de l'Isle Goroncourt.

He had thought of Melisande continually since he had had the letter.

He could not make up his mind what to do. Perhaps he would go to see Fenella. She had advised him once, and her advice had been good; moreover she had gained wisdom with the years, and he was sure she would be only too happy to help him solve his problem.

As he sat there the door opened and Wenna came in. She looked at him in some surprise and her sharp eyes went to the letter in his hands.

He said: "Oh, Wenna, her ladyship wants a wrap."

She had come near to the table and he noticed that she continued to look at the letter. He felt uneasy. He laid it down and immediately wished he had not done so. He said quickly: "It is getting chilly out there."

"I'll go and get it . . . at once," she said.

When Wenna went out with it, Maud said: "I thought he had forgotten. It was a long time ago that I asked him."

"Men!" said Wenna fiercely. "Thinking of nothing but themselves! Why, you'm chilled to the bone. You shall come in at once and I'll get 'ee a hot drink."

"Wenna, Wenna, what of my guests? You forget I'm not your pet now. I'm the hostess."

"You'll catch your death," prophesied Wenna, as she had prophesied a thousand times. But this time she was right.

The next morning her mistress was shivering yet feverish when she went in to her, and two days later she was dead.

There was great excitement in the *Auberge Lefevre*.

"It is Monsieur himself!" cried Madame. "Ah, Monsieur, it is a long time since we saw you. Come in. Come in. Your room shall be prepared for you. You will drink a glass of wine with my husband, will you not? Then we shall see about food for you. *Ragôut* . . . a little of that crimped sole that you like so much? Or the roast beef of your own country perhaps?"

"Thank you, thank you," he said.

"We shall make you comfortable here."

"I do not know how long I shall stay."

But Madame was away, calling her servants, preparing the warming pans, arranging for hot water to be carried to his room since he had a passion for the bath.

Madame herself would cook the meal. She would trust no other.

The Englishman drank a glass of wine with Armand.

He has aged, thought Armand. There is silver in his hair now.

They talked of town matters; but Armand was knowledgeable beyond the affairs of his own town. He shook his head. "There is a murmuring in the great cities, Monsieur. We hear it even here in the country. It is like a storm in the distance, you understand, Monsieur? This Louis Philippe and his Marie Amelie—are they going the same way as Louis XVI and Marie Antoinette? There are some who say they are neither for the aristocrats nor for the people. They meddle with the ministers of State, they bribe the juries and they dictate to the press. Frenchmen do not like this, Monsieur, and they are not calm like the people of Monsieur's country. They are happy, your people. They have a good Queen, have they not, kept in control by her pious German husband?"

The Englishman might have replied that England had her troubles; he might have mentioned the Luddites and the men of Tolpuddle, the rising struggle over the corn laws, the concession already granted to one class by another in the reform laws; he might have mentioned the terrible inequalities between rich and poor which were—to those who saw it in a certain way, which he did not—a shameful disgrace to any nation; but of course the inequalities in France were even greater. But the Englishman said none of these things. He preferred to listen to the Frenchman, to shake his head and condole.

Moreover he was thinking of the reason for his visit.

But he did not hurry. It was not in his nature to hurry. He had rehearsed what he would say when he was confronted with the girl whom he had not seen since she had dropped her *sabot* at his feet.

He ate the excellent fish which Madame had prepared for him; he scarcely noticed Madame's special sauce, but he assured her that it was delicious. Then he retired early that he might be fresh for to-morrow's task.

Melisande stood before her class of little children. Outside the sun was shining. There was a butterfly trying to get out of the windows—a white butterfly with touches of green on his wings. She was thinking of the butterfly rather than of the children.

Poor little butterfly! He was imprisoned in the room even as she was imprisoned in the Convent. She knew nothing of the world; she only knew a life which was governed by bells— bells for rising, bells for prayers, bells for *petit déjeuner*, for the first class, for the second, for the walk through the town and so on through the days; and every day was alike except saint days and Sundays, and any saint day was like any other saint day, any Sunday like another.

What were the excitements of the days? Little Jeanne-Marie had the colic; little Yvette had learned to read. Melisande loved little Jeanne-Marie; she was delighted in the triumph of little Yvette; but this was not living.

She spent much time in dreaming of wonderful things which would happen to her, of knights who rode to the Convent and abducted her; she pictured herself riding away with one of them to an enchanted castle, to Paris, to Rome, to London, to Egypt—all the wonderful countries of which she had read in the geography lessons. When she drew maps with the older children she would picture herself sailing up that river, climbing that mountain.

Sometimes when she was sent to the market with the garments or the garden produce which were to be sold, she would loiter and talk to the stall-holders. The eyes of old Henri would light up when he saw her, and she saw in the gaze of his young grandson that she was too pretty a girl to live in a convent all her life. She would linger at the *auberge* and try a piece of Madame's rich *gâteau*; Armand would let her see how he admired her while he awaited the answers to the questions he asked her with such burning curiosity. "And how long shall you stay at the Convent, Mademoiselle Melisande? Do you never hear news of some relatives in the outside world?"

Now she went to the window and opened it, but the silly butterfly did not seem to know how to get out even then. She seized it gently and released it.

"It is flying away, home to its children," said young Louise.

"To its little house and its baby butterflies," said Yvette.

She looked at the children, her green eyes momentarily sad. These children were obsessed by the thought of homes, of families in which there was a mother and father. They longed for a home—a real home however humble; they longed for brothers and sisters. She had ceased to long for such impossibilities; she wanted to escape into the world because she felt herself to be a prisoner.

As the butterfly flew away the door opened and Sister Eugenie came in.

Melisande sighed. The classroom in an uproar over a butterfly! She would be reprimanded for this. Why was it that her smallest misdemeanours always seemed to be brought home to her?

But Sister Eugenie did not seem to notice the disturbance. She was looking straight at Melisande, and there was a faint colour in her cheeks; her eyes, beneath her stern headdress, looked as excited as they ever could look.

"I will take the class," she said. "You are to go to *la Mère* at once."

Melisande was astonished. She opened her mouth to

speak, but Eugenie went on: ''Go at once. Oh, but first tidy your hair. *La Mère* is waiting.''

Melisande hurried out of the classroom along the corridors to the dormitory. Over the bed which was slightly bigger than the others hung a mirror. The bed and the mirror were hers; now that she was nearly sixteen, it was her duty to sleep in the dormitory with the small children.

Her hair, as usual, was untwining itself from the plaits which hung over her shoulders. No wonder Sister Eugenie had noticed it!

She hastily replaited it. What could the Mother want with her? She had dallied in the market square only yesterday; she had gossiped and laughed and chattered with Henri. Was that it? ''Now, now,'' had said Henri's grandson. ''No flirting with the young lady, Grandpapa!''

She had laughed with pleasure at the time; but what if the nuns had overheard? What a sin! What a penance would be hers!

She began to frame excuses as she went along to that room in which the Mother spent most of her time studying religious books and looking after the affairs of the Convent.

''Come in,'' said the Mother, when she knocked.

A man was sitting by the table. She caught her breath with surprise and felt the blood rush into her face. She knew that man. She would have recognized him anywhere because he was not like anyone else she had ever known. He was the Englishman who had sat outside the *auberge*.

''Melisande,'' said the Mother, ''come here, my child.'' As Melisande approached the table, the Mother went on: ''This is Mr. Charles Adam.''

Melisande curtseyed to the stranger.

''Speak to him in English, child,'' said the Mother. ''He would prefer that. Mr. Adam has come to see you. He has something to say to you, and he thinks it would be better if he told it to you himself. I am going to leave you that you may talk with him.''

''Yes, *ma Mère*.''

''He is your guardian, Melisande. Do not forget . . . in English. He will wish to know how proficient you have become in that tongue.''

The Mother rose and laid a hand on Melisande's shoulder; she gave her a little push towards Mr. Adam who had risen and was holding out his hand to shake hers.

The door closed on the Mother.

"This is a surprise to you," he said.

"My . . . guardian?" she said.

"Yes . . . yes."

"But you did not say. I mean . . . outside the inn . . . when I dropped my *sabot*. You did not tell me then. I should have been so excited. I did not know . . ."

She stopped. She was becoming incoherent as Sister Emilie said she was when she was excited, and it was only the fact that it was not so easy to translate her thoughts into English which stopped the flow of words.

"I am sorry," he said. "I could not explain then. It is difficult even now . . ."

"Of course, Monsieur." She looked at him with delight, taking in every detail: the elegant clothes, the hair slightly greying at the temples, the rather cold grey eyes, the stern mouth; she decided he was somewhat formidable, but everything that a guardian ought to be. He was not the sort of man about whom Thérèse need have the slightest qualm—nor the Mother, it seemed. How odd! Here she was alone in a room with a man for the first time in her life. Her lips curled up at the corners.

"So, Monsieur," she said, "you are my guardian."

"I . . . I knew your father."

"Oh, please tell me. I have so often wondered. What was my father like? Where is he now? Why was I left at the Convent? Is he still alive?"

"Your father was a gentleman," he said.

"And my mother?"

"Your mother died very soon after you were born."

"And my father also?"

"You . . . lost him too. He asked me to look after you."

"And it was you who sent me to the Convent?"

"The education which has been given you here is as good as any you could get. . . . I was persuaded."

She laughed and, because he looked surprised, she said:

"I am only laughing because I am pleased. No one has been really interested in me before."

"I had thought you might make the Convent your permanent home."

Her face fell. She felt as the butterfly would have felt if, after she had shown him the fresh air and freedom, she had brought him back into the schoolroom.

"I am not good enough to be a nun," she said. She was sad suddenly; her lids hid the brilliance of her eyes and all the joy seemed to have gone out of her face. "I did not feel the ecstasy of prayers and fasting. Little Louise said that when she worked on the angel's wing in the altar cloth she felt as though she had wings and was flying up to heaven. When I worked on the angel's robe, I just felt it was tiresome and hurt my eyes. You see . . ."

But of course he was not interested in little Louise and her feelings, nor in the weaknesses of Melisande.

She noticed that he ignored what she said and went on with his speech as though he were unaware of her interruption. She must keep quiet, for only by letting him do the talking could she know what he wished to say, and curb this aching curiosity within her.

"But," he went on, "it seems you are unsuited to convent life. So I have come to take you away if you wish to leave."

She clasped her hands together. They were trembling with excitement.

"I have one or two propositions to put before you." He looked at her eager animated face. "I am told that you know something of teaching. That means you could earn your living as a governess. I am told that you would be a good needlewoman if you would apply yourself to such work. It is possible that I may find a situation for you."

She was thoughtful. Perhaps, he thought, she saw herself escaping from one prison to another.

He made up his mind suddenly then. He had not until this moment been quite sure whether he could act so daringly. This was one of the most reckless moments of his life. It would be so simple to take her to Fenella. Fenella would have helped him as readily now as she had once before.

But Melisande was so charming—those shapeless ugly

garments could not hide that. She was Millie re-born . . . Millie turned into Melisande. Millie had been pretty and appealing, but this girl had real beauty. Millie was uneducated; this girl's intelligence shone through her beauty. That look of alert enquiry in the green eyes might have been inquisitiveness, but it was enchanting. How could he resist the temptation to bring his own daughter into his home, to watch her day by day? How could he allow her to take a menial post in another household? He seemed to hear Millie's voice saying: "I want her to have a *gros de Naples* gown and a mantle . . ."

She shall! he decided. He would, for once, forget to be cautious; he would override all difficulties.

"I have a situation for you," he said slowly.

"Oh . . . yes?"

He went on quickly: "My wife died recently. I have a daughter a few years older than you are. She needs a companion. Would you like to live in my house and help to cheer my daughter? The work would not be arduous. I should like you to be happy in my house. You would have all the comforts . . . the privileges . . . of my daughter herself."

Her eyes were shining, for he had changed. She had thought for a moment that he was going to lay his hands on her shoulders and kiss her.

"Yes please," she said. *"Please."*

"When will you be ready to leave?"

"Why, now!" she cried.

"I think in a few days' time would be more convenient. You will need time to prepare."

She was smiling, and she spoke as usual without considering. "I believe," she said, "that you were very fond of my father."

He turned away from her sharply; then suddenly he turned his head and said over his shoulder; "What makes you think so?"

"To have cared so much about me . . . whom you didn't know . . . to be so pleased because I am coming to live in your house."

When he turned back to her his face was without expression. "Let us hope," he said, "that everyone will be pleased."

It was impossible to keep the secret. The *auberge* hummed with it.

"What did I tell you?" cried Armand, delighted. "Now, Madame, you see that I am a man who can put two and two together."

But Madame was sad. "He will never come to see us again. And we shall lose Melisande too."

"You have grown fond of her," said Armand pensively. "She is a beautiful girl. You should rejoice since she is going to her father's house. She will have silks and satins, a handsome husband and a fine dowry."

"But we shall not see her in her silks and satins. We shall not see the handsome husband; and none of the dowry will be spent at our inn."

Armand was philosophical. "There will be others . . . other gentlemen who come to see their daughters . . . other gentlemen to sit with me and watch the children."

"That would be too much of a coincidence," retorted his wife.

"Indeed no," murmured Armand; "it would be life."

They watched them depart on the coach which would take them to Paris—that incongruous pair; the Englishman with the melancholy expression and the vivacious young girl in her sombre convent clothes.

Madame was openly weeping, and Armand wiped a tear from his eye as he returned to his bottle of wine.

It was not until they were in Paris that Charles changed his identity. Now it was safe, he thought; and he would have to tell her before they reached England.

"I was Charles Adam to the nuns," he said. "But that is not my real name. It is Charles Trevenning."

"Trevenning," she repeated with her French accent. "Is that so then?" How true it was that she spoke first and thought afterwards. "This . . . it was a . . ." She struggled for the word. "It was a necessary . . . ?"

"The position was a little difficult. My friends . . . being unable to see to these matters for themselves . . ."

"You mean my parents?"

"Yes. And I . . . with a child on my hands."

She nodded. "It was an awkwardness," she said. "A great awkwardness," she repeated, delighted with the word. Her eyes were sparkling. She had read forbidden books. There had been a lady staying at the *auberge* who had spoken to her and, being interested in her, had given her several books. She had smuggled them into the Convent. One grew tired of *Pilgrim's Progress* and the Bible. How enthralling were those books! What excitement to read of the outside world, where there was love, death and birth—all of which, it seemed so often, should never have taken place.

She was not as ignorant as people believed of life outside convents. She saw his point. Her parents had died and left him a baby. That was an awkwardness indeed. There would be scandal—and scandal was a frequent ingredient of the forbidden books. She understood perfectly why he had had to be Charles Adam. "But," she said, speaking her thoughts aloud, "the nuns would never have told."

"It seemed wiser," he said. "Will you remember then that I am Charles Trevenning, Sir Charles Trevenning. There is another matter. You must have noticed that you and I attract some attention. That is because people wonder about our relationship. It might be wiser if at this stage of our journey I call you . . . my daughter."

She nodded vigorously and with delight. "It is an honour," she said. "It pleases me."

He was relieved to find her so intelligent. He was becoming more and more drawn to her with every passing moment.

"And," he went on, "there is the matter of clothes. While we are in Paris we will try to find something more suitable for you."

She was enchanted by the idea of buying new clothes.

It was necessary to stay some days in the French capital, and he was determined to make her presentable before they left; he wished her to look like an English schoolgirl, who, having been met by her father after completing her stay at a finishing school, was going home.

He was sure that she attracted attention because of her incongruous clothes, because she talked too much, because she was excited by everything she saw. He believed that she would calm down. But he found that he could not make her into the girl he wished her to be; she was, above all things, herself. He pictured her vaguely in a discreet dress of dark tartan with a little cape about her shoulders; he saw her in a neat bonnet which would help to subdue the brilliance of her eyes.

When they entered the shop he said to the saleswoman in his stiff French: "This is my daughter. I want her to have a discreet outfit."

But he had reckoned without the saleswoman . . . and Melisande. The latter had already seen a beautiful gown with frills and flounces, with a low-cut bodice and leg-of-mutton sleeves. She stood before it, her arms folded across her breast.

"But it is too old for Mademoiselle," said the saleswoman tenderly.

"But it is so beautiful," said Melisande.

The saleswoman laughed understandingly while Melisande joined in excitedly; and they talked in such rapid French that he could not possibly follow the conversation.

"It is a travelling dress that is wanted," he began.

"Monsieur?"

"A travelling dress . . ."

"I want a dress of scarlet!" cried Melisande. "Of scarlet and blue and gold. I want all the brightest colours in the world, because I have lived in a convent and never worn anything but black . . . black . . . black. . . ."

"Black is for when you are a little older," said the saleswoman. "Then with those eyes that will be beautiful. Black . . . I see it . . . with the bodice cut low and frills and frills of chiffon."

"It is a travelling dress we want," he insisted.

But the saleswoman had taken Melisande away and as he heard the child's excited squeals of laughter and sat on the chair they had provided for him, he thought of Millie Sand at Hampstead and all she had wanted for this girl. Then he could smile at those excited voices. Could Millie see her daughter now? Of course she could. Wasn't it a tenet of his

belief that those who passed away could look down on those
who were left? Then she would be looking down and saying:
"I knew I could trust him."

He did not notice how the time was passing for he was
going over it all again—that long-ago romance of which this
girl, who had caused him such acute embarrassment and
would cause him more, was the living reminder.

And when at length she came and stood before him he
scarcely recognized her.

She was dressed in a travelling dress of black and green;
it nipped in her tiny waist; it gave her a slight and charming
maturity which had not before been visible. She was wearing
a green bonnet of the same silk with which the black dress
was trimmed. There were petticoats, she gleefully told him;
and there were other undergarments. She lifted her skirts to
show, but the saleswoman restrained her.

"Such spirits! It is a pleasure, Monsieur, to dress one with
such spirits. And there is a little dress with a wide skirt and
a *sous jupe* crinoline to accompany it . . . which would be
so useful for the special occasion, you understand?"

As he looked at Melisande he thought of the pride which
would have been Millie's if she could see her daughter now.
She had been educated as well as girls of the richest families;
and now she was charmingly dressed by a Paris House, the
most elegant in the world.

He said smiling: "The result is charming. And the little
dress . . . yes! She must have that also. And perhaps another
if that is what she will need."

The saleswoman was enraptured. Melisande was enraptured.

The clothes should be sent to their hotel.

"You have spent much money," said Melisande.

"You needed the things."

She jumped up and, putting her arms about his neck,
kissed him.

The saleswoman laughed. "It is understandable . . . Mademoiselle's gratitude to her kind Papa."

"The best of all Papas!" cried Melisande, her eyes gleam-
ing because of the secret they shared. They must act their
parts when they were travelling, her eyes reminded him; be-

cause if people thought they were not father and daughter there would be a scandal.

When they went into the streets heads turned to watch her. Perhaps, he thought, it would have been better to have left her in her convent clothes.

To travel with Melisande was like going over the familiar ground for the first time. How delighted she was with everything! The smallest things that happened to her became the greatest jokes. To travel on a railway! She had never believed she would enjoy such an adventure. How she delighted in her seat in a first-class carriage! And how sorry she was for those who must travel third! Her moods were changeable. They almost tripped over each other. Now she was delighting in the pleasures of Vauxhall—for he had been unable to resist the impulse to take her there—then she was weeping for the plight of the beggars, the crossing sweepers, the old apple women.

He was partly sorry, partly relieved, when they were on a train again steaming westward.

"It is time now," he told her, "for us to stop our little pretence."

"I am no longer to be your daughter?" she asked.

"I think we should be wise to adopt another relationship."

"Yes?"

"We will say that you have been introduced to me by a friend because you want a post, and as my daughter will be lonely, I have taken the opportunity of providing a companion for her."

"I see that you do not wish them to know how good you have been to the daughter of your friend. You do not like being thanked."

"But I do. I like it very much."

She shook her head and gave him her warm smile. "No. When I thank you for my clothes, for the happiness you have brought me, you do not like it. You try to change the subject."

"You thank me too often. Once is enough. And now you must please do as I say. I think it advisable for people to think that you are the protégée of a friend of mine. You have been brought up in France; you need a post, and I thought it would be an excellent idea for you to come and stay with my daughter as her companion. As I told you, she has just lost her mother. She was to have been married soon, and that, of course, will be postponed for at least a year. Meanwhile you can help with her clothes; you can walk with her, do embroidery with her, play the pianoforte with her and teach her to speak good French.''

''It shall be as you say,'' she said solemnly. ''I will do all that you wish. My tongue has often been indiscreet but it shall be so no longer. Every time it is in danger of saying what it should not, I shall remind it of all you have done for me, of all the happiness you have brought to me, to the Paris dressmaker, to the nuns and to Monsieur and Madame Lefevre.''

''Oh, come, I am not such a universal benefactor!''

''Oh yes, you are. To me—that is clear. To the dressmaker because you buy so much and make good business for her, to Monsieur and Madame Lefevre because you are rich and Armand makes up his stories about you, and you are Madame's special guest; and to the nuns because if you had not come for me I believe I should have run away and that would have given them much sorrow.''

''You see the rosy side of life.''

''I love all rosiness,'' she told him. ''It is because I must wear ugly black all the time I was at the Convent.''

Then suddenly she kissed him again.

''It is the last time,'' she said. ''You are no longer, from this moment, my father who has come to take me from my finishing school and buys me beautiful clothes in Paris; you are the wise man who takes the opportunity of bringing me as a companion to his daughter.''

Then she sat upright in her seat, looking demure, the picture of a young lady going to her first post.

They took the post-chaise when they reached Devon, for the railway had not yet been extended into Cornwall.

Melisande was thoughtful now. The bridge between the old life and the new was nearly crossed. She was thinking with some apprehension of the daughter who was a little older than herself.

They came along the road so slowly that it was possible for her to admire the countryside which was more hilly than any she had ever seen. The roads were so bad that again and again the wheels were stuck in ruts, and the driver and postilion had to alight more than once to put their shoulders to the wheel.

Melisande noticed that Charles was becoming more and more uneasy as they proceeded. She herself grew quiet, catching his mood. He was uneasy because of her, she knew; he wondered perhaps how his daughter would like the companion he was providing for her.

He told her stories of the Duchy while they waited for a wheel to be mended. He told of the Little People in their red coats and sugar loaf hats who haunted this wild country, of the knackers who lived in the tin mines; they were no bigger than dolls but they behaved like old tinners. The miners, in order to keep in their good graces left them a *didjan* which was a part of the food they took into the mines with them. If they did not leave the knackers' *didjans* they believed terrible misfortune would overtake them.

Her eyes were round and solemn; she must hear more of these matters. "But who were these knackers? They were very wicked, were they not?"

They could be spiteful, he told her; but they could be bribed to goodness if they were left their crout. They were said to be the spirits of the Jews who had crucified Christ.

"How shall I know them and the Little People if I meet them?"

"I doubt whether you will meet them. Soon you will see old miners. The knackers are like them, but they could sit in your hands. The Little People wear scarlet jackets and sugar loaf hats."

"What if I had no food to give them? I could give them my handkerchief, I suppose. Or perhaps my bonnet." Her eyes were mournful at the thought of losing her bonnet.

"They would find no use for the bonnet," he said quickly. "It would be much too big. And you may never meet them. I never have."

"But I want to."

"People are terrified of meeting them. Some won't go out after dark for fear of doing so."

She said: "I should be terrified." She shivered and laughed. "All the same I want to."

He laughed at the way in which she peered out of the window.

"These are just legends," he said. "That is what people say nowadays. But this is a land of strangeness. I hope you will be happy in it."

"I am happy. I think this is the happiest time of my life."

"Let us hope it will be the beginning of a happy life."

"I was far from unhappy in the Convent," she said, "but I wanted something to happen . . . something wonderful . . . like your coming for me and taking me away with you."

"Is that so very wonderful?"

She looked at him in astonishment. "The most wonderful thing that could ever happen to anyone in a convent."

He was alarmed suddenly. He leaned forward and laid his hand over hers. "We can't say that anything is good or bad until we see the effect it has upon us. I don't know whether I am doing the right thing. I trust I am, my child."

"But this *is* the right thing. I know it. It is what I always wanted. I wished and wished that it would happen . . . and you see, it has."

"Ah," he said lightly, "perhaps you are one of those fortunate people whose wishes are granted."

"I must be."

"Perhaps my daughter will take you to one of our wishing wells. There you can make your wish, and we will hope that the piskies will grant it."

She said: "I will wish now." She closed her eyes. "I am wishing for . . ."

"No," he said laughing, "don't tell me. That would break the spell."

"What a wonderful place this is! There are Little People, piskies and knackers. I am going to be happy here. I am going to be so good a companion for your daughter that you will be very glad you decided to bring me here."

She was silent thinking of all that she would wish for herself and others.

And eventually they went on with their journey.

It was dusk when they turned in at the drive of Trevenning. The woman at the lodge came out to curtsey and open the gate. Melisande wanted to ask a good many questions about the woman, but she sat still, her hands folded in her lap. She must remember that their relationship had changed. He was becoming more and more remote, more stern; she must continually remind herself that she was only his daughter's companion now.

She could see the hilly slopes about her, the great gnarled trunks of trees, the masses of rhododendron bushes, the pond, the great sweep of grass and then the house.

She caught her breath. It was bigger than she had imagined—almost as big as the Convent, she thought; but it was a home and would be homely. How rich he must be to live in such a house! No wonder he had paid the Frenchwoman's bill for clothes without a murmur.

The carriage drew up on the gravel before the front door. As she alighted from it she was aware of the stately grandeur of grey granite walls and mullioned windows. A manservant was waiting in the porch. He took his master's cloak and hat.

"Is Miss Caroline in?" asked Sir Charles.

"Yes, Sir Charles. She is in the library with Miss Holland and Mr. Fermor."

"Tell her I am home. No . . . we will go there ourselves."

They were in a lofty hall, the walls of which were hung with portraits and trophies from the hunting field; rising from this hall was a wide staircase; and there were doors to the left and right. Sir Charles opened one of these and, as she followed him, Melisande was aware of the watching eyes of the manservant.

Now she could see a room lighted with candles; books lined one of its walls; there was a thick carpet; she was conscious of velvet curtains and an air of magnificence.

"Ah, Miss Holland . . . Caroline . . . Fermor. . . ." Sir Charles approached the three people who had risen from their chairs and were coming towards him. Melisande saw an elderly lady in pearl grey, a tall young man and a fair girl who was dressed in deep black. Her hair, worn in ringlets, looked almost silver in contrast with her black gown.

Sir Charles greeted the three ceremoniously before he turned and beckoned Melisande forward.

"This is Miss St. Martin, your companion, Caroline. Miss St. Martin, Miss Holland, the aunt of Mr. Fermor Holland who is affianced to my daughter. And Mr. Fermor Holland . . . and my daughter, Miss Trevenning."

Caroline stepped forward. "How do you do, Miss St. Martin?"

Melisande smiled and the young man returned her smile.

"Welcome, Miss St. Martin," he said.

"I am sure Miss Trevenning will be delighted with your company," said Miss Holland.

"Thank you, thank you," said Melisande. "You are all so kind."

"Miss St. Martin has been brought up in France," explained Sir Charles. "It will be good for you, Caroline, to improve your French."

"You speak perfect English," said the young man, his blue eyes still on Melisande.

"Not perfect, I fear. Though I hope soon to do so. Now that I am in England I realize that there is a . . . a wrongness about my speaking."

"Not a wrongness," said the young man. "A charm."

Melisande said: "But you make me feel so happy . . . so much that I have come home. You are all so kind to me here . . . everyone."

Caroline said: "You must be tired after your journey, Miss St. Martin . . . or would you prefer us to call you Mademoiselle?"

"It does not matter. Miss . . . or Mademoiselle . . . please . . . say which is easier for you."

"I suppose you're used to being called Mademoiselle. I'll try to remember. I have had them prepare a room for you. Perhaps you would like to go straight to it?"

Before Melisande could answer there was a knock on the door and a woman came in, a small woman with black eyes and cheeks glowing like a holly berry in winter.

"Ah, there you are, Wenna," said Charles.

"Have you had a good journey, Sir Charles?" asked Wenna, and Melisande was struck by the odd expression on her face. She did not smile; there was no welcome in her face; she looked as though she hoped he had had a very bad journey indeed.

"Quite good," said Sir Charles.

Caroline said: "Wenna, this is the young lady whom my father has brought to be my companion."

"Her room be ready," said the woman.

In that moment Melisande was deeply bewildered. She was conscious of the uneasiness of her benefactor; of Caroline she knew nothing, for Caroline at this moment was wearing a mask over her features. The elderly lady was gentle and meek; she would be kind. The young man Fermor was kind too; he was offering her the kind of friendship which she had come to expect. She had seen it in old Henri's eyes, in those of his grandson, in those of Armand Lefevre and of many men who had smiled at her during the journey, who had opened windows for her or handed her something she had dropped. They had all smiled as though Melisande was a person whose friends they would wish to be. And that was how Fermor was smiling.

But now she had caught the eyes of Wenna upon her. They startled her, for they were almost menacing.

PART TWO

Trevenning

One

So Melisande was at Trevenning.

Sir Charles drew the curtains about his bed and lay down; he was shut away from the house, he felt, shut away from the room with a hundred memories of Maud.

Have I done right? he asked himself again and again. How could I send her to work in another household where she would be welcomed neither in the servants' hall nor as a member of the family but in that unhappy limbo somewhere between?

But he must act with the utmost caution. He had done a very daring thing in bringing her here. He must be careful to show her no special favours. He had been rather reckless during the journey; her charm had disarmed him; he had enjoyed letting people think that they were father and daughter. There must be no breath of scandal at Trevenning. He must have a talk with Caroline. He must ask his daughter to treat Melisande kindly; perhaps he could hint at a tragedy. He began to work out some plausible story; but he rejected that; he must not add to the mystery concerning Melisande.

He closed his eyes and tried to sleep. He felt the physical discomfort which came to him after a long journey; he seemed still to be swaying with the movement of the carriage, and when he closed his eyes he still seemed to see the passing countryside. He kept thinking of her, her sudden laughter, her joy in everything that was new to her, her pity for those who seemed unfortunate. She was a charming girl; if it had been at all possible he would have delighted in claiming her for his daughter. But there was one thing he feared more than anything else: it was that scandal should touch his name. It had always been thus with Trevennings.

When he thought of that he knew he would have been
wiser to have taken her straight to Fenella. He should never
have forged a link between Trevenning and the Convent Notre Dame Marie; his two daughters should never have met.

Yet, although he regretted his rashness, he was sure that
if he could go back in time, he would do exactly as he had
already done.

But—he promised himself—no more risks.

Caroline lay in bed thinking of the newcomer. She had not
drawn the curtains about her bed. She was uneasy. She had
not failed to notice the looks which Fermor had given the
girl and she thought she knew the meaning of those looks.

The girl had both beauty and charm; she had that indefin-
able something which Caroline was sufficiently aware of to
know that she herself did not possess it. She herself was
pretty; she had a fortune and she was in every way marriage-
able; yet Fermor had been unable to prevent himself showing
his admiration of the girl.

Her father had written of Melisande St. Martin as though
she were a woman of forty, prim, a woman for whom they
should be sorry. How could they be sorry for a girl such as
Mademoiselle St. Martin?

Already she had seemed to cast knowledgeable looks at
Fermor, had revelled in his admiration; already Caroline saw
her as a coquettish trouble-maker who would scheme with
all her might to make her position firmer. She was glad that
Fermor would soon be leaving Cornwall. He had stayed—
with his aunt Miss Tabitha Holland as chaperone—until her
father returned, to console her because she was so distressed
at the loss of her mother. He *had* consoled her, and she had
been happy until her father had arrived, for Fermor had been
tender rather than ardent; it was as though he had welcomed
the constant company of his aunt. That seemed strange when
she thought of the looks she had seen him cast at Peg and
Bet, the two maids, and had remembered that long-ago scene
with the parlourmaid. She had rejoiced in his restraint; she
looked upon it as a sign of the respect he had for her.

He had said however that he did not see why they should
wait a whole year. He had declared he would speak to her

father and his people. "Perhaps we could have a quieter wedding if that would offend conventions less." He was impatient of conventions; he was by nature headstrong and ardent; that was probably why he enchanted her. She had felt temporarily sure of him until that moment when she had seen him look at the stranger and delight in her.

But he will soon be gone, she assured herself. And who knows, perhaps I can find some means of sending her away before he returns.

In the servants' hall Meaker sat at the head of the table. Supper, when they all gathered together to exchange gossip and discuss affairs of the household, was the high-light of their days. Mrs. Soady, the cook, could be relied upon to provide a loaded table; there were pies and pastries to keep up their strength; and it was Mrs. Soady's delight never to let them know what was beneath the piecrust. Sometimes it would be a taddage pie made of delicious sucking pig; at others a squab pie with layers of apple, bacon, onions and mutton with a squab at the bottom of the dish. There would be giblet pies and lammy pies, tatty pies and herby pies. There would be no secret about the popular pasty nor that favourite star-gazy pie, for in the first place there was no disguising the shape of the pasty, and the pilchards' heads peeping out of the pastry betrayed the star-gazy for what it was. No table of Mrs. Soady's was complete without a dish of cream with which Mrs. Soady liked to see all her pastry anointed; and there was always plenty of mead and cider with which to wash down the food. And with Mr. Meaker at one end of the table and Mrs. Soady at the other, they were a happy family in the servants' hall at Trevenning.

There was one notable absentee that night, but Wenna did not always join the others at table. When Lady Trevenning had been alive and she was always waiting on her ladyship, Wenna would have her meals at odd moments. Now she had continued the practice in the service of Miss Caroline. Wenna was a specially favoured servant.

On this day there was no talk of affairs outside the house. Mrs. Soady did not, as she often did, talk of her sister, the wise woman, and the members of her wonderful family. Mrs.

Soady belonged to a 'pellar' family, and in such families supernatural power was handed down through generation after generation from an ancestor who had assisted a mermaid back to the sea. Mrs. Soady's sister, as well as being a member of such a family was a seventh child and a footling into the bargain (she had been born feet first) and everyone at the table had been reminded that being born feet first was an indication of great powers to come; so the Soady family were generally one of the favourite topics.

Mr. Meaker could not allow his family to be completely over-shadowed. They were not 'pellars,' but they were invalids and had suffered from all the most terrible diseases known to man. Mr. Meaker had not been so long at Trevenning as some of the servants; he had served other masters, and, according to his accounts, the houses in which he had served were not only much grander than Trevenning, but all the inhabitants had been martyrs to their various ailments. Such conversations, sponsored by Mrs. Soady and augmented by Mr. Meaker, went down very well with 'fairmaids' and pasties or one of Mrs. Soady's mystery pies.

But to-night, of course, there was no talk but of Miss Caroline's new companion.

Peg, who had shown her to her bedroom, was looked to for special information because she had actually helped the newcomer to unpack her bag. The trouble with Peg was that being rather silly she kept choking with laughter and had to be slapped on the back or given water or mead to drink in order that a threatened attack of hysteria might be counteracted. Mr. Meaker had warned her before about hiccups. A member of one of his families had started an attack just like Peg's, and it had lasted six weeks before it killed him.

"Now you, Peg," said Mrs. Soady with a trace of irritability, "don't 'ee be so soft, don't! And give over giggling. Now what was there in the bag?"

"Oh, not much, Mrs. Soady . . . but what she had was terrible queer. And she had a black frock and a green bonnet . . . *green*, I tell 'ee!"

"Well that ain't telling us nothing," said Mrs. Soady. "Mr. Meaker saw that much."

Mr. Meaker was glad to seize an opportunity. "And a

handsome wench, she was, Mrs. Soady. Healthy and shapely.'' He curved his hands to indicate the curves of Melisande, smiling as he did so.

''Give over!'' said Mrs. Soady. ''I'll warrant Mr. Fermor had his eyes on her.''

''He had indeed, Mrs. Soady,'' put in Bet. She looked slyly at Peg. Bet lacked Peg's buxom charms so she was glad Mr. Fermor had noticed the stranger, for that would put Peg's nose out of joint. Bet knew—if others didn't—what Peg was. Peg came from West Looe, Bet from East Looe; they were natural rivals. Peg always took Mr. Fermor's hot water up in the mornings, and sometimes she stayed a long time and came out flushed and giggling. Bet knew; and it would serve Peg right if others knew and Peg was sent packing to that cottage on the quay whence she came.

''And what did you see, Bet?''

''Well,'' said Bet, with a titter, ''I don't rightly think that Miss Caroline is all that pleased with the companion her father's brought from London.''

Mr. Meaker said: ''Master Fermor is a real gentleman. There's many like him. I remember Mr. Leigh up to Leigh House. Not the present Mr. Leigh, but his father. He was a man for the maidens. Some say it brought on his end . . . prematurely.'' Everyone looked with respect at Mr. Meaker who had the manners and speech of a gentleman and who liked to baffle them with the use of words unfamiliar to them. Mr. Meaker looked round the company and laughed. ''I remember old Lil Tremorney; she was in his bed . . . regular, so I heard, when she was employed up to Leigh House.''

''Now, Mr. Meaker, there's young people present,'' said Mrs. Soady, ''and young people as is in my charge.''

''I beg your pardon humbly, Mrs. Soady . . . I beg it humbly. . . . But facts are facts and best faced.''

Mrs. Soady wanted to get back to the subject which interested her.

''And from foreign lands they say she do come.''

''She do talk like to make you fair die of laughing,'' Peg put in; and others who had heard her speak confirmed this.

''She be French, I've heard,'' said Mrs. Soady. ''Like as

not Mr. Meaker will tell us how we calls a young woman that's French. T'ain't Miss, I do know for sure.''

Mr. Meaker, who was delighted to be called upon to give information, explained that French ladies if unmarried—and they could be sure this young person was—were called Mamazel.

''There now!'' said Mrs. Soady admiring Mr. Meaker's knowledge of the world. ''Fancy that.''

''When I was serving the tea,'' said Annie the parlourmaid, ''after dinner 'twas . . . in the drawing-room . . .''

''We know when you serve tea, Annie,'' said Mrs. Soady sharply.

''Well then I heard Mr. Fermor say to her: 'You're very charming . . .' I think it were . . . and I forget what else.''

''You should remember better,'' said Mrs. Soady. ''What did Miss Caroline say?''

''She were terrible put out—you could see that.''

''I can't think what's come over the master,'' said Mr. Meaker. ''If he were a man like old Mr. Leigh it would not be outside my comprehension to see him bring a young female into the house. But we know the master for what he is; and for the life of me I cannot see why Miss Caroline wants a young female companion.''

''And such a pretty one!'' said the footman.

''Well,'' said Mrs. Soady, helping herself to more taddage, and pushing the dish along the table to be passed to Mr. Meaker, ''I'd like to see our young lady married, that I would . . . and that quick.''

''What about the recent death in the family, Mrs. Soady?'' asked Mr. Meaker.

''I don't know, I'm sure; but I do know that that wedding ought not to be put off too long. There's no knowing what'll come to pass . . . and now we've got this young female in the house . . .''

She stopped for a mouthful. Everyone was eating, but while they savoured the delicious food, they were all thinking of Mr. Fermor and his roving eye which reminded Mr. Meaker of old Mr. Leigh. They were sorry for Miss Caroline; and they thought of the newcomer who was—in the footman's opinion—the prettiest, tiddliest little thing you'd find from Torpoint to Land's End.

Melisande lay in the big fourposter bed. Her clothes had been unpacked by Peg and were now hanging in the wardrobe. She had bathed in the hip bath with the hot water which Peg had brought her. She was living in luxury, she told herself.

The room was charming and a fire burned in the grate, although it was summer time, sending a flickering glow to reveal the velvet curtains and the carpet which were the colour of ripe rich plums. She had blown out the candles before getting into bed, for the fire gave her all the light she needed. She had drawn back the window curtains and peered out, but it was too dark to see anything.

What a different bed from the one which had been hers at the Convent! This was an ancient bed; most things in the house seemed ancient; it was a real fourposter, with an ornate tester, and silk curtains about it.

As she stretched luxuriously she reminded herself that she was really a sort of servant in this house. It would be necessary to please Caroline; and she would not be easy to please. The young man, Mr. Fermor—he would be very easy to please. Ah, if she were to be *his* companion, how much easier that would be!

She laughed at the thought. He had sat near her while she had drunk the strange tea in the drawing-room. She had been talkative, too talkative. "We never drank tea in the Convent," she had told him. "It has a strange flavour. I like it . . . oh yes I like it. I like everything that is English. It is all an excitement . . . ." And he had laughed and leaned towards her and asked questions about the Convent. She who did not know how to restrain herself, and had not even thought it necessary to do so, had rattled on, occasionally breaking into French. "I have learned English, yes. But to write it . . . that is easier. To talk . . . one must think fast . . . and the words do not always come. . . ." What shining blue eyes he had! She liked him. Yes, she liked him very much. He made her feel happier than anyone had since she set foot in England, more than Sir Charles had when he had been so kind.

Why, she was not sure. Was it because all the time he seemed to be telling her how much he wished to be her friend?

"You have an unusual name," he had said, "Melisande. It is charming. I wonder why you were called Melisande." "How can we know the reasons for the names when we do not know our parents!" she had said. And somehow that had shocked them all . . . all except the young man. "Mine is a family name," he told her, "handed down and down through generations. Fermor. It's as unusual as yours." That had made a bond between them. He was very friendly. He had said that they must have seen when she was in her cradle how charming she would be when she grew up, and they had given her the most charming name they could think of because of that. "It is you who are charming," she had said, "to say these charming things to me and make me feel so happy."

She had acted wrongly. She realized that. Sir Charles was not pleased; nor was Caroline. They were queer people, those two, not like herself and Fermor. That was another bond between them; they said what they wanted to say.

Perhaps she had been bold; she had talked too much. She had forgotten that she was but a servant in the house. "Be humble," Sister Eugenie had said. "Remember it is the meek who inherit the Earth."

Caroline had watched them all the time. She had said: "I am sure Mademoiselle is very tired." And the way in which she said Mademoiselle made Melisande feel that she was indeed a servant in this house. Then Caroline went on: "I am not going to allow her to be exhausted by your chatter."

She had made another mistake. "Oh, but I am not exhausted. I am so happy to talk here."

Caroline had purposefully pulled the bell rope and little Peg had come.

"Bring candles," Caroline had said. "Mademoiselle St. Martin is very tired. You can light her to her room."

The maid had led the way upstairs after Melisande had said goodnight to Sir Charles and Fermor. Caroline walked beside her as they ascended.

"What a large house," cried Melisande. "I had no idea that it would be so big."

"It has been the home of my family for years and years," Caroline had said, seeming more friendly now that they had left the young man in the drawing-room.

"That is very exciting for you. To say: 'My grandfather, my great-grandfather, my great-great-grandfather lived here. . . .' And *I* never knew my father . . . nor my mother."

Caroline had clearly been taught to ignore what might be embarrassing. She had pointed to the effigies which were carved on the walnut banisters. "They represent members of the family. But you need daylight to see them."

"I look forward to to-morrow. I am sorry that I arrive in darkness. I shall sleep to-night in a house I do not see. It will be a strangeness."

Caroline had been silent. She had been aware that Peg, who must be listening, was with them. She had been thankful for Peg's stupidity, for one did not want such conversation repeated in the servants' hall. She had been glad when they were in the bedroom and Peg had set down her candle and lighted those in the sconces.

"Go and fetch hot water for Mademoiselle St. Martin," had said Caroline. "Or would you like her to help you unpack first, Mademoiselle?"

"There is so little to unpack."

"Peg," Caroline had commanded, "unpack the bag, please."

"Yes, Miss Caroline."

While she had been doing this, Caroline had gone to the window and Melisande followed.

Caroline had said: "You can't see a thing. It's as dark as a shaft, as the mining people say." She drew the curtains then. "There, that's better. I hope you will be happy here. We are a sombre household just at this time. My mother . . ."

"Yes, I hear . . . from your father. I am so sorry. It is a very great sadness. I know how sad. My own mother I never knew, but that does not mean I cannot have the sympathy. When your father told me . . ."

Caroline had cut her short. "It was so unexpected. She was not strong but when it came . . . we were unprepared."

Tears had filled Melisande's eyes. She who had never

known a mother, who saw all mothers as idealized saints—
a mixture of the Mother Superior and Madame Lefevre—
believed the loss of a mother to be the greatest tragedy in the
world.

Caroline had said almost angrily: "But if she had not
died . . . I suppose you would not be here."

A short silence had followed during which Melisande had
thought: She is angry with me. This is a sadness. She has
taken a dislike to me.

Peg had unpacked the bag and gone for hot water. Caroline had turned to Melisande and said quickly: "My wedding
had to be postponed."

"I am sorry. That must make unhappiness for you."

"We are disappointed . . . both of us."

"I understand."

"Mr. Holland has tried to persuade his people and my
father that we should not wait. But there is . . . convention,
you know. It distresses us both."

"Convention?"

"Yes. The need to behave as people would expect . . . in
a manner which is due to our position."

Melisande had been about to speak but Caroline had gone
on quickly: "When my father wrote saying he was bringing
you, he seemed to imply that you were quite a different sort
of person."

"What sort of person?"

"He wrote saying that he had found a poor person who
needed a home, and as Mamma had just died and my wedding had been postponed, he knew I must be lonely, so he
had engaged her on the spot. He made her appear to be about
forty, very poor, grey-haired, very prim and . . . grateful.
At least that is the picture I had in my mind."

"I am poor!" Melisande had cried with a smile. "And if
I have not yet forty years then I shall one day. Prim I could
be; grateful I am. I hope I shall not always disappoint."

"Oh no . . . no. I am sure you will quickly understand us
. . . and fit in with us. Your English is a little quaint . . . but
I'm sure you will soon be as one of us."

Soon after that Peg had come back with the hot water, and
telling Melisande that if there was anything she wanted she

must pull the bell rope and someone would come and attend to her wants, Caroline said goodnight and left her.

So Melisande had undressed, washed in the hip bath, put on the cotton nightgown which she had brought with her from the Convent and got into bed. And now she found she was too excited for sleep. She could not stop thinking of the people whom she had met, and chiefly she thought of Fermor and Caroline; the one who so clearly wanted to be her friend, the other of whom she was unsure.

But life was exciting. To-morrow she would see the house; she would get to know it and all the people who lived in it.

As the firelight threw a flickering light about the room she thought of the cold bedrooms at the Convent. Even in winter there had been no fires in the bedrooms there.

She was just beginning to doze when there was a knock on her door. She started. The knock was repeated.

"Please come in," she called, and into the room came the woman she had seen when she had arrived at the house—the one whom they had called Wenna.

She stood by the door and for some inexplicable reason she alarmed Melisande. Perhaps it was because she looked fierce, angry. Why should she be angry with Melisande who had only just arrived at the house?

Melisande sat up in bed.

"I just wondered if you had all you needed," said the woman.

"That is so good . . . so kind."

Wenna came slowly to the bed and looked down on Melisande. "I shouldn't by rights have disturbed you once you were in bed. I didn't think you'd be there yet though."

"But I am glad you came. It is a kindness."

"Well, you comfortable, eh? This must be a bit strange . . . after the place you come from, I reckon?"

"It is very different."

"Did Peg look after 'ee? She do dream so. I wondered if she'd brought what you wanted. She do seem piskymazed half the time."

Melisande laughed softly. Why had she thought the woman was angry? Clearly she was trying to be kind. "Peg was very good. Everybody is very good."

"Then I didn't have no cause to come bothering."

"It was no bothering. It was a goodness."

"You come from across the water . . . from foreign parts?"

"Yes."

"And lived there all your life?"

"I lived in a convent."

"My dear life! That must have been a queer place to live."

"It did not seem so. It seemed . . . just the place where I lived."

"I suppose you was put there by your father . . . or your mother."

"I . . . suppose so."

"Seems a queer way of going on. Is it the foreign way then?"

"Well, they died, you see; and I had a guardian who thought I should be better in the Convent than anywhere else. I think that was why I went."

"My dear land! Fancy that! And you never saw your father?"

"No."

"Nor your mother?"

"No."

"But this guardian of yours . . . you had him. He was something, wasn't he?"

"Oh yes, he was something."

"Poor young lady! Did he come to see you often, this guardian?"

"No. He just arranged things for me."

"And I suppose he was a friend of our master's like?"

"I . . . I don't know. I don't know very much."

" 'Twas queer like, to keep you in the dark."

Melisande was uncomfortable. She wanted the woman to go, for now she had an idea that with all her questions she was trying to trap her into betraying her kind benefactor. That was something which Melisande had decided she would never do. All her life she would remain grateful to him.

"I only know that I have been looked after . . . fed and educated; and now that I am old enough this post has been found for me."

"I reckon you must feel pretty curious about all this. I know I would. I reckon I wouldn't leave no stone unturned."

"I lived with children most of whom did not know their parents. Thank you. It was good of you to ask. Peg has been very good and helpful. I am enjoying a comfort here."

Wenna was not going to be dismissed as easily as that.

She said: "Ah, a pity you didn't come earlier than this. This was a happy house not so long ago when my mistress was alive."

"It was a great tragedy. I have heard of it."

"She was an angel. I'd looked after her most of my life."

"I am very sorry for you. It is tragic."

"And then to die! She was always delicate. I knew she'd catch her death sitting out there in the cold. She ought to have had her wrap. I'll never forget it. She was like an ice-block when I went out to her. It need not have happened. That's the pity of it. I know it need not have happened." Melisande was conscious of the intensity of this woman, of the passionate anger within her. "Then," she went on slowly, "I suppose if it hadn't happened you wouldn't be here . . . would you? You wouldn't be in that nice comfortable bed with a fire in your grate. You'd be in that Convent where you'd been brought up. That's what would have happened if the mistress hadn't died."

Melisande was uncertain what to say. She had a wild fancy that the woman was accusing her of being in some obscure way to blame for the death of her mistress.

She stammered: "I suppose Miss Caroline would not have needed a companion if her mother had lived. She would have married very soon and . . ."

"Yes, she would have married, and when she married I should have gone with her. I shall go with her when she marries."

"You are very fond of her," said Melisande.

The woman was silent. After a while she said: "Well, there's nothing you want. Everything's all right?"

"Yes, thank you."

She went out. Melisande lay back staring at the door. What a strange woman! Melisande could not get rid of the fancy that she had not meant all she had said and that she had had some strange purpose in coming to her room.

She could not sleep for a long time, and then she would doze and awake startled to find herself looking towards the door. It was almost as though she expected it to open and Wenna to come in—for what purpose she did not know; she only knew that it made her uneasy.

The weeks began to pass—exciting, wonderful weeks for Melisande, filled with a hundred new experiences.

There was a new world to be explored.

It had been an exciting discovery to look from her windows and see the sea not more than a mile away. She had stood delightedly at her window on that first morning and looked out across the bay to the great strip of land which was like a battering ram flung out into the water; she saw the clouds gathered over the headland and because it was early morning and the sun was beginning to rise, those pink-tinted clouds made a coral-coloured sea.

She was then to live in a beautiful place, in a large luxurious house; she had to make the acquaintance of so many people. The house seemed full of servants and it needed all her gay carelessness of English convention to make their acquaintance. They were inclined to be aloof at first. They were deeply conscious of social layers. It was true she was not on the same shelf as the master and mistress, but neither did she belong on theirs. But Melisande inconsequentially did not see these differences. The servants were people; they lived in the same house as she did; she was eager to know them. First she charmed Mr. Meaker and the footman; and her delighted wonder in the pies and pasties of Mrs. Soady's making soon won her the regard of that excellent cook. The maids were amused and delighted with her; she was never haughty and she could be relied upon to give them her considerate help. The menservants thought her a real charmer and no mistake. She was undoubtedly a great success.

Her foreign ways delighted everyone. Her quaint speech amused while it gave listeners a sense of superiority which was pleasant. She would laugh with them. "Oh, I have said a funniness. Do tell me what *you* would have said." She would listen gravely and thank them charmingly. Oh, she was a caution all right, they all agreed; a charming caution. She must know this and that. She was full of energy and no matter was too insignificant for her attention.

If only she could have been so sure of her success in the drawing-room as in the servants' hall, Melisande would have been contented. But the family embarrassed her in some way or another.

Sir Charles had so many engagements that she saw very little of him. Caroline never seemed at ease in her presence. Caroline was the mistress and wished that to be clearly understood; but Melisande felt that the one thing Caroline would really have liked to ask her to do she could not, and that was to leave the house.

At the beginning Caroline said to Melisande: "I have never had a companion before. I have had governesses. I suppose a companion would be in the same class. My governesses always had their meals in the little room which adjoins the schoolroom. I think that is where you had better have yours. You wouldn't wish to have them with the family, would you? Except perhaps on special occasions. I remember my governesses had luncheon with us once a week. That was so that Papa and Mamma could ask questions about my progress. Sometimes they wanted an extra woman for a dinner party. Then one of the governesses would be asked. But on all other occasions they had their meals in this little room. It's difficult. You see, you couldn't be expected to eat with the servants."

Melisande laughed aloud. "No? I would not mind. They are my very good friends. Mrs. Soady and Mr. Meaker . . ."

Caroline's mouth tightened a little as it did when she found it necessary to repress the new companion.

"Most governesses would have been offended if they were asked to eat with the lower servants. And of course it would have been quite wrong. So I think it would be a good plan if you had your meals in that room. . . ."

So Melisande ate her meals alone in the room. It was of no importance although she would have liked the company of Sir Charles and Mr. Holland or the servants. She was fond of company and it was good fun to laugh and chatter.

Caroline said on that first morning: "I don't know what Papa expected you to *do*. Lady Gover has a companion. She reads to Lady Gover every afternoon; but then Lady Gover is almost blind, and in any case I shouldn't want to be read to. She makes Lady Gover's clothes too. Of course, there's Pennifield . . . and Wenna does a lot of sewing for me."

"That makes me very happy. I do not like to sew."

Caroline's smile was icy. "There will be sewing for the poor each day. My mother used to read aloud from a good book while I worked. Perhaps we may take it in turns to sew and read." She was implying that it was not for Melisande to say what she liked to do; if it was part of her duty to do such a thing she should do it.

Melisande looked at her pleadingly and pressed her lips tightly together to prevent her indiscreet comment. She wanted to say: "Please like me, because I cannot bear to be disliked. Please tell me what it is you do not like, and I will try to change it."

But she merely looked prettier than ever and that was exactly what irritated Caroline. If she had been ugly—forty, prim and grateful—Caroline would have thought of ways to be kind to her. Caroline did not want to be unkind; she was only unkind to those she feared; and she feared this girl for all her poverty and dependence.

She had spoken to her father that very morning, going to his study even though she knew he did not like to be disturbed there.

"Papa," she had said, "I cannot understand why you have brought this girl here. I do not want a companion. I have plenty to do preparing for my wedding."

"I think you should have a companion for a year or so— until you are married," he had answered. "I wish you to perfect your knowledge of the French language. You need a young lady companion when you go visiting."

"People will not receive *her*."

"They will receive her as your companion. She is a gentlewoman and well educated—better educated, I fear, than you are. She is quiet and modest and would, I am sure, be received anywhere."

"Quiet! Modest! I would not describe her so!"

"You are extremely selfish, Caroline. This girl needs a post. Doesn't that mean anything to you?"

"I am sorry for anyone who has to work, but that does not mean I want a companion. Why not find someone who does . . . someone like Lady Gover?"

"Lady Gover is very well satisfied with the companion she has. When you no longer have need of Miss St. Martin's services, I shall be obliged to find her another situation. In the meantime I should be glad if you would accept her as your companion and act as a well-bred young lady is expected to act—thinking a little of others less fortunate than herself."

Fermor was equally unsympathetic. When he said that it was a shame the poor girl had to eat alone, Caroline had retorted sharply: "You seem very interested in her."

"Interested! Well, she's a bit of a character. It's the way she talks. I find that amusing."

"She would find it uncomfortable if she were expected to have her meals with us, and I have no doubt that she thinks herself too good for the servants' hall. They always do. I remember there was always embarrassment about the governesses. One is always in danger of offending their susceptibilities. I suppose companions are the same. Genteel poverty is such a bore."

"Why not ask her which she prefers?" suggested Fermor. "I'm sure her ideas on the matter would be original."

"You forget that she is only a servant—although she's supposed to be a superior one."

He shrugged his shoulders; she sensed that he would have pursued the matter, but he was aware that she had noticed his interest in the girl.

Caroline had said that there should be an hour in the morning which they would devote to conversation in French.

During the first hour when this was in progress Fermor came into the library.

"You wanted me?" asked Caroline.

"No. I thought I'd take advantage of a little instruction myself. That is if Mademoiselle has no objection."

Melisande smiled warmly. Very ready, thought Caroline,

to accept admiration. "There is no objection!" she cried.
"There is only great welcome."

"Sit down then," said Caroline. "But do remember that
nothing but French is to be spoken during this hour."

"Mon Dieu!" cried Fermor, lifting his shoulders in an
attempt at suitable gesticulation.

Melisande laughed in great amusement, and there followed a torrent of French asking him if he had been in
France, if so in what part, and if he had found any difficulty
in making himself understood.

"Have pity!" he cried. "Have pity on a poor Englishman."

Caroline said sharply: "Really, Fermor, this is not what
Papa intended."

"A thousand apologies." He began to answer Melisande's
questions in French, so slowly and laboriously and with such
an appalling accent—which Caroline was sure was greatly
exaggerated—that Melisadane could not understand until he
had repeated some words several times. Then she would teach
him how to say those words, and they would both laugh
outrageously at his efforts.

Caroline watching them was tense with jealousy. She
thought: It will always be like that. I shall never be able to
trust him with an attractive woman. He'll never be different.
He would not have thought of me if our parents had not
arranged the marriage. He would have preferred someone
like this girl—as he is preferring her now.

"Monsieur speaks very bad French," Melisande was saying with mock severity.

"It is time you took me in hand," he said in English.
"Mademoiselle, it must not be only for an hour a day. You
must talk to me often, for clearly I cannot go about the world
in such ignorance."

How dare he! thought Caroline. He knows that I am
watching, but he does not care!

"But French, Monsieur!" cried Melisande. "You have
forgotten."

"Monsieur is very bad scholar, yes?" he said in broken
English. "He deserves much punishment?"

"Fermor," said Caroline sharply, "Papa would say you

are wasting time. He is most anxious for me to have French lessons. That is why Mademoiselle was engaged.''

''I'll be good,'' he said, smiling from Melisande to Caroline. ''I'll sit, meek and mild, and speak only when spoken to . . . and then it shall be in French . . . if I can manage it.''

''It is only by speaking that you can improve,'' said Melisande. ''You are very very bad, it is true, but I think you are eager to learn, and that is a very good thing.''

''I am very eager,'' he said, putting his hand on his heart. ''I am very eager to please you.''

The hour progressed—for Caroline most unhappily. She was glad when she could stop the lesson.

''Shall we go for a ride?'' she asked Fermor.

''The very thing! After all that brain work I need a little exercise.''

''Come on then.''

''What about Mademoiselle St. Martin?''

Caroline was aghast. How could he suggest such a thing! He was not treating her as a servant; he was behaving as though she were a guest in the house.

Melisande said: ''Alas, I do not ride a horse. It was not taught me in the Convent.''

He laughed. ''I suppose not. I can't help laughing. I just had a picture of nuns on horseback . . . in full gallop, black wings flapping. They'd look like prehistoric animals, wouldn't they? But I say, Mademoiselle Melisande, we can't allow this, you know. You can't ride! That's impossible! I mean of course, that we must put that right. Hunting is the noblest sport. Didn't you know that? You *must* ride. I'll teach you. You are teaching me to speak French. I'll teach you how to manage a horse.''

''But that would be wonderful. I should like to be a rider. You are very good. I am filled with happiness.''

''Then it's a bargain. Shake hands on it. When will you be ready for the first lesson?''

Caroline said quickly: ''You forget, Fermor, you're going back to London next week.''

''I'll stay a little longer. There's nothing I have to go back

for. I'll wait until Mademoiselle Melisande is cantering round
the paddock before I leave.''

"I think,'' said Caroline, "that as Mademoiselle St. Martin is employed by my father, and you propose teaching her
to ride on my father's horse, it might be advisable to ask his
permission first.''

"You are right, of course,'' said Fermor.

Caroline smiled faintly. "I'll ask him if he approves.''

"I'll do the asking,'' said Fermor. "Perhaps to-morrow,
Mademoiselle Melisande, you shall have your first lesson.''

"Thank you, but I should not wish to if it were not the
desire of Sir Charles and Miss Caroline.''

"Leave it to me,'' he said. "I'll see to it.''

Then smiling, he went out with Caroline, leaving her alone
in the library caught up by her intermingling emotions, deciding that life in the outside world was more complicated
than life in a convent.

As they rode out of the stable Fermor said: "What a bad
temper you are in this morning!''

"I?''

"Certainly you. Weren't you rather rude to that poor girl?''

"I thought what I said was necessary.''

"Necessary to hurt her feelings!''

"I wonder whether you would have been so solicitous of
her feelings if she had had a squint and a hare lip.''

"Would you have been so anxious to hurt her feelings if
she had?''

"That is not the point.''

"My dear Caroline, it is the point.''

"You can't teach her to ride.''

"Why not? I'm sure she'll make an excellent horsewoman.''

"You forget she is only employed here.''

"I may have forgotten, but you reminded me . . . remember . . . right there before her.''

The tears filled her eyes. She said: "I can't help it. It
makes me so unhappy to be . . . slighted . . . like that . . .
to be humiliated before a servant.''

He could be very cold sometimes; he was cold now. He

said: "It was you who humiliated yourself, treating her as you did."

He rode on in advance of her; she stared at his straight back and blinked away the tears. She thought: I am so unhappy. He does not love me. He never did. He will marry me because the marriage has been arranged. I would marry him if the whole world were against us.

They had reached the cliff path and she was glad that they had to pick their way carefully.

"We'll get down on to the beach," he said. "We'll have a gallop over the sand."

"All right," she answered.

She was thinking: Perhaps she'll be no good on a horse. Perhaps she'll have a violent fall . . . spoil her looks. She might even break her neck. That was a terrible thought and she was sorry she had had it. She did not mean to be unkind. If only her father had brought her a poor middle-aged woman who needed kindness, how kind she would have been!

She was more composed when they were on the beach, and she came level with him. He turned his head and seeing her thus was greatly relieved.

"Come on," he said; and they were off, past the great rocks in which were streaks of pink quartz and amethyst, sending the seagulls squawking out of their path.

He began to sing for very enjoyment.

"On Richmond Hill there lives a lass . . ."

She heard his voice mingling with the drumming of hoofs on the sand.

Melisande had been in the house six weeks when the thought came to her: I must not stay here. I must go away.

She was panic-stricken at the thought, for where should she go? How could she be happy away from here? If Caroline had wanted her she could have been happy; but Caroline showed her so clearly that she had no right to be here. The French lessons continued—they were more or less a command from Sir Charles—and they played duets on the piano, but this Caroline could do as well as she could and so, as far as music was concerned, Melisande could teach her nothing. They did a little embroidery together, but here again Caroline was so much more efficient with the needle. Sometimes in the evenings she would join in a game of whist, taking Miss Holland's place if that lady was too tired to play or was suffering from one of her frequent headaches. But even that had to be taught her, for she had never played the game before. She and Sir Charles would be partners on these occasions; she wished that Fermor would partner her. Sir Charles would admonish her gently: "Oh, Mademoiselle, that was rather impetuous playing. You see, had you waited I could have taken that trick . . ." She had the impression that he wished to be indulgent but that he was afraid of seeming too eager to excuse her; whereas Fermor would come boldly in to her defence. Whist did not therefore ease the tension; and she often wondered what she had to offer for her board and lodging, for a place in this lovely mansion.

To her it seemed such an exciting place with its great hall which, she had heard, had done service as a ballroom, and in which, in the old days, the whole family including the servants had taken their meals; she could have spent many interested hours in the galleries with the portraits of long dead Trevennings; there were parts of the house which had not changed since the days of Henry VIII; there was the magnificent carved staircase, and the large lofty rooms with their latticed windows and diamond-shaped panes, and those fascinating deep window seats. The servants' quarters were the most ancient; to descend to the great stone-floored kitchen with its huge fireplace and cloam oven, to see the cellars, the pantries, the butteries, was indeed to step back into the past.

There was so much that she had grown to love. She enjoyed rising early, leaping out of bed to stand at her window and watch the sun rise over the sea which seemed different every day. Sometimes it sparkled as though an extravagant god had scattered diamonds on its surface; sometimes it was overshadowed by mist, a creeping thing that seemed to be coming slowly onwards, but never came; she was excited to see it angry, lashing the rocks, contemptuously throwing up a broken spar, a mane of seaweed; to see it in a merry mood, tossing up the spume on the summit of its wave, catching it as a child catches a ball. She would look out across the sea to the Eddystone Lighthouse, like a slim pencil in the clear morning light, away towards Plymouth in the east and Looe Island in the west. It was a joy to ramble over the rocks, to stand alone watching the effortless flight of seagulls, to wander in the fields and lanes; she found great pleasure in walking down into the town and along by the quay, calling a greeting to the fishermen sitting at their cottage doors mending their nets, to walk out on the jetty and feel the salt sea air in her face; she liked to look back at the grey houses of the towns, the cottages on both sides of the river, some little more than huts, some much grander with their ornamental ridged tiles which she had learned were called the piskypows because they had been made so that the piskies might dance there during the night; and the piskies were friendly to those who gave them an alfresco ballroom.

There was so much to know, so much to learn; she was the friend of them all because they knew how anxious she was to be their friend. They would call her in to drink a little metheglin or mead, blackberry or gilliflower wine, to taste a piece of raisin cake, which they called fuggan—but that was for special occasions; there was always a piece of heavy cake or saffron cake for the young foreign lady at any time.

She had as many friends in West Looe as in East Looe. People were always glad to see her whom they called the little Mamazel. And although there were some in West Looe who would resent her friendship with the people who lived on the other side of the river, and some in East Looe who thought she owed allegiance to them—for the two towns liked to keep themselves apart—they forgave in Mamazel that which would have seemed duplicity in others.

Melisande knew of these resentments but she pretended not to. She was not, for the sake of East Looe, going to cut from her list of friends that wonderful old woman, Grandmother Tremorney, any more than she would, for the sake of the West, give up her friendship with old Knacker Poldown. Old Knacker—and he was so small and wizened that it was easy to understand why he had been so named—with his talk of the mines and the adventures he had there until he retired and came to live on the east side in a ground house with a pisky-pow on the roof, was too good to miss; but so was old

Lil Tremorney sitting outside her cottage, puffing at her pipe, with her tales of the lovers she had had.

Melisande had so many friends and she could not bear to leave them. Only yesterday she had been called in to Mrs. Pengelly's to see the new baby and taste a bit of the kimbly which had been saved for friends. It was a delicious cake made especially for the child's christening and she was honoured to receive her share.

How could she give up such things?

There was something else which she had to give up, and she had to admit to herself that it was what she would miss more than anything.

Fermor had been teaching her to ride for some weeks. Sir Charles had given his permission. He seemed secretly pleased and said he thought it was an excellent idea, and it was a good thing to let Fermor pay for his lessons in French. Fermor had declared that there must be a lesson every day, and he said he would not return to London until he had made Melisande into a proficient horsewoman.

He was kind and friendly, but she was becoming more and more conscious of an underlying wickedness within him.

One day during a riding lesson she realized that she could no longer shut her eyes to the danger of her position.

Her horse bolted suddenly and made straight for the cliff's edge. Immediately she was aware of the thudding of Fermor's horse's hoofs close behind her. In an instant he was between her and danger.

The horses were at a standstill, and for a few moments Melisande and Fermor remained stationary in breathless silence, with the scent of the sea and the heather in their nostrils, looking at each other. She was conscious of the deep feelings they aroused within each other.

Suddenly he became flippant. "Don't do that again," he said. "That horse is valuable."

She was still trembling. "It does not matter about me then?"

He came close and touched her arm. "You are more precious than all the horses in the world," he said in deep and solemn tones.

She was in no mood for more instruction that day.

"We'll go back to the stables," he said. "You're shaken."

They walked their horses soberly back to the stables. He helped her to dismount and as he did so held her while he gazed steadily into her eyes.

Then he bent his head and kissed her cheek lingeringly. He said: "You will ride to-morrow." It was a statement, not a question. "You're scared, Melisande," he went on. "You're very scared. When you're scared of something, face it, look it straight in the eyes. Don't run away from it. If you do, you'll remain scared all your life. Whereas if you look it straight in the eyes, you may find it is something you have been a fool to miss."

She knew that he was not referring to riding only.

She was certain now that she ought to go away.

"I must go at once," she said. "I have things to do." He did not seek to detain her and she hurried into the house.

She met Miss Pennifield on her way to the sewing-room. Miss Pennifield's face was flushed a patchy red, her lips were quivering, and in her hand she carried a dress.

"Is anything wrong, Miss Pennifield?" asked Melisande.

Miss Pennifield was obviously near tears. She held up the dress and shook her head wearily; she could not trust herself with words. Melisande followed her into the sewing-room; it was a relief to divert her attention to someone else's problems.

"This is the second time I've unpicked it," said Miss Pennifield. "There's no pleasing her."

"Can I help you?"

" 'Tis kind of you, Mamazel. I'm at my wit's end, I do declare."

She sat down and spread the dress on the table. "It's the sleeve. She says it don't fit. She do always say the sleeves don't fit. She's in one of her moods this morning. I do declare they get worse and worse. If only it was a flaring temper I could stand it, but it's a quiet sort of rage . . . brooding like and cruel."

"Poor Miss Pennifield! What's wrong with the sleeves?"

"First it be too bunchy here . . . then it be too bunchy there. There be no pleasing her. I don't know when I'll get through."

"I could finish off the skirt hem while you do the sleeves."

"Will you then? 'Tis good of you, and a relief to talk to someone. Sometimes I say to myself I'll be glad when Miss Caroline do marry and go to London, though I'll have one the less to work for. She wasn't always like this . . . come to think of it. I don't know. I think she's fretting for marriage like. There's some as is like that. Why it should be so, a maiden like myself can't say."

"Are these stitches all right? I was never very good with the needle."

"Keep them a bit smaller, my dear, and just a mite more even. We can't have her complaining about the stitches as well as the set. 'Tis Mrs. Soady's belief that Miss Caroline should be married quick. But I reckon she won't be no better then, for he ain't the sort that's going to grow more loving after marriage . . . as Mrs. Soady says. I couldn't say . . . being a maiden like."

"You have always earned your living at sewing, Miss Pennifield?"

"Why yes, my dear . . . sewing of a sort. . . . Lace-making too. Me and my sister Jane."

"You like it?"

"Oh, 'tis a hard life. Though better here in the country among the gentry than in the towns, I do hear. There was a time when me and Jane was both put to the lace-making to Plymouth. Travelled there we did through Crafthole and Mill-brook and Cremyll Passage on the coach, then over the Tamar. My dear life! What a journey! And we was put with a lady to Plymouth. There was eight or nine of us . . . all little things— some not more than five years old. Whenever I be a bit upset about bunchy sleeves and the like, I think of lace-making to Plymouth. Then I be satisfied with my lot. That's why I be thinking of it now, I daresay. Sitting there in a sort of cupboard it were . . . wasn't much more . . . a cupboard of a room . . . nine of us and the bobbins working all the time . . . and we dursen't look up for fear of wasting a second. So much we had to do or go without supper—and that weren't much; but it seemed a terrible lot to go without."

"Poor Miss Pennifield!" Melisande saw herself stitching shirts in the Convent needlework room. How she had hated it! And yet how fortunate she had been!

Her eyes were filled with sympathy and Miss Pennifield said: "Why, what a dear good little soul you be!"

"I wish I could sew better. I wish I could sew as quickly and neatly as you do."

"You come to it in time."

"Do you think I could? Do you think I could be a dress-maker? Perhaps I could. You see, Miss Pennifield, I cannot sew, but I know how to set a bow on a dress, or a flower . . . or how a skirt should hang . . . even though I cannot do the sewing. Perhaps I could be that sort of dressmaker."

"My dear life, who knows? But you wouldn't wish for to be a dressmaker, my dear. A young lady as speaks French so well, and English not bad . . . why, you be an educated young lady. You be a companion. That's like a governess. 'Tis a cut above a dressmaker."

"Miss Pennifield, tell me about you and your sister . . ." Melisande paused to consider herself. She had changed since she had been in the Convent and had chattered ceaselessly; she had wanted to talk about herself, her dreams and de-sires; she had not been eager to listen to others. She said quickly: "Don't tell me about the woman in Plymouth. That makes me sad. I want to laugh. Tell me about the happy times. There must have been happy times."

"Oh yes," said Miss Pennifield, "there was happy times. Christmas time was the best. Decorating the church. Mr. Danesborough, he was a merry sort of gentleman. But we moved away from his church when I was little, and we lived near St. Martin's then. Mr. Forord Michell . . . he were the vicar then. We'd decorate the church with holly and bay, and we'd go round a-gooding, which I'll tell 'ee, as you'd not know being not of these parts, was going round begging for sixpence towards our Christmas dinner. We'd go to all the big houses both sides of the river . . . this house and Leigh, Keverel, Morval and Bray . . . then we'd go to Tren-ant Park, Treworgey and West North. Then we'd go wassail-ing. We'd get one of the men to carve us a bowl and we'd decorate it with furze flowers, and we'd go begging a coin that we could fill the bowl and drink to the wassail."

Miss Pennifield began to sing in a small reedy voice:

"The mistress and master our wassail begin
Pray open your door and let us come in
With our wassail . . . wassail . . . wassail . . .
And joy come to our jolly wassail.

"Ah, there was a merry frolic, I can tell 'ee. We'd black our faces. We'd dress up and dance in the fields and some of us would be so far gone in merriment—and like as not with too much metheglin and cider—that we'd call on the piskies to come and join us. Oh, they was jolly frolicking times! Then there was Good Friday. I remember when we did all go down to the beaches with knives to get the horned cattle off the rocks, and we'd have sacks to put 'em in and we'd bring them back for a real feast. But May Day was the best day . . . if 'twas not Midsummer's Eve when we'd go out on the moors for the bonfires. Yes, May Day was best. Then we'd get together and wait till midnight, and there'd be fiddlers there too, and we'd all go to the farms nearby and they'd give us junket and cream or heavy cake and saffron or even fuggan. They dursen't refuse for, you do see, 'twas an old custom. The Little People don't like them that is too mean or too busy for old customs. Then we'd dance in the fields. We'd do the old cushion dances that was beautiful to watch. But it wasn't all feasting and dancing and games—oh, dear me no. Bringing home the may was a solemn thing. They'd been doing it for years—so I be told—before there was Christians in these parts, so said Mr. Danesborough, and he was terrible clever and knew much about these parts. When we brought home the may some of us would have whistles and we'd pipe it home like. Those was wonderful times . . . though there was much wickedness among them as took advantage of the dark. Though I know nothing of that . . . being a maiden like."

And so, as they talked, Miss Pennifield was laughing and gay again; she had forgotten that Miss Caroline had frightened her; and even when she took the dress back and Caroline admitted grudgingly that it would do, she still had that aura of happiness about her.

Melisande was subdued after Miss Pennifield had left her. What a sad life! she thought. To be a dressmaker! She tried to picture herself, old like Miss Pennifield, with eyes that seemed to be sinking into her head through too much sewing. Yet if she left this house, where would she go?

But to brood on unpleasantness was not a habit of Melisande's. She went to the kitchen and asked if she might have supper with them instead of on a tray in her room.

Mr. Meaker was in doubt; he was not sure that that was right, and he had been in some very big houses. Mrs. Soady, flattered and delighted, said, Who was to know? And it was a matter for Mamazel herself to decide. She set about making a special muggety pie for, as she confided to Mr. Meaker, she had heard that people set a powerful lot by French cooking, and she would show the little Mamazel that Cornwall could compete. Muggety couldn't fail to do this and there should be fair-maids to assist as well as a hog's pudding.

A place was found for Melisande at Mrs. Soady's right hand.

"We've got a guest to-night," said Mrs. Soady gleefully. "We must all be on our best behaviour like."

"No, no, no!" cried Melisande. "That I do not wish. I wish us to be ourselves. I am going to be very greedy, and I wish you to talk as though I am not here because I am so happy to listen."

There was much laughter and everybody was very happy. Squeals of delight went up when Mrs. Soady brought up a bottle of her best parsnip wine from the cellar.

"I hear the French be terrible wine drinkers," said Mrs. Soady, "and us mustn't forget we've got a French Mamazel at our table this day. Now, my dear, would 'ee like to start off with some of this here fair-maid? 'Tis our own dear little pilchards which I done in oil and lemon, and we do always say in these parts that it be food fit for a Spanish Don. Now, Mr. Meaker, pass the plates, do. I'm sure Mamazel wants to see us all do ourselves and the table justice."

"But this is delicious!" cried Melisande.

At first they all seemed a little abashed by her presence at the table, but after a while they accepted her as one of them and the conversation was brought to the subject of young

Peg, who had fallen in love with one of the fishermen down on west quay and couldn't get the young man to look her way. Bet was urging her to go along to the white witch in the woods, adding that Mrs. Soady, who belonged to a pellar family, was surely the best one to consult about this.

"A white witch?" cried Melisande. "But what is this?"

Everyone was waiting for Mrs. Soady's explanation which was not long in coming. "Well, my dear, 'tis a witch and no witch. Not one of them terrible creatures as travel around on broomsticks and consort with the Devil . . . no, not one of they. This is a good witch, a witch as will charm your warts away. You've no need to cross the fire hook and prong to keep off a white witch. They don't come interfering like. They do only help when you do go to them. They'll tell you how to find them as is ill-wishing you, or they can cure the whooping cough. They give you a love potion too and, my dear life, that's a thing to please some of the maidens."

"A love potion!" cried Melisande, her eyes sparkling. "You mean so that you can make the one you love love you! But that is a goodness. So a white witch will do that? I wonder why Miss Caroline. . . ." She stopped short.

There was silence about the table. They were accustomed to discussing the affairs of their employers, but they were not sure that they should do so with one whose station was midway between the drawing-room and the servants' hall.

Peg, Bet and the rest were waiting for a lead from Mrs. Soady or Mr. Meaker.

Mr. Meaker was for discretion, but Mrs. Soady—a member of a pellar family—was on her favourite subject, and this subject accompanied by a liberal supply of her own parsnip wine had excited her.

" 'Twouldn't do her no harm neither," she said.

The colour had risen to Melisande's cheeks. If Caroline could only make him love her as he should, there would be no need for her to think of going away from Trevenning. She could stay here, enjoying many of these informal suppers.

" 'Tis my belief," said Mr. Meaker, "that the gentry ain't got the way of going about these things. Charms don't work for the likes of them as they do for some."

"And 'tis easy to see why," said Mrs. Soady sharply.

"They do approach in a manner of disbelief, and if that ain't enough to scarify the piskies away, I don't know what is."

"Mrs. Soady," cried Melisande, "you do believe in these piskies?"

"Indeed I do, my dear. And my very good friends they be. They do know me well as coming from a pellar family. Why, when I was staying awhile with my sister on the moors, I went out one day and the mist rose and, my dear soul, I were lost. Now, t'aint no picnic being lost on our moors. Out Caradon way this was, and I don't mind telling 'ee I was scared out of me natural. Then sudden like I thought of the piskies, so I sang out:

> *'Jack o' Lantern! Joan the Wad!*
> *Who tickled the maid and made her mad,*
> *Light me home; the weather's bad.'*

"And do 'ee know, the mist cleared suddenly, but 'twas only where I was, and it didn't take me long to find my way home."

"Oh, please sing it again," pleaded Melisande. "Jack o' what is it?"

And Mrs. Soady sang it again; then the whole company chanted it, while the little Mamazel sang with them, trying to imitate their accents. Hers sent them into such fits of laughter that poor Peg nearly choked, and Bet grew so red in the face that the footman had to thump her on the back; as for Mr. Meaker, he had to have an extra glass of parsnip wine—he felt the need after the exhaustion he was suffering through laughing so much.

All this made everyone glad to have such a charming guest at the table, and they all set out to be as entertaining as they could.

Peg declared that she must go to the white witch, for she was sure young Jim Poldare would never look at her else. Then Mrs. Soady announced that Tamson Trequint, who lived in a little hut in Trevenning woods, was one of the best white witches she had ever come across. "Do 'ee remember my warts then? It was Tamson I went to on account of they. Where be they warts now? You're at liberty to find 'em if you can. She said to me: 'Search among the pea pods, my dear, for one as contains nine peas. Take out the peas and throw them away . . . one by one, and as you do it say: "Wart, wart, dry away!" And as them peas rot, my dear, so the warts will disappear.' "

"And did they?" asked Melisande.

"Not a sign of them from that day. And if that ain't white magic then tell me what is."

"Yes," said Peg, "but what about love potions, Mrs. Soady?"

"My dear life, you go along to see Tamson. It has to be after dark, remember. Tammy won't work a charm in daylight."

"But it is wonderful," murmured Melisande. "It is an . . . excitement. Would Tamson work a spell for anyone? Would she work a spell for . . . me?"

"Tamson could work a spell for the Queen. And a word from me, my dear, as belongs to a pellar family and has a footling for a sister . . . why, my dear life, of course her'd work a spell for 'ee!"

"Who would you be wanting a spell for, Mamazel?" asked Peg.

They were all looking at her expectantly and the footman said: "I do reckon Mamazel's face and ways is as good as any potion."

"Now that's a very nice thing to have had said to 'ee, Mamazel," said Mrs. Soady.

"You are all so kind to me . . . everyone. Here and in the town and the cliffs and the lanes . . . everybody has a kindness for me." Melisande stretched out her arms as though to embrace them all; her eyes were shining with friendship and parsnip wine. "You invite me to your table. You give me this . . . megettie . . . and these delicious fair-maids . . . you give me your parsnip wine . . . and now your white witch, that I may drink, if I wish, a love potion."

Peg, who laughed every time Melisande spoke, went off into fresh convulsions. After they had thumped her out of them, Mrs. Soady said: "We'll open that other bottle of parsnip, I think, Mr. Meaker. 'Tis an occasion. We'll drink to Mamazel's health, and we'll hope that the love potion she gets from Tamson Trequint will give her the one she's set her heart on. And Peg shall have her fisherman too. That's what we'll be drinking to.''

There was a sudden silence about the table. In the noise they had not noticed the door's being opened. Wenna had come into the room. She must have been leaning against the green baize door for some seconds while they had been unaware of her.

Melisande felt the black eyes burning as they rested upon her. They were like two fierce fires that would scorch through to her mind and discover what Wenna wanted to know of her.

''There was such a noise,'' she said. ''I got to wondering what was happening.''

They were all uncomfortable in the presence of Wenna— even Mrs. Soady and Mr. Meaker.

Mrs. Soady recovered her poise first. ''Why don't 'ee sit down and try a bit of this muggety pie? The crust be light as a feather. Peg, set another place do, girl, and don't forget the glass.''

''Parsnip wine!'' said Wenna, almost accusingly.

''It's what you might call a taster,'' said Mrs. Soady. ''Just a little I put by when I was making my last. I reckoned it had matured just right and we was trying it.''

Wenna was the spy. She would report to Miss Caroline anything of which she did not approve. The household was not what it had been in her ladyship's day. Mrs. Soady knew herself to be safe enough—although Miss Caroline could be spiteful—for she was forty-five and shaped like a cottage loaf and not the sort to trap Master Fermor into a bit of junketing in a dark corner. Peg had better look out—and even Bet. They were saucy girls, both of them; and Mrs. Soady wouldn't like to know—which meant she would—how far either of them had gone, inside the house or out. It was no use blaming them. There was some made that way. Peg was one and Master Fermor was another. She wasn't sure of the little Mamazel; but there was that in her to provoke such things—that was clear as daylight. And Wenna had overheard that bit about the love potion, and Wenna was an expert trouble-maker. Perhaps the little Mamazel had better be warned.

Wenna sat down at the table. She said: "Didn't Mamazel get her tray then?"

Melisande herself spoke. "I asked that I might come here. We have had a pleasant time. It is more pleasant to be with others than to eat alone. I am not one to find the great enjoyment in my own company, you understand? I like to hear the talk and the laughter . . . to know what is going on. It is a great enlightenment."

Wenna said: "None of the governesses did ever come down to eat in the servants' hall. That be right, Mrs. Soady, as you do know."

" 'Tis so," agreed Mrs. Soady. "But we did think it terrible friendly like, and Mamazel being such a foreigner, we didn't take aught amiss."

Melisande felt a wave of fear sweep over her as she looked at Wenna. Wenna was the skeleton at the feast. Wenna disliked her. Wenna would tell Caroline that she had found her here, and that it was most unladylike for a companion to sit in the servants' hall. Then it might be that Caroline would seize that excuse for getting rid of her. A companion must be ladylike. That was very necessary.

There was one thing which could make Caroline happy. If she were happy she would not seek to make trouble for all about her. If she could be sure that Fermor loved her she would be completely happy. A love potion was necessary for Caroline; but according to the servants, the gentry were denied these privileges because they did not entirely believe in them.

A love potion for Caroline, yes. But what of Wenna? What did she need?

Melisande could not guess. All she knew was that Wenna filled her with alarm.

Wenna knocked at the door of the study. She knew that Sir Charles hated to be interrupted, and she knew that she would be the last person he wished to see, for he had no more affection for her than she had for him; but she did not care.

"Come in," he said.

He was sitting in his chair at the desk which was immediately before the window. From where he sat he could look over the park; he could see Melisande riding on her horse—the horse, as Wenna believed, which she had no right to ride. Did servants learn to ride? Why should one be specially favoured? Wenna had the answer. She saw that tolerance, that indulgence, which came into his eyes when they rested on her—a certain secret pleasure because the girl was living in his house; she was supposed to be a servant but she enjoyed far too many privileges to be considered so. And soon others besides Wenna would notice this.

"I had to speak to you, master," she said. " 'Tis getting beyond a joke. 'Tis this girl you've brought here as Miss Caroline's companion."

His eyes went suddenly colder and quiet angry, but she stood her ground. She thought: Please God, Miss Caroline will be married and I'll go away with her. I'll stand between her and the wickedness of the man she's going to marry. There'll be dear little children and they'll be mine just as Miss Caroline were.

"Miss St. Martin?" he said.

" 'Twas her I spoke of, Sir Charles. I think you should know she's no fit companion for your own daughter, Miss Caroline."

"I don't believe that. Miss St. Martin is most suitable . . . most."

"She goes down to the servants' hall and drinks with them. I went there last night and found them all well nigh tipsy . . . and it was her doing. Nothing like it has ever been done before. She was egging them on. Drinking the health of the little Mamazel, they were."

A faint smile seemed to touch his lips, as though he were applauding her conduct, thinking how clever she was. The shame of it! thought Wenna. He has to bring the shame into his own house and think it right and proper!

"She has a very friendly nature. She has not been brought up in our English way. I doubt there was any harm in her taking a meal with the servants. She does not have any in the dining-room and probably feels lonely sometimes. She seems

to be very popular . . . not only with the servants. . . . I think
you must realize that as she is not entirely English . . ."

"She'll be riding with Master Fermor and Miss Caroline
one time of the day and drinking parsnip wine with the servants at another. It's wrong, master."

"You must understand that she has been brought up in a
convent. There, I imagine, there were no servants. The nuns
were servants and friends. Therefore she does not see distinctions as we do."

"I don't know nothing about that. All I know is that Miss
Caroline shouldn't have to treat her . . . like a sister."

The shaft went home. He looked uneasy. Now Wenna had
no doubts. She felt like an avenging angel. He should pay for
the unhappiness he had brought to her darling Miss Maud
. . . he should pay for the *murder* of Miss Maud—for murder
it was. If he had been thinking of her getting a chill instead
of what was written in foreign letters about this girl, Miss
Maud would be here to-day.

The misery of her loss came back to her in all its bitter
vividness.

How she hated him and his wickedness! She would not
rest until that girl was out of the house. That she should be
here was a slight to Miss Maud's memory. Perhaps he had
deliberately let her get that chill so that he could bring the
girl into the house and no questions be asked by those who
had a right to ask them.

No sooner had that thought come to her than she was sure
she had hit on the truth.

"I think," he said, after only the briefest pause, "that I
am the best judge of what is right for my daughter."

For your daughters, you mean! she thought. Ah, that's
what they are, both of them. One of them my dear Miss
Maud's child, and the other the spawn of the whore of Babylon.

Oh, Miss Maud, may my right hand forget its cunning if
ever I forget the wrong he has done you!

"I think that girl will bring trouble to the house," she said
aloud. "I've got a feeling. It's the same sort of feeling I had
before Miss Maud passed away. I just know. I've always
known such things."

He softened a little, remembering her devotion to Maud. He could be softened by memories of Maud. He felt guilty because he had forgotten to take her the wrap, although he assured himself that that had nothing to do with her death. She had always been ailing and the doctors had been prophesying her death for years.

"Send her away, master," said Wenna. "Send her away before something happens . . . something dreadful."

He was shaken by her intensity. Then he thought: She's a superstitious old woman. Are they not all superstitious in this part of the world? They are always imagining they are ill-wished, always dreaming that the Little People are at their elbows.

He said sharply: "You are talking nonsense, Wenna. Certainly I shall not send the girl away. Don't be so uncharitable. She is young and high-spirited. I am glad she is being taught to ride. She has given Mr. Holland French lessons. It is only fitting that he should reward her in his turn. You are prejudiced against her because Caroline spends so much time with her."

Wenna turned away muttering to herself.

"Wenna!" he said almost pleadingly. "Be kind to this girl. Do not resent her presence because you feel Caroline is growing fond of her. Remember that she would have a poor life if I sent her away from here."

Wenna replied: "I've said my say, master. It's something I feel within me."

Then she went out. She was thinking derisively: Caroline fond of her! Fond of her for trying to take Fermor away from her, as her mother took you from my Miss Maud! There shan't be another robbery like that one if I can stop it. And stop it I will. I'll see her dead first—your daughter though she may be, and the living proof of your sin and shame.

They had ridden into Liskeard. There were four of them: John Collings, son of the M.F.H. who had formed a friendship with Fermor, Fermor himself, Caroline and Melisande.

Caroline was angry. It was absurd, she was thinking, that they should have Melisande with them. Fermor had arranged that. There were two people at Trevenning who were determined, it seemed, to treat Melisande as a daughter of the house—her father and Fermor.

There sat Melisande on her horse—small and piquant. Sir Charles had given her the riding habit she was wearing. If she was to accompany Caroline she must be decently dressed, he had insisted. John Collings—as did so many people in the neighbourhood—thought Melisande was a poor relation, a distant connection of Sir Charles's. How could they think otherwise when the girl was treated as she was? No ordinary companion would receive such privileges. It seemed wiser to let people believe this was the case. Fortunately, thought Caroline, as she was still in half-mourning for her mother, there were few social occasions. Caroline felt that otherwise Melisande might have received invitations which would have involved awkward explanations.

It was September and there was a mist in the air, which thickened as they climbed to high ground. It hung like diamond drops on the hedges giving a fresh bloom to the wild guelder roses and a velvet coat to the plums of the blackthorn. Spiders' webs were festooned over the bells of the wild fuchsias which flourished in the road-side hedges. The silence was only broken by the clop-clop of their horses' hoofs or the cries of the gulls, mournful as they always seemed on such days.

Caroline glanced over her shoulder at Melisande who always seemed to enjoy everything more than normal people did. Now she was revelling in the mist which the others would deplore.

They were riding two abreast and Fermor was beside Melisande, John Collings with Caroline. Caroline heard Fermor teasing Melisande, provoking that sudden joyous laughter.

John Collings was saying that he hoped Caroline would soon be able to come to parties again and that he would see her in the hunting field. They missed her.

Caroline angrily felt that he was sorry for her, that he was as aware as she was of the pleasure the two behind found in each other's company. She was not listening to John Collings; her attention was focussed on Melisande and Fermor.

"The mist grows thicker," said Melisande.

"It'll be dense on the moor," said Fermor.

"What if we are lost in it?"

"The piskies will carry you off. They set a ring round you and, hey presto! they appear in their hundreds. Fee-faw-fum! I smell the blood of an English. . . . No, no, of a little Mamazel, as they call her in these here parts . . ."

Caroline could not resist breaking in. "He knows nothing about it, Mademoiselle St. Martin. He is not a Cornishman and he makes fun of our legends. And his attempt to imitate the dialect is very poor indeed."

"That's not quite true, Caroline. I don't make fun. I fear the piskies, the knackers and the whole brood. I bow my head when I pass old Tammy Trequint's shack, for fear she should ill-wish me."

"She would not do that!" cried Melisande. "She is a good witch. A white witch, she is called. She does not ill-wish. She will charm away your warts and cure your whooping cough . . . or give you a love potion."

"Interesting," he said. "Now I have no warts, no whooping cough . . ."

Melisande said quickly: "Mrs. Soady has told me of her. Mrs. Soady comes from a pellar family and is the sister of a footling."

"What nonsense the servants talk!" interrupted Caroline. "They should not say such things to you."

"But I like to hear. It is such an excitement. I feel a delight. To live so near us. A white witch! There are so many interesting things to learn in the world, are there not?"

Fermor leaned towards her slightly. He said: "There are many interesting things for a young lady to learn, but Caroline means—and I agree with her—that Mrs. Soady may not be the one to teach you such things, pellar family though she may have, and whatever it is that unnatural sister of hers may be."

"But I would learn from all. Everyone has something to teach. Is that not so? It is different things we learn from different people."

"You see, Caro," said Fermor. "She is wiser than we are. She leaves no cup untasted in her thirst for knowledge."

John Collings said: "There's a lot of superstition about

here, Mademoiselle St. Martin. Particularly among the servant class. You mustn't judge us all by them.''

''As a matter of fact,'' said Fermor, ''these Cornish are all superstitious . . . every one of them. You and I, Mademoiselle, do not belong here. I am as much a foreigner as you are. We may snap our fingers at the piskies. They daren't touch us.''

He began to sing in a loud and tuneful tenor voice:

''On the banks of Allan Water,
When the sweet spring time did fall,
Was the miller's lovely daughter,
Fairest of them all . . .''

And his merry eyes sought those of Melisande as he sang.

Caroline, setting her lips firmly, thought: Why does he? And before me! Doesn't he care at all? Is he clearly telling me that when we are married he will make no attempt to be faithful?

She began to talk to John Collings. How much easier life might have been if she had been affianced to someone like John. He had not town ways, town manners; he did not possess the allure of Fermor; yet how much happier she might have been.

He was still singing and he had reached the end of the song as they came near the outskirts of Liskeard.

''On the banks of Allan Water,
When the winter snow fell fast,
Still was seen the miller's daughter,
Chilling blew the blast.
But the miller's lovely daughter,
Both from cold and care was free,
On the banks of Allan Water
There a corpse lay she.''

Melisande could not refrain from laughing at the mock pathos in his voice. ''But it is so sad,'' she protested.

''And I cannot forgive myself for making you sad!'' declared Fermor. "It is just a song. There is no miller's daughter, you know."

"But there are many millers' daughters," said Melisande. "The one in the song . . . she is just in a song . . . just in the mind of the song writer. But many have loved and died for love, and that song is of them."

Caroline said: "The girl was a fool in any case. She should have known the soldier was false; she should not have believed in that winning tongue of his."

"But how could she know?" asked Melisande.

"One can tell."

"She could not."

"Then, as I say, she was a fool."

"In my opinion," said John Collings, "she might have waited until a more suitable time of the year. I mean to say . . . drowning herself when the snow was falling! Why could she not wait until the spring!"

"She was so unhappy. She did not wish to live until the spring," said Melisande. "That was a long time ahead. She was so sad that the snow was of no importance to her."

"What a controversy my little song has aroused!" said Fermor.

"When," put in Caroline, "it is intended as nothing more than a warning to foolish young women who listen to the honied tongues of deceivers!"

"All lovers have honied tongues," said Melisande.

"A provision of nature!" agreed Fermor. "Like a thrush's song or a peacock's tail."

"But how should a young woman judge between the true and the false?"

"If she cannot, she must take the consequences," said Caroline.

"I will sing you another song," declared Fermor, "to show you that it is not always the young women who must take care."

Immediately he began:

"There came seven gipsies on a day,
Oh, but they sang bonny, O!

"And they sang so sweet and they sang so clear,
Down came the earl's lady, O.

They gave to her the nutmeg,
And they gave to her the ginger;
But she gave to them a far better thing,
The seven gold rings off her fingers."

He sang on, of how the earl came home to find that his lady had gone off with the gipsies; and with mock feeling sang of the earl's pleading and of the lady's refusal to return to him.

"The Earl of Cashan is lying sick;
Not one hair I'm sorry;
I'd rather have a kiss from his fair lady's lips
Than all his gold and his money."

They were all laughing—even Caroline—as they came into the town.

"Three cheers for the lovelorn Earl of Cashan for chasing away the gloom of that corpse—the tiresome miller's daughter!" cried Fermor.

They went to a hostelry where the horses had a rest and a feed while they refreshed themselves before going to the horse market, for Fermor wished to look at horses and John Collings perhaps to buy.

They sat in the parlour with the sawdust on the floor, and a girl in a pretty mob-cap came to bring them tankards of Cornish ale. Hot pasties were served with the ale—fresh from the oven, savoury with onions.

"There seems to be merrymaking in the town to-day," said Fermor to the girl in the mob-cap, for she was a pretty girl, and Fermor would always have a word and a smile for a pretty girl, no matter how much he was taken with another.

"Well, sir," she said, "there's to be a flogging in the streets to-day. You'm here in time to see it. 'Tis old Tom Matthews. Caught red-handed, he were, stealing one of Farmer Tregertha's fowls. The whole town's turning out to see it done."

"What revelry!" cried Fermor. "Bring us some more of those pasties, please. They're good."

The girl bobbed a curtsey and went away.

"What does she mean?" asked Melisande.

John Collings said: "Oh, these people get excited about nothing. Just another felon, that's all."

"And he is to be flogged in the street?" asked Melisande.

"He stole a fowl and was caught," said Caroline.

"But . . . to be flogged in the street . . . where all can see! It is a great indignity . . . as well as a pain to the body."

"Well, let us hope it will teach him not to steal again," said Fermor.

"But in the streets . . . for people to see." Melisande shuddered. "To be beaten in private . . . that is bad. But in the streets . . ."

"It is a warning to other people, Mademoiselle," said Caroline. "There are some people who have to be shown that if they steal they will have to take the consequences."

Melisande was silent, and when the maid brought fresh pasties she found that she had lost her appetite.

When they came out into the streets they were just in time to see the dismal procession. The victim, stripped to the waist, was tied to the back of a cart which was slowly drawn through the streets. Behind him walked two men with whips; these men took it in turn to apply a stroke to the bleeding back of their victim.

Caroline, Fermor and John looked on with indifference; only Melisande turned shuddering away. Perhaps, she thought, he was hungry; perhaps his family was hungry. How can we know that he deserves such punishment?

She was as unhappy as she had been gay a short time before when riding along the misty road.

Fermor was beside her. He said: "What is it?"

She shook her head, but he came nearer, demanding an answer. She tried to explain, although she did not think he would see her point. "The hedges and the flowers and the mist . . . they are so beautiful. And this . . . it is so ugly."

"Felons must be punished. If they were not they would not hesitate to steal the coats off our backs."

They rode away to the stables and, while Fermor and John

were selecting a horse, Caroline said to Melisande: "You are too easily deceived, Mademoiselle St. Martin. You are too sorry for felons and . . . for millers' daughters. Stupid people and criminals have to suffer for their mistakes."

"I know it," said Melisande. "But that does not stop my being sorry."

"It is unwise to steal . . . no matter what. People have to be reminded of that."

It was unfortunate that on their way back through the town they should see mad Anna Quale, for it seemed to Melisande that the flogging of Tom Matthews was a minor tragedy compared with that of Anna Quale.

Anna had many visitors that day. Some had come in to the market and some to see Tom Matthews flogged; and they could not leave without a glimpse of Anna.

Outside the tiny cottage where she lived, a crowd had gathered. Anna's fame had travelled far, and there would not always be an opportunity of seeing her. She was mad; and her insanity was of a type which appealed to the ignorant crowd. Anna's was not a quiet introspective madness; it was not melancholy; Anna's mad fits were fits of rage in which she behaved like a wild animal, spitting and clawing at any who came near her, throwing herself against walls, trying to tear off her clothes, screaming abuse. Her fits occurred at ever-shortening intervals now, and it was considered a great treat to be an onlooker. She would throw herself to the ground, lash out with her arms and legs, bite her tongue; and her face would grow purple as she would utter shrieks and strange sounds. It was said that devils were in her; but the devils were not always so entertaining; sometimes they sulked and would not show their presence. Everybody hoped for a demonstration of the devils when they went to see Anna, and did their best to provoke them to action; but very soon Anna was to be taken away to Bodmin where she would be put in a cage and exhibited to passers-by in that town.

It was a terrible shame, said the people of Liskeard, that Bodmin should have all the fun. There were plenty of lunatics in Bodmin; you could see their cages any day you liked. It was unfair to take Liskeard's entertainers and give them to the Bodmin folk. However, Liskeard and its visitors were determined to get as much fun out of Anna as and while they could; and for the time being she was chained up in the cottage which had recently housed her parents and their large family.

The shrieks of laughter and shouts could be heard streets away.

"What's the excitement?" Fermor asked a man in a smock and leather gaiters.

"Don't 'ee know then, sir?" cried the man.

"That is precisely why I am asking."

" 'Tis old Anna Quale, sir. A regular caution, she be. And there be so many here on account of the flogging, sir. Did you see the flogging, sir?"

"We did. But what about Anna Quale?"

"They'm taking her away to Bodmin soon. 'Tis a crying shame."

Two more men had come up—old men, their faces eager and alight. Talking to strangers was the greatest joy they knew, for passing on knowledge which was theirs and of which the stranger was ignorant was a tremendous stimulation to self-esteem. They touched their forelocks, recognizing John Collings and Miss Caroline Trevenning, although the other lady and gentleman were unknown to them.

"Well, sir, 'tis like this here . . ." began one.

"No, Harry, you let me tell it. You do take too long. . . ."

"Now, look here, Tom Trewinny, you keep out of this."

"How'd it be if you shared the prize?" asked Fermor. "A sentence each, eh?"

They looked at him oddly. Gentry, for sure. But a foreigner with a fancy way of talking. Trying to be smart too; and they did not like foreigners.

John Collings said: "What is this all about, my good man? We're in a hurry."

"Well, sir, 'tis Anna Quale. She'm in the cottage there, and they be going to take her to Bodmin soon. We've always looked on Anna as ourn. Regular caution she's always been. You could see her lying in the market square, kicking and screaming and lashing out like . . . with all the devils calling out of her mouth. Then all of a sudden she'd go quiet . . . just like all the devils had come out of her. And they had too, sir, through the mouth. There's some in this town as has seen 'em. Then she'd get quiet and walk away.''

"So they're taking her away and the people don't like it?''

"That's how 'tis, sir. They'm taking their last look, you might say. You see, sir, she's chained up now . . . and has been this last day or so since the rest of them Quales was drove out of the town. They'm a bad lot, them Quales. Two of the girls in trouble and the mother and father no better than they should be . . . begging the ladies' pardon. We got a party together . . . with whistles and such like . . . and we gave they a riding out of the town. That left Anna, sir; and now she be alone they've chained her and they've ordained to send her to Bodmin.''

The crowd about the cottage had turned to look at the four on horseback and, since some of them had fallen away from the cottage door, Melisande had a glimpse of one of the most horrible sights she had ever seen in her life.

Standing just inside the room, into which it was possible to step straight from the street, was a creature who looked more like a wild beast than a human being.

Melisande saw bare arms, mottled purple, hanging at her sides, saw the dirty skin, showing through dirtier rags, the hair which hung about the creature's face, the slobbering mouth from which came a hideous muttering sound. But it was the eyes which Melisande would never forget as long as she lived. They were bewildered, tormented eyes, wild, defiant and yet somehow appealing for help.

And in that brief second a boy in the crowd, close to the door of the cottage, leaned forward. In his hand was a long branch with which he prodded the mad woman. She tried to grasp the branch, but as she nearly succeeded in doing so, the boy would pull it away. She lunged as far as the chain would allow; the ring about her waist must have caused her a good deal of pain; and as the boy again prodded her and she tried to catch the branch she cried out a second time in suppressed rage. It was clear that this had been going on for some time.

The crowd shrieked its merriment and the gentry looked on indifferently at the amusements of the poor. Only one person in that assembly experienced a passion as great as that of the tormented. Melisande, without a second's hesitation, without stopping to think of anything but the mad creature's pain, slipped from her horse, handed the reins to John Collings who happened to be nearest and was too astonished to do anything but take them, ran forward and snatched the branch from the boy's hand.

"Do not!" she cried. "It is wicked. So cruel!" In the stress of the moment she had spoken in French.

The boy, at first startled, had released his hold on the branch; he tried after that brief hesitation to retrieve it. He kicked out at Melisande, as he tried to reach for the branch which she held above her head; and as he did so, she brought it sharply down across his face.

A pair of hands seized her . . . two pair of hands. She was aware of angry distorted faces about her, of a sudden roar of fury. She heard the word: "Foreigner!" They were forcing her to the ground.

But Fermor had leaped from his horse, had thrown his reins to John Collings and was in the midst of the crowd.

"She be French!" someone was shouting.

"They French have tails. . . ."

"Now be a chance to see for ourselves. . . ."

"Stand back, you swine, you oafs, you country fools . . . stand back!" That was Fermor, eyes blazing, his arms swinging out. Someone staggered and fell, and Fermor had Melisande in his grasp.

"Get to your horse . . . at once!" he said.

She obeyed. None tried to stop her. Fermor was facing the crowd with that arrogant insolence which they knew so well and which they had respected and obeyed all their lives.

"How dare you!" Fermor was shouting. "How dare you molest a lady!"

He had backed away from them and in a second or so he had leaped into his saddle.

The crowd had moved forward in that brief time; their mood was angry. Fermor was gentry, but foreign gentry. These people had seen the blood of a felon in the streets that day; they had been disturbed while they were tormenting Anna Quale. They were protesting against interference. There was too much interference. Bodmin was trying to take

from them what was theirs by right; should they be interrupted at their pleasures by foreigners . . . even if those foreigners were of the gentry! It was only the presence of known
gentry—John Collings and Caroline Trevenning—that prevented them from acting in unison against the arrogant
strangers who had dared interfere; as it was, some were for
pressing forward, others for holding back.

Someone caught at Fermor's leg and was kicked and sent
sprawling for his pains.

"Stop this!" cried John Collings. "What the devil . . ."

"Tar and feather the foreigners!" cried a voice in the
crowd. "Chain 'em up with the mad 'un . . . since they do
like her so much."

Meanwhile Fermor had gripped the bridle of Melisande's
horse and was forcing a way through the crowd.

"Come on!" he urged. "We must get away . . . with all
speed."

And as he with all his might forced the two horses against
the surly people, they broke through and, once free of the
pressure, the horses were trotting, then galloping across
the market square, out and away.

After some minutes Melisande cried: "Stop! Stop! The
others are not with us."

He laughed but did not draw rein.

"I said the others are not with us," she repeated.

He continued to ride on for a few minutes. Then he stopped.
"Did they not follow us?" he asked. Then he laughed loudly.
"Out of evil cometh good."

"What . . . do you mean?"

They had left the town well behind, and he looked back
towards it. "It was a damned ugly crowd," he said. "Their
blood was up. They did not like us, Mademoiselle. They
liked neither you nor me. Tasteless oafs . . . don't you
think?"

"It was my fault."

"Ah, Melisande, you have a lot to answer for."

"What shall we do now?"

"There are several things we might do. First look for an
inn and quench our thirsts. That was a thirsty job. Then look
for the others. . . . Or congratulate ourselves."

"Congratulate?"

"On at last finding ourselves alone."

"Is that then a matter for congratulation?"

"I think so. I was hoping you would too. I at least feel a little gratitude towards the crowd. Let's ride on. I should not like to be overtaken by them."

"But . . . John Collings and Caroline . . . they will be looking for us."

"Don't let's worry about them. They'll be all right. John will look after Caroline."

"But we've left them there . . . with those people."

"They were only annoyed with *us*, you know."

"But you must be anxious . . . about Caroline."

"She's all right. Those people won't hurt their own. They have a hatred for those they consider strangers. You're one and I'm one . . . I no less than you. We're strangers in a strange land. We ought to console one another." He took her hand and kissed it. "I beg of you, smile. Be gay. I like to see you gay. Come on. We've escaped. Let us be gay."

"I am sorry. I am afraid of what they might do to Caroline."

"Why? She's safe. She'll be glad we've got away. It would have been very awkward if we'd stayed . . . very difficult! And Caroline does not like difficult situations. Let us find a tavern, shall we? Come on."

"No. We must go back."

"What! Back to those howling hooligans! By the way, you haven't said thank you. It is customary, you know, when people save your life."

"I do thank you."

"Are you truly grateful?"

"I am afraid I have caused much trouble."

"You're bound to cause trouble, Melisande. Merely by existing you would cause trouble. So a little more, such as we have had to-day, hardly makes any difference."

"You are not being very serious, I think. We should try to find the others. Of that I am sure."

"That would make you happy?"

"Yes please."

"As ever I am at your service. Come."

"Is this the way?"

"This is the way."

They rode on, and after a while Melisande cried: "Are you sure this is the way?"

"This is the way," he assured her again.

The mist had cleared considerably and she saw the moor about them, the heather glistening, little streams tumbling over the stones; the grey tors reminded her of poor Anna Quale, for they were like tormented beings.

"I have so long wanted to talk to you alone," said Fermor.

"Of what did you wish to talk?"

"I believe you know. You must know. You must realize that ever since I met you I have wanted to be . . . your friend."

"You have been very friendly, very kind. I thank you."

"I would be kinder than anyone has ever been. I would be the greatest friend you have ever had. Shall we pull up here and give the horses a rest?"

"But do they need a rest? They were watered and fed at the inn where we had the pasties. And I think we should get back to Trevenning. Caroline will be very anxious if we are not there when she returns."

"But I want to talk to you, and it is difficult talking as we go along."

"Then perhaps we should talk some other time."

"What other time? It is very rarely that we get away from them all. Here there is no one to be seen. Look about you. You and I . . . are alone up here. We could not be more alone than this, could we?"

He brought his horse close to hers and suddenly stretching out an arm caught her and kissed her violently. Her horse moved restively and she broke free.

She said breathlessly. "Please, do not. I wish to go back at once. This must not be. I do not believe we are on the right road."

"You and I are on the right road, Melisande. What other road matters?"

"I do not understand you."

"You know that is not true. I thought you were a truthful young lady."

"I cannot believe . . . that you mean what . . ."

"What do you think I mean? Why should you not? You must know how damnably attractive you are."

She was trembling. She wanted to hate him. She thought of the hurt to Caroline. Yet she could not hate him. She could not keep in mind his unkindness to Caroline, his careless indifference to the suffering of others; she could only think of his singing along the road the sad song about the miller's daughter, the merry one about the gipsy and the earl; she could only think of his blazing blue eyes when he had caught her horse by its bridle and forced a way for them through the crowd.

"Dear little Melisande," he was saying now, and again he tried to put an arm about her shoulder. As she eluded him he laughed, and she realized that it was that sudden laughter which disarmed her criticism. "This is an awkward position!" he cried. "Damme if I ever was in such an awkward one . . . and never did I so long to be on my own two feet. But what if I dismount? I believe you'd gallop away and leave me standing here. Shall I chance it? Shall I dismount? Shall I make you do the same? Shall I carry you to the grass there and make a couch for us among the bracken?"

"You talk too fast. I do not understand."

"Do not cower behind your unfamiliarity with the language. You know very well what I say. You love me and I love you. Why make any bones about that? Life is too complicated to argue about the obvious."

"The obvious?"

"My sweet Melisande, how can you hide it any more than I can?"

"And what of Caroline?"

"I will look after Caroline."

"By . . . hurting her . . . as the miller's daughter was hurt? What if she . . . ?"

"This is not a song. This is life. Caroline is no miller's daughter. If she were I should not be affianced to her. If Caroline discovers that I love . . . but why should she? You and I are not so foolish as to wish to make that sort of trouble. You may rest assured that she will not be found in the cold river. Caroline will understand that she and I must marry for the sake of our families; and all the arrangements for the future have been made for us. As for you and me . . . that is love. That is different.''

She drew back, her green eyes blazing. ''You are a very wicked man, I think.''

''Oh come! You wouldn't like me if I were a saint.''

She was thinking: I must get away . . . quickly. He is bad. He is one of those men of whom Thérèse thought, of whom Sister Emilie and Sister Eugenie thought when they would not look into the faces of men. It would be better if *I* had never looked into *his* face. She thought suddenly of the nun who had been walled up in the convent all those years ago; she wondered fleetingly if the man whom that nun had loved had been like this one, and she believed he must have been.

She quickly turned her horse and rode back the way she had come.

She heard him behind her shouting as she broke into a gallop.

''Melisande! You fool! You idiot! Stop! Do you want to break your neck?''

''I hope you break yours,'' she called over her shoulder. ''That would be a goodness . . . for Caroline . . . for me. . . .''

''I shan't break *my* neck. I can ride.''

Soon he was beside her, catching at her bridle and slowing down the horses.

''There, you see. You cannot get away from me. You never will, Melisande. Oh, just at first you will be very virtuous. You will say 'Get you behind me, Satan! I am a virtuous young woman of very high ideals. I have been brought up in a convent and all my opinions are ready-made.' But are you sure they are, Melisande? Are you sure of your virtue?''

''I am sure of one thing. You are despicable. You knew we were not going the right way. Deliberately you brought us here. I am sorry for Caroline.''

''That's a lie. You envy her.''

''Envy her! Marriage with you!''

''Indeed you do, my dear. A minute ago, when you were full of your convent ideas and you thought I was suggesting a break with Caroline and marriage with you, you could not conceal your delight. But wait . . . wait until you begin to think freely. Wait until you learn to be honest with yourself.''

"You . . . to talk of honesty! You . . . who have arranged this! Who brought us here?''

"Who started it? Who had the crowd at her heels? Do you realize that but for me you would be chained up with a mad woman now?''

"It is not true.''

"You've never seen an angry mob before, have you? There is a lot you have to learn, my dear Mademoiselle. It might have gone very badly for you if I had not been there.''

"John Collings would have saved me.''

"Well, I at least was the one who prevented disaster, wasn't I.''

"It is a truth. I have already thanked you.''

"So here is a little gratitude from you at last? Pity is love's sister, I've heard. What is gratitude?''

"I have thanked you for saving me from the crowd. Now let us return.''

"Be sensible, Melisande. Be reasonable. What will you do when Caroline no longer needs your services? Have you thought of that?''

"You mean when you marry her?''

"She might even decide before then that she does not need them.''

"Yes, that is a truth.''

"A truth indeed. You should look to the future. And that, my dear, as you so charmingly say, is another truth.''

"Look to the future! A future of sin is your suggestion.''

"That's an ugly word. I don't like ugly things.''

"But ugly things have ugly words, do they not?''

"You are too serious. Love should give pleasure. People were meant to be happy. Even companions were meant to be happy. I would make you happy. I would never let unhappiness touch you. I will give you a house in London, and there we shall be together. How can you stay here, buried away in the country . . . in a position which, to say the best, is uncertain?'' He broke into song:

"I would love you all the day . . .
Every night would kiss and play,
If with me you'd fondly stray
Over the hills and far away . . ."

"Let us return, please . . . the quickest way."

"Don't you like my singing? You do, I know. It draws you to me. Do you think I do not know?"

"Should you not be thinking of the effect of your singing on Caroline?"

"No. To Caroline I give marriage. I can spare nothing else for her."

"You are cynical."

"You mean I am truthful. Cynicism is a word the sentimental apply to truth. I could have made all sorts of false promises to you . . . as the miller's daughter's lover did to her. But I would not. Think how I could have framed my proposal. I could have said: 'Melisande, elope with me to London. I will go off first and a few days later you must follow me.' That would have shifted suspicion from me, you see. Then I should have met you, gone through a ceremony of marriage—not a real one you understand. There are such things . . . mock marriages. They have been going on for years. Then, you see, all would have been well until I was found out. Then you would have discovered that I was a scoundrel. Of course, I am a scoundrel, but I am an honest scoundrel. So I say to you: I love you. I love everything about you, even your prudery because it gives me something to overcome, and, by God, I will overcome it. I tell you the truth. I will never be a rogue in the guise of a saint. And I'll tell you this, Melisande: Look closely at the saints you meet in life. I'll warrant you'll find a little of the rogue in them. But you see, I'd rather be an honest bad man than a dishonest good one."

"Please to be silent," she said. "I have heard enough . . . too much."

Strangely enough he obeyed her and soon they saw the town stretched out before them.

"Better skirt it," he said. "They would recognize us and

we don't want any more unpleasantness, do we? We might not escape so easily this time, and although I'd be ready to tackle any of them single-handed for my lady's sake, I don't fancy facing a mob of hundreds.''

She recognized that they were now on the right road. Yet how changed everything seemed. Life had become no longer simple. She had so much to fear; Caroline, Wenna, a cruel and angry mob . . . and Fermor.

She took a quick glance at him. He was not in the least disturbed. She felt inexperienced and afraid. To whom could she go for advice? To Caroline? Impossible. To Sir Charles? He had been kind—he was still kind, yet he seemed remote. During those occasions when they were in each other's company she sensed in him an uneasiness. She believed that he avoided her; that he was anxious to prevent their ever being alone together. No, she could not ask him for advice. What of her friends in the servants' hall? They were too garrulous, too fond of gossip. This was not only her trouble; it was also Caroline's.

She thought of the nun, as she had thought of her so many times before. She saw the nun as herself, the lover as Fermor. She feared that she was as weak as the nun; and surely the lover must have been very like Fermor.

She ought to go away—not only for her own sake but for that of Caroline. But where could she go?

He was watching her, she knew; and he was laughing at her. She believed he was clever enough to read her thoughts, evil enough to laugh at them. He was a bad man. He represented Men as the nuns thought of them. It was because of men like this one that they wished to shut themselves away from the world.

They left the high road and were within a mile of Trevenning. He broke into another of his songs.

> *"Shall I, wasting in despair,*
> *Die because a woman's fair?"*

She tried to urge her horse to go ahead of his, but he would not have it so; he kept level with her and went on with his song.

"If she slight me when I woo,
I can scorn and let her go;
For if she be not for me,
What care I how fair she be?"

And so they came to Trevenning.

Wenna was sitting by Caroline's bed; she was stroking the girl's forehead with her cool fingers.

"What is it, my queen? Tell Wenna."

She was different from Miss Maud. She frightened Wenna. Miss Maud had tears for all occasions. Caroline hardly ever wept. There were times when Wenna thought there could have been comfort in tears.

Wenna could only guess what had happened. The four of them had set off together. Caroline and John Collings had come home first; after that Fermor had arrived with Melisande.

Caroline had seemed to wear a mask to hide her suffering, but no mask could deceive Wenna. God curse all men! thought Wenna. Oh, if only my little queen would have none of them! If only she'd throw his ring in his face, and tell her father she'd rather die than marry him! And what was he doing here! He ought to have gone back to London weeks ago. It was clear what he was doing. Thoughts danced in and out of Wenna's mind. She would like to see them both ridden out of the place. She'd play a whistle herself and dance to their riding; she would be the first to call obscenities after them.

When they had returned—those shameless ones—he had been blithe and gay, but she was afraid. She was not one to be able to hide her feelings. Her cheeks were scarlet, her eyes a more brilliant green than ever. Something had happened. Wenna could guess what. Oh shameful, shameful! In the open country, most like. There, soiling the good green earth, there among the flowers and grasses. It was doubly wicked that way.

Caroline had dressed herself in one of her loveliest dresses that evening. She had laughed and joked with her father— that old sinner—and the man she was to marry, that even greater young sinner. Oh, brave Miss Caroline, laughing with her heart breaking!

That imp of Satan had been put out of countenance though. She had had a tray sent to her room, and Wenna had seen Peg come out when she went to take it away, her lips greasy, still chewing. It looked as if Peg had had to finish her food for her. She had them all dancing to her tune. Mrs. Soady, Mr. Meaker, Peg and the rest . . . every fool of them.

I'd like to ill-wish her. I wish she was dead. I'd go along to a witch if I knew of one that did such things now, and I'd get a wax image of her and I'd stick pins in it every night, that I would. And I hope she finds trouble and he swears it weren't him. That I do. And I hope she dies. . . .

"Tell, my handsome. Tell Wenna. Caroline, my darling, tell Wenna."

"You know everything, Wenna, don't you?" said Caroline.

"Everything that concerns my lamb."

"Wenna, there's no one else I could talk to about this."

"Course there ain't. But there's Wenna. There's always Wenna. You'll be happier telling. What happened, dearie? What happened, my queen?"

"She wants him, you see, Wenna. She's doing all she can to get him, and he . . ."

"Well, my little queen, there's things I could say about him, but let's admit betwixt ourselves he's like all the men . . . perhaps no better . . . perhaps no worse."

"And she, Wenna, she's very pretty. She's more than pretty."

"There's the devil in her."

"Let's be fair. I don't think she means . . ."

"Not mean! She's been working for it. She looks at any, who'll be duped, with those great big eyes of hers. I never did like green ones. There's something of the devil in green eyes. I never yet knew any green-eyed person that hadn't got wickedness in them . . ."

"No, Wenna. That's not true."

"You're too soft, my precious. You're too good and kind. You're like your mother."

"I don't know whether she planned it, but he did . . . from the moment he saw that they could get away."

"What did happen? Tell Wenna."

"There was trouble in Liskeard. It was outside Anna Quale's cottage. The mob was there and she took it upon herself to interfere with them."

"She would!"

"They didn't like it, Wenna, she being a foreigner."

"The impudence! I wonder they didn't tear her limb from limb."

"They might have done. But he was watching her and I was watching him. He was off his horse before any of us could do anything . . . and he looked as if he would have killed anyone who laid a hand on her. He got her on to her horse and they galloped away. It seemed some time before John and I realized what had happened. It could only have been for a second or two though. Then John said: 'We'd better go. . . .' And the people just parted and made way for us . . . looking ashamed of themselves. It was because they knew who we were, I suppose. In any case, there was never any question of their touching *us*. We couldn't find those two, Wenna. We didn't know where they'd gone."

"They gave 'ee the slip then. They gave 'ee the slip on purpose."

"That was his intention."

"Hers too. Depend upon it."

"Then we came home and they came home. At least they came home not much more than half an hour after us."

"Half an hour be long enough for mischief, and they wouldn't want to call attention to themselves."

"Oh, Wenna, I'm so unhappy."

"There, there, my dearie. Why don't 'ee tell him you've done with him?"

"I can't, Wenna. I'll never be done with him."

"Why, you could stay here and there'd be Wenna always to look after and comfort 'ee."

"Wherever I go you'll be there to look after and comfort me."

"I know. Bless 'ee for that. We'll never be parted, my little love. But he's not the one for you."

"He is, Wenna. He is. There's one thing that frightens me. What if he is so much in love with her that he wants to marry her!"

"Not he! Who be she then? Somebody's bastard! Oh yes, you can be shocked, my pretty, but that's what she be. I know it. Some light o' love had a baby she didn't want, and she be it. Master Fermor's a proud man. So be his family. They don't marry the likes of her, no matter how green their eyes be."

"That sort of marriage has happened."

"She'd need the devil and all his spells to bring it off. He ain't given no sign that he's thinking of backing out of marriage with you?"

"No, Wenna."

"Well, don't 'ee fret about that. You'll marry him, my love; and to my way of thinking, one man ain't much worse than another. You'll have trouble with him . . . like this day. You'll always have that sort of trouble. But we'll fight trouble when it comes. We'll fight it together. Wenna would die for you, my precious. Wenna would kill for you. If I had her here now I'd take her throat in my two hands and ring it like I would the neck of a chicken for the boiling pot."

"Oh, Wenna, you're a comfort to me."

"Don't 'ee fret, my dear. Wenna's beside 'ee."

Caroline was quiet then. She lay still with her eyes closed while Wenna thought of the slender neck in her strong hands, and the green eyes, wide with horror, staring dumbly, asking for mercy which should not be given.

There was quietness throughout the house. In half an hour it would be midnight.

In her room, Melisande waited, her cloak wrapped about her, her shoes in her hand.

A board in the corridor creaked. Melisande was tense, listening.

Cautiously she opened her door and a small plump figure glided in.

Peg said: "Be you ready then, Mamazel?"

"Yes, Peg."

Peg whispered: "The back door be unbolted. Mrs. Soady

said not to forget to bolt it when we did come in. We'll pick up the food as we go out. 'Tis all ready. Come.''

They tiptoed downstairs, every now and then pausing to make sure that no one in the house was stirring; down the back staircase, through to the servants' hall, where they could breathe more freely, for if they awakened any of the servants that would be of no great importance as the adventure had the blessing of Mrs. Soady.

Into the great stone kitchen they went, where two neat packages lay on the table.

" 'Tis roast fowl,'' whispered Peg. ''Tamson Trequint be terrible partial to roast fowl. Mrs. Soady said she'd give a beautiful spell for a wing or a bit of the breast. Now then . . . be you ready?''

"Yes,'' said Melisande.

"Then come on.''

Out through the back door they went.

"Keep close to the house,'' whispered Peg, ''just in case someone has heard and looks from the windows.''

But they had to cross the park.

"Hurry,'' said Peg. ''We must be there by midnight. That be terrible important. A midnight spell be the best you can have. More like to work . . . so says Mrs. Soady; and her'd know, being a pellar.''

When they reached the high road, Melisande turned to look about her. The country was touched with the white magic of the moon; it cast a light path on the waters. The rocks looked like crouching giants; on the water there gleamed an occasional phosphorescent light, ghostly and fascinating.

"What be looking at?'' demanded Peg. ''What be over there by the sea?''

"It's so beautiful.''

"Oh, 'tis only the old sea.''

"But look at the shadows there.''

"Only they old rocks.''

"And the lights! Look! They come and go.''

" 'Tis mackerel . . . nothing more. Them lights do mean we'll have mackerel the next few days . . . like as not. Come on. Do 'ee want a midnight spell, Mamazel, or did 'ee come out to look for mackerel?''

It was eerie in the woods. Some of the trees gleamed silver like ghosts from another world, others were black and menacing like grotesque human shapes. Now and then there would be a movement in the undergrowth.

"What be that?" cried Peg.

"A rat? A rabbit?"

"I've heard of people what comes out alone at night being carried off."

"We're not alone."

"No! I wouldn't have come out alone . . . not for a farm . . . not for roast fowl every day of my life. That I wouldn't. The Little People don't carry 'ee off in twos, so 'tis said. All the same, I be scared. Better say Jack o' lantern."

Peg began in trembling voice:

"Jack o' Lantern, Joan the Wad,
Who tickled the maid and made her mad,
Light me home; the weather's bad . . ."

"But we do not want to be lighted home and the weather is not bad," pointed out Melisande.

"Well, we dursen't say 'Light me to the witch's cave.' I don't know that piskies be terrible fond of witches. I do reckon we might get pisky-led if we was alone. I'm terrible glad we'm not."

They pushed on, and Peg screamed when a low branch caught her hair and she could not immediately extricate herself. They both felt that at any moment they would see hundreds of little figures making a ring round them, tickling them until they were mad, leading them away to regions below the earth. But Melisande was able to release Peg, and after that, they took to running; and they did not stop until they reached Tamson's hut.

Wenna had heard the creaking of the stairs. Wenna slept lightly.

Someone was creeping about the house, she decided.

Wenna had her own ideas. She thought she knew. Wouldn't

it be just like him? She reckoned that the wicked Mamazel, the daughter of Babylon, was creeping up to his room. She pictured the terrible deeds they would perform.

What if she caught them together? That wouldn't do though. It would only bring sorrow to Miss Caroline. No! But she could go to the master with her tales.

She went to the door of her room. She slept in the room next to Caroline's.

Pray God, Miss Caroline don't wake, the poor lamb! she thought.

She waited. There was no sound now. Had she been mistaken? Had she been dreaming? But she would keep a sharp look out, she would. One little slip and she'd be off to the master. He couldn't keep a harlot in his house . . . not one who was going to rob his legitimate daughter of a husband. But perhaps he was shameful enough for that! Hadn't he brought that woman's daughter into the house to live alongside Miss Caroline?

She went back to her room, but as she was about to get into her bed she heard a sound from without. So, they were meeting out of doors. Why hadn't she thought of that!

She was at her window. The lawn was bright with moonlight. She listened. Yes. Surely footsteps. If only she were down there! But they were keeping close to the house. Where were they off to do their wickedness? On the sweet pure grass! Let them catch their deaths and die.

Now she saw them—two figures; one was Mamazel, the other was short and squat. Peg!

And what were they doing, and where were they going? They were making their way towards the woods.

Suddenly she knew, and the thought filled her with misgiving.

She knew why girls went out in pairs round about midnight. She knew why they made their way to the hut in the woods.

She sat at the window, waiting.

Melisande shuddered as they stepped into the hut. It was dimly lighted by a lamp which hung from the ceiling and smelt strongly of the oil. A fire was burning in a hollow in one corner of the hut. Two black cats lay stretched on the earthen floor. One rose and arched his back at the sight of the visitors; the other lay still, watching them with alert green eyes.

"Be still, Samuel," said a gentle voice. " 'Tis only two young ladies come to see us."

The black cat settled down on the floor and watched them.

On a table several objects lay in some disorder. There were pieces of wax, wooden hearts and bottles of red liquid which had the appearance of blood. There were charms made of wood and metal, a chart of the sky and a great crystal globe.

About the clay walls herbs were hung. There was a wooden beam across the ceiling of the hut and from this hung dark objects in various stages of decomposition. Two live toads were near the fire; a pot was simmering there; the steam which rose from it smelt of earth and decaying vegetables.

Tamson Trequint had risen. She was a very old woman whose untidy grey hair fell about her shoulders; her skin was burned brown by the sun and wind and she was very thin. Her eyes were black and brilliant and her heavy lids suggested an eagle.

"Come in. Come in. Don't 'ee be scared," she said. "Samuel won't hurt 'ee. Nor will Joshua. What have you brought me?"

Peg was too frightened to speak. Melisande forced herself to say: "We have brought roast fowl for you."

"So you be the pretty foreign one. Come here, my dear, that I may look at 'ee. You b'ain't frightened, be you? 'Tis the same with all these servant girls. They want my charms; they want their plough-boys and their fishermen. But they'm scared of coming to me to ask my help. What do you want, my dear? Speak up. You don't altogether believe in our ways, do 'ee? But you've come all the same."

"Is it true that you can give charms and potions to make people love," asked Melisande. "Can you make people love those it is good for them to love . . . even though they do not do so?"

"I can give a charm as will put a bloom on a young girl, my dear. I can smear her with jam like . . . so that the wasps come a-buzzing round. Are there witches where you do come from? Are there black witches like some . . . and white witches like old Tammy Trequint?''

"I do not know of them. I lived in a convent . . . away from such things.''

"I understand 'ee, my dear. You be like a bird as is let free. Mind someone don't catch 'ee and clip your pretty wings. Why do you come here?''

"I want a charm . . . a spell . . . a potion . . . if you will be so good as to give me one.''

"You want a lover. You should be fair enough without a charm.''

Melisande looked into the hooded eyes and saw that they were kindly for all their strangeness. She said quickly: "I am afraid of . . . someone. I wish his attentions to be turned from me. I wish them to go . . . where they belong. Could that be done?''

" 'Tis a love token in reverse, so to speak.''

"Can you give me such a one?''

" 'Twill not be easy. There's some who might come and ask such a thing and I'd know it would be no more than breaking a couple of twigs. But 'tis not so with you, my dear. We'll see. What does the other maiden want?''

Peg came forward. Her wants were simple. She wanted a love token to catch the young fisherman whom, try as she might, she could not catch without.

"Let me see what you've brought." She unwrapped the parcel of food. She sniffed it. " 'Tis good," she said. "Mrs. Soady have sent you and Mrs. Soady's my good friend.''

She put the food on the table and, picking up a piece of wax, with expert fingers, she forced it into a metal mould. This she put on the fire.

She said to Peg: "Think of his face, my dear. Think of him. Conjure him up. He's there behind you . . . a bonny boy. Close your eyes and say his name. Can you see him?'' Peg nodded. The mould was drawn from the fire and left to cool.

"Sit you on that stool, my dear. Keep your eyes closed and don't for a minute stop thinking of him. When he's cooled down you shall have him. Just sit 'ee still now.''

Peg obeyed.

"Now you, my dear. 'Tis not the same for you. 'Tis a double spell you need. Now first we must turn his affection from you like. I've got an onion here and I want you to pierce it with these pins. In the old days we'd use nothing but a sheep's or bullock's heart. But onions serve, and they be easy to come by. Now, my dear, take these pins and as you stick them in the onion you must conjure up his image. You must see him standing close behind you."

"This will not bring a misfortune to him?" asked Melisande anxiously. "There is no harm for him in this?"

Tamson laughed suddenly. "What be harm? Harm to one be good to another. If he do love you truly he might be happy with you. If he's to love this other, he might find sorrow there. Then that would be harm. So whether harm or good will come of this, I can't tell 'ee. I be a witch but a white witch. And I'll tell 'ee this, because I've took a fancy to 'ee: meddling with fate ain't always a good thing. 'Tis writ in the stars what shall be. Fate's Fate and there's no altering that; and when people come to me for spells they're after altering it. 'Tis devils' work to alter Fate. You got to call in magic. 'Tis more like to be harm that way than good."

"I know I must turn his thoughts from me. I know it would be a goodness to do so."

"Then stick in they pins."

The tears started to Melisande's eyes.

" 'Tis that old onion. But tears be good. Tears never done no harm. Is it ready, well riddled with pins? He's there. He's behind you. He's tall and handsome and gay. He loves many, but not one of them as he loves himself. Now we'll roast his heart, and as we roast it, you must say with me:

'It is not this heart I wish to burn,
But the person's heart I wish to turn . . .'

"Then, my dear, you whisper to yourself the name of her who should be his love, and you must see them together, and they must be joining hands while you do say those words. Say his name and her name . . . and see them bound together in love."

Melisande closed her eyes and repeated the lines after the

witch. She tried to see Caroline and Fermor, to see them embrace; but instead she was filled with a passionate wish that she might have been Sir Charles's daughter, that she might have been the one who was chosen for him. Caroline would not stay in the picture. He was there, singing on his horse, leaning over to kiss Melisande, laughing at her, mocking her. And she was there, riding away from him, yet reluctantly, knowing he was gaining on her. Then she thought of the nun who had broken her vows all those years ago and had died in her granite tomb.

"There!" said Tamson Trequint. "That'll do 'ee both. Now, my dear," she went on, turning to Peg, "here be your image. You stick pins in it every night, just where his heart is, and if you've seen him aright and you've done all I told 'ee, he'll be your lover before the coming of the new moon. Get on with 'ee now."

Peg said breathlessly: "Oh, Mrs. Soady did say she have a stye coming and what should she do?"

"Tell her to touch it with the tail of a cat."

"And Mr. Meaker be feared his asthma's coming back."

"Let him collect spiders' webs, roll them in his hands and swallow them."

"Thank 'ee, Mistress Trequint. Mrs. Soady said as something would be left for 'ee."

"Tell Mrs. Soady her's welcome."

They went out into the woods and the journey back was not so terrifying as the journey to the hut. They were too absorbed in what they had seen to think of the supernatural inhabitants of the wood. Peg was clutching her image and thinking of her fisherman. Melisande was less happy.

They crossed the lawns to the house.

"Quietly now," said Peg.

But Wenna, watching at her window, had already seen them.

Wenna had made up her mind. She would not remain passive any longer, for this was no time for passivity.

That wicked girl had not gone out to meet him; she was too artful for that. Like as not she was holding him off. She was more than wanton; she was cunning.

Wenna imagined her telling him that she was too good a girl to become one of his light o' loves. Clearly she had gone to the witch in the woods for a spell that would make him dance to her piping . . . dance to whatever tune she played; and her tune would be marriage.

So there was no time for delay.

Wenna went down to the kitchen.

Mrs. Soady was sitting at the table treating her eye with the cat's tail. The big tom-cat was on the table and Mrs. Soady was trying to make him keep still so that she could wipe his tail across her eyelid.

"What be up to?" asked Wenna.

" 'Tis this blessed stye again. My brother be a martyr to 'em, and they do trouble me now and then. I'm trying to cure the thing afore it grows so big as to close up my eye."

"Who told 'ee to do that then?"

" 'Twas old Tammy Trequint. She be very good. I remember how when Jane Pengelly's three had the measles she told her to cut off a cat's left ear and swallow three drops of the blood in a glass of spring water. My dear life, they was all cured by next day. That's Tam Trequint for 'ee."

Wenna thought: So you knew they was going to see Tamson then? You told 'em to go. You're as thick as smugglers, you two be . . . you and that Mamazel.

She looked at Mrs. Soady who was so fat that she appeared to be sliding off the chair on which she sat. Mrs. Soady's small benevolent eyes smiled at the world through her puffy flesh. There was a lot of Mrs. Soady. It came of feeding herself with tidbits all through the day. Not that she'd go short on her meals either! Mrs. Soady loved food. She also loved a bit of gossip—the tastier the better. Which did she love most, hog's pudding or news of the latest seduction, pilchards with cream or what Annie Polgard did to Sam? It was hard to say. Suffice it that both were irresistible.

There was something else about Mrs. Soady. She was the most generous body in the world. She could not enjoy her food completely unless she shared it with others; she could not enjoy her scandals unless she shared them also. It mattered not if it was her master's food she gave; it mattered not if she had sworn to keep the gossip secret. That was how it was with her.

"So you've been a-visiting Tamson then?'' said Wenna.

"No, 'tis too far for me and the way through the woods too bony, my dear. I send Tam a little something now and then. One of the maids takes it for me."

"So they've been to-day, have they?''

"Not so long ago."

"What's the trouble now?''

"Young Peg—she's after one of the fishermen.''

"That girl's a bad 'un."

"Oh, I wouldn't say that. She's just what you might call affectionate natured. Some is; some ain't. It turns up in a human being now and then, Wenna, my dear.''

"Did young Peg go alone, or did this here affection turn up in someone else?''

Mrs. Soady did not think she ought to tell, but it was going to be very hard not to; and Wenna felt too impatient to get the secret out of her like a winkle out of a shell. She said bluntly: "I saw them coming in. After midnight. 'Tain't right, you know, Mrs. Soady, young girls going out at midnight.''

"My dear, the spell only works at midnight, and going together no harm can come to them.''

"So Mamazel had to have a token, eh?''

"Well, why not? 'Tis a bit of fun. Though as Mr. Meaker said, a pretty girl like she be didn't ought to want a token. That's what he did say.''

" 'Tis easy to catch flies, my dear, but you want a net to catch a rare butterfly.''

"My dear!'' Mrs. Soady was overcome by such cleverness. "Do you think then . . . Oh, I don't know. 'Twas just a bit of fun. I remember what I was like when I was a girl.'' Mrs. Soady laughed softly at memories.

Wenna clenched her hands together. She thought: She's got to go. She must not stay here. And she did not care how she did it; she was going to drive Melisande from the house.

If she went to the master and told him all she knew of her, he would push aside all she had to say. Of course he would. What did he care if she took Master Fermor and broke the heart of his legitimate daughter? What had he cared for Maud? Hadn't he deliberately let her die because of his absorption with this girl?

Very well then. She knew how to attack where it hurt most. He was a dignified man. He was very proud of his position in the country. He might go off to gaiety in foreign parts and London Town, but no spot must tarnish his reputation here in Cornwall.

She said: "Mrs. Soady, I know something about this Mamazel."

"You know something!" Mrs. Soady's eyes glistened as they did when she chopped up apples, bacon and onions and laid them with mutton over a young and tender pigeon to make a squab pie. They could not have shone more over the drop of pig's blood that went into the making of a hog's or bloody pudding.

"I don't rightly know that I ought to tell."

"Oh, you can trust me, Wenna, my dear."

"Well, don't 'ee say a word then . . . not a word to a soul. Will 'ee swear?"

"I will, my dear. You can trust me."

Wenna drew her chair close to Mrs. Soady. "I happen to know whose daughter she is."

"Oh?"

"The master's."

"No!"

" 'Tis so. There was a woman up to London."

"You don't say!"

"Yes, I do then. He was always going up. Business, he said. Business? says I. I know what sort of business. And there was this girl, and they put her in a French convent; and then when she grew up, he wanted her here. Well, he couldn't very well bring her here while her ladyship lived. He's terrible strict about what's right and wrong . . . when it's going to be found out."

"How did you know all this? Did her ladyship know it, Wenna, my dear?"

"Well, she didn't know all. But I don't mind telling 'ee, Mrs. Soady, that just before Miss Maud died, there was a letter . . . a letter from foreign parts. He was worried about it. I saw him with it. He was wondering what he could do.

He was afraid to bring her here while Miss Maud was alive. Miss Maud asked him to bring her a wrap. . . . 'Twas on the night the engagement were celebrated. And what did he do? He went in and read that letter instead. And Miss Maud caught cold and died.''

''You mean that was what he wanted . . . so he could bring Mamazel here?''

''I didn't say that. 'Twas you who said that, Mrs. Soady.''

''My dear soul! I didn't mean it. I know the master to be a good man . . . none better. But you really think this be true?''

''I've every reason to believe it, Mrs. Soady. She's his daughter. She's what they do call his illegitimate daughter.''

''That be the same as a bastard,'' said Mrs. Soady in a hushed voice. ''Well, I never did!''

''Now, Mrs. Soady, I have took you into my confidence. You'll not breathe a word of it to a soul. 'Tis our secret.''

''Why, Wenna, my dear, you can trust me. Not a word. My dear life! The times we do live in!''

''Don't 'ee forget, Mrs. Soady. What the master would do if this got about, I can't say!''

''My dear life! My dear soul! And here's me forgetting that veer we be having for dinner.'' She rose from the table. Her little eyes were shining; she was not thinking so much about the young sucking pig she was to prepare, as of the strange goings-on of the master of the house.

She would be absent-minded for a while, and Meaker would know she had something on her mind; and old Meaker was almost as much a gossip as she was. He wouldn't let her keep it on her mind; he'd get her to share it.

It would not be long, Wenna reasoned, before the servants' hall would be in the secret; they would all be whispering of the extraordinary relationship between the master and Mamazel.

And soon it would get to the master's ears.

And then, Mamazel, my pretty dear, if I do know the master, you'll be something that has to be hushed up pretty quick; and things that has to be hushed up is put away where nobody can't see them. I reckon I have got rid of you good and proper, that I do!

Two

October brought the gales. The rain came driving in from the sea, bending the fir trees, beating against the houses, forcing its way through the windows and under the doors; the sea was grey and angry; the fishermen could not fish. They sat disconsolately in the Jolly Sailor, talking, as they talked every year, of the gales that kept a fisherman from his living. The sea mist, like a damp curtain, descended over the land.

"Everything be damp!" declared Mrs. Soady. "My shoes do get the mildew in them overnight."

Mr. Meaker complained of his rheumatics. Peg only was grateful for the weather. It meant that her young fisherman—for Tamson's charm had worked—could not go out, and everyone knew that fishermen kept from the sea needed a terrible lot of comforting.

Melisande was uneasy now and then. She would wonder whether her onion pierced with pins had been as effective as Peg's wax image. Melisande was by nature gay, and the first shock of finding herself in a somewhat alarming position had given place to a certain exhilaration. She must live for the moment. She was only just past sixteen and each week seemed an age in itself; she found she could not think very seriously of the future. As for Fermor she understood his feelings for her. She was certain that she herself was inclined to wickedness. Had not the nuns always told her so? Fermor was wicked and, like Satan, was tempting her to sin. Any wickedness at the Convent, so said the nuns, had invariably involved Melisande. So now, naturally enough, Fermor was tempting her because he opined that she would be very likely to fall into temptation. One should love the saints and abhor

the sinners; but one could not help being very interested in
the sinners; and she, poor little orphan, had been excited
because, for the first time, someone had spoken to her of
love.

No one had talked of love in the Convent. The baker had
given her the *gâteau*; and that was friendship. The affection
of the Lefevres was also friendship. Sir Charles had brought
her here, and that was kindness. But love was like parsnip
wine; it went to your head.

So, she decided, she must be forgiven for thinking of him.
He was merely tempting her as one of the devils with the
pitchforks depicted on the altar cloth, had tempted St. Anthony and St. Francis. She wondered if St. Anthony and St.
Francis had enjoyed being tempted.

Peg would often steal to her room to talk to her, for Peg
felt that there was a bond between them since they had gone
to Tamson's together. Peg would set down the tray and rock
on her heels while she talked of her fisherman, twirling her
hair, her eyes soft.

Peg thought suddenly that it was on account of Mamazel
that she had fallen in love with the fisherman. Before Mamazel had come she had thought a powerful lot of Master
Fermor. Peg had to be in love with someone, and Peg was
no dreamer; love for her had to be reciprocated. Master Fermor had been absentminded when she had taken in his hot
water, and it was because his thoughts were on Mamazel.
So Peg had promptly looked about and found her fisherman.

"I think my spell worked," said Melisande. "Tamson
Trequint is wonderful."

"Her's pretty good. Though Mrs. Soady's stye be no better. 'Tis that old tom-cat. He's a terrible creature. There's no
magic in him. Mamazel, I never heard of nobody ever wanting love turned from 'em before."

Peg's thoughts struggled for expression, but she could not
find the words. She wondered what became of people like
Mamazel. Governesses there were, she knew. There were
governesses at the Danesboroughs' and the Leighs'. But they
were not the sort whom love could touch. There were companions too. There was the one at Lady Gover's. They were
all middle-aged and Peg was vaguely contemptuous of them.

But what could governesses and companions do? There was no one to marry them. They couldn't marry the gentry like Mr. Fermor and Frith Danesborough; and they couldn't marry the miners and the fishermen. It was a sad thing to be a governess or a companion. But to be a *young* companion—that was a very queer position.

She wondered what would happen to Melisande when Miss Caroline married. Would Miss Caroline take her with her? She'd be mazed if she did. But could Mamazel stay at the house if she did not? Who could she be companion to?

It was too complicated for Peg, so she let her thoughts drift back to her fisherman. That was uncomplicated. If anything should come of it they'd marry and she'd go away to his cottage on the quay. Her story was set in a familiar groove. It was Mamazel's which could twist and turn in any direction.

"Mamazel," she said at length, "what'll 'ee do when Miss Caroline do marry?"

Melisande was silent for a while. Then she said: "I . . . I don't know."

Peg looked at her with vague sympathy, and Melisande did not want sympathy. She said almost defiantly: "It is a secret, is it not? It is the mystery. How do any one of us know what will become of her? It is that which makes of life an . . . excitement. When I was at the Convent, I did not know what was coming. And then one day . . . I leave . . . I leave the nuns and all that I have known for so many years. I have seen them every day and then . . . I never see them any more. It is all a change. There is a new country . . . a new house . . . new people. Everything is new. It is like stepping from one life to another. That can be a sadness. But it is an excitement to wonder what will happen next."

Peg stopped twirling her hair to stare at Melisande.

Melisande continued: "It may be that I shall go away from here. It may be that I go to a new country, to a new house, to new people." She added, still defiant: "That is how I wish it to be. That is an excitement. You do not know; it is all there before you . . . waiting for you . . . but you do not know."

There was silence. Melisande had forgotten Peg. She remembered her childish dreams. When the rich woman had

come to the Convent for Anne-Marie, Melisande had
dreamed that a rich woman came for her, took her away to
spend her life eating sweetmeats and wearing a silk dress.
That was a foolish dream but it had been pleasant dreaming
it. It had helped her over the monotonous days. Now there
were other dreams. Perhaps Caroline would fall in love with
John Collings and wish to marry him. Perhaps Fermor would
discover that he wished to marry Melisande. Perhaps he
would change a little. He would still be himself yet there
could grow in him a kindness, a tenderness. Anything could
happen in dreams, and dreams would not be suppressed.
They were as vivid now as they had been in the days when
she had dreamed of sweetmeats and silk dresses. Perhaps
these dreams were as flimsy, as unlikely of achieving reality?

In the house everyone seemed to be waiting for something
to happen.

Sir Charles, often shut away in his study, sitting back from
the window, seeing but unseen, watched the girl he had
brought into the house. He was aware of the conflict between
Fermor and Caroline, and that the most foolish thing he had
done in the whole of a fairly exemplary life was to have
become Millie's lover, and the next most foolish thing was
to have brought Millie's daughter into his home.

Melisande was her mother reborn, it seemed to Sir
Charles. In bringing her here he had sinned against his
daughter Caroline, as in loving Millie he had sinned against
his wife Maud. He recognized the passion Melisande had
aroused in Fermor; he understood it. But what could he do?
Could he send Melisande away? He believed that wherever
she went Fermor would follow. It seemed there was nothing
Sir Charles could do but watch and wait.

Wenna was waiting for the whispers to start. They had not
yet begun to spread. Here they were through October and
into November, and it was weeks since she had told the secret to Mrs. Soady. The cook was being unusually discreet.
Had she whispered the secret to Mr. Meaker and had he
warned her to silence?

Caroline was waiting fearfully. Fermor was affectionate;

he talked often of their marriage. She wished that she did not know so much.

Melisande too was waiting. She could not believe that life was not good. Dreams did come true if they were dreamed as vividly as Melisande dreamed them. They would not come true in the way she dreamed them, for she was no seer, no white witch who could see into the future; but nevertheless they would come true.

She wished that she had not gone to the witch in the woods. She had acted impulsively as usual. She should have waited. She should have asked for a spell to make Caroline turn to John Collings and to change Fermor into a loving husband for Melisande.

Surely this must come to pass. Life *was* a goodness; and Melisande was Fortune's favourite.

Fermor too was waiting. He was experienced and he knew what was passing through Melisande's mind. He was an eagle watching his prey. His emotions alternated between a passion which was almost brutal and an unaccustomed tenderness. He had laid plans for trapping her, but always that unaccountable tenderness would enter like a forbidding parent watching over a recalcitrant child. On the moors she had not known of her feelings. She was young—even younger than her years. That was due to the Convent life when she had been shut away from realities; but she would learn quickly. He could appraise her at times in the same cool manner in which he would select a horse. There was an air of breeding about her and there was too an air of simplicity. He intuitively knew that she was the result of a love affair between a person of breeding and another of humbler station in life—perhaps a lady and her servant, he ruminated; there were such cases. And her education had been given her by the aristocratic partner in her conception and birth.

Sir Charles was aware of the secret of her birth, Fermor felt sure. He had tried to extract that secret; but Sir Charles was determined to communicate nothing. He could imply with a look that he considered vulgar curiosity an unpardonable offence against good manners.

But Fermor hated inactivity. His desires must be satisfied while they were warm and palpitating. He was afraid of his

own feelings, though he scarcely liked to admit this. There
were times when he thought of marriage with Melisande. It
would be disastrous of course. Even here in Cornwall it would
be disastrous. What was he going to do with his life? Parliament was what his father had in mind for him. It could be a
life of absorbing interest and adventure. To have a hand in
government affairs, to make history—that appealed to Fermor. His father had friends in those quarters which would
make advancement certain. Peel, Melbourne and Russell
were his friends. There were many young men looking for
advancement; it would be ridiculous to make the way more
difficult by marrying the wrong young woman merely to satisfy a brief passion. Melbourne had figured in an unsavoury
divorce case, but Melbourne was a man of power who had
been Prime Minister. He had come through, but not exactly
untarnished—no one could do that—although he had survived the scandal. Yet it was growing clearer that, in an England where a young queen was becoming more and more
influenced by her priggish German husband, there would be
a tightening-up of class distinctions, and a misalliance could
ruin a man's career.

Moreover Fermor had been moved to passion before. Passion was fleeting. Many women had loved him and he had
loved many women. Was he going to be foolish over one?
Such folly was for callow young men, for inexperienced boys.

She must be made to see that that for which she hoped
was impossible.

His father was asking why he did not return to London. It
was imperative for him to attend certain social gatherings.
By shutting himself away in the country he was shutting himself away from his opportunities of making valuable friends.

So Fermor decided to end the waiting.

He went to Sir Charles's study.

Charles was nervous. He had expected a call from the
young man. He wondered what he would have done in his
place. He could never have married Millie, but Melisande
was an educated young lady. He could see the temptation.
Yet in his young days life had been easier. The conventions
had been less rigid in the Georgian era than in that of Victoria.

"I have come to tell you, sir," said Fermor, "that my father is urging me to return to London, and before I go I think we should have a definite date for the marriage. I know Caroline's mother has so recently died and that we are in mourning for her, but in view of the great distance between here and London and the rather special circumstances—our marriage was planned before the tragedy—I wonder whether you will agree that we might hurry on arrangements. Perhaps it would not be considered lacking in respect if the celebrations were quieter than was at first planned."

Charles looked at the young man. He is hard, he thought; harder than I was. He would not have fallen artlessly in love with a little mantua-maker.

Charles felt weary suddenly. It was for all these young people to live their own lives. Melisande must fight her own battles. It was foolish to blame himself, to feel he must shoulder all responsibility. To think as he had been thinking, was to blame or honour every father for what happened to his sons and daughters.

"Do as you think fit," he said. "As you say, these are special circumstances."

"Then," said Fermor, "let us have the wedding here at Christmas. Next week I shall return to London and be back in December."

Sir Charles agreed to this, and when Fermor went out, he was smiling. He had put an end to the waiting.

Melisande wished to be alone.

Her charm had worked after all. Caroline was at last happy.

They were working on the garments for the poor when Caroline said: "Let us not read this morning. I am so excited. The date for my wedding is fixed."

Melisande bent closer over the flannel petticoat which she was stitching.

"It is to be Christmas Day," went on Caroline. "There is not much time. Why, it is less than two months . . . six weeks. That is not very long. I want you to take a message to Pennifield this afternoon. Tell her she is to leave everything and come at once. She will be busy during the next few weeks. There is so much to do."

"Yes. There will be much to do."

"Fermor said it was absurd to wait longer. I fear people will *talk*. A wedding so soon after a funeral! But Fermor says these are special circumstances. To tell the truth I do not think he greatly cares what people say. But our wedding was arranged before Mamma died."

"Yes," Melisande answered, "it is a special circumstance."

Caroline looked at Melisande with something like affection. She thought: After six weeks I shan't see her again. Poor girl! What will she do? I suppose she will go to some other house. But she is so pretty that she is bound to be all right. She might even find some man in a good position to marry her.

Caroline was in love with the world that morning.

Melisande continued to sew in silence.

She envies me, went on Caroline's thoughts. She was sure he was in love with her. She does not know him. He always looked at girls with a speculative eye, and she is nothing more to him than the parlourmaid he kissed when he was fifteen. As his wife she would have to curb her jealousy, to remind herself that such affairs were of little importance to him. Some men drank more than was good for them; Fermor probably did that too. Others gambled. He was doubtless a gambler. He liked women too. One must shut one's eyes to his faults, for with them went so much charm, with them went all that Caroline wanted from life.

Melisande was glad to escape from the sewing-room and Caroline's exuberant chatter. She was glad to escape to her room and glad that Peg brought her luncheon tray to her there.

"My dear life!" cried Peg. "You ain't got much of an appetite."

"I have not a hunger to-day, that is all," she explained.

As soon as possible she set out for the little cottage where Miss Pennifield lived with her sister. Perched on the cliffs it was a minute dwelling place with cob walls and tiny windows. The industrious Misses Pennifield had made the sloping garden a picture with wallflowers, sweet smelling cabbage roses and lavender. There were many cottages like this one in the neighbourhood. There was only one floor which was divided by partitions, made so that they did not reach the ceiling in order that the air might circulate. At the windows were dainty dimity curtains and the coconut matting on the floor was very clean and neatly darned in places. They had some pleasing pieces of furniture which had belonged to their grandparents. There was a buffette fixed high in the wall and as this had glass doors their precious china could be seen. There were two armchairs and a table at which they worked. On the mantelpiece over the tiny fireplace were brass candlesticks, relics of the days when their family had been better off; there were two china dogs and some pieces of brass. Their home was their delight and their apprehension; they were always terrified that they would not have enough money to keep all their possessions. In hard times they had already sold one or two of their treasures. It was a nightmare of both sisters that one day they would grow too old to work and that they would lose their cherished home, bit by bit.

But there was no question of that to-day. The Mamazel had come to tell them of work.

Melisande sat at the table and listened to their twittering chatter.

"Well, there'll be dresses, I vow, and petticoats and all that a young lady would be wanting for her marriage. There b'ain't much time. Six weeks, did you say! Six weeks!"

Miss Janet Pennifield, who was not the expert seamstress that her sister was, and only helped on occasions, took in washing to help the family income. There seemed always to be clothes drying on the rocks and bushes at the back of the cottage.

Now she was brandishing a pair of Italian irons which she called 'Jinny Quicks' and used for ironing the frills on ladies' caps and the like.

"Well, I shall be able to bring home work, I don't doubt," said Miss Pennifield, "and you can give a hand, Janet. Oh, my life, 'tis soon to have a wedding after a funeral, but if Sir Charles consents, you may be sure 'tis right enough."

Melisande was aware that their merry chatter and their gaiety was tinged with relief. They had six weeks of hard work before them—six weeks of security.

"I should be scared if I be asked to do the wedding dress," said Miss Pennifield suddenly.

"You'll do it," said Janet. "You'm the best needlewoman this side of Tamar."

Miss Pennifield turned to Melisande: "You'll take a glass of Janet's elderberry."

"It is so kind, but I have much to do at the house."

"Oh, but Janet's elderberry . . . 'tis of the best."

She knew that they would be hurt if she refused; she knew that she must compliment Janet and tell her that it was the best she had tasted and ask them not to tell Jane Pengelly, because many a glass of elderberry had she had at Jane's and she had on as many occasions assured her that it was the finest in the world.

"There!" said Miss Pennifield. "You try that. Just a thimbleful for me, my dear, while you'm about it."

Miss Pennifield stared suddenly at Melisande, the glass in her hand shaking so that she spilled some of the precious elderberry. "But, my dear, I see now why you'm quiet!"

Melisande blushed faintly. Had she conveyed her pity for these two, with their few possessions and their desperate longing for security? "I . . . I . . ." she began.

Miss Pennifield went on: "What will 'ee be doing . . . when Miss Caroline do marry? I mean 'twill be a new place for 'ee then. Oh, my dear, 'twas careless of me. I didn't think. . . . Here we be laughing and drinking elderberry when you . . ."

"I will be very well, thank you," said Melisande. "But it is a kindness to think of me."

"I reckon you'll find a nice place," said Miss Pennifield. "There's many as would be glad to have 'ee, I don't doubt a moment. And being with Miss Caroline, well . . . 'tweren't all saffron cake and metheglin, was it?"

"No," said Melisande with a little laugh, "it was not."

"Though mind you, she be better now. Sir Charles is a good and kind gentleman. He wouldn't turn 'ee out before you was ready to go. 'Tis a pity Lady Gover be satisfied. I wonder if Miss Danesborough is in want of a companion. There's Miss Robinson at Leigh House. Now you'd be very happy there teaching Miss Amanda . . . if Miss Robinson were to leave.''

"It is a goodness to find these places for me. Let us drink. This is a delicious.''

Miss Pennifield insisted on refilling her glass. Janet was nodding her sympathy. They were embarrassed, both of them, because they had rejoiced in their good fortune which might so easily turn out to be bad fortune for the little Mamazel.

When she said she must go they did not seek to detain her and she was glad to hurry out into the damp warmth of the November afternoon.

She hesitated at the top of the cliff and looked down into the sandy cove bounded on one side by a formation of rocks and on the other by the short stone jetty.

The sea, silent in the misty light, was like a sheet of dull grey silk to-day. Without thinking very much where she was going she started down the cliff side.

There was a narrow footpath, very steep and stony. Now and then she paused to cling to a bush, and wondered why she had chosen this difficult descent. The path came to an abrupt end and was lost among a clump of thick bushes. She slipped, caught a prickly bush and gave a little gasp of pain. Ruefully she examined her hand and looked back the way she had come. She saw the narrow footpath winding upwards and it looked steeper than ever. She decided that she would continue with the downward climb. The tide was out and she would walk along the shore past Plaidy to Milendreath. It was a long way round, but she wished for solitude.

She looked out to sea. The gulls were swooping and drifting. Their cries were mournful and the thought came to her that they were saying goodbye to her.

The visit to the Pennifield cottage had depressed her. Of course she would have to go away. There would be no excuse for her to stay. She would have to go to another house—as a companion or a governess. It would all be so different. She thought sadly of Sir Charles's coming to the Convent, of the happy time in Paris. But Sir Charles at Trevenning was a different man from the one she had known in that first week of their acquaintance. As they had come nearer and nearer to Trevenning he had seemed more and more remote.

Perhaps she could ask Caroline or Sir Charles what was to happen to her when Caroline married. And standing there on the cliffs she was aware of a surging anger. Why should her destiny always be dictated by others? Why should she not manage her own affairs? Yet how could it be otherwise? She had discovered a little of what happened to the people who were alone in the world. She remembered some of the poor whom she had seen in Paris and London; she recalled the man whom she had seen whipped through the streets of Liskeard; and as long as she lived she would never forget the mad woman chained in the cottage.

"What will become of you?" Fermor had challenged. And he had one solution to offer her.

She could hear his voice:

"I will love you all the day,
Every night would kiss and play,
If with me you'll fondly stray
Over the hills and far away . . ."

But where was 'Over the hills and far away'? Whither would he take her if she put her hand in his and allowed him to lead her?

She was afraid . . . afraid of the pride within her, the desire to mould her own destiny. The Misses Pennifield, shaking their heads over her, had pictured her eagerly trying to please new employers, and there was no mistaking their pity. They *knew*; and she herself was ignorant. She was in that station of life to which they had been called; but she had received some education and perhaps because of that she found it harder to accept her lot. She had seen Lady Gover's companion, a sad elderly lady whose face had no animation in it, no love of life. Melisande had seen the same dull, deprecating look in the face of the Leighs' governess.

That was the life of virtue. Fermor was offering another life—the life of sin. And now here alone, with no one in sight, she knew that the nuns had been right to fear for her.

As she stood still considering which way to go, a high-pitched voice suddenly said in perfect French: "Mademoiselle, you cannot get down that way."

"Who is that?" she cried in French, looking about her.

"You cannot see me, can you? I am a bandit. You should be very frightened, Mademoiselle. If I wished, I could kill you and drink your blood for supper."

The voice was that of a child and she said with a laugh: "I wish you would show yourself."

"You speak French very well, Mademoiselle. No one else here does . . . except me and Léon."

"I should. I was brought up in France. But where are you? And is Léon with you?"

"No, he is not here. If you can find me I will take you to safety."

"But I can't see you." ·

"Look about you. You cannot expect to see without looking."

"Are you in that clump of bushes?"

"Go and see."

"It is too high up."

There was a slight movement on her right and a boy appeared. He was small and looked about six years old; his bright dark eyes glowed in his olive-skinned face and he wore a wreath of seaweed round his head. He had an air of extreme arrogance.

"You are not a pisky, are you?" asked Melisande.

He said with the utmost dignity: "No. I am Raoul de la Roche, at your service, Mademoiselle."

"I am glad of that. I need your service. I should be glad if you could show me an easy way down."

"*I* know a good way down. *I* discovered it. I will take you if you like."

"That is kind of you."

"Come this way."

It was difficult to believe he could be as young as he looked. He had such an air of seriousness. He noticed her eyes on the seaweed and took it off.

"It was a disguise," he said. "I was hiding in my cave there, and I wore it to frighten people . . . if they should come. *I* did not wish them to come. *I* have been watching you. You did look scared. Only *I* can climb up here.''

She was amused by his emphasis on the personal pronoun; it conveyed a certain contempt for the rest of the world and a great respect for Monsieur Raoul de la Roche.

''Do you live here?'' she asked.

He led the way, answering: ''We are staying here for *my* health, Léon and I. *My* health is not good, they say. Are you here for your health?''

''No. I am here as a companion, which means . . .''

''*I* know,'' he said quickly. ''Léon is *my* companion.''

''Oh, but you see, I'm a paid companion.''

''So is Léon, and he's *my* uncle too. *I'm* called old-fashioned. I make people smile. It's because I've lived with grown-up people, and I like reading better than games, really.''

''You're very unusual, I'm sure,'' said Melisande with a smile, for his arrogance was amusing.

''Yes, I know,'' he said. ''They're trying to make me more usual. . . . Not quite usual, of course, but more usual. That's why I'm here with Léon.''

''Where is Léon now?''

''Down there.''

''He doesn't mind your climbing about?''

''Oh, no. It is good for me. I do it to please Léon. I play bandits and disguise myself with seaweed to please him. It is good for me, the doctors say.''

''But you enjoy it, I'm sure. You sounded as though you did when you called out about drinking my blood.''

''A little perhaps. Otherwise I should not do it. You are French also?''

''I suppose so. I lived in France . . . in a convent. I am not sure whether my parents were French or not.''

''You are an orphan. *I* too am an orphan.''

''Then we are of a kind.''

''This is a steep bit. *You* may slip.''

''I'll follow in your footsteps.''

''When I am strong I shall swim. That will be good for my health. You should tell me your name. I must introduce you to Léon.''

"It is St. Martin. Melisande St. Martin."

He nodded and went on. "There is Léon over there. He has seen us."

A tall thin man was coming towards them; there was a book in his hand; between him and the boy there was a slight resemblance.

"Léon!" cried the boy. "This is Mademoiselle St. Martin. She may be French. She does not know. She is an orphan as I am. She was lost but *I* showed her the way down."

"Good afternoon," said Melisande.

When he smiled he was very pleasant. "Good afternoon," he said. "So my nephew has made your acquaintance."

"He was kind enough to bring me down."

"I am glad he was of use."

"It was easy to *me*," boasted the boy.

"Raoul, Raoul!" admonished the man softly, but he smiled indulgently. He turned to Melisande. "Forgive his exuberance. He is really delighted to have helped."

"I am sure he is. You are living here for the winter, he tells me."

"Yes, we have taken a house. It is a great comfort to meet someone with whom we can talk with ease."

"*I* find it a great comfort," said the boy. "I told Mademoiselle St. Martin that the people here speak either very bad French or no French at all."

"Well, that is good for you," said Melisande. "It will teach you to speak English all the quicker."

"And when they do speak we can't understand," said the man. "I thought I had a fair knowledge of English, but I cannot understand that which is spoken here."

"It is a mixture of Cornish and English," said Melisande.

"I shall engage Mademoiselle as *my* interpreter!" said the boy.

The man said quickly: "I very much doubt that she would be willing to give you her services. You must forgive Raoul, Mademoiselle St. Martin. He is ten years old and we have brought him here to make him strong on cream and pasties. We have come for the climate which is supposed to be warmer than the east of England. Last winter we were in Kent. That was very cold. How I am talking! You must forgive me. It is because I have had to pick my words and stumble for so long.''

"There are just the two of you?''

"We have brought our servants with us. They are not French.''

"They are Kentish, and from London some of them,'' said Raoul, who clearly did not like to be left out of the conversation. "*I* thought they were hard to understand until we came here. The people here are far worse speakers.''

"Well, I must say thank you for bringing me down,'' said Melisande, turning to Raoul.

"But you must not go yet!'' said the boy, making it sound like a command.

"Oh, but I have to get back. I work here. I came out to take a message, and it is going to take me longer to get home round by the shore as I intended. So I must say goodbye.''

"Let us walk with Mademoiselle,'' said Raoul.

"Let us ask first if she will allow us to do so.''

"I should be delighted,'' said Melisande.

"*I* shall not be tired,'' said the boy. "I have had my afternoon sleep.''

They walked over the rocks to the patches of sand.

"I hope we shall be able to meet again some time,'' said the man. "Could you visit us, I wonder?''

The boy's darting attention had been caught by the living creatures in a rock pool and he stooped to examine them.

"I am only a companion here; you understand that?''

"I too am a companion of sorts.''

"The little boy explained.''

"He is delicate,'' said the man quietly. "He is clever and imaginative and full of high spirits, but bodily weak. I am afraid he has been rather spoiled because of this . . . and because of other things. It is my task to look after him. I gather that you—a poor young lady—are companion to a rich woman. I—a poor man—am companion to a rich little boy.''

"He said you were his uncle.''

"The relationship is not so close as that. He thinks of me as his uncle. I am really only a second cousin. You see, you and I are in similar positions. I look after him. I teach him. I guard his health. That is my task."

"It must be very pleasant."

"I am fond of him, though at times things are a little difficult. As you have gathered he has been a little spoiled; but at heart he is the best little fellow in the world. Tell me, Mademoiselle, do you expect to stay here for a long time?"

"I don't know. I came here not very long ago as a companion to Miss Trevenning. Trevenning is the name of the house. Perhaps you know it. She is to be married soon . . . after that . . . I am not sure."

"And when will she be married?"

"On Christmas Day."

"That is some weeks ahead."

"Why yes."

"I am glad. We must meet during that time. Compatriots in a foreign land must be friends."

The boy had come up. He was animated as he discussed the creatures he had been studying in the pool. His face was slightly pink and he was breathless; the knees of his knickerbockers were damp.

The man said: "But you have got wet. We must go back at once."

"*I* do not wish to go back. *I* wish to stay and talk with Mademoiselle."

"But you must go back at once. You must change your clothes. Why, Mrs. Clark would be angry if you stayed out in wet clothes."

The boy's face was stubborn. He said: "It is not for Mrs. Clark to do anything but what *I* wish her to."

The man turned to Melisande as though he had not heard the boy's remark. "Mrs. Clark is our housekeeper," he explained. "A wonderful person. We are very fond of Mrs. Clark."

"All the same," said the boy, "she may not say when I have to go in and when I may stay out."

"Come," said the man, "I am sure Mademoiselle St. Martin will forgive us if we hurry away."

"Indeed I will, and I must hurry myself," said Melisande. "I must say goodbye . . . quickly. Goodbye."

"Au revoir!" said the man. "We shall be on the beach to-morrow."

"If it is possible I may see you then."

She did not look at the boy's sullen face. She felt a sudden pity for the man who was poor and in charge of the spoilt rich little boy. She felt sorry for all those who were poor and must pander to the rich.

"Thank you," she said to Raoul, "for showing me the way down."

His face brightened. He seemed to have recovered from his sullenness. *"Au revoir,* Mademoiselle. *I* shall look for you to-morrow."

"Then goodbye. *Au revoir."*

She hurried on, making her way rapidly until she came to Plaidy beach, where she left the shore and scrambled up the steep path away from the sea.

She heard a laugh and her name was being called.

She recognized Fermor's voice.

"Who was the friend?" he called, sauntering towards her.

"Friend?"

"I'll tell you right away. I saw the encounter. I heard you were going to the Pennifields' and came to meet you. I was at the top of the cliffs and saw you with your friends."

She felt that mingling of pleasure and apprehension which being alone with him could not fail to bring.

He had come very close. "You look as though you think I'm one of the gorgons and about to turn you to stone."

She stepped backwards and said quickly: "It is so strange that they should be French, and that I should have met them like that."

"How did it happen?"

"I was going down the cliff and found it rather difficult. The little boy came out of a cave in which he was playing bandits. He helped me down."

"And took you to Papa?"

"It is not his father—a second cousin."

"You've quickly become acquainted with the family tree. You enjoyed the company of the second cousin."

"You have very good eyes."

"My eyes are as those of a hawk . . . where you are concerned."

"You make me feel like a field mouse waiting for the swooping. You should not have such ideas. I am not to be seized and carried off by a hawk. Now I must hurry back to the house. I am late."

"You spent too much time with your new friends, little field mouse. Perhaps I should say shrew mouse. You are becoming shrewish."

"It is good that you think so. Field mice are poor pretty things; but shrew mice are not so pretty. Perhaps they are not so well liked by hawks."

"They are even more popular. And did you know that the best sort of hawks are noted for their patience?"

"Are you still thinking of that offer you made me?"

"I have never ceased to think of it."

"What . . . even now . . . with your wedding day fixed!"

"It is a thing apart from weddings."

"You have made that very clear to me. I wonder if you have explained to Caroline also?"

"You must not be a silly little shrew mouse. You must be grown-up. Of course Caroline knows nothing of it."

"What if I told her? If you ever try to see me alone again I *will* tell her."

"What!" he said lightly. "Blackmail?"

"You are the wickedest person I have ever met in the whole of my life. I did not know anyone could be so wicked."

"Then it is time you learned. You could reform me, you know. Now, there is a task for you. If you will love me—if you admit you love me, for of course you love me—you will see how charming I am . . . how good, how tender, how devoted."

"I wish to hurry back."

"Do you imagine I cannot keep pace with you?"

"I would rather be alone."

"But I would rather be with you."

"Do you never do what others want? Is it always what you want?"

"Well, what about yourself? Are you doing what others want? Now if you were as unselfish as you would like me to be, you would say: 'Well, I know I shouldn't, but because he wants me so much I must please him. That would be unselfish, and I am so good, so kind—in fact such a little martyr, that I must sacrifice myself since my own desires count for nothing.' "

"You twist everything. You are flippant. If Caroline knew you as you really are she would not love you."

"But you love me, in spite of all you know of me?"

She walked quickly but he quickened his pace. She broke into a run.

"You can't keep that up . . . not on these steep paths." He caught her arm.

"Please do not touch me."

"You have commanded too long." He laughed as she would have wrenched herself free. "You see, it is of no use. If you struggle you will merely become exhausted, and here we are alone. You may call for help and who will come? Your brave little bandit and the handsome second cousin are far away. And if they did hear you they would find it a different matter rescuing you from me than from the cliff path. You are at my mercy."

"You tell so many lies."

"No. It is you who pretend. You cannot distinguish between what you want and what you think you ought to want. When I said: 'You are at my mercy!' your eyes sparkled at the thought. Do you think I don't understand! You could say then: 'It was not my fault!' What joy! To be forced to what you dare not do yet long to. What could be better? Shall I give you that satisfaction? I love you so much that I am greatly tempted to please you so."

"You say the most cruelly cynical things I have ever heard. I did not know there were people like you."

"How could you? How long have you been in the world? We don't haunt the Convent precincts hoping to seduce holy nuns."

He allowed her to escape and she began to walk on rapidly.

"I wish to be serious," he said, catching up with her and taking her arm. "We have so little opportunity to talk. I am going to London at the end of the week. Ah, that saddens you."

"No. It is a pleasure for me. It is the best news I have heard for a long time."

"The coward in you is delighted, but is that the true Melisande? No! I do not believe it. In reality you are sad. Now there is no need to be sad, only sensible. Tell me, what will you do when you get away from here?"

"That is my affair."

"Let us be sensible and make it mine too."

"I do not see how it can be yours."

"You need to be protected."

"I am able to protect myself."

"When I say you need a protector I use the word in the fashionable sense. You may protect yourself with your wits, but they will tell you that without help they cannot provide you with the necessities of life. For that you need a human protector."

"Please understand that I shall be my own protector."

"How? In the house of some disagreeable woman?"

"Are all women who employ governesses and companions disagreeable?"

"Most are—to their governesses and companions."

"Well, that appears to be my lot in the world and I must bear it."

"So you will be resigned to that state of life to which God has called you?"

"I must make it good."

"It will not be good. It is hateful for a girl of your spirit. It is so undignified. I wish I could marry you. Why weren't you Caroline and Caroline you? How virtuous I should have been then! I should have been a model wooer. Goodness is a result of circumstances. Has that occurred to you? I believe that if a marriage between us had been arranged I should have been a faithful husband."

"People become good by adjusting themselves to their circumstances, not by arranging the circumstances to suit themselves. That is the difference between good and bad surely."

"Now, Mademoiselle, you are not the Mother Superior of that Convent of yours, lecturing a miscreant. If the world does not suit me, I must make it suit me. Look, my dear,

you are young and inexperienced; you have dogmatic ideas
about life. I am being very serious now. Let me find a house
for you where you can live discreetly. It shall be secure as a
marriage. Everything you want in the world will be yours.''

"This is like Satan and his temptations. You think to show
me the kingdoms of the world.''

"The kingdoms of the world are well worth having.''

"At the expense of what one knows to be right?''

"When you have endured the indignities your careless employers will not hesitate to put upon you, when you have
suffered at their hands—even been unable to find employ-
ment at all—then perhaps you will not despise those kingdoms of comfort . . . and more than comfort . . . of affection
and friendship as well as passion and all the love I will give
you.''

"You speak with much persuasion, but you cannot disguise your wickedness. If you were unhappily married and
spoke thus to me there would be a difference. But while you
plan to marry you make these plans . . . with the cold blood
. . . on the eve of your wedding.''

"There is nothing cold-blooded about me. You will, I
prophesy, ere long discover that.''

She was silent and he went on gently: "Melisande, of what
do you think?''

"Of you.''

"I knew it. Now that you are in a truthful mood, admit
that you think of me continually.''

"I think a good deal of you . . . and Caroline. I wish that
I had lived more in the world. I wish I could understand you
more.''

He put his arm about her. "Give yourself time to understand me. Try to cast aside most of what these nuns have
taught you of the world. It is all very well for them, living
their shut-in lives. What were their lives—living death, mere
existence. You don't know what is to be found in the world—
what joy, what pleasure. I will show you. Yes, I am offering
you the kingdoms of the world. But you see, my dearest
Melisande, life is not the simple thing of black and white
that those nuns have painted for you. They believed they were
teaching you the truth. They know no other. Poor little cow-

ards . . . afraid of the world! People like you and I should be afraid of nothing.''

''But we are both afraid. I am afraid of what I have been taught is sin. You say that you wish they had chosen me to marry you. Then, if you are not afraid, why should you not make your own choice? You are afraid . . . even as I am. You are afraid of opinion . . . of the convention. You are afraid of marrying outside your own social class. That, it seems to me, is more cowardly than being afraid of what one has been taught is sinful.''

He was nonplussed for a while. Then he said: ''It is not fear. It is the certain knowledge that a marriage between us would be impossible.''

''You may dress it up as you like. You can call it certain knowledge. I call it fear, and I call you a coward. You are not afraid to face any man single-handed; you are not afraid of an angry mob. That is because you are big and strong . . . in your body. But in your mind you are not strong; and it is in your mind that you are afraid. You are afraid of what people may say and do; you are afraid they will not help you to the position you want. That is a fear. It is a worse fear than being afraid because the body is not strong enough to fight.''

''You mistake wisdom for fear.''

''Do I? Then please go on being wise . . . and so will I!''

He said: ''I've hurt you. I've been too frank. In other words, I've been a fool. I've shown you too much of myself. I don't know why I did it. I ought to have waited . . . to have caught you unaware.''

''You are too interested in yourself, Monsieur. You think yourself irresistible. That is not the case as far as I am concerned.''

He caught her angrily and kissed her. She could not hold him off, but she knew that she did not want to. She was shaken at having to admit to herself that, if he had made his proposals at a time other than when he was planning marriage to Caroline, she might have been unable to resist them.

She must fight him. He must never know how near she was to submission. She must continually see him as he really was, not as she was trying to believe he must be.

"Do you think I don't understand you?" he said as though reading her thoughts.

"You are clever at self-deception, I do not doubt."

"You attack me with your tongue, but you betray yourself in other ways."

"You have a high opinion of yourself. If it pleases you, keep it, Monsieur."

"Do not call me Monsieur as though I am one of your prinking Frenchmen."

"If I were so misguided as to do as you wish, we should spend our lives in quarrelling."

"Our sort of quarrels can be more stimulating than agreement."

"I do not find them stimulating . . . only an irritation."

"That is why your cheeks grow scarlet, your eyes blaze and you are a hundred times more attractive when you are with me than with anyone else."

"I must return. Caroline will wonder what has happened to me. I should not take all day to visit Miss Pennifield and ask her to make dresses for Caroline's marriage to you." She hurried on.

"Melisande!" he called. "Don't go yet."

She answered over her shoulder: "You had better not come any farther with me. You would not wish Caroline to see you with me, you brave man."

She heard herself laugh, but it was shrill laughter. She hoped he did not notice that there was a note of hysteria in it.

"Melisande," he repeated. "Melisande."

But he did not follow her now. We are too near the house, she thought; and he has too much wisdom. Poor Caroline! And poor Melisande!

Fermor had gone to London and Trevenning was a different place without him. It is as though an evil spirit has departed, thought Melisande; but how dull was the place without him!

Life had become more simple, it seemed. Everybody appeared to be happy. Caroline spent hours with Miss Pennifield, trying on the garments for her trousseau. They had discovered that Melisande, whilst being a poor needlewoman, could make suggestions about dresses, add an ornament—or take one away—so that the effect was transformed.

"It is your French blood," said Caroline, now sweet and friendly. "The French are wonderfully clever at such things."

"Mamazel certainly has the touch!" cried Miss Pennifield. "Why, Miss Caroline, when you are married you will be wanting her with you to help you with your clothes."

Poor blind Miss Pennifield! thought Melisande. Unwittingly she had shattered the peace.

But the gloom quickly passed and Caroline forgot her fears, and when Miss Pennifield retired to the sewing-room and Caroline suggested that she and Melisande should read together from a French book, she said: "By the way, I hear there are some French people in the neighbourhood. Everyone is agog. They find them amusing."

"I know," said Melisande; "we have met."

"Really?"

"Yes. It was when I went to Miss Pennifield's cottage last week. I tried to get down the cliffs but it was very steep; the little boy was playing there and he guided me down. His guardian, who is also his cousin, was on the beach. The little boy introduced us."

"That must have been fun."

"Yes, it was fun. They were very pleased to speak French. They said they could not understand the English of the people here and I explained they were Cornish . . . not English."

"It must be pleasant to meet people from your own country."

"It was a . . . niceness."

"I expect you all chattered away in great excitement."

"Perhaps. I have met them since. They were lonely and, as you say, it was good to speak French. I have seen them once or twice since."

"You must know more about them than anyone else." Caroline smiled. "I have heard that the boy is rich and used to having his own way with everyone. He's the master of the household and knows it. Mrs. Clark is quite a gossip. They say here that she is a regular Sherborne."

"A Sherborne? I do not know that."

"Oh, it's an old saying that goes back to the days when there was only one newspaper which came all the way from Sherborne. It was the Sherborne Mercury, I believe. They say here, when anyone is a bit of a gossip, that he or she is a regular Sherborne."

Melisande laughed. She had never been on such happy terms with Caroline.

"Well," went on Caroline, "Mrs. Clark says they belong to an old French family—aristocrats. One branch lost its possessions in the revolution; the other survived and escaped. The boy belongs to the rich de la Roches and the man to the poor branch of the family; but if the boy should die the fortune will go to the man. Mrs. Clark is full of sympathy for the man; she says the boy is a handful."

"The regular Sherborne is, I should say, quite right. The boy is amusing but it is not good for one so young to know his power. The man is very kind and tolerant."

"Have you met them often?"

"Once or twice."

Caroline smiled to herself. She was very interested in the foreigners and particularly in the man. It pleased her that he and Melisande had become friends. It seemed to her that this man might provide a solution which would prove satisfactory to everyone concerned.

This was a great occasion. Everyone in the house was talking about it. Sir Charles, Miss Caroline and the Mamazel had all been invited to dine at the rectory with the Danesboroughs.

" 'Tis the first time," said Mr. Meaker, "that I ever heard of a companion going out to visit social like with the family . . . unless, of course, she was a poor relation."

Mrs. Soady sat at the head of the table cutting up the pasties so that the savour of onions made everyone's mouth water. She said nothing, but the curve of her lips told them all clearly that if she had chosen to speak she could have startled them.

Mr. Meaker seemed slightly irritated. If she knew something it was a matter of servants' hall etiquette to impart it—at least to Mr. Meaker.

"Well, Mrs. Soady," he said, "you don't think it be strange then?"

Mrs. Soady paused with the knife and fork gracefully poised above the pasty. "Mr. Meaker, I can't say. I be as surprised as you, and that's all I'm in a position to say."

"I've been in some big houses," said Mr. Meaker, "and I repeat: I've never seen it before unless it was a poor relation."

"As a regular thing you be right, Mr. Meaker."

"Of course," said Peg, "she's very pretty."

"And educated better than a lady," put in Bet; "though that might go against her—some holding that education ain't all that ladylike."

"Mr. Danesborough," said the footman, "is never one to stand on ceremony . . . parson though he may be."

"And related to a lord," added Mr. Meaker.

Everyone was looking at Mrs. Soady who, as she served up the pasties, was smiling knowingly at her secret.

"It do make you think," said Peg, "that this Mamazel . . . *be* somebody."

That made Mrs. Soady dimple.

She do know something! thought Mr. Meaker. 'Tis something about the Mamazel.

From now on it was going to be Mr. Meaker's special task to prise that secret out of Mrs. Soady.

To Melisande it was a great occasion. It was to be the first time she wore the dress bought in Paris for such an occasion, the dress with the frilled skirt and its accompanying *sous jupe crinoline.* She had cleverly made a rose from pieces of silk and velvet which Miss Pennifield had given her. This she tucked into her corsage, and it gave a youthfulness to the Paris gown, and the green of the rose's stalk and leaf matched her eyes.

Caroline came into the room. She was wearing a blue silk dress, a charming dress she had thought it and one of her most becoming, but as soon as she looked at Melisande she felt it to be dowdy. How could Melisande afford such a dress? And why should a simple gown look so much more becom-

ing than all the blue silk frills and tucks which had taken so
many of Miss Pennifield's hours to create?

Caroline felt that if Fermor had been in the house she
would have hated Melisande.

"What a lovely dress!" said she. "It's quite plain . . .
apart from the flower. Oh, it is a lovely flower!"

"You have it," said Melisande.

"No, no. It is for your dress. I can see that." Caroline
forced herself to smile. "Mr. Danesborough has a special
reason for asking you."

"A special reason?"

"Wait and see. A surprise. A rather nice one, I think."

Melisande looked very excited and Caroline thought: She
is so young, so fresh and charming. No wonder she attracts
him. But for him I should have enjoyed keeping her as my
companion.

Melisande was thinking: What a pity! It is Fermor who
makes the trouble. She is pleased because there is to be a
nice surprise for me. And what is it? What can it be? What
a nice quiet happiness there is without him!

Later, riding in the carriage with Sir Charles and Caroline,
she felt that she belonged to them, and that was what she
could only call a great pleasantness.

Sir Charles talked to them both. He was eager to know
how Caroline was progressing with her French lessons.

"She progresses well," said Melisande.

"And you are enjoying your riding?"

"That has been a great enjoyment," she told him.

Melisande waited eagerly. Perhaps now he would tell her
that soon she must go. Surely they must tell her soon and,
now that they were here talking so intimately, that would be
a good time?

But neither he nor Caroline said anything about her leaving
them.

"I daresay Caroline keeps you and Miss Pennifield busy
with the sewing for her wedding."

"Yes, Papa. Mademoiselle St. Martin has very good
taste."

"Undoubtedly she has."

He closed his eyes to indicate that he did not wish for more conversation. He was disturbed to be travelling with them both like this. They brought back such memories to him of Maud and Millie, for each was sufficiently like her mother to remind him. He was greatly disturbed by this beautiful young girl. He was wondering what he was going to do with her when Caroline went away. He had a daring scheme. He was thinking of installing her as housekeeper. What would the servants have to say to that! She was popular with them, but to set a young girl in such a position, so that she was the equal of Mrs. Soady and Mr. Meaker! It might cause trouble. It might even do worse. It might cause conjecture. He was terrified of that.

He had hoped in the first place that Caroline would take her away with her when she married. That would have been the best solution. Eventually he might have found a suitable husband for her. But, of course, she could not go with Caroline. He had reckoned without Fermor.

It was a very daring proposition this—to keep her in the house, to create a position for her. He would have to proceed very warily, for there was one thing he could not endure: scandal which might result in exposure.

He was glad that Wenna would leave with Caroline. He would certainly be glad to see the back of that woman.

Caroline had told him of Melisande's encounter with the Frenchman. Danesborough had, in his usual manner, quickly made the acquaintance of the young man and his precious charge. It was Sir Charles who had suggested that Caroline's companion should be invited to meet the young Frenchman; and Danesborough, who had asked de la Roche for dinner, extended the invitation to Melisande without hesitation.

Danesborough was a broad-minded man; and Sir Charles had pointed out that, although she was in poor circumstances, Melisande was a girl of education.

They had arrived at the Danesboroughs' and in the drawing-room, Mr. Danesborough with his sister, who was the chatelaine of the household since the death of Mrs. Danesborough, greeted them warmly.

There were other guests and among them Melisande saw, with surprise and pleasure, Léon de la Roche.

"Ah, Mademoiselle St. Martin!" cried the jovial Mr.

Danesborough, "I am so glad you have come. Monsieur de la Roche has been telling me how you and he were introduced by young Raoul."

"It is so," said Melisande. "He rescued me and introduced me. It was a double kindness."

Mr. Danesborough was clearly enchanted with her. Sir Charles, he said, had told him of her learning but had not prepared him for her beauty. He had promised Monsieur de la Roche that he should take her in to dinner; Mr. Danesborough implied that he envied Monsieur de la Roche.

And here was Léon de la Roche himself. To Melisande he looked different in this new setting—remote, less friendly, a pale stranger; but there was no doubt of his pleasure in seeing her.

"I am delighted," he said in his own tongue.

She answered in French: "I had no idea that you would be here. You must be the surprise. Caroline told me there was a surprise. A rather nice one, she said." She laughed. She felt young and carefree. This house held no memories of Fermor, and chatting with Léon she could forget all about him. She began to chatter of how excited she was to come out to dinner. "I have never before been out to dinner. It is my first dinner party. Of course, I have had supper with the servants in the servants' hall. Such things there are to eat! And that is great fun. But this is grand . . . and how different you look! And I too, I daresay."

"You look charming. You always look charming. But tonight you are very beautiful."

"It is the dress. It is beautiful. I longed to wear it, but this is the only suitable occasion there has been. I hope there will be other suitable occasions . . . many, many of them."

"So do I. It is a delightful dress."

"It is French. That is why you like it. The flower is English though. Made with these hands from cuttings given by Miss Pennifield. So perhaps it is half French? She gave the material; I made the flower. I have been wondering if I can earn my living making flowers."

"You go too fast. Why should you earn your living making flowers?"

"If it should be necessary," she said. "Who knows? It would be a little accomplishment."

"But you have many accomplishments."

"I do not know them. You are to take me in to dinner. Mr. Danesborough told me."

"I am delighted."

"Isn't it fun . . . meeting properly like this . . . not just a chance encounter on the seashore, and I promise to be there if we can arrange it and it does not rain!"

"It is. But it was also fun on the seashore . . . the greatest fun."

"And fun to be talking French as loudly as we like. Few, if any of them, know what we are saying."

"It makes us seem apart. I can't tell you how glad I am to find you here. Mr. Danesborough is an interesting man. He called on us and told me a good deal about the neighbourhood . . . past and present. Raoul has taken a fancy to his son Frith who came with him."

"His son?"

"He's not here to-night. He's home for the holidays, I think. Too young for dinner parties. Although I doubt whether he is much younger than you are."

"It is an advantage to be out in the world. Then you come to dinner parties and renew acquaintance with interesting people whom you meet on the beach."

They went in to dinner together. It was delightful, thought Melisande, to walk in a sort of crocodile, your hand resting lightly on the arm of a gentleman. It reminded her of another crocodile—by its very difference.

The table was a magnificent sight to Melisande, with its flower centre-piece and cutlery. Everything was wonderful to-night, she decided. She refused to think of Fermor; she refused to think beyond to-night. She found herself between Léon and Sir Charles, and felt immediately at home.

Sir Charles was talking to a lady on his right, but she could not but be aware that he was listening to what she and Léon were saying, although she doubted whether he could follow their rapid French.

"How is Raoul?" she asked.

"Quite well. This place suits him. He likes it, so we shall stay here."

She smiled. "It seems strange . . . a small boy to make the decisions."

"It is an unusual position. Sometimes I think he would be better surrounded by children of his own age."

"Those who did not let him have so much of his own way perhaps. Has he been long in your charge?"

"Since he was five years old. That was when his mother died. Poor Raoul! He belongs to a tragic family. His grandmother was a young woman at the time of the revolution. She was at the court—a close friend of Marie Antoinette. She was imprisoned and suffered much hardship. It undermined her health. But by some extraordinary good fortune she was released. She was one of those who escaped the guillotine. But there were many who lived and suffered through the revolution."

His expression was mournful, and she thought: What a sad face he has! She longed to make him smile. The smile of a sad person, she decided, was a charming thing, because it came so rarely. She was again thinking of Fermor with his brash gaiety. How different was this man! His gentle melancholy appealed to her the more because she had known Fermor.

"Raoul is yet another victim," he said.

"Raoul! After all these years!"

"His grandmother escaped, but months in the Conciergerie had ruined her health. She was only seventeen when she was freed, and then she married. She died just after her daughter was born. That daughter was Raoul's mother. She too was fragile. You see, the same disease, the disease of the Conciergerie, was passed on to her. She married. Raoul was born; she died as her mother had, and her sickness began to show itself in Raoul."

"That is terrible!" said Melisande. "To pass on a weakness so. It seems as if a bad thing will live for ever."

"There is hope for Raoul. More is known of these things now. When his father—my cousin—died, he left Raoul in my charge. He asked me to look after him, to educate him, to watch over his health. I have done so for four years."

"That is good of you."

"I don't want to masquerade under false colours. I was poor . . . very poor. My family, you see, lost everything during the Terror. Estates . . . fortune . . . everything gone. I had nothing. My wealthy cousin, in leaving me in charge of his son, was also providing for me."

"Well, perhaps you are fortunate. You have the little boy and your good health."

"You are a comforter," he said, smiling his gentle melancholy smile.

"You have a longing for a different life?"

"We lost much. As you so properly remind me, I have good health, and that is the most important of all possessions. The *canaille* left my family that—which is more than they did poor Raoul's. You are not eating. I distract you from your food."

She smiled. "And it is all so good! This delicious fish! This sparkling wine! How I love it! But your story is more exciting than fish or wine. To-morrow and the next day . . . food and drink are forgotten. But I shall remember your story as long as I live."

"Do you remember other people's stories so vividly then?"

"Yes."

"I wonder why?"

"Is it because so little has happened to me? Perhaps. I still remember old Thérèse, at the Convent, who used to peer at everyone, and how it was said in the town that she was really looking for her Jean-Pierre whom she had loved so long ago. . . . I remember Anne-Marie who went away with a rich woman in a carriage. Yes, I think I remember every little detail of what happened to other people. Perhaps it is because, when I hear these stories, I feel that I am the person to whom they are happening. *I* was old Thérèse, peering about for her Jean-Pierre; and I was Anne-Marie going away in a carriage. I was poor Raoul's grandmother growing ill in the Conciergerie. When things like that happen you cannot forget . . . even if they only happen in your mind."

"You are interested in other people's lives because you have a sympathetic nature."

"That is flattery perhaps. Sister Thérèse said I was inquisitive . . . the most inquisitive child she ever knew, and inquisitiveness is a sin—or a near-sin.''

"I think that in you it is a charming sin.''

"How can a sin be charming?''

"Most sins charm, don't they? Is that not why people find them difficult to resist?''

Fleetingly she thought of that charming sinner whom she was trying in vain to banish from her mind. But there he was—recalled by a few words.

"I think,'' she said, ''that this is becoming an irreligious conversation.'' She laughed. The wine had made her eyes sparkle and Sir Charles, turning to her, looked into her animated face and said: ''May I know the joke?''

"I was saying to Monsieur de la Roche that I am very inquisitive, and that is a sin or a near-sin; and he says that sins usually charm and that is why they are difficult to resist.''

"And are you so very inquisitive?''

"I fear so.''

There was a lull in the conversation during which Mr. Danesborough was heard to refer to Joseph Smith, the founder of that strange sect called the Mormons, who had been murdered that year.

They all found the Mormons a fascinating topic, and the subject was taken up with animation round the table.

"Of what do they speak?'' asked Léon de la Roche.

"Oh, the Mormons—a religious sect of America. I know little of them except that their religion allows them to have many wives.''

"I have no doubt,'' Mr. Danesborough was saying, ''that Mr. Brigham Young will follow in Smith's footsteps.''

"They say he already has ten wives,'' said the lady on Mr. Danesborough's right.

"Disgusting!'' said Miss Danesborough.

Mr. Danesborough said that he was not sure that a thing could be condemned until all the facts were known, whereupon everyone looked at the parson with mild exasperation and affection. He was the most extraordinary of clergymen; and it was doubtful whether his queer views would not have

.landed him in trouble, but for his wealth and family connections.

"But surely," protested the lady on his right, "it says in the Bible somewhere that a man should only have one wife."

Sir Charles said unexpectedly: "Solomon had a good many; and hadn't David?"

The young man next to Caroline said: "Men have murdered their wives because they wanted another. Now if, like the followers of Brigham Young, they could have as many as they could afford, such murders might be avoided."

Melisande caught Caroline's eye then and she knew that the conversation had set them both thinking of Fermor. Were they both thinking that if they were Mormons they might both be preparing for marriage?

Melisande spoke her thoughts aloud. "But I suppose even Mormons only marry one woman at a time."

She had spoken in English and shocked glances were cast in her direction. This was a most improper conversation to be carried on at the table of a clergyman, and Mr. Danesborough was as guilty as anyone; but even if the men liked to make bold comments, it was not expected that ladies should do so.

Miss Danesborough hastily changed the conversation, and Léon de la Roche bent towards Melisande and said: "Now that we have met formally, you must visit us. Mrs. Clark would be pleased to give you luncheon or dinner. If you came to luncheon Raoul would be delighted, I am sure."

"Thank you. I will ask Caroline. If she can spare me, I should very much like to come."

"We will invite Miss Trevenning too. Perhaps then there will be more hope of your coming."

"I shall look forward to that."

When they were in the drawing-room and the men were still at the dinner table, Melisande told Caroline that Léon proposed asking them to luncheon. "Would you wish to go?"

"Why, of course," said Caroline.

"I am glad."

"I am to come as a sort of chaperone?" said Caroline with a friendly grimace.

"He did not say that."

"Well, I have no objection. You can't, you know, go calling on gentlemen alone."

How charming she is! thought Melisande. How friendly! It is because Fermor is not here.

And later during the evening the invitation was given and accepted. Caroline and Melisande were to have luncheon with the de la Roches in two days' time.

They were silent riding back in the carriage, and when they returned to the house, Caroline said to Melisande: "Come and help me. I don't want to wake Wenna at this hour."

So Melisande went to Caroline's bedroom and unhooked her gown and brushed her hair for her.

"It was a successful party," said Caroline, looking at Melisande's reflection in the mirror. "Everyone was admiring you. Did you know that . . . Melisande?"

Melisande blushed with pleasure, not because of Caroline's remark but because for the first time she had used her Christian name.

"No," she said.

"Please call me Caroline now. We don't want to stand on too much ceremony, do we? They were admiring you, Melisande. I believe everybody thought you were a connection of the family."

"Do you think so . . . Caroline?"

"I am sure of it. I wonder if Monsieur de la Roche thinks it."

"No. I told him I came from the Convent."

"Well, it clearly made no difference to him. He is rather interesting, don't you think?"

"Very interesting."

"And certainly taken with you!" Caroline laughed lightly and Melisande knew that even now she was thinking of Fermor. She wished Léon to be interested in Melisande and Melisande in Léon . . . and it was because of Fermor.

The door opened and Wenna looked in.

"Why didn't you call?" she began, and stopped, seeing Melisande.

"Oh, Wenna, I didn't want to disturb you. Mademoiselle is helping."

Wenna said: "You should have called. Wouldn't you like me to . . ."

"No, no," said Caroline impatiently. "Go back to bed at once, Wenna."

"All right, all right. Goodnight then."

Both girls said goodnight and the door was closed in silence.

Then Melisande said: "She does not like me. I wish it were not so. She watches me . . . sometimes there is a hatred."

"That's Wenna's way, and of course it is not really hatred."

"That way is, for me."

"Melisande . . . don't worry about Wenna. Everything will be all right."

Caroline, smiling into the mirror, saw two weddings—her own with Fermor and Melisande's with Léon de la Roche. After the wedding she and Fermor would never see Melisande again.

"Yes," she repeated, "everything will be all right."

At the supper table in the servants' hall the relationship between the French Mamazel and the French Mounseer was being discussed with eagerness. Mrs. Soady sat, lips pursed, as she always did when this subject was under discussion, smiling to herself as she listened to the chatter about her.

Every now and then Mr. Meaker would dart a look at her.

It was not like her to keep a secret for so long. It must be a very special secret; she must have been warned; the need for silence must indeed have been deeply impressed upon her.

"It's a clear-cut case of romance," said the footman.

"It's a lovely story," said Peg. "And Mamazel's so pretty she might be a princess in disguise."

That remark made Mrs. Soady's lips twitch. This secret, Mr. Meaker had already guessed, had something to do with the Mamazel.

"Though," said Bet, "you'd hardly call that mounseer a prince, would you?"

"Well," admitted Peg, thinking fondly of her fisherman,

"he might not be everybody's fancy, but by all accounts he's a very nice gentleman."

Bet said that when she thought of a prince in disguise she thought of someone like Mr. Fermor. "You know," said Bet, "always singing and laughing, and big and strong and ever so goodlooking."

"Good looks," declared the footman earnestly—he had no pretensions to them himself—"are a matter of opinion. . . . To snails other snails are good looking. There's no accounting for tastes."

"But they're not snails!" pointed out Peg. "And Mr. Fermor's so very goodlooking. He makes most others seem plain . . . terrible plain."

"Yet," said the parlourmaid, "if two snails do find each other handsome, perhaps two French people do. I reckon 'tis because she's a mamazel and he's a mounseer that they like each other all that much."

Mr. Meaker said, as he passed his plate up for a helping of nattlin pie: "I hear the boy's not all that pleased about this friendship between our Mamazel and his uncle."

All eyes were on Mr. Meaker who slowly piled cream on to his nattlin.

He filled his mouth and masticated slowly. "These painted ladies," he said, studying the potatoes on his plate, "ain't all that much better than painted lords."

"Oh, yes they be," said Mrs. Soady sharply. "Painted ladies be the best sort of 'taters I ever knew. And how did you get to hear about the little 'un and our Mamazel, Mr. Meaker?"

"Well, I had cause to go into the town, and while I was refreshing myself at the Jolly Sailor who should come in but Mr. Fitt, him that is coachman to the Mounseer . . . or I should say to the little 'un. That's a strange household, seeing that this boy is the master, having all the money, and Mounseer nothing more than one of these tutors, though he be a relation. The little 'un is a Duke or a Count or something . . . though that may be different in French. This Mounseer is his guardian, but he has little of his own, so I did understand."

"And what did Mr. Fitt say about the little boy and our Mamazel?" persisted Mrs. Soady.

"Well," said Mr. Meaker, picking up his glass of mead and taking a gulp before proceeding, "it seems that the boy is spoilt . . . very spoilt. It seems that though he first found our Mamazel and took quite a liking to her, he don't like any to have the stage but himself—so to speak. And the Mounseer has been spending too much time with Mamazel for the liking of his little lordship."

"Spoilt brat he be!" said Mrs. Soady. "Who do he think he is? Why, 'tis a beautiful romance, I'll swear, and no more than Mamazel deserves."

"Why yes, Mrs. Soady, 'tis rightly so, but you see the boy be the master . . . or so Mr. Fitt tells me. If he lives till he's twenty-one he'll have a fortune, and the Mounseer will be left a little money. If the little 'un dies, 'tis the Mounseer that the fortune goes to."

Bet said with a giggle: " 'Tis a wonder he do take such care of the little 'un!"

"Now, Bet!" said Mrs. Soady sharply.

"That's foreigners for you!" said the footman.

"The things they be up to!" said Mrs. Soady. "The idea of leaving a fortune to a little 'un like that."

" 'Tis a queer set-up," admitted Mr. Meaker. "It was a very interesting conversation I had with Mr. Fitt."

Mrs. Soady was watching Mr. Meaker. There he was, enjoying all the attention that was focussed on him and thinking himself so clever, so full of knowledge.

If he did know what I do know! thought Mrs. Soady. Him and his Mr. Fitt!

And when they were alone together she said to him: "You and your Mr. Fitt!"

Then she sat down in a chair and laughed.

"What's so funny about Mr. Fitt?"

"I could tell you something, Mr. Meaker, that would make your eyes pop out of your head."

"Reckon you could, Mrs. Soady."

"It 'ud startle 'ee more than anything Mr. Fitt could tell 'ee."

"Reckon it would, Mrs. Soady."

Mrs. Soady, tempted, trembled on the brink of disclosure.

Mr. Meaker bent towards her, his eyes beaming, flattering, begging for the secret.

"Oh well," said Mrs. Soady, "reckon you ought to know. You're the head of the men servants, and 'tain't right you shouldn't know. But, mind 'ee, Mr. Meaker, 'tis between us two."

"Why, yes, Mrs. Soady. Won't get no farther than me."

"You've been wondering why Mamazel is treated as she is. You've been asking yourself why she's been treated like one of the family. Well, I'll tell 'ee. She is one of the family."

"One of the family, Mrs. Soady?"

Mrs. Soady chuckled. "A member of the family all right. She's the master's own daughter."

Mr. Meaker's eyes were round with wonder and appreciation.

"Though," said Mrs. Soady, "what they do call illegitimate. In other words . . ."

"A bastard!" whispered Mr. Meaker.

The weather was mild all through November and into December. There was great activity in the house. The preparations for the wedding on Christmas Day went on and, although they had first decided that it must be a quiet wedding, the original plans grew and so many guests were asked that it would be quite a grand occasion after all.

Letters came from Fermor to Caroline. Melisande would watch her receive them, take them to her room and emerge starry-eyed. He must be a good letter-writer. He would be. But nothing he would say could be trusted. Melisande had gathered that only once did he refer to her in those letters. Caroline had read out to her what he had said: "Felicitations to your father, old Wenna, and all men and maidens who inhabit Trevenning—not forgetting the 'little Mamazel'." That was all.

Sometimes it was more than a pleasure, it was a necessity to escape from the house and the bustle of preparation. How shall I feel when he comes back again? wondered Melisande. How shall I feel on the day he marries Caroline?

It was a comfort to find Léon waiting for her on the shore

at that spot where they had first met and which had now become an accepted meeting place. If there was nothing to detain her in the house, she would often make her way there. If the boy was inclined to come out, they would both be there; if not, Léon would come alone. Melisande could not help feeling relieved when Raoul did not come; he was bright and intelligent, often amusing, but every now and then a certain resentment would leap into his manner. He liked Melisande but he did not care to see her take too much of Léon's attention; when he thought this was happening, his manner would become a little overbearing. Léon was, she was sure, the most patient man in the world. Raoul was avid for information, and often she was able to turn that resentment into interest for small creatures they found in the rock pools. By giving him her attention she could soothe his vanity and his arrogance, and she spent hours in the library at Trevenning trying to discover interesting facts which she could impart to the boy. He might have been a charming child, she often thought, but the vast fortune which was to be his and the power it gave him over the people about him had completely spoiled him.

Melisande was glad therefore one day during the second week of December to arrive on the shore and find Léon alone. He was stretched out on the sand, his back propped up against a rock; and when he saw her he leaped to his feet. There was no mistaking the pleasure in his face.

"I was so hoping you'd come," he said.

"It is just for half an hour. I must not stay longer. It gets dark so early."

"I'll walk back with you, so you needn't fear the dark."

"Thanks. But I shall be expected back soon. There is a good deal to do. Do you realize that it is only two weeks to Christmas?"

"And the wedding. I suppose the bridegroom will soon be coming."

"We don't expect him until a day or so before Christmas."

"Melisande. . . . May I call you that? It is what I call you in my thoughts."

"Please do."

"Then to you may I be Léon?"

"Yes, when we are together like this. I think when others are present it should be Monsieur de la Roche and Mademoiselle St. Martin."

"Very well. That shall be our rule. What will you do after the wedding, Melisande?"

"Sir Charles has spoken to me. He has suggested I might stay."

"After Miss Trevenning has gone?"

"Yes. I can make myself useful in the house. There is much I can do, he says. His daughter will be gone and she will take Wenna—one of the servants—with her; the house will be depleted, Sir Charles says, for Caroline and Wenna had certain duties. He suggests that I take over those duties. I think I shall enjoy this, and it is great good fortune."

"He seems a very kind man."

"He *is* a kind man. Few know how kind. But I know. I have seen that kindness. He says that there will be duties for me, and that I seem to be making a home there. He says the Danesboroughs like me . . . and others. He mentioned you. He said that now I have friends here, I would not wish to leave."

"It's the best news I've heard for a long time."

"For you?"

"For me. I have wondered what it would be like here if you left."

"Don't you like this place?"

"I have liked it very much since we met. Our friendship has made a great difference to me." He picked up a stone and threw it into the sea. They watched it hit the water, rise and fall again. "Well, now our friendship goes on."

"I hope it will go on for a long time. But you will not stay here for the summer."

"In the summer I suppose we must go to a different climate. We should go to Switzerland . . . high in the mountains."

"That sounds very pleasant."

He smiled his melancholy smile. "I am ungrateful, you are thinking. I am disgruntled. Sometimes I rail against fate. I say, 'Why should some be born to riches, others to poverty?' "

"I am surprised that you should have such thoughts."

"All poor men have them. It is only the poor who worry about inequality and injustice."

"You long to be rich?"

"I long to be free."

"Free? You mean from Raoul?"

"My position is a difficult one. I often ask myself if I am good for the boy. I ask myself, 'Is this living? What are you? A nurse? A tutor? A woman could play the first part better, and there are scholars who could make far better tutors than you could.' "

"But it was the wish of Raoul's parents that you should be the nurse, the tutor. He is of your own blood. No one could love him as you do."

"You are right and I am ungrateful, as I said I was. It is because you are so sympathetic that I pour my troubles into your ear."

"What would you do if you were rich and free? Tell me. I should like to hear. You would return to France?"

"To France? No. My old home is a government building now. It is in Orléans. I have been there . . . not so long ago, walked through the streets past those old wooden houses, stood on the banks of the Loire and thought: 'If I were rich I would come back to Orléans and build a house, marry, raise a family and live as my people lived before the Terror.' I used to think that. But now I know that I would not go back to Orléans. I would go miles away . . . to a new world. Perhaps to New Orleans. The river I should look at would not be the Loire but the Mississippi, and instead of building a great mansion and living like an aristocrat, I should have a plantation and grow cotton or sugar or tobacco. . . ."

"That's more exciting than the mansion. For what would you do in the mansion?"

"I should grieve for the past. I should become one of those bores who are always looking backwards."

"And in the New World it is necessary to look forward . . . to the next crop of sugar, tobacco or cotton. What do they look like when they are growing, I wonder? Sugar sounds nicest. That's because you can eat it, I suppose."

He laughed suddenly.

"Which would you grow if you could choose?" she asked.

"You have made me think that I should like to grow sugar." He smiled at her. "Melisande, you are so different from me. You are so full of gaiety. I am rather a melancholy person."

"What makes you melancholy?"

"The terrible habit of looking back. I always heard my parents say that the good old days were behind us and that we should never get back to the splendour of those times. They made the past sound wonderful, magnificent, the only life that was worth living. I suppose they heard it from their parents."

"It is an inheritance of melancholy."

He took her hands and said: "I want to escape from it. I long to escape from it."

"You can. This minute. These are the good times. Those were the bad times. Wonderful times are in the future . . . waiting for you."

"Are they?"

"I feel sure of it. Wouldn't Raoul like to grow sugar?"

"The climate would kill him."

"I see. So you cannot go until you are no longer needed to look after him."

"No. But when he is twenty-one, I shall come into a little money. Then he will no longer need me. I shall be free."

"That is a long way to look forward. Still, in the meantime you have Raoul to care for, and you know that, although he is sometimes a rather difficult little boy, he is an orphan, and you . . . you only . . . can love him and help him and look after him as his parents wished."

After a while he began to talk of the New World with an enthusiasm which astonished her, for she had never seen him as animated as this before. He had wanted to go there, he explained, since he had realized that France would never be the France for which his parents had made him yearn.

"The old France is gone," he said. "There is a King on the throne, but what a King! The son of Egalité, a man who gave up his titles to join the National Guard. What could be expected of such a King? No! It shall not be France for me."

"Tell me about the plantation you would have. Let us pretend that the climate *would* be good for Raoul, and that you are now making plans for leaving."

"The climate could never be good for Raoul."

"But I said, pretend it would. You say you are melancholy and I am gay. When I am sad, I pretend. I have always pretended. It is the next best thing to reality. It is better to imagine something good is happening than to brood on what is bad and cannot be altered. Now . . . how should we leave?"

"First we should cross the Atlantic. Are you a good sailor?"

"I am the best of sailors."

"I knew you would be. I have some friends in New Orleans. We should make for them. You would have to look after Raoul while I worked hard, learning all I had to learn about managing the plantation."

"That would be easy. I daresay there would be much to entertain us, and Raoul is interested in everything."

"We should employ negroes to work for us; and I think that, once I was proficient, the thing would be to get the plantation going and then . . . build the house."

She was smiling dreamily, seeing not the sea and rocks, but a plantation of her imagining. It was a sugar plantation. She did not know what a sugar plantation looked like, but she imagined rows and rows of canes and laughing people in gay colours with dark shining faces. She saw them all dancing at the Mardi Gras.

He broke in on her dreams. "If ever I go, will you really come with me? Would you marry me, Melisande?"

"But . . ."

"Forget I asked it. It was too soon. I see that. It is a mistake. I was carried away by your enthusiasm."

There was a short silence before he said: "I am right? It is too soon?"

"Yes," she answered. "I think it is too soon."

"What do you mean, Melisande?"

"That as yet you are my friend and I have been happy . . . and very comfortable . . . knowing you. It is too soon for big decisions. We do not, as yet, know each other very well."

"I know enough."

"You do not even know who my parents were."

"I did not think of knowing them. It is of knowing you that I am sure."

"You are a great comfort to me and that is a very good thing to be."

"I'll comfort you all the days of your life."

"I believe you would. You are gentle, and only sad when you look backwards."

"If you married me there would be so much to look forward to that I should no longer want to look back."

"A new life," she said dreamily, "in a new world."

"That would not be for years. You forget . . . Raoul."

"How would Raoul feel if you married me?"

"A bit hurt at first perhaps. He has had my undivided attention for so long. But he is fond of you and would grow fonder. You have charmed him as you have charmed all others. At present he is too self-centred to see anyone very clearly apart from himself; but we should soon overcome any opposition."

"Léon, he is not a bad little boy. It is just that he has too much power . . . and he is too young to handle it. He could change, I think."

"It would be so good for him to have us both. More . . . normal. We could both be parents to him. It is so difficult . . . a man all alone."

"Yes, I see that. But it is not Raoul we are discussing, Léon. It is ourselves."

"And I have spoken too soon."

"Yes, that is it. You have spoken too soon. Could we put this aside . . . until later on? Leave it for a few weeks, Léon. That is best. Let us talk of other things and suddenly . . . soon . . . I shall know. I feel it. Do you understand?"

"Yes, Melisande, I understand."

She jumped up. "It will soon be dark and I am late. Please . . . I must go at once."

They walked back to Trevenning, but they did not talk any more of marriage. But when he left her he said: "We must meet often . . . every day. We must get through this business of knowing each other as soon as possible. You are very beautiful and I am very impatient."

"Good night," she said.

He took her hands and kissed them.

"I am very fond of you," she said, "and a little of Raoul. I think it could be a happy thing if we were all together."

He would have put his arms about her but she held him off. "Please . . . we must wait. It is too important and, as yet, we cannot be sure."

She left him and, as she did so, she seemed to hear Fermor's mocking laughter. Two proposals—and how different!

"Life is a strangeness," she murmured in English.

Three ways were open to her now. Which should she choose?

Take the one you long for! she seemed to hear a voice urging her. Be bold. Say goodbye to the dull life. Live gaily and recklessly. That is the way. She could imagine the tuneful tenor voice:

> *"I would love you all the day,*
> *Every night would kiss and play,*
> *If with me you'd fondly stray*
> *Over the hills and far away . . ."*

Over the hills and far away to a sinful life . . . to adventure. She thought: Clearly if I were wise I should marry Léon.

It was Christmas Day.

Melisande lay awake, though it was early and the house not yet astir.

Caroline's wedding day had come.

Fermor had returned only yesterday, having been, he said, delayed in London. As soon as she heard his voice she felt excitement rising within her; as soon as she looked from her window and saw him laughing as he was greeted by the grooms and servants, she knew great disquiet.

Now on this early morning she would look facts in the face and see them as they really were. She had dreamed—she who lived so much in dreams—that something would happen before this day was reached. Her romantic thoughts, winding along pleasantly to a happy ending, had given John Collings to Caroline, and had found a charming girl for Léon; that left Melisande and Fermor who, by a miraculous stroke of good fortune, had changed his nature; he became serious-minded without losing any of his gaiety; he became tender without losing any of his passion; he began loving instead of lustful.

In her dreams Melisande lived in a perfect world.

But now—on Caroline's wedding day—reality had risen indisputably over fantasy, and ruthlessly was preparing to stamp it out.

In the wardrobe was the dress of green silk, made to her own design, which Miss Pennifield had helped her to sew; at the neck were little bows of black velvet, and there was a big rose of black silk and velvet to wear at the waist. "Black!" Miss Pennifield had cried. "Why, it looks like mourning. Black is for funerals, not for weddings. Why don't you make a nice pink one? Roses are pink, not black, my dear. And I'll find 'ee some lovely pieces." "There can only be black," she had said. "It is a need . . . for a green gown." And she thought: For me too.

She was not quite seventeen, and that was young to despair. She wondered how old the nun had been at the time of her incarceration. She, Melisande, would this day be walled in—walled in by the death of hope.

She had not seen him alone since his return. He had not sought her, she knew, for had he wished to see her he would have found some means of doing so. He had come with wedding presents . . . for Caroline. He talked with Caroline; he rode with Caroline; and that was fitting.

So clearly Melisande had meant nothing to him but a possible partner in a light adventure which he thought they might share together; Melisande had turned away and he was shrugging his shoulders as he passed on.

Now she could hear the first stirrings in the house. In the servants' hall they would be up very early. Mrs. Soady, a sedate priestess in her kitchens had been withdrawn and absentminded for days, her mouth watering at the pies and pasties she was making, the cakes, the puddings. There was hardly time to gossip with a wedding so near.

Melisande rose. She must go down to help them. It was better than lying in bed and examining lost dreams.

* * *

Caroline lay awake. She had scarcely slept all night.

The day had come—the day she had feared would never come. She had left the wardrobe door open that she might see the white dress which had been the despair of both herself and Miss Pennifield. On the dressing table was the white lace veil which had been worn by her mother and her grandmother.

She was trying to think of the future and she could only think of the past, of seeing him in London when they were children, of his teasing contempt of her, of a housemaid's whispered words on a staircase, of Melisande. But she was foolish to brood on these things. He had scarcely looked at Melisande yesterday.

She had meant to tell him, when they had ridden out alone, of the friendship between Melisande and Léon de la Roche and how it seemed to be moving towards an inevitable conclusion. But she had been afraid, lest it should spoil the happiness of her wedding eve.

She could not lie in bed . . . waiting. She wanted the day to come; she wanted the ceremony to be over. For two weeks they were to stay in this house, for they had decided that there should be no honeymoon. That was a concession to convention which they had decided to make. Sir Charles had agreed that they might marry although a year had not elapsed since the death of Caroline's mother, but gaily to go off on a honeymoon was too flippant, too disrespectful. The matter had been talked over with several people, and all had agreed that the married pair should stay quietly at Trevenning for a few weeks, and then leave sedately for London.

Caroline had not cared about a honeymoon—all that mattered was that she and Fermor should marry—but now she realized she would have felt less apprehension if they could leave the house to-day . . . after the ceremony and the reception.

Yet she and Melisande had become friends, and she knew that Melisande was no scheming woman. She was an impulsive girl, eager to please—a friendly, charming girl. But how much happier Caroline would be if she could say goodbye to her. With Fermor's return her jealousy had come back.

But she must not invent unhappiness. She got out of bed and going to the dressing table put on the veil. She saw from the mirror that she was very pale and there were shadows of sleeplessness under her eyes. She scarcely looked like a happy bride. Yet everything for which she had hoped promised to be hers.

The door had opened and Wenna looked in.

"My dear life! Out of bed! What be doing? Why, my queen, you look so tired. Didn't 'ee sleep then? And trying that thing on. Don't 'ee know 'tis unlucky?"

"Wenna . . ."

Wenna ran forward and took Caroline in her arms.

"I'm frightened, Wenna."

"What of, my little one? Tell Wenna what's frightening 'ee? It be *he*. I do know."

"No. It's the future, Wenna. Everything. Nerves, Wenna . . . wedding day nerves. They say people get them."

"It ain't too late, you know, my precious. If you do say the word . . ."

"No, Wenna, no! Never!"

Wenna was resigned. "I'll be with 'ee, my precious. All the days of my life I'll be there beside 'ee."

The ceremony was over and there was gaiety in the house. How could it be otherwise? It was true that not a year had elapsed since the death of the mistress, and everyone knew that a year was the shortest period which should elapse between a funeral and a wedding in the same house—but it had pleased the guests to forget this.

The infectiously gay bridegroom banished all gloom. Handsome, dashing, he seemed all that a bridegroom should be.

As for Caroline, she was subdued, pale and obviously nervous, which, said the guests, was all that a bride should be.

Sir Charles was grave and clearly delighted with his daughter's marriage; the bridegroom's parents, rich and fashionable from London, were equally pleased with the match. From the surrounding county all the best families had come as guests to Trevenning; and as the friends of the bridegroom's family were also present, the house was full. Never had there been such a dazzling ceremony in the great hall, decorated as for Christmas, with holly, ivy, box and bay leaves. Christmas Day and the wedding day of the daughter of the house! What could be more demanding of ceremony? Let gloom be banished! It was so easy to say: "I know her mother has not been gone so very long, but this is what she would have wished." They could be happy, laughing, dancing, singing, as long as they could remind themselves that in doing so they were merely carrying out the wishes of the dear one who had departed.

On the great table were bowls of punch; there was metheglin, mead, dash-an-darras, and shenegrum—that concoction of boiled beer, Jamaica rum, lemon, brown sugar and nutmeg—without which no Cornish Christmas was complete.

The table was loaded with Mrs. Soady's greatest masterpieces. There were boars' heads, and every sort of pie that could be made; besides the usual meat pies there were fish pies containing mackerel, bream and pilchards. There were pilchards offered in every way known to Cornish connoisseurs. There were sucking pigs—both veers and slips; and of course there was hog's pudding—that Cornish delicacy—of which the Londoners took sparingly.

Harassed serving men and maids scurried about the house; from the kitchen came the last minute cakes and pies which Mrs. Soady felt must be made in case they should be short.

And after the banquet, the servants descended on the hall like a swarm of locusts and cleared everything away that the guests might dance and disport themselves as was fitting for a wedding in the family on Christmas Day.

The old dances were danced and all the company, led by the bride and groom, joined in the Quadrille and Sir Roger de Coverley; and the Cornish guests, at the request for Cornish dances, formed up and showed the foreigners the furry dance to the accompaniment provided by musicians specially engaged to play for the company.

It was a merry party.

Léon had been invited; he stayed close to Melisande and it was clear that he was enjoying the spectacle of a Cornish Christmas and wedding party.

"If you married me," he said, "there would not be such a grand occasion as this, alas."

"The grandeur would be of no importance," she told him.

"You are a little sad to-day."

"Sad? On such a day! Why should I be?"

"Perhaps because Miss Trevenning will go away now that she is married. Are you apprehensive too . . . on her account?"

"Apprehensive when she is in love? That is clear. Don't you agree?"

"Yes, I agree."

"And so is he. Can you see that?"

"He? Oh, he is in love with himself."

She looked at him sharply.

"I am envious perhaps," he said. "Not of him as he is . . . oh no! I do not envy him his wealth or his bride. But I wish that I had that assurance which wealth gives. I wish I had a bride who was in love with me as his is with him."

"Be careful!" she warned. "This is Cornwall where strange things happen. Piskies and fairies lurk unseen. It may be that your wishes will be granted. You may have his wealth and you may—as you say he has—fall in love with yourself."

"No doubt he found that easier than I should. For one thing he is so handsome; and for another he is so pleased with himself."

"Anyone truly in love is pleased with the object of that love, and whatever it may seem to others it is handsome to the lover. I hope Caroline will be happy."

"You speak as though you think she will not."

"I am being foolish then."

Fermor seemed to sense that they were talking of him. He smiled in their direction and then came over.

"Are you enjoying the wedding feast, Mademoiselle St. Martin?" he asked.

"Very much. I don't believe you have met Monsieur de la Roche?"

"I have seen him."

"I do not remember seeing you," said Léon.

"I was at the top of the cliff; you were below. But I recognized you. I have, they say, hawk's eyes. They see a good deal.''

"This is Mr. Holland, as you know," said Melisande to Léon.

"Indeed yes. We all know the bridegroom."

Fermor said: "I heard that you and Mademoiselle St. Martin are delighted to speak French together. How pleasant to meet compatriots in a foreign country!"

"It has been most pleasant."

"I really came to ask Mademoiselle to join in the dance. It is not right that young ladies should hold aloof from the festivities. I have hardly had a word with her since my arrival yesterday. I have to apologise for my neglect and to beg her forgiveness.''

"Not only do I forgive," said Melisande, "I applaud. It is fitting, is it not, Monsieur de la Roche, that a bridegroom should neglect all but his bride?"

"It is an accepted rule of conduct, I believe."

"You have been a bridegroom?" asked Fermor; and Melisande fancied she detected the faintest streak of insolence.

"I have not; but I understand."

"Trust a Frenchman! But I won't be forgiven as easily as that. Every man—married or bachelor—has a duty to the community. *Toujours la politesse,* I believe you say in your country.''

"In France," said Melisande, "*la politesse* always stands aside for *l'amour.* Thank you for asking me. Thank you for apologising. Please go back to your wife with a clear conscience. That is what all expect.''

"Oh, but I must look after our guests, you know."

"Monsieur de la Roche looks after me and I after him."

He looked at her sardonically. "I guessed it, but I don't intend him to keep that pleasure all to himself. Come . . . dance with me.''

He would have drawn her into the centre of the hall where the couples were forming for a barn dance, but at that moment there was a knocking at the door, a shouting from without, and in the next few seconds the guise dancers were trooping into the hall.

Fermor said: "Another old custom! Who are these people?"

Jane Collings, who heard his remark, called out that they were the guise dancers who always came to the big houses at Christmas time.

"So it *is* another old custom!"

"Very ancient. Older than Christianity!" said Jane.

The guisards were unrecognizable, for most of them wore masks, and those who did not had blackened their faces in order to hide their identity. Some were dressed up to represent characters for whom the Cornish had a special sympathy. There were two as Sir Jonathan Trelawny as well as a Charles the First and a Monmouth. They acted their parts to the amusement of the guests, and after that they danced the ancient dances which they had been practising for weeks before Christmas.

Before they had finished their performance the wassaillers arrived, and with them the curl singers. The hall was full now; and there was general singing and dancing and drinking of dash-an-darras to the health of the bridge and groom.

It was necessary for this last ceremony that Fermor should stand beside Caroline. As he did so he looked towards Melisande, and it was not easy to know what he was thinking. Melisande shivered. The scene seemed to her a strange one. The black faces of the dancers made them grotesque, and the masks worn by some of them were ugly, almost menacing. Yet she knew that beneath them were the faces of kindly simple people. There was the bridegroom, elegant in his wedding clothes from London, the handsomest man in the room, over six feet in height, an ideal bridegroom as she had heard him called; yet, thought Melisande, that handsome face was a mask more misleading than any worn by the revellers.

She turned suddenly to Léon.

"What is it?" he asked.

"I will marry you. I think . . . we shall be happy together."

"Melisande . . ."

"Yes, if you still wish it, I will."

He gripped her hand. "I do not know what to say. I am overwhelmed with happiness."

"I believe it is the right thing for us," she said. "If I should wish to tell anyone that we are to marry, may I do so?"

"I want them all to know. Shall we announce it now?"

"Not here. They would not be interested. It would be an anticlimax. Who are we? Just consider—*our* betrothal announced at such a grand wedding!"

"When shall it be?"

"Not for a little while. There will have to be many arrangements, won't there."

"I will break the news gently to Raoul. Will you mind his being with us?"

"*I* shall not mind, but what of him? How will he like the idea?"

"He'll get used to it. Perhaps we could get married here . . . before we leave. Then we could all go away together. So, my dear sweet Melisande, we shall not be parted after all . . . never again."

Fermor's eyes were on them. "It is a great comfort for me to know that you are near," she said.

"I wish we could be alone somewhere."

"We shall meet to-morrow perhaps."

"At the usual tryst. Our own spot. In the years to come we shall visit it often. I shall always remember your coming down the cliffs with Raoul . . . down to where I stood on the sand."

"It was like coming down to safety."

They could no longer talk. As was the custom Caroline was about to sing for the guests.

She was flushed, shining with an inner happiness. Wenna watched her.

She's happy to-day, thought Wenna. But is one day's happiness worth a life-time's misery?

Caroline was saying: "I haven't much of a voice, as you know, but I will do my best, and here is a song you all know and perhaps you'll help me by joining in."

Caroline's voice was sweet but weak, so there must be absolute silence for her. She sang:

"A well there is in the West Country,
And a clearer one never was seen;
There is not a wife in the West Country
But has heard of the well of St. Keyne."

Several of the guests sang lustily:

"But has heard of the well of St. Keyne."

And they went on to sing with Caroline of the stranger who came to the well and, being tired out, drank of the waters, and how he heard of the waters' magical power from the old man who had seen him drink.

" 'Now art thou a bachelor, stranger?' quoth he,
'For an if thou hast a wife,
The happiest draught thou hast drunk this day
That ever thou didst in thy life!' "

Melisande listened intently while Caroline and her helpers continued.

" 'St. Keyne,' quoth the Cornishman, 'many a time
Drank of the crystal well,
And before the angel summoned her,
She laid on the water a spell.

'If the husband of this gifted well
Shall drink before his wife,
A happy man thenceforth is he
For he shall be master for life.' "

Fermor had sidled over to Melisande and Léon. He whispered: "We're foreigners . . . all of us. These Cornish are a bit overpowering."

"I wish," said Léon, "that I could understand the words. It is so difficult to follow . . . for one with my not very excellent English."

"Mademoiselle will doubtless explain. She understands, I am sure. She has become so proficient with our English that there is little she does not understand."

"Listen to the last verses," said Melisande; and they all turned to look at Caroline.

" 'You drank of the well I warrant betimes?'
He to the Cornishman said;
But the Cornishman smiled as the stranger spake
And sheepishly shook his head.

'I hastened as soon as the wedding was done,
And left my wife in the porch;
But i' faith she had been wiser than me,
For she took a bottle to church.' "

There was a burst of applause. Many of the Cornish began to chant the last words again, looking slyly from Caroline to Fermor as though they wondered which of them would drink first of the waters of the well.

"The song is . . . what you call an appropriate one?" said Melisande.

"I suppose you would say so," said Fermor.

"And you have drunk of this water? Or do you intend to?"

"Dear Mademoiselle, do you think I need the help of this St. Keyne or whatever her name is? No. I rely on myself. Have no fears that I shall be unable to look after myself."

Melisande thought he was like a satyr, mocking her, assuring her that he had vowed to bring her to surrender; and that he could be thus on the day of his wedding seemed to her the depth of infamy.

There was a sudden silence all about them. The guests had finished with St. Keyne. It was the bridegroom's turn, they were declaring.

"First the bride . . . then the groom. 'Tis an old Cornish custom."

He sauntered towards the musicians.

"Ladies and gentlemen," he said, "how can I follow such a spirited rendering as we have just heard, with one of my little songs? You will excuse me . . ."

"No, no!" they cried. "You must sing. The bride has sung. The groom must sing too."

His reluctance was feigned, Melisande knew. Everything

about him is false, she thought. He wants to sing. He wants
them to admire his voice. He is all conceit, all arrogance.
Now that she knew him, she knew him for the devil, as
Thérèse and the Sisters thought of the devil.

He sang to them in his powerful voice and there was im-
mediate silence in the hall; and only Melisande knew that
the song was for her.

> "Go, lovely rose!
> Tell her, that wastes her time and me,
> That now she knows,
> When I resemble her to thee,
> How sweet and fair she seems to be.
>
> Tell her that's young,
> And shuns to have her graces spied,
> That hadst thou sprung
> In deserts, where no men abide,
> Thou must have uncommended died.
>
> Small is the worth
> Of beauty from the light retired;
> Bid her come forth,
> Suffer herself to be desired;
> And not blush so to be admired.
>
> Then die! that she
> The common fate of all things rare
> May read in thee:
> How small a part of time they share
> That are so wondrous sweet and fair."

Listening, Melisande felt that he was luring her—in spite
of all she knew of him—to some fate which must be avoided
and which she yet feared would overtake her.

She turned to Léon at her side.

She was relying on him to help her withdraw from that
quicksand into which she had already taken a step.

In the servants' hall the Christmas bush hung suspended from
the ceiling; every servant had gathered some of the evergreen

leaves with which to decorate the wooden hoops. The walls were adorned as lavishly as were those of the great hall itself with holly, mistletoe and evergreen leaves wherever it was possible to put them.

Mrs. Soady sat at the head of the table, a contented woman. It was near midnight; the guests were growing weary, and the servants were free now to settle themselves about the table. Now and then, of course, one or the other of them would be called to the guests, but the calls were less frequent.

Mrs. Soady, who had had her fill not only of her favourite foods but of her favourite wines, was saying it was a Christmas they would all remember as long as they lived, when Peg came in to announce that Mamazel and the Frenchman were still together and that she had seen them holding hands.

Mrs. Soady nodded. Metheglin made her very sleepy— the nicest possible sleepiness that made her love all the world, that made her want to share her pleasures with all.

" 'Twouldn't surprise me," said Bet, "if there was to be another wedding hereabouts."

"Oh, I don't know about that," said the footman. "This Frenchman he looks after the little boy, and the little boy be a duke or something—though only a French one. Well, this Mounseer . . . if he be a relation—though a poor one—he'd be close to dukes, you do see."

"And what's that got to do with it?" asked Mrs. Soady, faintly truculent. The footman was bringing discord into happiness. Mrs. Soady was as fond of the little Mamazel as though she were one of the children she herself had never had. Mrs. Soady wanted the Mounseer to marry the Mamazel. She liked weddings. Look what a Christmas they had had through this one!

"Well, Mrs. Soady," pleaded the footman, "you do know these families be terrible particular."

"I can tell you," said Mrs. Soady, "that Mamazel have come from as good a family as any French mounseer, and be fit to marry with dukes . . . French ones leastways."

Mr. Meaker was alert. He was flashing warning glances. It was all very well to impart such weighty secrets to the senior member of the male staff, but to announce it to housemaids, parlourmaids and such chattering maidens, that would be folly such as even Mrs. Soady would not indulge in except under the influence of Christmas feasting and good metheglin.

Mrs. Soady intercepted Mr. Meaker's glances. She brushed them aside. She was excited now.

"You little know who Mamazel be," she said to the footman.

"Who then, Mrs. Soady?"

Many pairs of alert eyes were fixed on Mrs. Soady.

Mr. Meaker groaned inwardly. He knew Mrs. Soady could not resist the temptation. She was leaning back in her chair smiling.

"Well then, this be all between ourselves. 'Tis a secret as must never be mentioned outside these walls. Now, I'll tell 'ee . . ."

And she did.

It was early morning before the celebrations ended.

Melisande went to her room. She felt very tired. Pictures of the evening kept flitting through her mind. She saw herself standing beside Léon, heard his whispered words and herself giving the promise to marry him; she saw herself out in the cold night air waving as his carriage drove away. But most vivid of all were the pictures of the bride and bridegroom standing side by side acknowledging the toast, of Fermor strolling over to speak to her, of Fermor standing smiling at her as he sang for her.

Her head was aching, and as she was about to snuff out the candles panic seized her. On impulse she ran to the door and turned the key in the lock. She left the candles burning and getting into bed lay, looking at the door.

And as she lay there she thought she heard sounds outside—slow stealthy footsteps.

It could not be Fermor. He would not leave Caroline on their wedding night. It was someone going downstairs for something. She must remember that there were many people in the house.

But it seemed to her that the footsteps paused outside her door. She was trembling and tense, aware of immense relief because she had locked the door.

Then she saw something white lying on the carpet. The faint creaking of boards outside her door told her that whoever had come along the corridor had slipped that note under her door.

She got out of bed and picked it up. A little flower fell from it.

On the paper was scrawled in a bold hand which she knew at once must be his: "They say these flowers cure madness. They bring a state of calm reason. It is only a Christmas rose, but all flowers are the same inasmuch as they share the common fate of all things rare."

She wrapped up the flower in the paper and burned them in the candle flame.

He was callous and brutal. She was thankful that she could turn to Léon and never think of him again.

In the early hours of the next day, the storm began to rise. The rain lashed the windows and the wind moaned and howled about the house.

Melisande was unable to sleep for long; all through the hours of that morning she had dozed and been awakened by the gusts of wind that seemed to shake even Trevenning to its foundations.

Each time she woke it was as though in a panic. Afterwards she thought that the storm had been like a dramatic herald of tragedy.

When she rose from her bed and stood at the window, she could see the roaring raging sea tossing the foam in the air; she could see it frothing about the rocks that looked like angry black guards defending the land against the seething monster.

Everyone was sleepy after the revels of the preceding night. Sir Charles warned his guests that it would be unwise to go near the edge of the cliffs in such weather; in a wind like this one, people had been blown over and into the sea.

No one ventured out of doors, for all through the morning the rain was beating down; but in the afternoon it stopped, though the wind was as furious as ever.

Melisande was about to go out to meet Léon when Sir Charles intercepted her.

"Surely you are not going out in this?"

"Just a little way."

"I shouldn't if I were you . . . unless it is very important."

"Well, I suppose it is not really important. It could wait until to-morrow."

He smiled at her in the wistful way he did when they were alone. "Then let it wait. The gusts are terrific on the cliffs. By to-morrow it may have calmed down. Our storms soon tire themselves out."

She thanked him and went back to her room. She stood for some time at the window watching the angry waves. The storm continued and it grew too late to think of going out that day. But how she wished next day that she had gone out to meet Léon. She could not help feeling then that had she gone everything might have turned out differently.

There was more merrymaking in the great hall and in the servants' hall that night, but Melisande joined neither party. She pleaded a headache and stayed in her room. She could not have borne to exchange words with Fermor at that time.

That night she slept well, being tired out; and when she awoke in the morning, the sun was shining and the fields and stubby fir trees were a glistening green; the sea was almost as calm as a lake—a pale blue-green.

When Peg brought her breakfast to the little room in which she had her meals, she knew at once that something had happened. Peg's face expressed that excitement which was in people's faces when they had exciting news to impart, whether the news was pleasant or unpleasant. But as Peg caught her eye she set her face into tragic lines, so Melisande knew that this was tragic news.

Peg burst out: "Oh, Mamazel, there be terrible news. One of the men has come straight back with it. Mrs. Soady said to prepare you gentle like."

"What is it, Peg?"

How long she seemed to take to speak, and why did Melisande immediately think of Fermor and Caroline. Peg's next words dispelled that picture which was forming. "It's the little boy . . . the little duke . . . the French duke."

"What, Peg?"

"A terrible accident. It were yesterday afternoon when the winds was so fierce. He was out with the Mounseer. They was on the jetty. 'Twas a foolish place to go when all do know it be special dangerous. He were blown into the sea."

"Both . . . of them?"

"No, only the little one. He were lost . . . in the sea."

"And Monsieur de la Roche?"

"Well, he could do nothing, you see. It seems he b'ain't no swimmer. Not that he'd have had all that chance if he'd been as fine a life-saver as Jack Pengelly."

"But . . . tell me, Peg. Tell me everything."

"The little body was washed up in the night."

"Dead!"

"Couldn't be no other . . . seeing as he'd been in the sea nigh on ten hours."

"And . . ."

"The Mounseer . . . he's heart-broken, they do say. You see, the little 'un was blown over and he not being able to swim could only run for help. He got hold of Jack Pengelly and *he* dived in twice. 'Twere like a boiling cauldron, they do say. Mark Biddle went in too. 'Twere no good."

"I must go and see him."

"Mrs. Soady said she reckoned that's what you'd want to do."

Melisande picked up her cloak and ran downstairs. She heard Mrs. Soady talking as she came into the servants' hall. Mrs. Soady was saying: "Well, that's what I heard, and 'twould seem to be so. Out on the jetty on an afternoon like that! And the little 'un going in and him just running for help. Of course, there's a fortune in it. So perhaps . . ."

No! thought Melisande. *No!* It's not true.

Mrs. Soady had abruptly stopped talking.

"So, my dear, you have heard the news?"

"Peg told me. You mustn't think . . . He wouldn't . . ."

"Oh, 'twas a terrible tragedy. They do say the Mounseer be well nigh heart-broken. Where be going, Mamazel?"

"I'm going to see him. I must see him."

"William will take 'ee in the carriage. I be sure Sir Charles would not say no to that. Bet, you run and tell William."

"Thank you, Mrs. Soady."

"There, my dear, don't 'ee take on. 'Tis the sort of thing that do happen in these terrible storms. There's been many lost on that jetty. A snare it be, and should by rights be roped off on such days."

"What did you mean when you said there was a fortune in it?"

"My dear life! Did I say that? You must have misunderstood me. I just said what a bit of bad fortune, I reckon, and how the Mounseer was heart-broken at what have happened."

Melisande stared before her. She thought: They will say cruel things about him. Even kind people like Mrs. Soady will believe those cruel things about him.

Mrs. Soady looked at Mr. Meaker and shook her head. There were times, thought Mrs. Soady, when silence was a virtue. Least said was soonest mended. She didn't like this. She didn't like it at all; and she had taken the little Mamazel under her wing and would protect her from the wickedness of the world.

Bet came in to say that the carriage was waiting, and hastily Melisande ran out to it.

The journey seemed to take hours. She pictured it all . . . the two of them battling against that violent wind. Had the boy asked to go out on to the jetty? Or had Léon suggested it? No, Léon would not suggest it. He would have been persuaded. If I had gone . . . if only I had been there, she thought, this might not have happened.

She looked through the carriage windows at the smugly smiling sea. It was like a monster who had had his fill, who had brought tragedy, and having shown his power was content to be still and gentle for a while. The houses looked fresh in the morning light. The well-washed tiles gleamed blue and green in the pale sunlight; the moisture still glistened about the pisky-pows.

When she reached the house, Mrs. Clark took her to Léon's room and left them there. "Comfort him," she whispered; "he's in a sad way."

So, Melisande went to him unceremoniously and, seeing his haggard face, held out her arms to him. He came to her and they embraced. Then he held her at arms' length.

"So you have heard."

"Oh, Léon . . . please . . . *please* don't look like that. It's terrible. But we'll grow away from it . . . together."

He shook his head. "I can never grow away from it."

"You will. Of course you will. It is because it is so near that it seems overwhelming."

"I was there, Melisande. I was there."

"I know. I have heard."

His face was dark and bitter. "What else have you heard?"

She caught her breath. "What else? Why, nothing. Just what has happened."

"You cannot hide it, Melisande, though it is like you to try. You know what they will say, what they are already saying. You have heard. I see it in your face."

"I have heard nothing," she lied.

"It's a brave lie. But you are brave. At the moment you are sorry for me. Pity overwhelms you. But the brave despise cowards, and you see one before you now."

She took him by the arm and looked up into his face. "It is terrible . . . doubly terrible because you were there. But there was nothing you could do, Léon. There was nothing else you could do but what you did."

"I could have plunged in," he said fiercely.

"But you cannot swim."

"I could have tried. Who knows? At such times men can make superhuman efforts, can't they? I might have saved him."

"You couldn't. You did the only thing possible. You brought Jack Pengelly to the spot. Jack knows the coast . . . knows the sea. He's a strong swimmer. He has saved lives before. What you did—though it might not have been dramatic—was the wise, the sensible thing."

"You are trying to comfort me."

"Of course I am trying to comfort you. What else could I do? You need comfort. You have lost a dearly beloved child."

He said ironically: "And gained a fortune."

"Don't say that."

"It's the truth. You know the terms of my cousin's will. It seems they are general knowledge. Do you think I don't know

from the way people look at me! Raoul is gone . . . and they
are saying that I killed him.''

"That's nonsense. Nobody shall say that. It's a stupid thing
to say. Everybody knows how you cared for him, how you
spoilt him with your devotion and your care.''

"So that I allowed him to go on to the jetty . . . and to his
death.''

"He was so self-willed. He always did what *he* wanted. I
can picture it . . . exactly as it happened. You said, Don't
go; and he said, I will. I can picture it so clearly. I knew him
and I know you, Léon. Léon, if we are going to be happy,
there must be no bitterness.''

"So we are going to be happy?''

"You asked me to marry you, remember, and I accepted.
Do you wish to withdraw that proposal?''

He said quietly: "So . . . you would marry me now. You
said we did not know each other very well. You said we must
get to know each other before we married. I said we must
do it quickly. This is the quickest way to improve our knowledge of each other. You have discovered a coward. I have not
discovered anything. I always knew that you would be loyal
to lost causes. You would give your allegiance to the weak
who need you.''

"No, Léon, *no*! You are so unhappy. Of course you are
unhappy. Do not let us add to that unhappiness.''

"There will always be gossip about me, Melisande. Everywhere I go, those people who know me and my position
will wonder. That is how it will be.''

"We shall not let it bother us even if it is so.''

"Melisande, I could only marry you if you believed in
me.''

"Of course I believe in you. No one who knew you and
saw you with that boy could think for a moment that you
could do a cruel thing. If anybody says it, it is because they
are evil. . . .'' She thought of Mrs. Soady then, and Mrs.
Soady she knew well to be a kindly woman. She was shaken.
Kindly people often loved to gossip.

But she was determined to hide these thoughts. She would
not believe such ridiculous gossip. Now that she saw how he
needed her, she was determined to marry him soon.

"You say that now," he said, "but if others say these things you might begin to believe them. I could not endure that."

Tenderness swept over her. She saw his weakness. There was that in him which would always look to what was bad in life, would always expect the worst. She must, even in this moment, compare him with Fermor. What should Fermor have done? Of course he would have been able to swim. He would have plunged in and saved the child. He would have had a crowd of spectators to applaud and admire. And if he had been unable to swim? If he had—like Léon—found himself in that dreadful position, he would have felt no need to fear. He would have somehow seen himself more than life-size. But it was the very difference between them which had made her turn to Léon.

She loved Léon, she assured herself; she loved him with a newly found tenderness; and because this terrible thing had happened to him she was going to share it with him.

Gently she talked to him, making plans for their future. She was going to take care of him. Soon they would go away from here—but not too soon. It must not seem as if he were running away. If it were true that people said evil things, he must face that evil; they would face it together.

She knew that she had brought a great comfort to him before she left him and the carriage took her back to Trevenning.

Ten uneasy days followed.

It was known that Melisande was to marry Léon de la Roche. No one said anything derogatory in her presence regarding Léon, but she knew that the gossip was rife.

Mrs. Soady shook her head. She was not pleased with the engagement now. "Murder," she said to Mr. Meaker, "be like shenegrum; and there's nothing like shenegrum to give 'ee a taste for more shenegrum."

Mr. Meaker was grave too. He reckoned that money was often the motive for murder amongst the nobility. The poor had no money to make it worth while. But, said Mr. Meaker, the Mounseer would be rich now and, when a man got rich so quickly through someone's death, you had to look about and into things; and looking about and into things made you start wondering.

No, they did not like the thought of Mamazel's marriage at all. It made an exciting topic of conversation; it was the only topic of conversation. They delighted to talk of it; but they could not say they liked the thought of the marriage.

The whole neighbourhood was talking. A death. A Fortune. A man who couldn't swim. The two of them alone on the jetty . . . the most dangerous spot they could find.

The nods, the grimaces, the furtive glances betrayed their thoughts to Melisande.

And one day the footman came into the servants' hall with an air of great excitement. He whispered to Mr. Meaker, and Mr. Meaker whispered to Mrs. Soady. All that day they whispered of what the footman had seen. The tension grew when Mr. Meaker on the very next day saw what the footman saw; and later others saw it too.

There were conferences round the table. What should be done? "Wait a bit," cautioned Mr. Meaker. So they waited. "But," said Mrs. Soady, "I shall not wait much longer."

Melisande had no idea of these secret matters, there was one thing every person in the servants' hall was agreed upon; the Mamazel was not to be told . . . yet. It was something which would have to be broken to her very gently.

Caroline was kind to Melisande, for she too had heard some of the rumours. This was a terrible thing of which Léon de la Roche was accused. Caroline was happy and she wished to see Melisande settled. She was greatly comforted to know that Melisande was betrothed to Léon. It was so suitable; such a neat ending to what had at one time threatened to be a frightening situation.

Preparations were going on for her journey to London. She would be delighted when they left. In the meantime she wanted to be as kind to Melisande as possible.

"I hope you will be happy," she told Melisande, "as happy as I am."

Melisande could not meet her eyes. She kept thinking of Fermor and Caroline together; and she thought of the note she had found under her door on the wedding night, and the Christmas rose which had come with it.

"We are so delighted about your engagement . . . Fermor and I. You looked strained, Melisande. Not worried by all this talk? My dear, people always talk. They're envious. Monsieur de la Roche will be a very rich man now. I am glad. It is so *comforting* not to have to worry about money."

"He would rather not be rich," said Melisande. "We would rather things were as . . . they were before."

"I am sure you feel like that. I know he was fond of the little boy . . . and you too. But don't worry about the cruel things people say, Melisande."

"You are very kind." Melisande felt the need to explain to someone. She went on hurriedly: "Raoul . . . he was so self-willed. You see, he would say '*I* want to do this!' and he would do it. Léon was too lenient with him. It was a difficult position. Léon did not wish him to go on to the jetty. But you see, Raoul had been so used to having his own way."

"I have heard he was a very self-willed little boy. But, Melisande, don't concern yourself with silly gossip. I would not if I were in your place. Suppose someone trumped up a silly story about Fermor. . . . I would not believe it."

Poor Caroline! thought Melisande. Poor Caroline and poor Léon! How cruel the world was to some people.

She hoped that Caroline would never be wise enough to understand what sort of a man she had married.

"We shall not concern ourselves with gossip," said Melisande. "As you say, it is folly. I shall see that we do not."

And at the end of those ten days Léon told her that he had to go to London on business. He expected to be away for a week or more.

Melisande was glad. It would be good for him to get away. In London no one would know what had happened.

After he had gone it was as though a great burden had been lifted from her shoulders.

Was she glad on her own account as well as on Léon's?

It was three weeks after the wedding—a lovely day, a preview of spring, with the primroses already brightening the hedges; the birds were singing, believing that spring had already come.

The bride and bridegroom had not yet left for London. Their departure had been delayed once or twice. Fermor had seemed in no hurry to go, and Caroline was eager to fall in with his slightest wish.

Melisande went out into the lanes to pick some of the early primroses. Absorbed in her task she did not immediately realize that she was being watched; but, looking up suddenly, she saw that she was near a gap in the hedge where there was a gate leading into a field. Fermor was leaning on the gate.

"Good morning!" he said.

"How long have you been there?" she demanded.

"What a greeting!" he mocked. "What does it matter?"

"I do not like to be watched when I do not know it."

"It was not more than two minutes. Am I forgiven? I saw you come here. You have avoided me constantly so that I have been obliged to creep up on you unawares . . . as if you were a wild colt."

"I must be going," she said quickly.

"So soon?"

"I have much to attend to."

"Really? You cannot visit Monsieur, can you, now that he is away?"

She did not answer.

"So you really are going to marry him?"

She turned and was hurrying away when he leaped over the gate and caught her arm. "Don't do it, Melisande," he said. "Don't do it."

"Don't do what?"

"Marry a murderer."

Flushing scarlet she wrenched her arm away.

"You may hit me if you like," he said. "You think I deserve it, don't you?"

"I am afraid it would give you a great satisfaction to see me lose my temper, and I do not wish to satisfy you in any way."

"That's a pity, for I would do anything in the world to satisfy you. I think of you continually. That is why I risk your displeasure by begging you to have nothing to do with him."

"What do *you* know of *him*?"

"That he is a murderer."

"And I know that you are a liar. Do you think that anything you said would carry any weight with me?"

"You must forget your resentment. I could not marry you, Melisande. It was impossible. Don't be angry with the inevitable. But I must prevent your marrying him. Your life would be unsafe with such a man. I tell you he deliberately killed the boy."

"I do not want to hear any more."

"I knew you were headstrong. I knew that you were foolish. But I didn't know that you were a coward, afraid to face the truth."

"You forget. I clearly showed you that you are a coward."

"I did not accept that estimation of my character."

"Nor do I accept yours of mine. I don't believe anything you say. I don't trust you. You are cynical and brutal and I despise you."

"I would rather have your fiery scorn than the lukewarm pity which is all you have for him. The feelings you have for me are at least stronger. That is the hope I cling to."

"You are a fool as well as a brute then, if you would cling to any hope as far as I am concerned."

"Wait until I tell you what I know. Melisande, you've got to listen. This man was poor and now he will be rich. That's true? You agree?"

"I have no wish to discuss this with you."

"You always run away when you are afraid."

"I am not afraid."

"Then listen to what I have to say, and prove it. I know exactly what happened on the jetty. The wind was howling and it had stopped raining. Everything was set fair for him. He said to the boy, 'Let's go for a walk,' and the boy agreed. They went out. 'Come on to the jetty,' he said, 'it'll be fun watching the waves from there.' The boy agreed. How should he knew he was going to his death? And then, how easy it was. . . . A little push . . . a little wringing of the hands . . . and then running for Jack Pengelly. What chance had the child in a sea like that!"

"You were there, I suppose. You saw it all."

"I was not there, but nevertheless I know what happened.

If the boy fell in, what would be a man's natural reaction? He would at least attempt to rescue him surely.''

"A man who could not swim would be a fool to jump into such a sea. The only sensible thing to do was to run for help, and that is what he did."

"If a man could not swim; that's the point. But, my dear Melisande, Monsieur Léon could swim. He could swim very well."

"It is not true."

"It is true. I have seen him swimming."

"Where?"

"A mile or so along the shore . . . in a very quiet cove."

"I don't believe you."

"I thought you wouldn't."

"So there is nothing more to say."

"Yes, there is. The next day I went to the cove again. It was just before midday. He was there again . . . swimming. This time I took the precaution of having one of the grooms with me. Jim Stannard. I have asked him to say nothing yet. But you can go along and ask him now. You'll hear what he has to say."

She looked at him incredulously, but a terrible fear was with her.

She said: "Of course I don't believe you."

"And Jim Stannard?"

"I have no doubt you have bribed him to do your will."

With that she turned and left him.

She returned to the house and went straight to her room. Peg brought up her luncheon tray. She did not appear to see her, and Peg, ever curious, loitered.

"Is anything wrong, Mamazel?"

Melisande looked at her and did not speak. She had not heard her. She was thinking: Could it be true? But how could I trust him?

Could it be that the whole thing was planned? There was so much money involved. She thought of Léon and his plans for a new life. He could swim—so said Fermor. Then either he was a coward who had been afraid to attempt to save Raoul . . . or he was a deliberate murderer.

Peg was watching her.

"Mamazel, you've had a shock. You'm frightened, Mamazel."

"I'm all right, Peg."

Peg stared at the carpet. Peg was fond of Mamazel. It frightened Peg when she thought of all the gossip that was going on in the servants' quarters. Seeing Mamazel in this state she couldn't keep quiet any longer.

"Mamazel," she said, "don't you marry him! Please, Mamazel, it would be wrong."

Melisande stood up and went over to Peg. She said: "Peg, what do you know? If you know anything, you ought to tell me. You are my friend, Peg. You should not keep me in the dark."

"Mrs. Soady says as you ought to be kept in the dark. It's Mr. Meaker who ain't sure. He says he's going to see Sir Charles. To ask Sir Charles . . ."

"Peg, I have a right to know. Is it anything to do with . . ."

"It's to do with the French gentleman. Oh, Mamazel, you mustn't marry him. That's what everybody's saying . . . because . . . you see, Mamazel . . . we've seen him. I've seen him myself. Bet and me went one morning. Mr. Meaker, he's seen him and so's the footman. He was swimming in the sea in that quiet cove. . . . Mr. Meaker said that he might have had a chance to save the boy . . . and . . . he pretended he couldn't swim. We don't like it, Mamazel. We don't like it."

"So . . . many of you have seen. Why did I not see?"

"Well, they didn't tell you, Mamazel. They couldn't very well. But they'll all tell you now. There he was . . . swimming in the sea. And only a week or so since he said he couldn't. It's queer. It's frightening, Mamazel. Mrs. Soady's well nigh beside herself. She says foreigners b'ain't like we are. They do terrible things."

"Peg, I know you're my friend."

"We all are, Mamazel. We'd like to see you happy like. . . . And it's all fixed you should stay here . . . we hope you won't marry him. Mr. Meaker says nothing can't be proved . . . but he hopes he goes away from here and us never hears no more of him. There'll be a good marriage for 'ee later on. There's as good fish in the sea as ever come out, so Mrs. Soady says. And the master 'ull see you have as good a wedding as Miss Caroline, shouldn't wonder . . . you being his own . . . his daughter . . . same as Miss Caroline, only with a difference like. Mr. Meaker says they don't always make all that difference in the best families. I reckon Sir Charles will do something fine for 'ee. But don't 'ee marry that foreigner . . . after what has happened.''

"Peg! Peg, what are you saying? *I* . . . I am Sir Charles's daughter?''

"Oh, 'tis a secret, I do know, but it must mean the master be fond of 'ee. That's why he have brought you here and set you above the servants like. No governess was ever treated like you have been, Mamazel. So now we do know, we don't mind like . . . being so fond of you.''

This was too much to happen in a short hour. To know that Léon, who had declared he could not swim, could do so and might have saved Raoul's life; and to learn that Sir Charles was, in reality, her father.

She tried not to let Peg see how agitated she had become. She thanked Peg for her kindness in trying to comfort her. Then she turned to her tray and Peg went out.

She did not attempt to eat. She went straight to Sir Charles's study.

She knocked and was thankful to find that he had not yet gone to the dining-room.

He was startled by the way in which she stared at him.

She burst out: "I have just heard an extraordinary thing. Is it true that I am your daughter?''

She watched the colour drain away from his face. "Who told you that?''

"One of the maids.''

He repeated blankly: "One of the maids. Which one?''

"They all know, apparently. It seems that everyone knows . . . except myself.''

"This is absurd.''

"Then it is not true?''

She noticed that he hesitated and great sorrow filled her. She *was* his daughter and he was ashamed to acknowledge her. He was alarmed because his secret had been discovered.

Fermor she knew for a bad man; Léon, of whom she had been fond, was now proved to be a coward or worse; and Sir

Charles, the man to whom she had looked with admiration, was weak and could not acknowledge his own daughter because he feared the damage to his reputation.

The nuns were right. The world of men was an evil one. No wonder they had retired from that world; no wonder they averted their eyes from men.

Now she felt that she too wanted to escape from all men, to shut herself in, to readjust her ideas. They all had feet of clay, every one of them, and she was not sure that Fermor—so blatantly wicked—was any worse than the others.

Sir Charles was recovering from his shock. She saw now that her fallen idol's one idea was to protect his reputation.

He said: "This is absurd and ridiculous. It must go no farther."

"You will have to deny it," she said, and there was a faint smile about her lips. "There is so much that makes a scandal," she went on fiercely, maliciously. "You came to the Convent, you brought me here. You have not treated me entirely as a servant, not entirely as a member of your family. This is a foolishness, a carelessness, and so there is scandal."

He did not see the scorn in her eyes. He was too concerned with his predicament. "To deny it," he said, "would be to admit such a thing could be. No. There is only one solution. You will have to go away from here at once."

"Yes," she said, "I thought that."

He came over to her. The old kindness showed in his face. He was oblivious of the disappointment that was edged with contempt in hers. "Don't worry. I will arrange something. I have friends. I will see that everything is conducted as . . . it should be. I will see that you are well cared for." He smiled, rather cunningly, she feared. He went on: "This engagement of yours . . . and the death of the child . . . I am afraid it is rather unfortunate."

She said: "So you have heard. . . ."

"Mr. Holland has told me, and it has been confirmed by the servants, that Monsieur de la Roche was seen swimming only a short while after the accident, so . . . ."

"I have heard," she said.

"So much scandal. So much gossip . . ." he said. "It is so unfortunate. And you?"

She cried out: "I want to go away. I want to go away from everything . . . everyone. I want to hide myself where no one can find me."

He laid a hand on her shoulder. "I understand. You shall go away from here. I shall not tell . . . him where you are . . . if that is your wish. It is as well for you to go away. You will want to think of so much, and it is always possible to see things clearer when one is a long way from them."

She smiled. "It is convenient . . . these two things together," she said.

He answered her: "I will arrange everything. You need have no fears of the future. I will see that you are well cared for. You may leave everything to me."

"You are very kind," she said, "to one who is . . . not your daughter."

She could bear no more and, turning, she ran out of the room.

She, who wanted to love all the world, despised too many people in it. There were three men whom she had wanted to love: Sir Charles, the rescuer, the man of dignity, the man of honour who trembled for his reputation; Léon who acted a part, gentle Léon, such a contrast to Fermor, sinister Léon who said he could not swim and had allowed a little boy to die when his death would enrich him and bring him all his desires—that dignity of which he had talked with passion, that security, that plantation in New Orleans; and Fermor, who had no sense of honour, who had nothing but his own violent appetites, who would stoop to any meanness, any unkindness to satisfy his carnal desires.

Yes, she wished to get away, to shut herself in with herself, to understand more, to leave this world where men looked like heroes and, beneath their shining armour, were cowards or brutes.

She lay on her bed for a long while. Caroline came to comfort her—Caroline her sister. Poor Caroline, who was as defenceless as herself in this wicked world of men.

PART THREE

Fenella's Salon

One

When Fenella Cardingly received the letter from her old friend Charles Trevenning she lay back in bed gently fanning herself with it and smiling as she did so.

Polly Kendrick, her personal maid and constant adorer, came and sat on the edge of the bed and looked at her expectantly, like a spaniel hoping for a walk or a titbit. Polly's treats were the pieces of gossip Fenella threw to her from time to time. Polly was goodhearted and grateful, but Fenella knew that not even her private affairs were held sacred by Polly. Polly must know everything; she gave faithful service in exchange for her share in her mistress's confidences.

Fenella, mischievous by nature, liked to keep Polly in suspense, so she continued to look round the ostentatiously luxurious bedroom, still smiling, still fanning herself with the letter.

The bed was a large one; Fenella herself was large and she liked her possessions to be in proportion. It was a modern bed; Fenella was modern. The back piece was inlaid with mother of pearl designs. In these could be seen nymphs—large nymphs of the same proportions as Fenella's own—and gods who bore a striking resemblance to some of the famous figures of the day; no shepherds these, but fine handsome gentlemen of dignity and poise. The sheets were of silk—pale blues or pale mauves; the quilt was of the same blue and mauve decorated with gold thread. The bed itself was set upon a dais and the steps which led up to this were carpeted in blue; there were heavy blue curtains which could be drawn, shutting off the steps and dais from the rest of the room. The walls about that alcove in which the bed was placed were covered with tapestry in which nymphs and gods, similar to

217

those on the bed-back, were depicted. Once there had been
mirrors where the tapestries now hung, but Fenella had had
these taken away some years ago. She had told Polly—to
whom she told most things—that when gentlemen came into
the sanctum she could delude them into believing that they
resembled the figures on the bed-back. They took on greater
stature, she had declared, new virility; but the mirrors had
lately proved a deterrent and the tapestries were so much
more effective. "You go on," said Polly at that, for her devoted affection made up for her lack of respect, "it's your
own figure that's made you take the mirrors away, Madam
dear." Fenella had laughed and not denied it. She *was* growing old; but there was still much in life to delight her; her
life was as rich and colourful as her establishment.

In the bedroom there were many vases and statues—all
presents from admirers—and every object was of high value.
The painted ceiling was decorated with nymphs and gods
similar to those already in evidence.

To Polly—child of the slums of St. Giles's—the house of
Fenella Cardingly was an exotic palace over which Madam
reigned as supreme Caliph; but Polly was the Grand Vizier
of especial powers; and Fenella's life was not more full of
pleasure and excitement than was Polly's.

Polly was small—no more than four feet eleven inches in
height; she was so thin that she resembled a child, except
that her face betrayed her age; her features were small and
wizened, but her close-set darting eyes were so bright that
they gave her a look of intelligence while they betrayed her
overwhelming inquisitiveness. Beside Fenella, five feet nine
inches, with her large bust and hips, dark hair—which Polly
declared grew darker every year—large round brown eyes,
jewelled and clad in colourful garments of fantastic design,
Polly was an excellent foil. Polly Kendrick and Fenella Cardingly lived in their magnificent world, and neither of them
could imagine what life would be like without the other.

Fenella's carriage had run over Polly one day; this had
happened at the time when Fenella had been disastrously
married, and before she had reigned in her own right in the
social world she had made her own. In those days Fenella
had been the wife of Ralph Cardingly, and it was not until

he died that she had found her own personality and had created this world of excitement, extravagance and impudence
of which she was the undisputed queen.

To the poor waif of the slums whose daily lot had been
starvation and bestiality, Fenella had become goddess-
mistress; and to Fenella the loyalty of this poor little woman
had become very precious indeed. From the beginning they
had played an important part in each other's lives. Polly had
been saved from a life of misery; Fenella had been goaded
to greater daring in order to shine more brightly in the eyes
of her slave.

And what excitement Polly glimpsed through the love affairs of their young ladies! They were hers, she considered,
as much as Fenella's. All lived fantastically in Fenella's temple, for Fenella had, with Polly's help, created a fantastic
world about them.

Fenella grew rich. She sold lotions for the beautifying of
women, and concoctions to restore virility to men. Any
member of either sex could trust Fenella. They could come
to her temple unseen and leave it, as she said, new men and
women. That she had a dressmaking establishment in the
upper rooms of her large house was well known. Her young
ladies—the six goddesses of grace, as she called them—wore
the clothes designed in her workrooms when they mingled
with her guests. They were all different types and she was
constantly replacing them, for so many of her goddesses left
her after a brief stay. Her temple was but a resting place, she
was fond of saying.

She rarely went out nowadays, but when she did and she
by chance saw a lovely girl in a shop, or even in the street,
she would offer to take her in and train her. It was a great
opportunity for those girls. To meet Fenella was to meet
fortune. These girls who, had they not met Fenella, would
have had little but poverty to look forward to, invariably
found a protector when they were in Fenella's care and, if
they were wise—and Fenella brought up her girls to be wise—
they would learn how to protect themselves in readiness
for that occasion when the protector no longer protected.
There were other young ladies whose fathers paid considerable sums of money that Fenella might teach them poise,

grace, and how to charm; and when these young ladies passed out of Fenella's charm school, which they would do by way of the entertainments she gave, they would invariably find the sort of husbands their parents wished for them.

It was typical of Fenella that she entwined the respectable with the not so respectable. She could be a duenna for young ladies of fortune whose parents had not the entry into society; and she could be procuress as regards her poorer beauties. She had her open dress salon and also her discreet trade in those commodities which people wished to buy in secret. In one of the rooms of this establishment was her Bed of Fertility. It cost a great deal of money to occupy the Bed of Fertility for one night. The room in which it was placed was very similar to that in which Fenella sat reading the letter. There were dais and rich curtains; and the tapestry which lined the walls depicted the progress of lovers through many stages. There were beautiful statues and pictures—all of lovers. Some, it was said, would pay the price of a night in that chamber merely to see the pictures. But, said Fenella, the bed was for the married who wished for children and had been disappointed in that respect. To sleep in it meant that almost certainly a child would be conceived. The motive behind Fenella's letting the apartment was a righteous one.

That was how it was in their domain over which she presided. Respectability by itself was dull; eroticism was revolting. But what a combination Fenella had to offer! Eroticism paraded side by side with respectability!

Now, watching her, Polly knew from Fenella's smile that something was about to happen. She waited patiently.

"Well," said Fenella, "why do you sit there?"

"Madam dear has had some news?"

"You will know soon enough."

"Oh . . . so it's a new arrival."

"Who said so?"

"Madam dear, you can't diddle Polly."

"You're an inquisitive old woman."

"Two years younger than yourself, Madam dear. So I wouldn't talk about old women if I was you."

"That's where you're wrong. You were born old; I was born to be eternally young."

"Don't you believe it, Madam dear. You look every bit of forty-five."

"Go away, you insect."

"First tell me what's in the letter?" begged Polly.

"Just to get rid of you then. Pour me some coffee."

"Cream, Madam dear? You're getting fatter, you know."

"I like my fat and I like my cream. Well, Polly, you shall know. We're to have a new young lady."

"Madam dear! When?"

"Soon, I think."

"And who is she?"

"A dear little bastard."

"Ah, one of *them*."

"You remember the Cornishman?"

"Yes, I remember him."

"We owe him a duty, Polly. He came here one day hoping to stay the night. I was in love with someone then—I forget who, but that is not the point . . . except that he went away—the Cornishman, I mean—and became involved with a little seamstress. There was a child . . . this child."

Polly made delighted clicking noises with her tongue.

"So we're responsible, eh?"

"He is sending her here. Melisande St. Martin. He reminds me that I helped to christen her."

"It's a pretty name."

"She might have been Millie but for me. Heaven knows *what* she might have been but for me."

"She would never have been born but for you . . . according to you."

"I had her sent to a French convent. She is an educated young lady now."

"What are you going to do . . . find a nice husband for her?"

"We'll do our best, Polly. That's why he is sending her to us. She's to come here to learn dressmaking. If she's pretty we'll soon get her married. If she is not . . . well then she can work in the sewing-rooms."

"That'll be seven of them. You never had seven before. I don't like sevens. We lived in number seven . . . in Seven Dials. There was seventeen people in three attics and seven

of 'em died of fever. My mother died having her seventh
baby. . . ."

"Don't be so superstitious, Polly."

"Why, you're as superstitious as any!"

"Never. There's a reason for everything. Always remember that."

Polly jerked her thumb upwards. "What about the bed
then? What reason is there between them sheets, eh?"

"People go to the Bed of Fertility believing they will succeed. That's half the battle, Polly. Believe in getting something, and you're half way to having it. That's what I've done.
Go and tell the girls they're to have a new little friend. But
first bring me pen and paper and I will write to my dear friend
at once, telling him that we are expecting his little Melisande."

Melisande was travelling first-class in the train which carried
her across the country eastwards away from Cornwall. She
felt bruised and bewildered, and there was growing within
her a resentment against those people who had seemed to
take her life in their hands and send her whither they wished.
Was she to have no say in her own way of living?

A thought had come to her that when she reached London
she might run away, that she might not look for those people
who would be meeting her there; she might tear up the paper
with the address on it which she carried in her pocket; and
she might never let any of them interfere with her again.

Had she been of a different nature she would have gone
back to the Convent. She believed that was what Sir Charles
had hoped she would do. How pleasant that would have been
for him! He could have washed his hands of her—such a neat
ending that would have been! She would not give him that
satisfaction. Moreover how could she live as the nuns and
the Mother Superior did? They had taken a brief look at life
and had found it as disturbing and disillusioning as she had;
they had decided to devote their lives to the service of God.
But she was of a different nature. Life in the quiet Convent
was even less attractive to her—she had to admit—than living
on the defensive against wicked men.

"But one learns," she said to herself. "One learns to understand these wicked men. One learns how to fight them. Had I been wiser I should have been duped neither by Fermor nor by Léon. Had I been wiser I should have understood why Sir Charles came to the Convent and took me away. I should have known, when he did not acknowledge me as his daughter, that he loved his position and his reputation more than his own child. If I had known these things there would have been no shock, no disillusion.''

The strange fact which had emerged from her unhappy experience was that Fermor, the self-confessed villain, was no more to be despised than the others. These are the men, she decided, the creatures who made convents necessary, for if men were like saints there would be no need for holy women to shut themselves away.

Fermor was a wicked man, a would-be seducer; but she remembered that he had said he would rather be a bad man with a streak of goodness in him than a good man with a streak of badness. Perhaps Fermor's type appealed to her more than the hypocrites, and that was why she still thought of him with regret. Now she would admit that the happiest time at Trevenning had been when she was with him. If there was badness in him, there was also badness in her, for while she had enjoyed his company had she not known that he was betrothed to Caroline?

How right he had been when he had told her that time passed for her as it did for the lovely rose. Time had passed. She would never see him again; and she would admit, now that she was far removed from temptation, that she, not being good like the nuns, wanted to live in that gay world he could have shown her, to share with him that excitement which he had promised.

She could scarcely think clearly even now of the days between her discovery and her departure.

She had been bewildered, and when she was bewildered she was usually hasty. She would not have believed Léon guilty but for her knowledge of men which had come to her through Fermor and Sir Charles. Fermor had always laughed at her simplicity. And had she not seen Sir Charles, squirming when confronted with the truth, losing all nobility in that undignified fight to protect his reputation?

If she herself had done wrong she would hate to admit it perhaps; she would certainly seek to justify herself. But to deny one's own child! She would never be guilty of that.

And Léon? She could not shut out the memory of his talking with such fire of what he longed to do. And the boy had stood between him and those desires. She could not believe that he had planned to murder Raoul. She believed that he had succumbed to temptation in a weak moment. She could picture it all so clearly; the raging winds, the storm, and the little boy—the spoilt little boy who would insist on going where *he* wanted to—running along the jetty and being blown over. To plunge in and try to save him would have been to risk Léon's own life; to leave him to drown was to realize all those dreams. So much money was involved. She could not forget his tortured face, his ready belief that people were talking of him . . . surely before he could have known they were. *Qui s'excuse s'accuse,* the nuns used to say; he had excused and accused himself.

A week after the accident he had been seen swimming, by several people on several occasions in a quiet spot.

She was glad that he had gone away and that she had not been compelled to see him again. The note she had written to him was short and to the point.

DEAR LÉON,—I know now that you can swim. It seems that several people have seen you swimming. I realize that I have been very foolish. I did not understand you. I do now. The temptation was too great for you. You will understand why I do not think we should see each other again.

MELISANDE.

She had explained everything to Caroline; and she had asked both her and Sir Charles in no circumstances to tell Léon where she was.

She knew then that she was afraid of seeing Léon, afraid that he would somehow appeal to her pity and—as so many people seemed to do—arrange her future for her. There was one thing which was very clear to her. She must escape from Léon. She wanted to escape from Léon more than anything.

Now she must make a clean break with the past.

She thought then how strange her life was. She had lived close to the nuns, knowing them intimately; each day was like another; and then suddenly she had been whisked away to an entirely new life. Now she must go to another new life, a completely fresh set of people. The various sections of other people's lives must surely overlap.

Only yesterday she had said goodbye to Mrs. Soady, Mr. Meaker and the other servants, to Caroline, Fermor and Sir Charles. They had all appeared sad to see her go; and she had a feeling that they were sure—as she was—that they would never meet again.

Sir Charles had called her to his study soon after that sad encounter when she had told him of the servants' gossip. He had been stern, remote, almost as though he disliked her. He told her of the arrangements he had made for her; she was to go to the house of a dressmaker and learn the trade. It would be very useful to her, and Madam Cardingly was a clever woman who would look after her and teach her many things besides.

She asked no questions. She showed no interest. She was wishing she could run away.

He had tried to give her money before her departure and she had haughtily refused it. Now she realized that that had been foolish. She should have taken it—surely he owed her that!—and launched out on her own.

He did prevail upon her to accept a little. "You may need it during the journey, you know."

"I have a little money which I have saved while I have been here."

He had smiled pleadingly. "Do please take this. I should be so glad if you would. . . ."

And she had softened and accepted.

The train had crept into the station and here she was in London.

She alighted and looked about her. A porter came to her assistance because she had stepped out of a first-class carriage. She saw the notice: "Porters are not allowed to carry for third-class passengers." She shivered. Here was a further reminder of the position of the poor.

"I am being met here," she told the porter.

He touched his cap and, as she was about to pass on, a little woman came hurrying towards her. She resembled a witch, thought Melisande, with her small wizened face and her darting eyes.

"Now you're Miss St. Martin, I'll bet," said the little woman, grinning at her; and her face was transformed into a friendly one by that eager grin.

"Yes."

"Then you're my pigeon. I'm Polly Kendrick come to meet you."

"Polly Kendrick! I have not heard of you."

"No, you're expecting Madam Cardingly. Madam don't go out much. I've come in her place."

"It is a goodness."

"Ah, you're foreign. Madam was telling me. An educated young lady from France. And pretty too. Screaming cats! You're going to make the young ladies look after their beaux!"

"The young ladies!"

"We've got lots of 'em. Here, don't want to stand about, do we? I've got Madam's carriage waiting for us. Here, you," she said to a porter, "bring the lady's baggage. Now, come on. All the way from Cornwall, eh? And travelling alone? Hope no one tried to kidnap you. That would be a lark . . . before you got to Madam's, wouldn't it?"

Melisande was smiling; there was something about this woman to make her smile. The eager interest had made Melisande feel that she was wanted.

They got into the carriage and the driver whipped up the horse.

Polly Kendrick did not stop talking. "Now I can see you proper. My word, you're a beauty, you are! Madam's going to like that. Madam's got a weakness for the pretty ones." Polly nudged her. "So have I. Madam says she likes 'em because they're a reflection of her own youth; they're what she was once. *I* like them—she says—because they're what I never was. There's Madam for you. Full of that sort of talk. Clever, Madam is. The cleverest I ever struck. None like her. Never was. Never will be. Madam will look after you.

Madam 'ull see you're all right. Madam's going to love having you with us . . . it's them others as is going to get their pretty noses put out of joint. It makes me laugh. Miss Genevra with her baby blue eyes; Miss Lucie with her curves. . . . They're going to meet a rival. But that's life for you. Can't have it all your own way, can you? Now, *what* is your first name?"

"Melisande."

"It's pretty. . . . Madam christened you. You can trust Madam to find the right name."

"Madam christened me?"

"Oh yes, Madam christened you all right." Polly nudged and bent closer. "This is a secret. Your father came to see Madam, and she had another lover, so he went out and met your mother. She was a little dressmaker and your father met her at Vauxhall where she was being pestered. Well, your father fell in love with her and they had a little love nest. Result: little you."

"I . . . I see."

"Didn't you know? Screaming cats and fighting dogs! My tongue runs away with me. Never mind. Keep it dark I told. But I think, don't you, dearie, it's best to know. I've had a good life and it's all on account of keeping my eyes and ears open. Madam says that's all very well, but it's opening my mouth, as well as me ears and eyes, that'll get me into trouble. There's Madam for you."

"And Madam christened me?"

"Why yes, because when you was born and your poor dear mother died, your poor dear father didn't know which way to turn. So Madam named you Melisande and had you sent to a convent in France. There's Madam for you!"

"So Madam has been a sort of foster-mother . . ."

"Madam's foster-mother to the world. God bless her. But what am I going to call you, dearie? I know, Melly. That's pretty, ain't it? Little French Melly. Why, dearie, your eyes are green . . . real green. None of our young ladies has real green eyes. You'll be the first."

"Please tell me of these people. I have no idea where I'm going. It is a bewilderment. I know that I am to go to Madam

Cardingly to learn the dressmaking—though I do not think I
shall be very good at the work.''

"You . . . dressmaking! With them eyes!''

"With these hands, I thought.''

"Oh! I'll tell Madam that. Madam will like that. She likes
the sharp retort. The gentlemen like them too . . . as long
as they're not too sharp like. They're as good as other things
. . . some other things . . .'' Polly went off into laughter
again. "No, I expect Madam will want a pretty girl like you
to show off the dresses. That's what her goddesses do. Of
course, she wasn't sure what you'd be like. If you'd been like
me . . .'' The thought sent Polly off into more laughter.
"Well then, you'd have had to work with your hands all right.
But being like you are . . . your face is all you'll need.''

"I do not understand this.''

"Well, seeing we're nearly there, there won't be time to
tell you. Madam's waiting to see you. She won't thank me
for keeping you from her. She said to take you straight to her
when we came in. You're to drink tea with her. Madam's
very fashionable. She drinks tea in the afternoons as well as
after dinner.''

The carriage had drawn up in a quiet Georgian square. As
they alighted Melisande looked up at a tall house with six
steps leading to the wide porch, on either side of which were
pillars decorated with intricate carvings. There were balconies on the first and second floors and on these balconies
were flower-boxes at this time full of evergreen plants.

The door was opened by a man in livery.

"One of our new young ladies, Bonson,'' said Polly with
a wink.

Bonson bowed and gave Melisande a warm smile.

"Come on, dearie,'' said Polly, "Madam don't like to be
kept waiting.''

On the hall floor was a red carpet which swept up the wide
staircase. At the turn of the staircase was a tall window with
a window seat facing the next flight. Here there was a statue
of a beautiful woman with long curly hair hanging over her
shoulders.

"A gentleman said it reminded him of Madam,'' said

Polly. "That's why she keeps it there. He gave it her, of course."

"It's lovely. Is she as lovely as that?"

"In her time, dearie; none like her. Time passes. That's a sad thought for you beauties. When I think of time passing I can't help laughing. Time can't take much from me. What you never have you never miss, so they say. But you miss it all right; what you can't do is lose it."

They had left the great hall with the hanging candelabra, the mirrors and the fine pieces of furniture, and had mounted the stairs.

"Madam's a one for mirrors," whispered Polly. "Though not so much now as one time. Here we are."

She flung open a door.

"Madam," she cried. "She's here. Our seventh and the loveliest of the lot."

Melisande was aware of splendour, of more thick carpets, of heavy furniture, of statues and huge ornaments, of heavy velvet curtains. There was a perfume in the air; there was a great mirror on one side of the room which made it appear larger than it was. Between the velvet curtains she caught a glimpse of the balcony and beyond it, the green of the square.

Fenella Cardingly was stretched on a *chaise longue*, her large body covered by a blue silk wrap; this robe was open at the throat to show the beginning of a magnificent bust; a jewelled ornament of diamonds and sapphires held the cloth together. The black hair was elaborately dressed and there was a flashing ornament on it. She held out a white hand, sparkling with gems, and said: "Welcome, my dear child! Welcome, little Melisande!"

Polly was pushing Melisande forward as though she were some treasure she had discovered and was eager to show.

"There," said Polly, "do you like her?"

"She's charming," said Fenella. "Kneel down dear, so that I can see you better."

Melisande felt as though she were kneeling to the Queen. Fenella took her face in her hands and kissed her forehead.

"I hope you'll be happy, my dear."

"You are very kind," said Melisande.

"That's what we intend to be. And it's going to be a pleasure to have you. Polly, go and tell them to bring us some tea. I want to talk to Melisande for a little while.''

Polly grimaced and hesitated. ''Get along, you insect!'' said Fenella.

Polly went out reluctantly.

''I expect she chattered during the ride from the station. Here, my dear, bring a chair and sit close to me so that we can have a chat.''

Melisande obeyed.

''Are you surprised to find us as we are?''

''It is a great surprise. I thought it was to be a dressmaker's shop.''

Fenella laughed. ''So that's what he told you, eh? A dressmaker's shop.''

''No, he did not tell me that. He said that I was to be with a dressmaker. I pictured the shop.''

''Dresses are made in places other than shops, my dear. We call them *salons*. Why, you *are* pretty! You'll pay for dressing. You're going to do very well here.''

''Thank you, Mrs. Cardingly.''

''I am called Madam Fenella, dear. It is more suitable than Mrs. Cardingly. It is usually Madam for short. You look unhappy! Are you? Charles told me there had been a sad love affair in Cornwall.''

Fenella waited. Then Melisande said: ''I would rather not speak of it . . . if you do not mind.''

''Of course you don't want to speak of it. That'll be later. Don't fret about that now. What did your father tell you about us?''

''My father? You mean Sir Charles? He did not admit that he was my father.''

Fenella laughed. ''That was like him. He was always afraid of criticism. There's reason in it. If you are as bold as I am, you ignore other people's opinions. If not, you bow to them.''

''You know that he is my father then?''

''That is precisely the reason why he has sent you to me. He wants me to look after you.''

''And you . . . ?''

''My dear, I said I would do anything in my power for

Charles, but now I have seen you I would add . . . and for you. You are of great interest to me.''

"I think I know why."

"Polly?"

"She talked to me."

"Trust Polly! I often threaten that one day I'll have her set on in a dark alley and have her tongue cut out. Don't look shocked, dear. I wouldn't do it really. But her tongue is an embarrassment to her as well as to me. Here we live in our own special little world. It is a happy world, and we are a happy family in it. We're a large family. You will soon meet my other girls. I have my little seamstresses and my goddesses. You'll be one of the goddesses. We mustn't strain those lovely eyes or prick those pretty fingers. Men don't like pricked fingers, dear, though it shows industry. But industry is not what most men are looking for—except of course the industrialists, and we don't receive many of that sort here.''

"But if it is dresses I am to show, is it not the ladies who will see them?"

"There'll be ladies *and* gentlemen to look, dear; and the ladies always like dresses that the gentlemen look at longest—though, of course it is not really the dresses the men are looking at. That is something ladies never seem to understand. You'll do well here, I know.''

"Please tell me what my duties are?"

"Chiefly to show the dresses. You shall help in the workroom too . . . but that is only if you have an aptitude.''

"But shall I be of use . . . if I am not good with the needle?''

"Sewing is a poorly paid trade, my dear. Showing dresses needs more skill.''

"I am afraid I am not skilled at all.''

"Stand up, my dear. Now walk across the room. That's right. Head erect. Genevra will teach you how to walk. You have natural grace and that is a good thing. There'll be a few tricks to learn.''

"You mean, Madam, that I may earn my living by walking about!''

Fenella nodded.

"But that seems to me an easy way of earning the living.''

"My dear child, often what appears to be the easiest way of earning a living brings in the biggest spoils. Look at me. I spend a good deal of time on this couch, but I earn a living. The best way to gain a living in this world is to let others earn it for you. That is what clever people do. That is what you may learn to do. Who knows!" Fenella laughed and stopped to say: "Here comes the tea."

It was wheeled in by Bonson.

"Will *you* pour, dear?" said Fenella. "Then we can be *quite* alone. Cream for me, please."

Melisande's hands were not too steady as she poured and passed the cup to Fenella.

Fenella was watching intently. What grace! What beauty! she thought. And even the dress is charming.

Fenella found young girls enchanting. Planning their future was like planning her own. They made her feel young again. And here was a charming girl, quite the most beautiful of all her beautiful girls, and what an interesting history! The daughter of a rather staid old Cornish gentleman, and the result of brief folly in his youth. It was romantic and amusing—two qualities which appealed to Fenella.

"You are bewildered," she said. "It is all so strange . . . and so different from what you expected. Never mind. That's a matter for rejoicing. Did you expect me to be a terrible old woman who would make you sew thousands of stitches every day and stand over you with a stick if you should fail?"

"I was afraid. You see, I am not good at the sewing. Although I make very good flowers. I made this one on my dress."

"It's effective. That helps the dress. I can see you will be useful in our workrooms too. You are going to be very useful. You will be happy here, I know. I knew it as soon as I saw you. You remind me of what I was at your age. I was bigger, of course; and our colouring is different; but there is something about you. . . . I want you to settle in . . . cosily. One of the girls will show you round. We entertain often, and now that I have met you I know that you will grace our evening parties. In the showroom you shall try on our dresses and we shall see what suits you. We shall dress you and you shall mingle with our guests. The result will be that many women will want to buy the gown that you are wearing. Worn by you these gowns will look so beautiful that they will not believe the beauty comes from you; they will think it is mainly due to the gown.''

"It sounds as though this will not be real work.''

"You'll see. You will find our *ménage* a little different from Trevenning, I don't doubt. If there is anything you don't understand, you must come to me. You will share a room with three other girls. I am sorry you can't have a room to yourself. This is a big house but we are a big family. Genevra, Lucie and Clotilde will be your room companions . . . for the time being. Lucie will soon be going. She is to marry. Sooner or later they all marry. I can't keep my girls. Do you know anything about politics?''

"No . . . or very little.''

"Then you must learn more. You must learn about art, poetry and music. There is much conversation in my salon, and it is better for a girl to be intelligent *and* beautiful. She does better for herself. Genevra is a very beautiful girl, but she knows very little, and she will not or cannot learn . . . what I would have her learn; yet she has a natural cunning which she uses instead. She can look after herself.''

"Do they know that I am . . . the unaccepted daughter of Sir Charles Trevenning?''

"They do not know his name, dear. It is wiser not to tell. You can never be sure into whose ears the information will fall. They'll know you're illegitimate. Clotilde is the illegitimate daughter of a lady of high rank. Her mother asked me to take her . . . much as your father did. Lucie is another . . . although not so highly placed and the daughter of a gentleman and a village girl. She is to marry with her father's consent. We are delighted with Lucie. My girls find what they want in my establishment, and that is what I want.''

"You are very kind, I can see.''

"Oh, I have been fortunate. I like to share my good fortune. I teach my girls to be self-reliant. When I was a girl of your age I was married. I had a fortune and what I thought was a fine future. My husband was unfaithful to me and, worse still, he spent all my money.''

"I cannot think why any women wish to marry.''

"Most wish it, my dear; some because they are fools; others because they are wise. The fools long for a man to protect them; the wise long for a man whom they can govern. Petticoat government, my dear, is what I like to teach my girls; how to rule the world of men. The essence of the power which we wield is our secrecy. The only way to subdue masculine egoism is never to offend masculine vanity by letting it be known that you are in control. It is a simple method when dealing with simpletons. Half the world is made up of rulers; the other half, of slaves. You must decide to which half you are going to belong."

"This is all very strange to me. I have never heard anyone talk like this before."

"You have lived with nuns."

"And they hate men. They shut themselves away from them."

"I don't hate men; I like them. I understand them. In fact I'm very fond of them. But I never let my fondness blind me to their weakness. Consider us and consider them. We let them think we are vain. We are the ones who are continually peeping into mirrors, who are concerned about gowns and ornaments. Poor souls! They call that vanity when they feel they themselves are so perfect that they need little adornment. But you will learn. When you have finished tea I am going to ring for one of the girls to show you your room. They will help you to dress and, unless you feel too tired—or would rather not—you may come to the salon this evening. What clothes have you? Have you a suitable gown for evening wear?"

"I have one for special occasions. My . . . Sir Charles bought it for me when we were in Paris."

"Is it as becoming as that one?"

"It is beautiful, but I have had few occasions to wear it."

"Let Genevra see it and she will tell you if it is suitable for the salon. If it is, and you wish to let them bring you down, you may come. But if you would prefer to stay in your room and rest after your journey, please do so. It will be necessary for you to be discreet in the salon. We will say that you are convent-bred, which is true, of course; you have come from the country because your family feel that you should not stay there where there are so few opportunities of meeting people. What do you know of literature?''

''I have read *Pilgrim's Progress* and some of Jane Austen's novels while I was in the Convent. When I was in Cornwall I read *Sartor Resartus* and *The Last Days of Pompeii*.''

Fenella grimaced. ''No Byron?''

''No . . . no Byron.''

''You must be very quiet to-night . . . if you come down. After all, you are French. You can pretend you don't understand if conversation gets beyond you. Genevra uses her impudence as a defence against her ignorance. At first you can pretend not to understand the language. To-morrow I shall set you a course of reading. I can see you are intelligent and will quickly learn. You should be able to discuss the works of Tennyson, Peacock, Macaulay, and this new man Dickens. As to politics we're predominantly Whig sympathizers here. Negro emancipation, Income Tax and the Chartists are matters of which, I suppose, you know very little?''

''Very little indeed, I'm afraid.''

''Well, at the moment you will become delightfully French if these subjects turn up. I doubt whether many will feel equal to conducting a conversation in French on such subjects. I feel very strongly about the working conditions of women and children in the mines and factories. We have some old Tories who argue fiercely about that. You ask what your duties will be. You must keep up to date with current affairs. My young ladies must not only be beautiful; they must be entertaining. Now, my dear, I can see that I am bewildering you. I am going to ring for one of the girls to show you your room. She will show you the house and tell you all you need to know. Go and pull the bell-rope, will you?''

Melisande obeyed, and the summons was answered by a maid who was asked by Fenella to find either Miss Clotilde, Miss Lucie or Miss Genevra, and send her along.

In a short time there was a knock on the door and there entered one of the most beautiful girls Melisande had ever seen.

She was fair-haired and her eyes were a startling blue; she had a small piquant face and a slightly tiptilted nose; while she was slender there was a hint of the voluptuous in her figure; and there was about her an air of suppressed amusement.

"Ah!" said Fenella. "Genevra!"

"Yes, Madam?" The accent was unexpected; in it was the unmistakable tang of the London streets.

"Genevra, here is Melisande St. Martin who is going to be with us. I want you to look after her . . . show her round . . . see that she is comfortable."

"Why yes, Madam." She smiled at Melisande.

"Take her along now, Genevra."

Melisande followed Genevra.

Polly came in as soon as Melisande had left.

Fenella smiled ironically. "Well?"

"Talk about a little beauty!" said Polly. "I bet she reminded you of what you were . . . like all the charmers do."

"No insolence now!"

"What are your plans for her?"

"He wants me to find the right sort of husband for her—a lawyer would be his choice."

"He don't look all that high, does he?" said Polly sarcastically.

"Don't forget he's a countryman. He's got a keen sense of the fitness of things. She's a girl of obscure birth, and therefore she's suitable only for a professional gentleman—a barrister say. There'll be a nice dowry for her—a great attraction."

"And a nice picking for us, Madam dear?"

"We'll be paid for her board and lodging while she is here, and we'll be given a useful sum when we have delivered the husband."

"It beats me how you do it," said Polly admiringly. "No one but you could. Look at you! Nobody could call you a prude, Madam dear; and yet country gentlemen with nice ideas put their daughters into your charge. Young ladies from convents mix with harlots . . . for that Kate and Mary Jane are no less . . ."

"Now, Polly, this is where you show your mediocrity. Moderation is always desirable. Put girls in a nunnery and you'll find some of them run away—and amok. Think—but

how can you know of such things? But take it from me that
in the nunneries there are women dreaming of lovers—and
in the past there were orgies, positive orgies—simply because of repression. And in the brothels harlots sigh for the
singing of anthems and the absolution of sins. No, no Polly,
life is made up of too many ingredients to present a simple
concoction. To savour it we must be wise . . . we must relish
all flavours. Look at me. I have had my lovers . . ."

"I'll say you have!" said Polly admiringly.

"I have had my lovers, and because I know men of all
kinds in all their moods, I am more suited to look after the
daughters of gentlemen than a Mother Superior who knows
nothing of the world. We should temper austerity with voluptuousness, virtue with broadmindedness."

"Now, Madam dear, I am not one of your circle with
advanced views. I'm not a gentleman buying a powder to
make the ladies love me, nor a lady wanting lotions to knock
years off my age. I'm not a sterile old couple wanting a night
in your magic bed."

"Be silent, you ugly old woman. What do you know of
such things? How could you be a gentleman in search of
virility! And let me tell you no amount of lotions would be
of any use to you; and what would be the good of knocking
years off your age! You were as repulsive at fourteen as you
are at forty. As for a night in my magic bed—who in their
right senses would want to perpetuate you?"

Polly sat down on the *chaise longue*, her eyes shining with
affection and adoration.

Fenella smiled back at her.

They were completely delighted with the fascinating world
which they had created. They were content with each other.

Melisande had been at the house in the square for a week. It
was the most extraordinary week of her life; it was just what
she needed to help her to forget her experiences in Cornwall.
Nothing could have been more different from Trevenning
than the house of Fenella Cardingly. It seemed that Fenella
had said: "Such and such a thing is normal; therefore my
house will do the opposite." That made an exciting if bewildering *ménage*.

The room Melisande shared with the three girls was a large and airy one overlooking the square. It was on the third floor of the tall house; there were two other floors above it, as well as the attics where the servants had their sleeping quarters. In the room were four narrow beds with coloured sheets and counterpanes—greens and mauves. A long mirror was fixed on the wall, and there were others on the dressing tables. The chairs and commode were eighteenth century and elegant; the rugs of mauve and green. The room always smelt of mingling perfumes used by the young ladies who inhabited it.

These young ladies accepted Melisande as one of them. Their numbers, they said, were always being depleted and made up again. Few girls stayed with Madam long. They married or went away for other reasons. The girls laughed when they said 'other reasons.' They were continually laughing at something which was said.

Exciting and amusing things happened to these girls; indeed everything that happened to them seemed to be amusing and exciting. Melisande had never known there were such people. They had no modesty, it seemed. They would walk about the room wearing nothing but a pair of shoes and a necklace, admiring themselves in the long mirror or listening to the comments of the others.

In the Convent when one of them had taken a bath, Melisande remembered, they had been warned not to look at themselves. God and the saints were watching, they had been led to understand; and any sly peep would have been recorded against them. But these girls were frankly curious about themselves and others; and when Melisande told them of the Convent attitude to nudity they were amused and laughed heartily.

"Well," said Genevra, who never minced her words and was not quite a lady, "if old Sir Francis didn't like to look at me, he'd be the first man who didn't."

"*Saint* Francis," corrected Lucie, who, as the daughter of a well-born man and a village girl, chose to remember the paternal parent rather than the other.

Genevra retorted: "Saints or Sirs, you can't trust any of

them. I reckon those old nuns weren't worth looking at any way."

After those bewildering evenings, when Melisande mingled with Fenella's guests wearing dresses which had been selected for her, the girls would lie in their beds talking of the evening. They talked with a frankness which at first amazed Melisande. They were frank about themselves. Melisande learned that Genevra had known terrible poverty in her early days. Genevra made no secret of her beginnings. Her mother, as a girl, had worked in a factory from the early hours of the morning until late at night; she had been shaken out of her sleep of exhaustion to start work again, beaten as she was dragged along to the factory, for she was ready to fall asleep on her feet; she had stood at her work through long hours, brutally treated by the overseer who had given her two children—Genevra and Genevra's young brother.

One morning, in the attic which had been their home, Genevra had awakened to find her mother still in bed; she had shaken her and been unable to awaken her when she had realized with cold surprise that she was dead. Genevra could not feel sorrow. Her mother had ill-treated her. The overseer, who sometimes visited the attic had begun to notice the extraordinary beauty of Genevra. Genevra had no great horror of incest—nor even any knowledge of it as such—but she was terrified of the overseer. She was conscious of the sudden change of manner in a man from whom hitherto she had received nothing but blows.

She knew that her brother had been sold, when he was three, to a master of chimney sweeps. One thing Genevra would never forget as long as she lived was the piteous crying of her brother as he was taken away. She had seen him once afterwards—that was a year later—deformed, grimed with soot, and burned on his arms and legs. That was her brother— her little brother who to her he had seemed so pretty when he was a year old and she was three.

"Something happened to me," said Genevra. "Don't ask me what. I only knew that whatever happened to me, I wasn't going to work in a factory."

But Genevra took her tragedy lightly. Her life was a gay one. Others suffered in this terrible world, yes; but not Genevra; and if Genevra did better than others it was not due to luck, it was due to Genevra and her own unbounded energy and superior powers.

She talked more than the others.

"When we were in the attic a lady used to come sometimes. She'd bring us soup and bread. We used to have to say after her:

'Though I am but poor and mean
I will move the rich to love me
If I'm modest neat and clean
And submit when they reprove me.'

"I never forgot that. I made up my mind I'd make the rich love me. There's a bit of sense in it, but like most things they tell you, you have to make it suit yourself."

"You moved the rich to love you!" said Clotilde, and they laughed again.

"I'm clean, I'm sure," said Genevra. "Could you call me neat?"

"No," said Lucie. "Gaudy."

"And modest?"

"He whom we're thinking of wouldn't look for modesty. Do you submit when he reproves you?"

"But he reproves me for not submitting."

The 'rich' to whom they referred was a noble lord with a vast estate in the country. He had taken one look at Genevra and had found her enchanting; he had pursued her ever since. Genevra kept the little company informed of the progress of her love affair.

Before she met Fenella her name had been Jenny; but there were too many Jennys, said Fenella; and she christened her Genevra. Jenny had picked Fenella's pocket one day when Fenella had paid a visit to a mercer's shop. There had been Jenny near the entrance of the shop—a very hungry Jenny, pausing to look at the beautiful lady descending from her carriage and wondering whether there was a handkerchief she could quickly steal and take along to a man in the rookeries who would pay for such things. Jenny had been caught, but Fenella had intervened and had her brought to stand before her while she sat in the shop. Jenny, never at a loss for words, had poured the whole story into what her quick wits told her would be a sympathetic ear. Fenella heard of the overseer and his unwholesome advances, the brother crippled by his employers, and Jenny's present hunger.

Fenella had said they were to let her go and that she might present herself at the house in the square. Jenny had done this, had received a bath and delightful clothes to wear. Fenella had then changed her name to Genevra, and to Fenella Genevra gave her love and loyalty. To Fenella she owed all, including her friendship with the noble lord. She had persuaded the rich, in the forms of Fenella and the lord, to love her; and in the first place it had been due to being neither modest, neat nor clean, nor even submitting when reproved, for she had stood glowering at Fenella in the shop, until she realized that Fenella's intentions were kindly.

Lucie's story was different. She had been brought up quietly in the country with a governess. She had been two months with Fenella, and here she had been introduced to an earnest young man who would marry her.

Clotilde's story was different again. Clotilde was the daughter of a lady of high rank and her footman. She had been brought into the lady's house and had spent part of her childhood there. Clotilde was lighthearted; she lacked Lucie's desire to stress her high-born streak, and Genevra's pressing need to set poverty behind her for ever. Clotilde fell in and out of love with speed; there was no restraint in Clotilde. Had she not been partly of noble birth, and had not regular sums of money been paid to Fenella by her mother, she would have joined Daisy, Kate and Mary Jane in their apartment from which only Genevra's special attractions and strength of character had saved her.

The segregation of those three was not complete. At certain times they all mingled freely, but the girls understood that they had come to Fenella in different ways. Daisy, Kate and Mary Jane adored Fenella. She had saved them, as Genevra said, from what was nearer a fate worse than death than some things she had heard so described. She had saved them from drudgery and starvation, from the appalling misery of the days of famine which made up those hungry forties. She had found them—one in a shop, one in a sewing-room, and another in the streets—poor thin scraps of female life; yet in them Fenella had seen that beauty which delighted her. So she had brought them into her house. She fed them; she gave them a little education; and they showed off her dresses. Fenella could not guarantee their marriage; marriage was not for such girls unless they were exceptional. Occasionally they entertained and were entertained by gentlemen, and that was very pleasant for the girls and the gentlemen. Fenella received benefits from such encounters, as did the parties concerned. It was an amicable arrangement and considered by them all far better than the starvation and drudgery which the factories and workshops had to offer. Fenella's girls grew plump and happy. Said Fenella: "Better to sell their virtue than their health. Better to sell what they have to sell to a lover than to an industrialist. They eat, sleep and live comfortably in my house, which is more than they could do by working in a factory."

Genevra belonged to their category, but Genevra had shown herself possessed of especial gifts. Genevra had the attention of a noble lord, and Fenella was amused and delighted to see how a cockney girl of only that little education which she had been able to give her, could score in the battle between the sexes.

For Melisande the days in Fenella's house had been pleasant, the evenings somewhat alarming.

Each day they would rise late after one of the maids had brought them cups of chocolate. They would lie in bed talking of the previous night's entertainment with their usual frankness. Afterwards they would read books which Fenella had chosen for them. Sometimes luncheon would be taken with Fenella, who would talk politics and literature or discuss the previous night's gathering. In the afternoon they would take the air in the Park, riding there in Fenella's carriage or walking about on the gravel paths with Polly as their chaperone. There they often met gentlemen who had attended Fenella's social evenings. When they returned they would go to the dress salon and the dress they should wear that night would be selected for them. Then they would retire to their rooms and be helped to dress by two French maids—

servants of Fenella's—who were immediately attracted by Melisande, gave her the best of their attention and delighted to talk French with her.

Melisande was recovering from the shocks she had received during those last days in Cornwall. Her natural high spirits had risen to the surface; she was adaptable and, just as she had quickly become the companion of Caroline, she was fast becoming the charming, vivacious and intelligent young woman Fenella intended she should be.

The nuns would have raised their hands in horror. Melisande herself wondered whether she was like a chameleon which took its colour from its background. Here she was, delighting in clothes, laughing with the girls, enjoying recounting her conquests as they did.

For, of course, they would not let her remain silent. They wheedled certain information from her although she had determined that these things should remain her secret. She had never been discreet at any time. Yet she did not tell them that Sir Charles was her father. She felt compelled to respect his desire for secrecy. But she told of Léon and of Fermor; and she felt that these girls, with what seemed to her their vast knowledge of the world, might help her to understand these two men.

"You must have had a lover," they insisted one morning as they lay in bed sipping their chocolate.

"I thought I was going to be married," she told them. "That was only a little while ago."

Genevra put down her cup of chocolate. "And you didn't tell us! What stopped it? Was he a duke or something?"

Lucie said: "Did his people stop it?"

But Clotilde merely waited patiently to hear.

Melisande then told the story of her meeting with Léon, his desire for freedom, the sudden death of little Raoul and the fortune Léon had consequently inherited.

Lucie cried: "A fortune? And you gave that up! You're not very clever, Melisande."

Genevra said: "You should have waited, Melly. You should have heard what he had to say."

Clotilde, her eyes looking—as they invariably did—as though she were brooding on intimacy with one of her lovers, said: "If you had really loved him, you wouldn't have gone away without seeing him. There was someone else, wasn't there?''

Melisande was silent; but they all began to chant: "Was there? Was there?''

"I don't know."

"But you must know," insisted Clotilde. "Though," she added, "it might be that you only know *now*.''

And then Melisande told them of Fermor, of the wickedness of him and the charm of him, of the proposition he had made while he was betrothed to Caroline, of the Christmas rose he had slipped under her door with the note written on his wedding night.

"He is a rogue," said Lucie. "You were wise to have nothing to do with him.''

"Was he really as handsome as you say?" asked Genevra.

Clotilde answered for Melisande. "Not quite. She saw him with the eyes of love. It makes a difference.''

"Tell me," said Melisande, "what should I have done?''

"Waited to ask Léon for his explanation, of course," said Lucie.

"Married him and gone to the plantation in—wherever it was," said Genevra.

"You should not have run away from the one you loved," murmured Clotilde.

And after that they began to talk of Fermor and Léon as they talked of their own lovers.

"But it won't be long," promised Genevra, "before you have others to choose from.''

The salon in which Fenella entertained her guests was brilliant that night. The girls—as they so often did—were to join the company after dinner. There they would mingle with the guests, wearing the most spectacular dresses of Fenella's designers. Fenella's beautiful girls ranked with the food and wine as one of the attractions of her evenings.

There was nothing to warn Melisande that this evening was to be any different from others. It was true that she was wearing a wonderful dress—the most beautiful and daring she had yet worn. It had been chosen for her on account of its colour which was emerald green; it was of silk-faille with a pointed bodice, and even her small waist had to be more tightly laced than usual that she might fit it; the skirt was composed of masses of very fine black net through which ran a gold pattern, and this net covered the emerald green silk-faille; the bodice was very low-cut and her back, down to her waist, was bare apart from the flimsiest covering of black and gold net. The dress had been cut to accentuate every curve of the feminine form.

Genevra wore a similar dress in blue which matched her eyes. Lucie was demure in grey and Clotilde seductive in red. Daisy, Kate and Mary Jane would come down later if required.

As they went into the salon most of the guests turned to look at them. Fenella watched them from her throne-like chair. She could not make up her mind which dress she preferred—the green or the blue. It was strange that the green seemed simpler than the blue; or was it that each dress took something from the character of its wearer? Genevra was a girl in a thousand, pondered Fenella. It was just possible that she might marry her lord. But was she clever enough for that? It was a pity that Melisande had to be married to a barrister or someone of that stratum. She must select him soon and let him begin his courtship. Melisande must not know that it was arranged. There was a tilt to her chin which suggested that she might refuse to enter into such a relationship. No, the girl was simple and charming; she was a little bruised at the moment, and that would necessitate a careful approach. Genevra could safely look after herself. The slums of London produced hardier plants than did convents.

A young man was coming towards her. She did not recognize him; and she was certain that he had received no invitation from her to attend. Such intruders hardly ever annoyed her (although sometimes she feigned irritation, for boldness was a characteristic which she greatly admired), especially when they were as good-looking as this young man.

He was well over six feet in height. And what arrogance! What haughtiness! Yet there was a twinkle in the blue eyes. It was an impudent face but the arrogance was offset by the humour she saw in it. She warmed at once to the young man.

She held out her hand to him; he took it and put it to his lips. "Your humble servant!" he said.

She raised her strongly marked eyebrows. "I have not the pleasure, sir, I am very much afraid."

"You do not know me? But I know you. Who could be of London and fail to know its priestess of fashion and beauty?"

"Have done!" she said lightly. "And tell me on whose invitation you came here."

He put on an air of mock penitence. "Am I then unmasked so soon?"

"What have you to say for yourself?"

"What can the uninvited guest say except that he so longed for paradise that he determined to dash through any flaming swords that might attempt to keep him out."

"I can see," she said, "that you are a young man who knows how to make out a good case for himself. What is your name?"

"Holland," he said. "Is it too presumptuous for a man to visit his father's friends? My father has been a frequent visitor to your wonderful house."

"Bruce Holland," she said with a smile.

He bowed. "I am his son . . . his only surviving son, Fermor Holland, at your service."

Fenella was beginning to enjoy herself. There was nothing she liked better than audacity, and she thought she was understanding why he was here, and longed to know if her surmise was correct. Her eyes went to a charming figure in a green dress.

"Fermor Holland," she repeated slowly. "Now I believe you recently became a husband."

He bowed to acknowledge that this was so.

"Have you brought your wife with you to-night?"

"Alas, she was unable to accompany me."

"Her good manners doubtless prevented her, since she was not invited."

"Doubtless," he agreed.

"Let me see . . . she was the daughter of Sir Charles Trevenning . . . another of my friends, a dear Cornish squire."

''We are flattered that you are so interested in us, Ma'am.''

''Ma'am!'' she exclaimed. ''That is for the Queen.''

''You are a Queen,'' he said. ''All-powerful, all-beautiful, Queen Fenella!''

''What a flatterer you are! You are not going to tell me that you came here to see me!''

''But I am.''

''And whom else?''

''Whom else could the eyes perceive when they are dazzled by such surpassing beauty?''

''So you wish to renew your acquaintance with Mademoiselle St. Martin?''

He opened his eyes wide but he was speechless.

''I don't blame you,'' she went on. ''She is charming. But she is not for you, my dear young man. You may stay this evening, but you must not come here again until I have consulted with your father-in-law. Now, go along, and remember . . . I did not invite you here. You are here because you have committed the unpardonable sin of the uninvited guest. I do not see you. And you may not stay long. I believe I should forbid you to speak to Mademoiselle St. Martin. But I know that would be useless.''

''Then I have your permission to seek her?''

Fenella turned her head away. ''I'll be no party to this. You are not here at my invitation. You are a graceless young man. I can see that. Your father was the same. And it is solely on his account that I am not having you turned out. Now, go along and remember . . . you must not stay long.''

He bowed over her hand.

She watched him go, her eyes sparkling.

She thought: A charming young man! Amusing . . . exciting. There are not many like him nowadays . . . for men are not what they used to be.

He was standing before Melisande, and she was thankful that she was not alone. She was with a young man who had partnered her during the evening, as well as with Genevra and her lord and Lucie and her barrister.

''You look as if you've seen a ghost, Mademoiselle St. Martin,'' said Fermor.

"I . . . I had not expected to see you here," stammered Melisande. "I had no idea you knew Madam Cardingly."

"My father is an old friend of hers."

"Introductions needed," said Genevra in a whisper which could be heard by all.

Melisande tried to steady her emotions. She was excited, joyful and afraid. She knew in that moment why she had not seen Léon and asked for his explanation. It was because she was in love with Fermor.

She made the introductions. Genevra's eyes shone; Lucie lowered her lids over hers.

"I feel as though I know you well," said Genevra. "Melly has talked of you."

"I am doubly enchanted," he said. "It is so gratifying to be talked of."

"But how do you know *what* we have heard of you?" demanded Genevra.

"It must have been pleasant since you are so delighted to see me."

"It might be curiosity to see if you are as black as you've been painted. Teddy," she said to her lord, "you should prepare to be jealous. I like this Mr. Holland."

Lucie and the barrister, Francis Grey, greeted him politely, and he was warm and friendly towards them as he was to Genevra and Teddy, but he showed a definite coolness towards Melisande's partner.

Melisande said: "And Caroline . . . is she here?"

"She could not come."

"What a pity! Perhaps next time?"

"Who knows?"

He could not take his eyes from her. She seemed quite different from the Melisande he had known in Cornwall. She looked older than seventeen; in Cornwall she had looked younger than her age. He believed she would be more vulnerable in this atmosphere of sensuous luxury.

They made a charming group—the three young girls in their gay dresses, the four young men in their evening dress of the latest fashion. Fenella, watching them, saw the tension between Melisande and Fermor and shrugged her shoulders, thinking: Ah well, I shall soon find her an eligible husband.

Melisande's present partner was a pleasant enough young man, but his position was hardly secure. He was a Peelite in the government, and Peel was going to fall over the Corn Laws. Fenella must not delay. The serpent—such a handsome, charming serpent—had entered Eden.

The young Peelite was talking earnest politics now. "Of course Sir Robert was right. Of course he'll come back. I know that his action has split the Party but . . ."

"How charming you look," Fermor whispered to Melisande. "What luck . . . finding you here!"

"Did Madam Cardingly invite you? She must have known . . ."

"No, she did not invite me. I discovered where you were and, as soon as I made the discovery, that was where I had to be. I did not wait to be invited. I came, I saw Madam Fenella, and do you know, I believe my charm has conquered her. Or perhaps it is my obvious devotion. Who was it said, 'All the world loves a lover'? Shakespeare, I believe. He usually knew what he was talking about. Well, here I am."

She ignored him and answered the man who had been her escort before Fermor had arrived. "I don't think he can come back. The Tories will never allow that."

"A man such as Sir Robert can do the seemingly impossible."

"Where there's a will, there's a way,

So they say . . . so they say . . ." sang Genevra.

"You combine wisdom with charm," said Fermor, eyeing Genevra with an appreciation which set Teddy's moustache bristling.

"Perhaps," said Genevra, "it is better to be born wise than beautiful. Beauty needs such wise handling if it is to flourish."

"It flourishes in the richest soil," said Teddy, "just as flowers do."

"You see how wise Teddy is!" said Genevra.

The politician was growing peevish. Melisande said: "How will you be affected when Lord Russell takes over?"

"Sir Robert will soon be back in his old position," insisted the young man.

"Mademoiselle St. Martin," said Fermor, "may I take you in to supper?"

"It is not yet supper time."

"Then may I have a few words with you . . . alone? I bring important news. It is the sole reason for my being here."

She lifted her eyes to his face and he smiled boldly.

Genevra said: "Come along. We will disperse. Important news should not be allowed to wait. Come along, everyone. We will join you later when the important news has been imparted. I hope it's good news; is it?"

"I think so," said Fermor. "And I thank you for your tact which is almost as great as your wisdom and beauty."

Genevra made a mock curtsey and slipped her arm through that of Teddy who was clearly glad to be moving away from the arrogant man with the startlingly blue eyes. Lucie and Francis went with them; and the earnest politician had no help for it but to do likewise.

"Very clever, was it not?" said Fermor when they were alone.

"It is what I would have expected of you."

"I am glad you have such a high opinion of my cleverness."

"I suppose there is no news?"

"Why should you suppose that?"

"Because I have also learned to have a high sense of your duplicity."

"You have learned to speak English more fluently."

"I have learned a lot of things."

"I can see it. Soon your wisdom will equal that of the charming Genevra. Your beauty and charm already excel hers."

"Please . . . I am not young any more."

"Have you grown so old?"

"One grows old by experience . . . not by years."

"You've hardened."

"That is good. Do you not think so? I am like a fish who has grown a shell; I am like a hedgehog with his prickles."

"I never saw anyone less like a shellfish or a hedgehog."

"It is a metaphor . . . or is it a simile?"

"I can think of more attractive ones to fit you."

"Please, what is it that you have to tell me?"

"That I love you."

"You said you had important news."

"What could be more important than that?"

"To you? Your marriage perhaps."

He flicked his fingers impatiently. "Is there somewhere where we can talk in private?"

"There is nowhere."

"What about the conservatory?"

"It is not for us."

"Why not?"

"You must understand I work here. I show dresses. This dress I wear does not belong to me. I wear it so that it shall be admired and ladies of wealth wish for one like it. I do not entertain my friends in the conservatory."

"Not if they are exalted guests of your employer?"

"I have no instructions regarding you."

"Why are you here?" he asked.

"To work . . . to earn my living, of course."

"Work! You call this work. What are all these girls? Don't you know? Do you think I don't know?"

"We show dresses. Some work in the showrooms."

He laughed. "I thought you had grown up."

"Sir Charles sent me here," she said.

"Indeed! That you might follow in your mother's footsteps?"

She flushed hotly and turned away. He caught her arm.

"You must forgive me," he said. "Remember you love me for my frankness . . . among other things."

"*I* love *you!*"

"Of course. I'm not a saint. I explained that. I don't offer you marriage; nor do I murder little boys for their fortunes."

"Be silent!" she said in a low voice. "And go away. Don't come here again to torment me."

"Not to torment, but to please you . . . to make you happy. Do you really not know what this place is?"

She looked at him in silence.

"What innocence!" he exclaimed. "Is it real or is it feigned?"

"I do not understand what you are talking about. What do you mean . . . about this place?"

"It is not a convent where holy nuns congregate, is it? How do the girls spend their time? On their knees asking for grace? Their methods are not those of nuns. You must know that. Oh, I am coarse and crude . . . but I know you will forgive me."

"You upset everything. I was happy here. I believe I could have been happy at Trevenning . . . but for you."

"You might have married your murderer. Would you have been happy, do you think? Like a sheep in a field . . . shut in . . . knowing no other world but that bounded by four hedges? And then he might have decided to murder *you* . . . having acquired the taste for murder. But you were not in love with him. If you were, why did you not wait for his return? Why did you not give him a chance to explain? Shall I tell you? It is because you do not love him. It is because you know there is only one man for you, and I am that man."

"What a pity there is not only one woman for you—and that woman your wife!"

"That would make life so simple, wouldn't it? But can we expect it to be so simple as that?"

"I believe Caroline does."

"Yes, you have grown up. You get angrier. You have a temper, Melisande, my pretty one. Guard it. Tempers are dangerous things. Do you remember when you leaped from your horse and snatched the branch from the boy who was torturing the madwoman? That was temper . . . righteous anger. You nearly had the mob on you then. But you didn't stop to consider. Or perhaps you knew that I was there to protect you. What would have happened if I had not been there to snatch you from the mob? I'll always be there, Melisande, when you need me. With a fiery temper like yours, that blazes into fury, you need a protector. Once more I offer myself."

"The offer is not accepted. It is supper time now. Goodbye."

"I am taking you in to supper."

"I am not here as a guest, you know."

"You should not be here at all. You should let me rescue you from the indignity of your position."

"To place me in a position of greater indignity! I see no indignity in my present position."

"That is because you are so innocent."

"I don't think Madam Cardingly knows what sort of man you are, or she would not allow you to come here."

"It is precisely because she knows the sort of man I am that she welcomes me here. Come, let us go in to supper."

At the supper table buffet they were joined by others, and Melisande was glad of this. The conversation was general. It ranged from politics—always a favourite topic at Fenella's gatherings—to literature. Melisande had quickly learned to be discreet and, if she could not profitably add to the interest of the discussion, she would keep silent. Fenella often said that it was better for a girl to be quiet than foolish.

One of the ladies of the party now admired Melisande's dress and wondered how it would look in claret colour. It was Melisande's duty to discuss the claret-coloured dress the lady might wish to be made for her, to suggest slight alterations to suit a more mature figure than her own. Melisande was a success at her job and nothing delighted her more than to give advice which resulted in a sale. Then she could feel justified in her comfortable existence in this strange household.

The conversation was turned to the Poor. Everybody talked about the Poor nowadays. It was as though they had just discovered the Poor; although Fenella had been aware of them for so long, she had only recently managed to make them a subject of general interest. There were always, in every gathering, those who would cry: "But Christ said, 'The Poor ye have always with you' and that means there must always be poor. Why all this fuss about something which is natural and inevitable?" There were others who quoted *The Song of the Shirt* and *Oliver Twist*. These were now discussing *The Cry of the Children* and the new novel *Coningsby* by that Jew who was, it was said, about to lead the Tory protectionists.

Some of the more frivolous were discussing Fanny Kemble's latest performance; but Melisande remained quiet, not this time because she could not have joined in, but because of Fermor's presence.

He lifted his glass of champagne and drank to their future.

"I do not see what future you and I could have together unless . . ." she began.

"Unless you come to your senses?" he finished for her. "My dear, you will. I promise you."

"Unless," she went on, "you reform your ways. Then perhaps I may meet you with Caroline."

"Reform . . . reform!" he sang out. "It is all reform. Everybody would reform everything these days. Are they not content with their Corn Laws? Must they start on human beings?"

She said quietly: "You don't think about other people at all, do you? You are the utter egoist. You see only a small world with Fermor Holland in the centre of it."

"Don't be deceived. We are all in the centre of our small worlds—even your learned friends here with their chitter-chatter of art and literature, of politics and reform. 'Listen to *me*!' they are saying. 'Hear what *I* have to say!' I say that too, and because my song is a different one, that does not prove me to be any more self-centred than the next man."

"I wish you had not come here."

"Be honest. You are delighted that I have come."

She was silent for a while, and because he was smiling she said: "It is startling to see someone reappear from a life which one had thought left behind for ever."

"You always knew I'd come for you, didn't you? It'll always be like that, Melisande. I shall always be with you."

The champagne had made her eyes sparkle. She had drunk more than she was accustomed to. Was she a little tipsy? That was an unpardonable sin in Fenella's eyes. "Drink is a goodly thing," was one of her maxims. "One must drink to be sociable. One must acquire the art of drinking, which is to drink just enough. To drink too little is unfriendly; to drink too much is gross."

As a result of her heightened emotions Melisande was seeing everything with a new clarity. What was she doing here? What sort of place was this to which her father had sent her? Was it merely, as he said, to learn dressmaking? It was certainly not to learn dressmaking. It was to wear beautiful clothes, to attract admiration. Why? She caught sight of Daisy now. Daisy was wearing a pink dress, very décolleté, in which she looked like a full-blown rose. She was making an appointment with a thick-set man. In a little while they would slip away and Daisy would not be seen until next day. "Do you know what sort of place this is?" Fermor had asked.

Why did Fenella keep girls here? What was it all about? Was it the sort of place to which a conscientious father would send his daughter? Was Fenella Cardingly the kind benefactress she had made Melisande believe she was? What were those places called, where girls like Daisy, Kate and Mary Jane lived and worked? What was the label attached to the women who looked after such places, who arranged such meetings? Was this a high-class brothel? Was Madam Fenella a procuress? What was the ultimate purpose of sending a girl here?

But it was this man who had put evil thoughts into her head. Fenella *was* good and kind. This was a happy place. Did she believe that, because she wished to believe it, because if she believed otherwise she would not know how to act?

Nothing could make her alter her opinion of Fenella's kindness. She had come here, bruised and wounded, and Fenella's strange house had comforted her as she had not believed it was possible to be comforted.

Fermor took her glass from her and set it down. She stood up.

"Let us go back to the salon," he said.

He took her arm and gripped it fast. She found as they moved away, that she was glad of the support. They were alone in the corridor.

He said: "It is impossible to talk in that room with so many people about us. Can we not be together alone . . . for five minutes?"

"Do you know," she said, and her voice sounded vague and not her own, "why I have been sent here?"

He nodded. "And I want you to leave here. It is not good for you to be here, in this kind of place."

"I do not understand you."

"Is it possible that you don't know?"

He had opened a door and looked inside. Finding Fenella's small sitting-room unoccupied, he drew her in. He shut the door and put his arms about her.

"I can't leave you here," he said passionately.

"If there is anything that is wrong in this place, you have brought it. Until now . . ."

"Did I bring the prostitutes, the Bed of Fertility? What is going on in this house now . . . at this moment? What mysteries should we discover if we were to look, I wonder?"

"But you said that Madam Cardingly is a friend of your father's . . . and she is also a friend of Sir Charles."

"My father is of his generation. I'm fond of him. I'm also like him. He would come here but he would not expect my mother or my sisters to do so. Sir Charles has sent you here to acquire a husband, I'll swear. Fenella's is the only market for bastards."

She twisted free. "Good night," she said.

He laughed, and caught her. "Having at last found this solitude, do you think I will lose it? The home I would offer you is respectability itself compared with this place."

"I do not believe you."

"Let us stop quarrelling. Let us enjoy these few moments alone. Oh, Melisande, if I had known how strong was this passion I have for you, I would not have married Caroline."

She retorted angrily: "You say that, now that your marriage has taken place. It is safe to say it now."

"I mean it. I have thought of you constantly. And, you see, you can't hide your feelings from me. We were meant for each other. Don't let us deny it."

"But I will deny it . . . I will." Her voice shook. To her horror she found that she was crying.

He lifted her and carried her to a sofa. There he sat, holding her in his arms. Now he was gentle, tender; she wished he would not be so, for in such a mood he was irresistible.

They were silent for a while. All her denials, she knew, were of no use. She had betrayed herself. She sensed his triumph. She could only sit still with his arms about her, drying her eyes with his handkerchief.

"It might have been quite different," she said, "if you really mean that you love me enough to marry me."

"I do mean it," he said. "But what's done is done. Let us build with what is left to us."

"And Caroline?"

"Caroline need never know."

She stood up suddenly. "I must go," she said. "I shall be missed."

"What does it matter?"

"I am employed here to show this dress."

"From this moment no one employs you. My love, you are free."

"I feel that I shall never be free."

"We must settle this. Come away with me . . . to-night. To-morrow I will find a house. There we shall be together . . . and nothing shall part us."

"You do not understand. I am saying goodbye."

His eyes glinted. "You change quickly. A moment ago you led me to believe . . . ."

"You led yourself to believe."

She ran out of the room. It was not easy to slip back into the salon unseen. Genevra and Lucie had noticed her entry. Genevra came to her and kept close to her for the rest of the evening. Genevra, the child of St. Giles's, felt protective towards the girl from the Convent.

Fenella drank a cup of chocolate before she slept. Polly brought it and sat on her bed watching her drink it.

"You're worried, Madam dear," she said.

"Rubbish!" said Fenella.

"Is it that couple in the Bed? They'll never get children. A hundred beds such as ours would be no use to them." Polly giggled. "Fifty guineas a night! One of these days someone will ask for his money back."

"It rarely fails, Polly. You know that very well."

"It will to-night. And what if one of these reformers gets busy on *you*, ducky? What if they start talking about fraud?"

"Don't be silly, you insect. As if I can't look after all reformers."

"Well, we have been in trouble at times, you know."

"And got out of it. Now, Polly, three of the best men of law in this country are my very close friends. Politicians are my friends. Everybody who has any power is my friend. They would not wish any scandal to upset our little world of delights, would they? If there were a scandal about our Bed, they wouldn't be able to come here, would they? So there will be no scandal. It is not that which worries me."

"Oh, so there *is* something worrying you?"

"I'd tell you if I could trust you to keep your mouth shut."

"Don't worry. I'll find out for myself. Is it our little French Melly? I thought there was something strange about her after the party was over. She'd been crying too, and Genevra was looking after her as though she was Mary and the other her little lamb."

"A young man came here to-night. He's upset her. He mustn't come here again. He's up to no good."

"What about letting one of the others look after him? Kate's latest hasn't been after her quite so much lately. Every week his longing for our Katey grows weaker. Poor Katey, she's going to need a consolation prize."

"I wish it were possible. He's charming, but I don't think he'll be satisfied with anyone other than the girl on whom he's set his heart."

Polly grimaced. "And has Melly set her heart on him?"

"Our Melisande is a good girl, Polly Kendrick; and she knows his wife. Otherwise . . . I'm not sure. But I've got to be sure. Polly, we've got a job to do. Her father sent her to me to be married, and I've never yet failed anyone who entrusted his child to me. We've delayed too long over that girl. I'm fond of her. I wanted to keep her with us for a bit. But she's got to be married . . . soon. Then this blue-eyed cavalier won't be my affair. I'm afraid of him—he's so charming. Polly, he's formidable!"

They continued to discuss Melisande and the night's uninvited guest. They laughed and talked about the couple in the Bed of Fertility; they went over the chances of Genevra's marrying her lord; and they ended up by mentioning certain young men who would be eager to marry Melisande, for the adequate dowry her father would provide, together with her undoubted charms, would make her an excellent match.

* * *

Melisande saw Fermor frequently after that night. He presented himself at the house three or four times a week, and, although Fenella told Polly, every night after such occasions, that she would command him to discontinue his visits, she never did so. She found handsome young men charming, and handsome young men in pursuit of beautiful young women irresistible.

"When we have Lucie married," she told Polly, "our next marriage shall be Melisande's."

"Always providing," put in Polly, "that little French Melly don't elope with her lover beforehand. Even you, Madam dear, might find it hard to marry her off if she was to do that."

"Nonsense!" said Fenella to that, but she was uneasy. She added: "I must do something about the child at once."

She comforted herself that it would be useless to ask Fermor to stay away, for he would find other means of seeing the girl.

She sent for Lucie.

Lucie was a good girl who had never given any trouble. Why was it that Lucie was the one of whom Fenella was the least fond? She could rely on Lucie; if all girls were like Lucie there would be little to worry about. She was now calmly going into a marriage of convenience, sensibly realizing that, after the ceremony, she would enjoy a status hitherto denied her, wisely not looking too high—as that absurd and adorable Genevra was doing—but taking the sensible way to security.

Dear Lucie! thought Fenella hypocritically.

"Lucie, my dear," she said. "I want to have a little talk with you. It is about Melisande."

"Yes, Madam?"

"She is very like you, I always think. Her position is similar, and it would give me great pleasure if you took her under your wing. I should like to see her as happily settled as you will be. I want you to make a special friend of her, talk to her about your coming wedding. Polly shall take you both to look over your new house. You see, Lucie my dear, girls like

Genevra and Clotilde could so easily put wrong ideas into the head of an impressionable girl.''

''I will do all you say, Madam.''

''Andrew Beddoes is a friend of your future husband's, I believe.''

''They know each other because they are in the same profession.''

''It would be rather pleasant if the friendship were cultivated. You and your charming Francis, Melisande and Andrew.''

''Why yes, of course.''

''I should like it all to come about naturally . . . romantically.''

Lucie smiled. She was grateful to Fenella. Some might cavil at the darker side of the activities which went on in this house, but it was an establishment like no other, Fenella was a woman like no other. She helped girls who found themselves in unfortunate positions; naturally her methods must vary according to the girls. When she was securely married, Lucie would wish to sever all connection with Fenella Cardingly's establishment; until that happy day, she was ready to obey Madam Fenella.

''I shall do my best,'' said Lucie. ''Melisande is quite unlike the other girls. Being convent bred she is very innocent. Marriage with Mr. Beddoes would be good for her.''

When she had gone, Fenella said aloud: ''*Dear* Lucie!''

Her conscience was salved. There was no need to worry about that charming young man. Let him come to the house as his father had. Melisande's future was about to be happily settled.

Polly, the chaperone, escorted the two girls out of the house. She knew that he would be waiting. He was always popping up, she told Madam. Madam only laughed when she was told. He was so charming, she said.

Lucie was saying to Melisande: ''I am so glad you are coming with me. The others . . . they're not serious. And at times like this it is pleasant to have a friend.''

''It is good of you to let me come,'' said Melisande. ''I hope you will be happy, Lucie. Oh, I do hope that.''

"Why not? I shall have everything I want. Mr. Grey will rise in his profession. I shall see to that." Lucie's face under the large bonnet was serene. Prim, Genevra called it. Not prim, thought Melisande, but contented. Melisande sighed. Lucie would never act in such a way as to bring disaster to herself.

"Come along, my dears," said Polly. "It's a sharp step to our Lucie's new home, and Madam won't expect us to be too long away. My goodness gracious me, who's this?"

He came forward bowing. "Three ladies . . . out alone! You must allow me to be your escort."

Lucie was shocked; she looked at him coldly. "We are well chaperoned, thank you, Mr. Holland."

"I'm here to look after the young ladies," said Polly. "I'm as good as any gentleman."

"Better!" he said, giving her one of his winning smiles. "I know it; you know it; the young ladies know it. But does the rest of the world know it? My dear Polly, your size belies your valiant heart, and I shall take it upon myself as a duty to accompany you."

Polly clicked her tongue and shook her head. Fermor took Lucie's hand and kissed it. Lucie softened. After all, she thought, what harm can come of it in the street?

He then took Melisande's hand and kissed it. He kept it in his and said: "A guardian apiece. What could be better than that?"

Lucie could only walk beside Polly.

Melisande said to him as the other two stepped ahead: "You are not wanted. You know that. Have you no pride?"

"On the contrary, my pride swells to enormous proportions when I consider how much I am wanted. Polly dotes on me; so do you. As for the prim little Lucie, I have such belief in my powers that I think I can melt even her stony heart."

"I wish you would not come to the house so often."

"You would be hurt if I did not."

"I should be happier if you did not."

"But you think often of me, you must admit."

"I often think of Caroline. Is she very unhappy?"

"She is well and happy, thank you."

"Unaware of your conduct?"

"She can have nothing to complain of so far. Melisande, let us have done with this bantering. Let us be ourselves, say what is in our minds. I am in love with you . . . you with me."

"No!"

"I said, let us tell the truth. Promise me to answer one question truthfully. Will you, or are you afraid to do so?"

"I am not afraid to answer truthfully."

"If I were free to marry you and asked you, would you marry me?"

She hesitated and he said: "You promised the truth."

"I am trying to tell the truth. I think I should, but I should be very uneasy."

He laughed contentedly. "That is all I wanted to know. The uneasiness would not worry me. We should not be too easy in our minds, should we? We should be anxious . . . anxious to preserve that which is so precious to us both. Melisande, for once let us not quarrel. Let us pretend that this is *our* home which we are going to see . . . our marriage which is about to take place. Can you imagine that?"

"Perhaps," she admitted.

Here in the street it was possible to throw caution away. The pleasure of such contemplation surprised her. Here, with him beside her, it was so easy to believe in.

He had slipped his arm through hers. It did not matter. Polly was going on ahead with Lucie. Besides, Polly would only have said: "The daring young man!" and she would have said it indulgently. Like her mistress she had a fondness for daring young men.

He looked down at her; she looked up at him; longing and love was in their eyes. They said nothing. It was wonderful to have such moments as these, thought Melisande; to step right out of the world of reality into the world of imagination. There was no Caroline in this world; Fermor was himself, yet becomingly different. They were two lovers on their way to visit their new home.

He sang softly so that only she could hear, and the song he sang was wistful and tender, simple and moving:

"O, wert thou in the cauld blast,
On yonder lea, on yonder lea,
My plaidie to the angry airt,
*   I'd shelter thee, I'd shelter thee.*
Or did misfortune's bitter storms
Around thee blaw, around thee blaw,
*   Thy bield should be my bosom,*
To share it a', to share it a'."

If they could have walked on through the streets of London for ever like that, how happy she would have been!

They turned into that street in which stood the charming little house which was to be Lucie's home, and as they did so suddenly the spell was broken.

It was a moment of horror for Melisande. She had turned, sensing that they were being followed, and so she saw the woman who was walking behind them and might have followed them since they left the house in the square. For one moment Melisande's eyes met a pair of bright malevolent ones. Wenna was in London with Caroline, and Wenna had come to spy on her and Fermor.

She shivered and looked quickly away.

"What is it?" said Fermor.

She looked over her shoulder, but Wenna was not to be seen.

"I . . . I saw Wenna," she said. "She must have followed you."

"That old horror!"

"She will tell Caroline that she has seen us together."

"What of it? How could I refuse to escort you and your friends?"

"I don't like her. She makes trouble. She hates me."

"She hates me too. She makes no secret of it. She clings to Caroline like a leech and snarls at me like a bulldog."

"I am frightened of her."

"You? Frightened of an old woman . . . a servant!"

"After to-day you must not come to see me any more."

"Let 'after to-day' take care of itself."

They stepped into the hall of the little house. It was in process of being prettily furnished, and Lucie went from room to room in delight, calling attention to the carpet which had been delivered and laid in the drawing-room, asking them to admire the ormolu mirror—Madam Fenella's advance wedding present.

But looking into the mirror, Melisande seemed to see Wenna's brooding face looking at her threateningly. She felt that Wenna had followed her, watched her, seen this love of hers for Caroline's husband trembling on the edge of surrender.

Then she knew that this must be her last meeting with Fermor.

Two

So Lucie was married.

Fenella was pleased. Lucie's wealthy parent was pleased. Lucie was settled in life, and this was another triumph for Fenella. More ladies and gentlemen would put their bastard children in her charge, since the stigma attached to those children made it impossible for them to be launched through the usual channels. Fenella was doing such a useful service.

Fenella, the fabulous, the incredible and the mysterious, might be a product of an earlier era when life was lived in a more colourful manner; but the new era had scarcely begun, and Fenella would flourish for many a day as yet to come.

At the wedding the bridegroom's best man was Andrew Beddoes—a serious, quiet young man who selected Melisande for his attentions and stayed by her side during the drinking of toasts.

He was pleasant and courteous and seemed such a contrast to Fermor that she was glad of his company.

He talked of his friendship with the bridegroom, of their profession, of the luck of Francis Grey, who was as happy as a man could be.

Melisande liked him for his warm appreciation of Lucie's bridegroom.

He talked interestingly of his hopes for the future. Francis was going ahead. Mr. Beddoes was certain that he would succeed with Lucie to help him. In such a profession a man *needed* a wife, and a wife like Lucie could help so much. There was a great deal of entertaining to be done. Lucie was so poised, so elegant and so modest, and yet completely confident.

"You speak as though you are in love with Lucie yourself," said Melisande.

"No," he said gravely, "not with Lucie." He smiled and said how kind Melisande was to listen to him.

"But I am so interested. I hope you will be as lucky as Francis Grey."

"I hope that too," he said.

After the wedding she saw more and more of Andrew Beddoes. He came often to the house, where Fenella welcomed him with special warmth. She allowed him to walk with Melisande in the Park with the newly married pair as chaperons.

There were times when they visited Lucie and her husband. Then the men would talk of Law, and Lucie would expound on the delights of housekeeping. It was a pleasant household, and it seemed to Melisande that Lucie had grown more attractive since she had married.

Fermor was angry when he saw what was happening.

Fenella did not deny him admittance to her house. She told herself that it would be good for Andrew to meet a little competition. She and Polly watched his sober courtship and the fiery one of Fermor with amusement and delight.

"It's dangerous," Polly said. "You never know what a young man like that will do. It wouldn't surprise me if he abducted Melly. He's quite capable of it."

"I know. I know," said Fenella. "But he'd have to get her consent."

"He might do that."

"But have you noticed she's changed? There was a time when I thought she was ready to fall into such a trap. But not now. Something's happened. She's wary. She may have discovered some of his wicked secrets. Depend upon it, he's got some."

"You think she'll take Andrew?"

"She's fundamentally a good girl, Polly. I ought to know. Don't I know girls? She longs for that bad one, and I believe he would have won, but she knows his wife. I feel sure that he's made some mistake somewhere. He must have made love to Melisande *before* his marriage. It's all very well to be bad, but badness must have some disguise. He's too blatantly wicked. That's his youth, I expect. He's too arrogant as yet and thinks he can get away with anything. He should have waited until *after* his marriage. Then he could have come along, very sad and dejected and told her his wife didn't understand him.''

"That old tale?"

"All tales are new to those who haven't heard them before. He should have made her sorry for him. Melisande is generous; she's all heart. She'll act first and think afterwards. But in behaving as he did he made her think first. She's thinking now. She's thinking hard. And Lucie's working for Andrew Beddoes. Our dear Lucie has no imagination and, like all the unimaginative, she sees others as a pale shadow of herself. She's happy. She's got her home and lawyer. She's got what she wanted. Therefore she decides that's what Melisande must want.''

"But something's happened to change Melly. It was that day I told you about. They walked behind Lucie and me . . . like a pair of lovers. Then, as we went into the house, I noticed she was as white as a sheet. She's been different since then.''

"It may be that his wife saw them together."

"What! Followed them! Ladies don't do such things, Madam dear.''

"Jealous women do; and ladies can turn into jealous women, Poll, my dear. It was something like that, I'll warrant. Well, it will do Master Fermor good to know that he can't have it all his own way. He's like his father. Men used to be like that when I was young. Hard livers, hard drinkers, hard lovers. Times are changing, my insect. We're getting prim. I shouldn't have been able to start a salon like mine in these days. This young Gladstone is not our sort at all, and he's one of the men of the future. I don't like the virtuous, Polly. They pry. They see evil rather than good. No! Men are not like they used to be. But Fermor's a chip off the old block of mankind. He's of *our* time . . . not of the coming age. Times are changing and we're sticking, Polly. We don't belong to the age that's just beginning.

'Wedlock is a hard pinching boot
But fornication is an easy shoe.'

"Yes, some years ago that was printed quite casually in one of the papers, and it was not meant to shock. It was the way we thought in those days. Most people think the same now; they always think the same; but we're entering a new age, Polly. We're becoming a people who wrap ourselves up in decorum and think that if we lay it on thick, what's underneath doesn't exist. But it's there just the same. It's there.''

"So he's one of the old lot, is he?'' said Polly. "He finds his wife a hard-pinching boot and he thinks our Melly would be an easy shoe. I don't doubt it. I don't doubt it at all. But our little girl took fright, and that's going to send her to Mr. Beddoes. I hope it's right. I only hope it's right.''

"He's bewitched you as he has Melisande. That's what men were like in the old days.''

"Well, we'll see. But I'd like our little French Melly to be a happy little girl, that I would.''

"She will. She'll marry Beddoes and live happy ever after. And we shall have done our duty.''

"And earned our money.''

"Don't be vulgar, Polly. In time she'll understand that sober marriage and a bank balance are worth all the blue-eyed wooers in the world . . . in the long run, of course.''

But Polly sighed; and Fenella sighed; they were romantics at heart.

So the meetings between the lawyer and Melisande were encouraged and, a month or so after Lucie's wedding, Andrew Beddoes asked Melisande to marry him.

"I know it seems sudden to you, Miss St. Martin,'' he said, "but I think it is partly due to seeing the happiness of my friend, Francis Grey. I won't deny that I have given this matter a great deal of thought. I have even discussed it with Grey. He is fond of you, and his wife loves you dearly. We could be near neighbours of theirs and we—he and I—might even consider joining together in a business relationship.''

"I . . . I see,'' said Melisande.

She looked at his clear, honest-looking eyes, at his serious face. Fermor had made her expect more passion in a proposal; but this was, of course, a different proposition from that which Fermor had made. She thought of Léon, whose proposal had been of yet another nature. Was she as fond of this lawyer as she had been of Léon? It was hard to say. Then she had been innocent and inexperienced. She knew now that Léon had aroused her pity and that she had turned to him in order to escape from Fermor. Once again she was seeking escape from Fermor. She did not pity this self-assured young man, but she did admire him. He was always courteous; he did not anger her; he was so energetic in his desire to advance in his profession. How many times had she compared him with Fermor—and always to Fermor's disadvantage! Andrew would be a faithful husband, she was sure; Fermor never. Andrew was determined to make his way in the world. What ambitions had Fermor? Few it seemed, but to seduce her. There had been talk of his going into Parliament. She wondered whether he was too lazy. He already had a large income and one day would inherit more. Fermor seemed to have no ambition but to look about the world, decide on what he wanted, and proceed to take it.

In every way Andrew was admirable; in every way Fermor was disreputable. A wise girl would have had no difficulty in deciding; unfortunately Melisande was not wise.

But she was learning more and more about this establishment in which she found herself. She listened to the chatter of the girls. Lucie had warned her that it was not wise to stay too long with Fenella. If one did sooner or later one might become as Daisy, Kate and Mary Jane. They were such jolly girls—so full of fun and laughter—but what did the future hold for them? Jane and Hilda, two seamstresses, had been desirable once; they liked to talk to the three jolly girls while they remembered wistfully that that was how they were once. Now they sat sewing for a living, and the privilege of doing so they owed to the benevolence of Fenella Cardingly.

She must get away from this house. She was sure that Sir Charles was ignorant of its nature. She did not believe he would have sent her there had he known. Lucie was right. A girl must not stay too long at Fenella's. She had only yesterday wandered into the room which was set apart from the rest of the house, and in which was the Bed of Fertility. She had smelt the heavy perfumed air, had seen with shocked dismay the statues and pictures. It was an embarrassing experience.

Now this young man was offering her escape—not only from Fermor and the tragedy which any weakness on her part would surely bring to Caroline, but from Fenella and her mysterious establishment.

"Well," said Andrew, "what is your answer, Mademoiselle St. Martin?"

"I . . . I don't know. I want time to think of it."

"Of course, of course. I have been rash. I have spoken too soon."

She smiled at him. He would never be rash; he would never speak too soon. From his point of view at least, she knew there would be no doubt. She was not surprised. Young as she was she had been much admired.

"How long would you like to consider this?" he asked eagerly.

"Oh . . . a few days. . . . Perhaps a week."

"Then you will give me your answer not later than a week from to-day?"

"Yes, but there are things you should know about me."

"Nothing could change my feelings about you."

"You are very good, Mr. Beddoes," she said. "I shall always remember how good."

He kissed her hand and left her; and she decided then that she would be very foolish if she did not accept his offer of marriage.

Fenella sent for her. Fenella was well satisfied. She lay on her *chaise longue* and held out her hand. Taking Melisande's she patted it.

"Dear child, Mr. Beddoes has spoken to me. You know of what."

"I can guess."

"He is a good man, my dear."

"I know he is."

"And you will agree to marry him?"

"I have not yet made up my mind. He has given me a week to decide."

"I hope," said Fenella, picking up the ivory fan which was within her reach, "that you will decide to be wise."

"Sometimes that which appears to be wise turns out unwise."

"Not with a man like Andrew Beddoes, my dear. He knows where he's going. He will be a successful lawyer in a few years' time. Doubtless he will make a fine name for himself. He might get a knighthood. That wouldn't surprise me at all."

"Is it easier to live with people who have titles than those without?"

"Ha! It is an easier matter to live with a successful man than a failure. Don't be deceived by ideas about bread and cheese and kisses. They don't work after the first few weeks, and we want to see you settled for life. I won't deny I hoped you might marry into the peerage. A girl with looks like yours might have done so twenty years ago. But now, my dear, society is changing. The men who could offer you a grander marriage than this one wouldn't offer you marriage at all."

"Is it not a question of affection?"

"That comes into it. But you are fond of him?"

"I admire him."

"Admiration is as good a basis as love. We seek to turn those we love into the perfect beings of our imagination. Those whom we admire we emulate. Yes, mutual admiration is a very good basis for marriage."

"Madam, I am rather bewildered. Why did my father send me to you? Why did he say I was to be apprenticed to a dressmaker when . . ."

"He could not have explained me nor my establishment to you, dear. Nobody could. I hope you have been happy here. Perhaps you have seen certain things which it was not good for you to see. Here each lives her own life. What is good for one may be bad for another. The chief quality we have is tolerance. You can't go far wrong in being tolerant, dear. Then you don't condemn; you don't blame. You say simply: 'That way is not the way I wish to go.' No more than that. Nobody is unhappy here. That is how I weigh the good and the bad. Happiness is good; sorrow is bad. If I give happiness, that is good enough for me."

"I see. And you would be happy if I accepted Mr. Beddoes?"

"It is the best thing that could happen to you. I should be pleased; your father would be pleased."

"My father!"

"He wishes to see you happily settled, of course."

"Does he . . . care then?"

"Care! Of course he cares! He writes regularly asking me of your progress."

"I did not know."

"He cannot write to you. It is not in his nature to do so. He is a man of pride, of fixed conventions. You were the result of an indiscretion which he feels would disgrace him if it were known. You may call him a coward. But be tolerant, Melisande. Always try to look through the eyes of others; that breeds the best things the world has to offer: kindness, tolerance, understanding and love."

Melisande knelt down and kissed Fenella's hand.

"I think," she said, "that I will marry Mr. Beddoes."

After that night and the day which followed it, Melisande often thought that if only one had time to prepare for shocks, so much that was tragic might be averted.

The French maid was dressing her, Clotilde and Genevra.

Genevra was chatting with abandon in front of the maid, since the latter certainly could not understand Genevra's English.

Genevra was laced and standing in her petticoats waiting for her dress of silk and lace to be slipped over her head. Clotilde lay back languorously in her chair. Melisande was standing before the mirror while Elise laced her corset. She was laughing as she gripped the back of a chair while Elise pulled tighter and tighter.

"That's enough," said Genevra. "*Assez, assez!* You'll make the poor girl faint into the arms of Mr. Beddoes. But I'll wager another gentleman would be there first to catch her."

"Is it true," asked Clotilde, "that you will marry this Mr. Beddoes, Melisande?"

"It is not yet decided."

"It is a mistake," said Clotilde. "I see it in your eyes. A great mistake."

"How can you be sure of that?" demanded Genevra. "One man's meat is another's poison. One girl's pleasure another's pain."

"Mademoiselle is ready?" asked Elise.

Melisande said she was, and the ivory velvet gown was slipped over her many petticoats.

"Ah," said Elise, "*c'est charmante*. Mademoiselle will be the belle of the *soirée*."

"Traitress!" cried Genevra. "What of little Genevra!"

"Is charming also," said Elise. "But Mademoiselle Melisande . . . ah, *parfaite*!"

"I have the prettier dress to-night," said Melisande.

"Is it fair?" cried Genevra. "Your prey is trapped. I have yet mine to win. Do you know Teddy's family are trying to force him into marriage with a *lady*?"

"He'll not be forced," said Melisande. "You'll see to that."

"Poor Teddy!" sighed Genevra.

Clotilde said: "You are in love, Melisande, and it is not with the lawyer."

"I think," said Melisande, "and everyone thinks, it would be a good marriage."

"But a good marriage is not necessarily a happy one."

"Love!" said Elise. "*L'amour, ma chérie* . . . it is the best in the world and the . . . how do you say . . . the *droit de naissance* of Mademoiselle."

"Love, love, love!" cried Genevra. "Can you live on love? Can you eat love? Does it make a roof over your head?"

"Nothing else matters," said Clotilde.

"Agreed," said Genevra. "*If* you already have the food and the roof. What if you have not?"

"All is well lost for love," said Clotilde.

"All is well lost for a crust of bread if you're starving. You, my dear Clo, have never starved. That's quite clear to me. You have never seen the inside of a factory, have you? I have. I say: 'Give me the food, give me a roof, give me freedom from earning a living, and then . . . if there's anything more to be handed out . . . give me love.' I say to Melly: 'Marry your lawyer. Play my game.' It's the same, you know, only I'm playing for higher stakes. I'll be 'my lady' one of these days. I started lower but I'm going farther up; but it's the same old ladder we're climbing. Fermor Holland has charm. I don't deny he's a temptation. But don't be foolish, my child. It wouldn't last, and then what would happen? The best would be that you'd be passed on like an old dress. First for the use of the lady, then my lady's maid, then the parlourmaid, then the housemaid . . . then the old slut who mops the kitchen floor . . . and after that the dust bin. No, dears, I know too much. I've seen too much. Don't let yourself get passed down. Marriage is enduring; love passes. Don't be deceived by the sugar and spice. The lawyer is a sensible man. Would he marry you but for the fact that your father's making it worth his while?''

"My father!'' cried Melisande.

"Of course, ducky. You're one of the lucky ones. You're like our Lucie. Her father bought her a nice promising lawyer; your father's doing the same. It's only the poor like myself who have to fend for themselves. That's why I'm fighting for Teddy. Teddy don't want a dowry, so all he's got to want is Genevra. It's hard, but it's been done before, and what others can do so can I.''

"A dowry . . .'' Melisande was repeating.

"I listen. I keep my eyes open.''

"Your manners are shocking,'' said Clotilde. "Nothing will improve them, I fear. Even when you become a peeress you'll be listening at keyholes.''

"They say listeners never hear any good of themselves,'' said Genevra with a grimace. "Who cares? It's as well to know what people say of you—good or bad. And whoever says good of anyone behind their backs? My little habits have helped me along. That's why I know what a kind papa our Melisande has got. You're a lucky girl, Melly dear. He's a very fond papa. Madam told Polly that's he's gone thoroughly into the history of your Mr. Beddoes and has satisfied himself that the young man is a suitable husband for his little ewe lamb. On the day you become Mrs. Beddoes a substantial sum will be handed to the lawyer and much good business will be put in his way. I'd say he was getting a double bargain. Dear little Melly *and* a fortune! I'd say he's coming off slightly better than Lucie's Francis. Why, what's the matter, dear?''

"I did not know this," said Melisande.

Clotilde, Genevra and Elise were watching her. Her face was white and her eyes like blazing green fire. But she was silent for a while.

Clotilde said: "Genevra . . . you fool!"

"No," said Melisande then. "No, no! Thank you, Genevra. You are the wise one who listens at doors. Thank you. I see I am the fool, Clotilde, because I believed that he wanted to marry *me*. I did not know of this dowry. You say I have a fond Papa. I suppose that's true. How much is it worth to marry me! A large sum, you say. Then I am not worth very much by myself, am I. It is not a complimentary, is it . . . that such a large sum has to be offered as . . . a bride?"

She began to laugh. Genevra was beginning to be alarmed by what she had disclosed. Clotilde was the first to recover herself.

"Melisande," she said, putting an arm about her, "it is a custom, you know. All young ladies of good birth have a dowry. It is merely part of a custom."

"There is no need to explain these matters to me," said Melisande, her eyes flashing. "I know now. I have been blind-folded. Those who are supposed to love me put bandages on my eyes. Thank you, Genevra, for tearing them away. Oh, how I wish I were as clever as you! How I wish I had lived with you in your garret and seen what men really were, in the beginning. We are different, Genevra. You saw clearly and I have been stupid . . . stupid all the time. Now I see. Now I understand. And it is the *good* men I despise the most. The lawyer who is so anxious to marry me . . . for my dowry! He is yet another. Thank you, Genevra. Thank you for explaining what I ought to have known."

"Here," said Genevra, "you'd better calm yourself, ducky."

"You see, dear," said Clotilde, "they only want the best for you. Don't blame them for that. Don't blame him."

"I should have been told. Don't you see . . . it is the pretence, that hypocrisy that I cannot endure. They deceive me, all of them, except . . ."

"I've been a fool," said Genevra. "I thought you knew this. You must have known about Lucie."

"I am a fool. I know nothing. I am blind . . . blind. . . . And I do not see until the truth is pushed under my nose by kind people like you." She put her arms about Genevra and Clotilde. "Oh, Genevra, Clotilde, you are my friends. You do not pretend to be good. I hate all men and women who pretend to be good, for they are the bad ones. I hate that man now. I never loved him, but I admired him. I respected him. What an idiot!"

Elise said sharply: "Do not, Mademoiselle. I beg . . . be calm. You must not laugh so. It is bad."

Genevra put her arms round Melisande and hugged her. "Don't worry, Melly. We'll look after you. I'm sorry I said what I did. I thought you knew . . . honest."

"It is for the best perhaps," said Clotilde. "It was wrong, that marriage. I knew it."

"Melly," said Genevra, "you've got the light of battle in your eyes. What are you going to do?"

Melisande looked from one to the other. Clotilde knew. The battle between security and adventure had been won for adventure.

Melisande threw out her arms suddenly. "I am free!" she cried. "Now I will be no one but myself. I will not be sold with a dowry to make up the weight. I feel as though I have been laced too tightly and now I am free. Now I shall do what *I* wish . . . not what others wish for me."

"You look wild," said Genevra uneasily. "Are you sure you want to appear to-night?"

"I have something to do to-night, Genevra. I am in love . . . in love with my new life."

The ivory velvet encasing the slim figure was a triumph, thought Fenella; and never had Melisande appeared to be so beautiful. What had happened to her to-night? Her eyes were like flashing emeralds.

She seemed so sure of herself. She had thrown aside that modesty which had been so appealing, and yet she was more attractive without it.

Poor Mr. Beddoes was looking bewildered, as though he scarcely recognized his bride-to-be.

Melisande was saying: "I must have a word with you, Mr. Beddoes; I have something to say to you."

"You have your answer for me?"

"Yes." She smiled at him. She had lost her pity. It was not mere dislike she felt for Mr. Beddoes. To her he represented Hypocrisy, her newly found hate. From now on she would be one of the bold and adventurous. She hated shams. She hated the man who said: 'I love you' when he meant 'I love your dowry and the good business which would be put in my way if I married you.' She loved the bold adventurer who promised love and passion without lies.

"I can see what it is," he said. "Oh, Melisande, we shall be happy."

"If a substantial sum of money and influential clients could make us happy, we should be very happy indeed, should we not?" she flashed.

"Melisande?"

"You look surprised. Why? I know that is what this marriage means to you. What have I . . . I myself to do with it? It might have been Genevra, Clotilde, Daisy, Kate . . . anybody Madam Cardingly put before you. But it was Melisande St. Martin whom you wished to marry, for her father has provided for her so adequately."

He stammered: "I do not understand. I am very fond of you, Melisande."

"I know you are in love. . . . How comforting it must be to be in love with a sum of money!"

"You bewilder me."

"I am glad someone else is bewildered. I myself have been bewildered for so long. If you had said to me, 'Let us marry. Your father promises me a sum of money if I will take you off his hands and salve his conscience concerning you' I should have respected you more. But you came to me and talked of love.''

''But I do love you, Melisande.''

She laughed. ''How much would you have loved me if my father had been a poor man unable to make it worth your while to marry me?''

''Surely this is an unnecessary conversation?''

''It is necessary to me. I am enjoying it. It eases my anger; it soothes my wounded pride to be able to talk to you in this way. You have had your hopes of a financially attractive marriage. Pray leave me my little satisfactions. Give me a chance to say that I despise you . . . not for wanting the money my father would provide, but pretending to want me.''

''Are you telling me that your answer is no?''

''That must be clear. If it is not, take warning; you will have to be much sharper in your profession, if you are going to succeed without my dowry. But perhaps you will find other offers open to you. Certainly I am telling you that my answer is no.''

Fermor, who had been watching, came over and laid his hand on her arm. ''Good evening, Mademoiselle St. Martin,'' he said. ''Good evening, Mr. Beddoes. Did I gather that you wished to speak to me, Mademoiselle?''

She turned her blazing eyes upon him. ''That is so.''

''I am gratified. Mr. Beddoes will excuse us, I am sure.''

They walked away, leaving the bewildered Mr. Beddoes staring after them.

''Such lovers' quarrels should not be conducted in public,'' he said.

''It was no lovers' quarrel.''

''Melisande, what has happened to you to-night?''

''I have grown up. I am beginning to be wise . . . as Genevra and Clotilde are wise. I have been foolish. I wonder you didn't lose patience with me long ago.''

''I am always losing patience with you. Haven't I wanted you fiercely from the moment I saw you, and haven't you been maddeningly coy?''

''I am myself . . . now. I am in love with truth.''

''And with me too?''

''In love with truth is to admit my love for you. Always

before I have been in love with rightness and what I believed to be good. But now I am in love with truth, and I love you because you are without pretence of goodness.''

''I hope you won't be shocked, my darling, when you discover my heart of gold.''

''There is so little chance of finding it that I will risk the shock. I am bad too. Oh yes, I am. I have wanted to be with you. I have said: 'Caroline? What of Caroline? She should not have married him knowing that he did not love her.' What do I care for Caroline? I want to leave this house at once.''

''We'll go to-night.''

''Now?''

''This minute. Now I have made you admit the truth, we'll not wait another hour.''

''Where shall we go?''

''There are places. To-morrow we'll find a house, and there we shall live.''

''You mean I shall live there. You will only partly live there. You have your home.''

''Will you believe me now if I say how much I wish it could have been different? I wish I could live there all the time.''

''Yes,'' she said, ''I do believe you. You will tell Caroline?''

''Tell Caroline! Certainly not.''

''Why not? To tell her would be truthful.''

''It might be, but it would also be the utmost folly.''

''What if she were to discover?''

''Then we should have to make her see reason.''

''I am still frightened when I think of Caroline. Then I know that I am the same poor thing who has been deceived so many times . . . by Léon, by Mr. Beddoes . . . and perhaps by you!''

''The view of the world would certainly be that I am deceiving you. But the world has a queer twisted way of describing things sometimes. I would never willingly deceive you in accordance with our understanding of the word deceive. We cannot tell Caroline. It would hurt her unnecessarily. There is no reason why she should know. Can we leave now?''

"Fermor, I'm afraid suddenly. It is Caroline who is making me afraid. She would know."

"She would not know."

"Wenna followed us that day. Caroline will know through her."

"I didn't see Wenna. You imagined it."

"Wenna is here in London with Caroline. You know that. What more natural than that she should follow us? I can't come with you to-night."

"You shall come. You have promised."

"I will not come. I cannot come to-night. I must think of Caroline to-night."

"You said we had done with all pretence."

"This is no pretence. To-night I am intoxicated."

"You have drunk nothing."

"With freedom," she said. "I must not come while I am in this state."

"So," he said, "you do not mean what you say?"

"I think I mean it. I will not stay in this house after to-night. I am going to be free, and my first free act will be to come to you. I will come to-morrow, I promise; but not to-night."

"Why not? Why not?"

"Perhaps I know I should not. People are looking our way. Madam Cardingly and the girls . . . and some of the men . . . are watching us. Let us seem natural. I want no one to guess that I am running away to-morrow."

"How I love you!" he said. "Now I shall show you how much."

"Love is the best thing in the world. I know it."

"To-morrow you may change your mind. You must leave this place to-night."

"No. But I will come to-morrow. I swear."

"I will meet you here at two-thirty. That is the time when you take a walk. Slip away before the others. I will be waiting in the square. I will have a place ready for you. Afterwards you can choose what you want. Oh, Melisande . . . at last!"

"At last!" she repeated.

"Swear to me now that you'll not change your mind."

"I will meet you in the square to-morrow without fail. I swear."

"How long time takes to pass! It is not yet ten o'clock. Fifteen hours must pass before my dreams are realized! It is tormenting to be near you and not to be alone with you."

"You alarm me sometimes," she said. "You always have. I feel like a child watching a fire . . . longing to touch . . . knowing she'll be burned, because she has been warned, and yet not knowing what the burning will be like."

"You'll not be hurt," he said. "To some are given the gift of meeting one woman . . . one man . . . in a lifetime, and that is the one . . . the only one. You are that one for me. If I had known it when we first met we would not have missed so much."

"There was always Caroline though, wasn't there? She was there before we met. We should have brought unhappiness to her."

"She would have married someone else."

"I cannot forget her. Sometimes I think I never shall as long as we live."

"You must not think of her. I must not think of her. Think of ourselves and all the happiness we shall have. Should we miss that for the sake of one person who cannot know such happiness in any case?"

"She could if you loved her."

"How could I love anyone but you?"

"Perhaps love grows sated. How do I know? What do I know yet? I am beginning to know. Perhaps I am being wrong. Perhaps I am going to suffer. There was a nun, long ago in the Convent, who loved. I think of her. I always did as a child. She took her vows and had a lover. She suffered terribly. Perhaps I too shall suffer . . . even as she did. They walled her up and left her to die in a granite tomb."

"What a morbid thought! Someone ought to have walled up her judges instead of her."

"We have to see everything through others' eyes as well as our own. They thought they were right. She knew she would be punished. Perhaps she willingly accepted punishment. I should want to do that if I had done something which deserved punishment. I should wish to take it in resignation as the nun did. That is why I must think of Caroline to-night.''

''If you attempt to draw back to-morrow,'' he said, ''I shall come and take you by force.''

''That would be so easy for me, wouldn't it? None could blame me then. All the burden of sin would be yours.''

''Sin! What is sin? Sin, in the eyes of most people is doing what *they* don't approve of. Darling, have done with talk. You have promised . . . to-morrow.''

''I will be there to-morrow.''

''And you'll not draw back?''

''What would be the use? You have sworn to force me to do as you wish.''

He touched her hand lightly, for others, sent by Fenella, were joining them.

They talked; she was very gay; she seemed intoxicated. Many were enchanted with Melisande that night, and six women decided they must have an ivory velvet gown; it gave such a glow to the skin, such a shine to the eyes.

And the long evening passed.

She was demure next morning, quiet and brooding. Genevra and Clotilde watched her anxiously, but she betrayed nothing.

Fenella sent a message to say that she wished to have a chat with Melisande when the girls returned from their afternoon walk. Fenella would never have that chat, for Melisande by then would have left the house for ever.

She feigned sleepiness while they drank their morning chocolate. ''Poor darling!'' said Genevra. ''Last night wore you out. Never mind, ducky. Got to resign ourselves to what's what, you know.''

''Yes,'' said Melisande, ''we have to resign ourselves.''

''And have you given dear Beddoes the go-by, or have you decided to take what's offered you?''

''I shall never marry Mr. Beddoes.''

Clotilde smiled sagely. ''I wish you all the best of luck, my dear,'' she said.

And they did not worry her after that. She read with them

during that long morning and, when they were preparing themselves for a walk in the Park, she slipped downstairs and out of the house.

Clotilde saw her go. She stood at the door watching her meeting with Fermor; and Clotilde smiled knowingly and went back to wait for Genevra and Polly.

Neither Fermor nor Melisande spoke much during that short walk to the furnished house which he had found for her.

She was walking away from one existence to another. This was what she wanted—to be with him, not to banter and quarrel as they had always done before, but to exult in being together. It was true that a shadowy third person walked beside them. Melisande could never forget Caroline . . . Caroline in her black mourning dress, with her fair ringlets over her shoulders; there was an intensity about Caroline, something which suggested a capacity for deep feeling—for love, for suffering, for tragedy.

He had taken her hand and gripped it tightly as though he feared she might run away.

"I can't believe it's true," he said, "even now." He turned his face to hers and began to sing quietly but on a note of exultation:

" 'Hark! Hark! the lark at heaven's gate sings . . . ' "

"Don't!" she said. "Please. I am so happy."

And she thought: Or I should be if I could forget Caroline.

"Here we are," he said.

They stood before a small house. She looked at the latticed windows, the dainty white lace curtains, the miniature garden, the iron gate and the path which led to the front door.

He opened the gate and they went through.

"You like it?" he asked.

She nodded.

"Here's the key." He held it before her. "Our key, darling." He put his arm round her and laughed aloud. He did not release her while he opened the door. He drew her into the hall. She noticed how bright and clean everything looked

and she wondered how he had found such a place so quickly.
There were fresh flowers on the table.

"All ready," he said. "All waiting for you." He stopped
for nothing—not even to shut the door—before he lifted her
off her feet.

"Fermor . . ." she began.

"Put your arms about my neck and tell me you don't want
to run away."

She did so. "It would be no good if I tried, would it? You
wouldn't let me, would you?"

He was trying to kick the door shut, but it would not close.
Indeed it was pushed open, and suddenly they were not alone
in that little hall.

Two people had come in and shut the door behind them.
Fermor put Melisande on her feet, and she stood still in
horrified despair.

It was Wenna who spoke first. Caroline stood in silence.

"There! There! What did I tell 'ee? There they are . . .
caught in the act, you might say."

Fermor said angrily: "What are you doing here?" And he
was addressing Caroline.

Wenna came forward; she looked like a witch in her town
clothes, thought Melisande. Her hair escaped in wisps from
under her black hat, and her dark clothes made her skin seem
browner. There was sweat on her nose and upper lip; her
cheeks were fiery red and her black eyes narrow and full of
a furious hatred.

"We caught you proper," went on Wenna. "I knew what
was going on. I knew what kept you away from home."

"You insolent woman!" said Fermor. "You are dismissed
from my service."

"Your service! I was never in it! I serve Miss Caroline,
and with her I stay. There, my queen, now you do know
what he is, and I reckon if you'm wise you and me'll go
home where we belong to be, away from this place of sin
and vice."

"Nothing could please me more," said Fermor coldly.

"Fermor," whispered Caroline, "how could you do
this?"

"Caroline, you must see reason."

Wenna burst into loud laughter. Fermor strode to her and grasped her by the shoulder. "Will you be quiet or shall I shake the life out of you?"

"Try if you like!" said Wenna. "Kill me! Then you'll be hanged for murder. It would be worth dying to take you with me."

He threw her from him.

"Take her away, Caroline," he said. "I don't know how you could behave in this way . . . following me . . . spying on me. I'll not endure it."

"How like you!" said Caroline sadly. "You are caught; you are in the wrong; so you seek to turn the tables and put others in the wrong."

"You think it right then to follow your husband, to bring your insolent servant to abuse me!"

"Oh, Fermor, this has nothing to do with it. You followed her to London. You found out where she was. You . . . you are in love with her, are you?"

"Yes."

"And this is to be your home?"

"It is."

"And our home? What of that? What of your life with me?"

"My dear Caroline, you have no one but yourself to blame. It is a wife's duty to look the other way when there is something she should not see."

Melisande could bear no more. She would never forget the suffering she saw on Caroline's face. She cried: "No, no. It is not so, Caroline. It is not so. It was to be . . . but I shall go away. You married him, and it is my place to go away. I did not mean to hurt you like this. I thought you would not know of it."

"You see what a good little girl she is!" sneered Wenna.

"I could never trust you," said Caroline. "I always knew you would make trouble. Everything changed when my father brought you into the house. I was happy before that."

"I will go away," said Melisande. "Caroline, I will go right away. He shall come back to you."

"When you have finished arranging my future," said Fermor in tones of cold fury, "I have something to say."

"What can you say to excuse this?" demanded Caroline.

"I had no intention of excusing it. My relation with Melisande makes no difference to our marriage. What more can you ask than that?"

Caroline laughed bitterly.

"You have lived too long in the country," he said. "You have been brought up in the narrow way of life. You have to be reasonable, my dear. You must understand and then you will see that everything can be happily settled."

Melisande looked at him and saw that the tender lover had disappeared. This was Fermor at his worst. He was hurting Caroline and he did not seem to understand, or was it that he did not care? He was hard and brutal. Perhaps everything seemed so simple to him. He had made a marriage of convenience; his family was pleased; her family was pleased. What more could be expected of him? Melisande had despised Mr. Beddoes for wishing to make such a marriage. What of Fermor?

Now she saw him as utterly selfish, capable only of fierce desire, never of the smallest sacrifice. Had she turned shuddering from Mr. Beddoes, a cautious and practical man, to another who was simply a brute?

She was still unawakened then? She was still unsure. Here on the very edge of surrender she was turning aside.

Caroline swayed slightly and put out her hand to the wall. Wenna cried out: "My pet . . . my little queen!"

"It's all right," said Caroline, "I'm not going to faint. I won't live . . . like this. I'd rather die."

"Don't talk so, my little love," soothed Wenna. " 'Tis tempting evil."

"So much that is evil has happened," said Caroline. "I would rather be dead than here at this moment in this house of sin."

Fermor said: "At the moment it is merely a house . . . as blameless as any other."

"I can't bear it," said Caroline. "You are so cruel . . . so hard . . . so callous . . ."

She turned away and ran out of the house.

Wenna said: "A curse on you! A curse on you for your

wickedness! May you both suffer as you have made my girl suffer . . . and more!''

Then she went out after Caroline, calling: ''Wait for me. Wait for Wenna.''

Melisande had shrunk against the wall. Fermor, flushed and angry, said: ''Not a pleasant beginning.''

''I cannot stay,'' said Melisande. ''Not now. I cannot stay. I cannot forget them . . . either of them.''

He came to her and put his hands on her shoulders. ''You'll not go now.''

''Yes, Fermor, I must.''

''Because of that cheap bit of melodrama?''

''Cheap! Melodrama! Couldn't you see that she was heartbroken? Couldn't you see that she loves you, that you must go back to her and that you and I must never see each other again?''

''That is playing their game, foolish one. That is playing right into their hands. That's what they expect. We'll snap our fingers at them.''

''You may. I will not.''

''But you will. You came here and you'll stay here. You've left a note for Fenella. Your message will stand. You can't go back. You've left all that. You're here with me now and that's where I intend you shall stay.''

He held her against him and she cried out: ''No, Fermor. No.''

''Yes,'' he said. ''It shall be yes. I'll have no more of your changing your mind.''

''How dare you try to force me to stay?''

''You said you wanted to be forced.''

''Everything has changed.''

''Nothing has changed. You came here and you'll stay here.''

''I'll not. I hate you. I think I always hated you. You are more cruel than anyone. You have broken her heart and you don't care. You simply don't care. You laughed at her.''

''You fool, Melisande. Did it deceive you then?''

''I know,'' she said. ''I know. I am going away . . . somewhere . . . anywhere . . . but not with you.''

There was a loud knocking on the front door. Melisande

opened it before he could stop her. Wenna stood before her—
not the same Wenna who had left them a few minutes ago.
This was a broken woman with a haggard face and a terrible
fear in her eyes.

She said hoarsely: "There's been an accident."

That was all, and they followed her into the street.

A crowd had gathered. Melisande felt sick. She knew that
the figure lying in the road was Caroline, and when she saw
the carriage drawn up by the kerbside, and the people about
it, she knew what had happened.

"Wenna . . . Wenna . . ." she cried, "is she . . . badly
hurt?"

Wenna turned on her in fury. "She did it on purpose,"
she said. "I saw her. She went straight under the horse. You
did this . . . you murderess!"

Melisande did not speak. She felt her limbs trembling.
They had reached the edge of the crowd and she heard Wenna
say: "This is the lady's husband."

Someone said: "I'm a doctor. We must get her to the
nearest hospital."

Even Fermor was shaken now. "How . . . how badly hurt
. . . is she?" he asked.

"As yet I can't say. My carriage is here. We'll go at once.
You and the maid come with me."

Fermor turned to Melisande. "Go back to the house," he
said, "and wait." Then he followed the doctor.

Melisande stood apart; she could hear the blood drumming in her ears. "Murderess!" it seemed to be saying.
"Murderess!"

A woman with a shawl over her head said: "Feeling
faint, Miss? It gives you a turn, don't it? The blood and
all that. Never could stand the sight of blood, meself."

Melisande wanted to talk to somebody, she felt alone, cut
off from all her friends. Fermor was lost to her, Fermor on
whom she had been relying.

She said: "Is she badly hurt?"

"Dead as a doornail, they say. It stands to reason . . .
went right over her. Neck broke, like as not."

"No . . . no!"

"There, don't you take on. Look! They're getting her into

the doctor's carriage. That's her husband, that is. Funny, her running out like that. Quarrel, I reckon it were. Poor fellow! White to the gills, ain't he? And what a handsome looking gentleman, eh? Well, she'll be took care of. The likes of her would be. Likes of us has to look after ourselves. And if she's dead it won't be a pauper's funeral for the likes of her.''

"Don't say that. She won't die. She can't die.''

"She will and she can. Why, Miss, what's the matter with you? Look as if you're the one that's got knocked over. There they go. That's the servant and the doctor. Ah well, that's all over. Another of life's little tragedies, eh?''

A small woman, very neatly dressed, was standing near.

"Such a terrible thing,'' she said. "I saw it happen. She went straight out in front of the carriage. I can't understand why she didn't see it coming.''

"Her husband was there,'' said the woman with the shawl. "Might be they'd had a quarrel like . . . and she in a fit of passion . . .''

"It's a great pity,'' said the other, "that some of these people haven't more to occupy their minds.''

"Like us working folk,'' said the first woman.

"I'm a lady's maid myself,'' went on the small woman, "and I know her sort. Spoiled, some of them. . . .''

They went on to talk of her sort. Melisande moved away. She felt she could bear no more. She watched them aimlessly talking for a few minutes before each went her different way. The crowd was breaking up as there was no more to see, and in a very short time there was only Melisande left. Behind her was the little house. She had never felt so alone, so wretched in the whole of her life.

What now?

She had only one desire at the moment, only one need; and that was to get right away from that house, right away from the old life. She had left that when she had walked out of Fenella's house and she would not go back. She could not go back, now that she knew that the girls were not there to work but to be shown like cattle in a market place—a good bargain with a make-weight dowry. She must never see Fermor again. If Caroline were dead, Wenna was right in saying that, between them, she and Fermor had driven her to her death. If Caroline was alive, she would be between Melisande and Fermor for ever.

She began to walk aimlessly away from the house which was to have been her home with Fermor.

She had brought with her the little money she had. It would help her to live for a short while. She would work . . . really work this time at some honest job.

She thought of the lady's maid who had spoken to the woman in the shawl. Perhaps she herself was qualified to become a lady's maid?

On and on she walked, not realizing where she was going until she came to two small houses side by side. They looked neat and cosy and were different from the others in the row; in the window of one of these little houses was a card which bore the words: "Room to Let."

She noticed how clean were the curtains, how bright the brass of the knocker . . . as she lifted it.

A woman in a starched apron opened the door.

"You have a room to let," said Melisande.

"Come in, Miss," said the woman.

And Melisande began a new phase of her life.

PART FOUR

The Lavenders'

One

From the moment Melisande set eyes on the clean little woman and entered her clean little house she had experienced a sense of relief. Mrs. Chubb's house, she felt, as soon as she stood in the narrow hall with the pot of ferns on the table and the homely pictures on the walls, was as unlike Fenella's as any establishment could be; and surely Mrs. Chubb, with her bright hazel eyes and white hair, the picture of an honest hard-working woman whose life was without complications, was herself as unlike Fenella as this cottage was unlike the house in the square.

A young lady, arriving in a somewhat dazed condition and looking for a room which she wanted to occupy immediately, must give cause for some speculation in such an orderly mind as that of Mrs. Chubb; but, as Mrs. Chubb told Melisande afterwards, she took to her in a flash, and she was sure right away that whatever Melisande's reason for coming to her in such a state might be, Melisande herself was All Right.

The room was on the upper floor of the two which comprised Mrs. Chubb's house. It contained a narrow bed, a chest of drawers on which was a swing mirror, a wash-hand-stand, and what Mrs. Chubb called "appurtenances."

Melisande asked the price. It seemed reasonable.

"I'll take it," she said.

Mrs. Chubb's bright hazel eyes were questioning. "I suppose your trunk'll be coming, Miss?"

"No . . ." said Melisande. "There is no trunk."

"You a foreign lady?"

"Yes . . . in a way."

"Ah!" Mrs. Chubb nodded wisely, as though that explained everything. But it did not alter Mrs. Chubb's opinion of her new lodger, for she prided herself on making up her mind about people the instant she saw them, and nothing was going to change her opinion of her powers in that direction.

A bit of trouble, a love affair like as not, or running away from home? Well, well, Mrs. Chubb would see. Mrs. Chubb—again in her own opinion—had a sympathetic way with her, and there was nothing that overcame reserve like sympathy.

"When will you be moving in, Miss?"

"I'll stay now."

"Oh! Would you like me to get you a cup of coffee? If you'll forgive me saying so, Miss, you look as if you've had a bit of a shock."

"Yes," said Melisande, "I have indeed had a bit of a shock. Please, I should like the coffee."

"What about you coming in and having it in my parlour? Then we can talk about the ways of the house."

"Thank you."

The parlour was small and clean. It was rarely used. It was Mrs. Chubb's delight, and she never entered it without looking round with an air of proud possessiveness and a quick glance over her shoulder—if she was not alone—to see the effect of such splendour on others.

There was a blue carpet on the floor; there was a heavy mirror and a mantelpiece crowded with ornaments. There were two what-nots loaded with knick-knacks, every one of which had its significance for Mrs. Chubb. There were chairs and a sofa; and near the window was a table on which stood a fern similar to the one in the hall.

"There! Sit you down!" said Mrs. Chubb. "And I'll bring you the coffee."

Melisande looked round the room when she was alone, at the pictures—most of them in pastel shades depicting groups of plump young women and graceful men—and the daguerrotype showing two people looking rather self-conscious; as one of these was undoubtedly Mrs. Chubb, Melisande supposed the other to be Mr. Chubb.

But her mind was too full of what happened to allow her to consider Mr. and Mrs. Chubb for long. She had found a haven—if only a temporary one—and she now felt that she had time to think of what she must do.

She must never see Fermor again. She could never be happy with him, for she would never forget Caroline's face as she had stood before her. If Caroline had killed herself, she, Melisande, was to blame. Murderess! Wenna's words would always be with her. She would hear them in her sleep, she fancied; they would break through into every happy moment.

She could not go back to Fenella's. She hated the house now. It seemed sinister with its rich furnishings and air of voluptuousness. She would not allow them to assess her as they had done, to set her up in the market place.

All love was drained from her; she could feel nothing but hatred and contempt; and she felt now that she hated herself most of all.

Mrs. Chubb came in with the coffee.

"There! You like the room?"

"Very much. That is a picture of you and your husband?"

"That's right. Me and the dear departed."

"I am sorry."

Mrs. Chubb wiped her eyes with the corner of her apron. She looked at the picture and recited as she must have done so many times before: "A better man never lived. His only concern was to provide for me after he had gone."

There was a respectful silence. Then Mrs. Chubb released the corner of her apron and smiled brightly. "There! All right?"

"It is very good, thank you."

"You're welcome."

Mrs. Chubb's way of breaking down reserve was to talk about herself. Confidences were like gifts between nice people, she believed; they had to be exchanged.

"That was just before he died," she said nodding at the daguerrotype. "It's two years come June since I buried him."

"I . . . I see."

"A good man. We was in service together. That's how we met. But Mr. Chubb, he was the go-ahead sort. He wasn't going to stay in service all his life. Saved, he did. He had a legacy—he was thought the world of by the lady and gentleman—and he put it into two houses. He was a planner, he was. That's for you, Alice, he used to say, for after I'm gone. So he put the money into two houses—this one and the one next door. I get the next door's rent—and better tenants there never was. Mr. Chubb saw to that. And here I am with a roof over my head and taking a lodger to help things out. That's what Mr. Chubb did for me.''

"You were very lucky.''

"My luck came when I met Mr. Chubb. I say to young ladies who haven't got to the married state . . . I always say: 'May you meet another like Mr. Chubb.' I say it to you now . . . that's if you haven't reached that state, Miss.''

"No,'' said Melisande, "I haven't.''

Mrs. Chubb was relieved. She didn't believe in trouble between husbands and wives.

"Feeling better now? You're looking it.''

"Thank you, yes.''

"And you'll not be having your things sent?''

"No. I have no things.''

"Well, they're very nice, what you're wearing. But you'll want some things, won't you?''

"Perhaps I can buy them.''

"Oh, I see. This shock like. . . . You've quarrelled with your people, have you? I'm not nosy. Mr. Chubb used to say: 'Alice, Mrs. Chubb, my dear, you're one of the few women without a nose.' That was his joke. He was full of jokes. It's just to be prepared for callers . . . that's all, Miss.''

"I don't think there'll be any callers.''

"All on your own, eh?''

"Yes. You . . . er . . . you have been in service, have you?''

Mrs. Chubb was smiling broadly. Here it came. Confidence for confidence. Sympathy had the same effect on reserve as hot water on a bottle stopper that wouldn't open.

"Head housemaid, and Mr. Chubb, he went from pantry boy, footman to butler. He was a man to rise in the world.''

"Do you think I could be a lady's maid . . . or companion?''

"No doubt about it, Miss. Being foreign . . . that's what they like lady's maids to be. Can you crimp the hair and do that sort of thing? I remember there was a foreign lady's maid in our last place. Such an outlandish name she had. And she did well for herself.''

''You see, I shall have to earn a living.''

Mrs. Chubb nodded. As a lady's maid she wouldn't be needing the room, would she? So she had only taken the room until she found a job. Mrs. Chubb was disappointed, but only mildly, for she liked what she called experiences as well as lodgers; and thanks to the wisdom of Mr. Chubb, she could rub along all right without letting her upstairs room. Moreover instinct had told her that she was going to like this girl, and instinct would not be disobeyed.

''Any experience, Miss? That's what they all want.''

''Well, I have been a companion.''

''They'll want references.''

The girl turned pale. Oh dear, thought Mrs. Chubb. Been up to something!

Instinct flinched but stood firm. She's all right. Mrs. Chubb dismissed her suspicions. I'd trust a girl with a face like that. Obviously it was some brute of a man who, unchivalrous and unChubblike, had forced his attentions upon her. That explained everything. That was why she had run away.

''Unless,'' said Mrs. Chubb, ''you had a very good recommendation from someone.''

''I . . . I understand. How does one start looking for such a post, Mrs. Chubb?''

''So that's what you're going to start doing?'' Well, said Mrs. Chubb to herself, I do like honesty. Most would have pretended they wanted the room for ever. I told you so, said instinct. She's honest.

''I . . . I want to. In fact . . . I must . . . soon, of course.''

''Well, sometimes they put notices in the papers . . . and sometimes one of the other servants recommends a friend . . . or perhaps one lady will speak to another for a girl. It's done all ways.''

''I shall have to start looking in the papers.''

Mrs. Chubb made a decision. She said: ''There's Our Ellen.''

''Who is that?''

''Our Ellen. Our girl. Mr. Chubb's daughter and mine.

She's in service . . . in a grand house near the Park. She's got a good job, our Ellen has. She's housekeeper in one of the best houses, with a big staff under her. Now Ellen's got friends all over the place. If any lady was wanting a maid, Ellen would hear of it. Ellen's got her father's head for business. Ellen's doing well for herself.''

"You think she would help me?''

"Ellen would do what her mother asked her to. Are you in any hurry?''

"Well, there will be my rent and board. I have only five or six pounds . . .''

"That's a fortune!'' said Mrs. Chubb.

"It's all I have and I must find something before it goes.''

"Ellen will be coming to see me next Wednesday afternoon. That's her day off, and home she comes to her mother. Never fails. We'll have a talk with Ellen.''

"You are very good,'' said Melisande.

Mrs. Chubb saw the tears in the girl's eyes.

Poor dear! thought Mrs. Chubb. Poor pretty dear!

She determined that Ellen must set the poor pretty creature on her feet, not only for the sake of the girl herself, but for the honour of the Chubbs.

Little by little Mrs. Chubb gleaned as much of the story as Melisande felt she could tell her.

She heard of Melisande's life in the Convent and the father who had eventually decided to launch her in the world. Melisande mentioned no names at all. "I was first taken to his house where I had a post as companion to his daughter, but there was gossip. I was treated too well, and the servants guessed I was his daughter.''

Mrs. Chubb nodded at that; she was well aware of the sagacity of servants and their unflagging interest in the affairs of their employers.

"So he sent me to a friend of his. A husband was chosen for me, but I could not accept him.''

"It's a good thing,'' said Mrs. Chubb, "that I know the upper classes and what's right and wrong to them. Now if I was like my next door tenant . . . why, bless you, my dear, I'd be inclined to think it was something you'd made up.''

Melisande did not attempt to describe the nature of Fenella's establishment; she felt it would be something Mrs. Chubb would never understand; nor did she tell of Fermor for, if there was one man in the whole world who lacked the chivalry of Mr. Chubb, that man was Fermor, and Melisande could not afford to lose the sympathy of her new friend—now her only one—by trying to explain that in spite of obvious villainies, she still hankered after him. How could Mrs. Chubb, who had been cherished by a saint, understand the fascinations of a man like Fermor? Mrs. Chubb might even withdraw her good opinion of Melisande if she tried to explain.

A few days after Melisande's arrival at the house, Ellen appeared.

Ellen was a big woman, plump and forceful. "She's got more of her father than me in her," said Mrs. Chubb admiringly.

Ellen, clearly accustomed to parental admiration, sat like a queen in state in the parlour, so that it seemed smaller and more overcrowded than usual. She talked of her own affairs for so long and in such details—speaking of the Lady and Him, and people with names like Rose, Emily, Jane and Mary, all of whom Mrs. Chubb seemed to know very well indeed, for she inquired feelingly after Mary's bad leg, Rose's flirtatiousness, Emily's headaches and Jane's slatternliness—that Melisande feared they would never begin discussing her affairs.

But Mrs. Chubb had not forgotten her.

"Now Miss St. Martin here, Ellen—she wants work, and we've been wondering what you could do for her."

Ellen paused in her flow of talk and turned her heavy body to study Melisande critically.

"She's foreign," said Mrs. Chubb, like a defending lawyer. "That ought to go some way, didn't it, Ellen . . . for a lady's maid?"

"Oh . . . lady's maid!" said Ellen, and grimaced.

"She's a lady, and educated in a convent."

"Most of them's governesses," said Ellen. "But she's got more the look of a lady's maid than a governess."

"It's good of you to be interested," said Melisande. "Your

mother has kindly said you would be, and that you know more than anyone in London when there are such vacancies.''

Ellen smiled and waved her hand as though to deny such power, but in a perfunctory way necessitated by modesty rather than the need to admit the truth.

''If you should hear of something for me,'' went on Melisande, ''lady's maid or governess, and could say a word for me, I should be so grateful.''

''If there should be something going, you can be sure I'd hear of it, and I don't mind admitting that a word from Ellen Chubb would go a long way.''

''You are most kind. Your mother has told me what power and knowledge is yours.''

Mrs. Chubb was beaming; she did not know who pleased her more—her lodger-protégée, with her pretty face and charming ways, or her omnipotent, omniscient daughter.

They talked for half an hour of Melisande's qualifications, of her convent education, of her few months' companionship to a lady in the country where she had helped that lady dress and do her hair, had read to her and helped her with her clothes.

''But,'' said Mrs. Chubb, with winks and distortions of the face, ''Miss St. Martin wants no reference made to that young lady.''

The winks and distortions meant that there was a good reason for this which Ellen should hear when they were alone.

Ellen looked first grave, then confident. Grave because experience and references were two of the necessities when it came to the ticklish business of getting a job. However, so great was the power of Ellen Chubb that it might be possible—with this power working for Melisande—to dispense with what, in any other circumstances, would have been sheer necessities.

Ellen left the house that day on her mettle.

And, six weeks after Melisande's arrival at Mrs. Chubb's house, she was engaged as lady's maid to Mrs. Lavender.

Two

The Lavenders lived in a tall narrow house which overlooked Hyde Park.

It was not a large house, and more space seemed to have been allotted to the staircases than to the rooms. It was a dark house, and as soon as she entered it, Melisande felt that it was a poor exchange for the clean conviviality of Mrs. Chubb's cottage.

Mrs. Lavender, like the house, was tall and thin. She had a dark, brooding personality. Her hair was the vivid red of a young woman's; her face was an ageing one. It was a discontented, suspicious face. The interview she had with her did nothing to lift Melisande's spirits.

She was met at the door by a manservant whom she afterwards knew as Gunter. Gunter and his wife lived in the basement. Mrs. Gunter was cook-housekeeper, Mr. Gunter butler and handyman. There was one other servant—an elderly woman named Sarah.

Mrs. Lavender received Melisande in her dressing-room, which she called her boudoir. It was an elaborate room lacking the taste displayed in Fenella's rooms yet somehow reminding Melisande of them. Mrs. Lavender's were fussy, whereas Fenella's had been grand. Mrs. Lavender herself wore a frilly négligé which did not suit her elderly face. She was lying back in an armchair when Melisande was shown in by Gunter.

Melisande stood uncertainly while Mrs. Lavender's eyes travelled over her.

"You are very young," said Mrs. Lavender.

"Oh no. . . . Not . . . so young."

"Say Madam when you address me."

"Not so young, Madam. Eighteen."

That did not seem to please Mrs. Lavender. She said suspiciously: "I am told this is your first post."

Melisande was silent.

"It is not my custom to take servants without references. But I have heard from a friend's housekeeper that you are trustworthy and so am prepared to give you a trial."

"Thank you, Madam."

"You are French, I hear."

"I was brought up in France."

"What is your name . . . your Christian name?"

"Melisande."

"I shall call you Martin."

"Oh . . ."

"The wages will be ten pounds a year. This is your first post. I expect I shall have a good deal to teach you. As you will live in and have no expenses I consider I am being very generous."

"Yes. Thank you . . . Madam."

"Well then, you may start to-morrow. Pull the bell and Gunter will show you out."

Melisande obeyed.

Gunter was inclined to be sympathetic. As they were on the stairs he turned and winked at her. "Got it?" he asked.

"Yes, thank you."

He grimaced, as though he thought it might prove to be a mixed blessing.

He put his hands to his mouth and whispered through them: "Tartar!"

"Yes?" said Melisande.

"Oh . . . you're foreign. What about popping in to see Mrs. Gunter before you go?"

"You are most kind."

Mr. and Mrs. Gunter were pleased to entertain her in their basement room, and Mrs. Gunter in a burst of friendliness—or perhaps compassion—brought out a bottle of her ginger wine that they might drink to the success of Melisande in her new home.

Melisande was touched by their friendliness and very glad of it, for it warmed the chilling atmosphere of the house. She supposed that, had she not still been feeling rather dazed and careless of what became of her, she would have been more depressed about her future. Yet, at this moment, nothing seemed very real to her, nothing seemed of any great importance. Caroline and Fermor, with Wenna an accusing figure in the background, haunted her by day and night.

"There," said Mrs. Gunter, who was many inches taller than her husband, considerably broader, and showed a protective attitude towards him, which she was now preparing to extend to Melisande, "you sit down, and Gunter'll get out the glasses."

The Gunters' room was furnished humbly. "Our own pieces," explained Mrs. Gunter. "We never move without our bit of home, and as I say to Gunter, what's nicer than a bit of home? So you're coming to work here, eh? Steady!" That was to Gunter who was filling the glasses too full. "Can't afford to spill our best ginger. It's not so easily come by."

"I start to-morrow," said Melisande.

"I wouldn't like to be in your shoes," said Gunter.

"I'd like to see you try to get into them!" said Mrs. Gunter, giving Melisande a push to stress the joke.

Melisande laughed.

The Gunters were a merry pair. Gunter now began to mince round the room. "And how would Madam like her hair done to-day, eh? A little curl here? A little curl there?"

"Looks like he's already been at the ginger," said Mrs. Gunter, with another push. "It goes to his head . . . and my legs."

"I think," said Melisande, "that I'm going to be very glad that you will be here with me."

"Well, that *is* a nice thing to say," said Mrs. Gunter. She added in a whisper: "She can't keep her maids."

"It's not so much her . . . as him," said Gunter darkly.

"Him?" asked Melisande.

Mrs. Gunter looked evasive. "Oh, he's a lot younger than her . . . regular little dandy, he is. She thinks the world of him. 'Archibald, my dear!' " mimicked Mrs. Gunter.

Mr. Gunter pranced round the room and embraced his wife.

"Gunter'll be the death of me," said Mrs. Gunter.

They were serious suddenly, looking at Melisande with concern.

"What is it?" she asked. "You think I shall not do this job? You think I shall not give the satisfaction?"

"Well," said Mr. Gunter. "I'd say you will and I'd say you won't."

"Give over!" said Mrs. Gunter sternly. "You see, Miss, she's a bit of a tartar. She's nearing sixty and she'll want you to make her look thirty. It can't be done. And every time she looks in the glass, she knows it. She's got the money. Now you'd say that when a woman marries, all she's got's her husband's. That's the law. Well, her father knew a thing or two about that and he got the money tied up in some way. Some sort of thing I don't understand. But it means the money can't go to Mr. Lavender. It comes to her . . . regular . . . to *her*, you see. Mr. Lavender can't lay his hands on it. It was a shock to him when he found out how he'd been bested. It works all right though, don't it, Gunter? It keeps him sweet and dancing attendance. Whereas . . ."

"Whereas . . ." said Mr. Gunter, going off into laughter.

"If he got his hands on the money it might be quite a different story. As I say to Gunter, sixty can't mate with thirty and all go merry like. There's bound to be troubles. Sometimes she's not all that sweet, and who does she take it out on but us. And you, my dear, will be at her beck and call more than any of us. I think it right to warn you."

"Thank you," said Melisande.

"You don't seem very scared," said Mrs. Gunter.

"I did not expect that I should find it easy."

The Gunters looked at her sharply, and Melisande went on, with emotion: "I shall never forget your kindness. It is so good to meet kindness in this world."

Unable to reply in words to such a display of feeling, the Gunters looked shyly at each other as though to say: Foreign ways!

The verdict after she had left was that she was queer but nice. And talk about goodlooking! Far *too* goodlooking.

"My word," said Mrs. Gunter, "*she's* not going to like that."

"No," said Mr. Gunter, "but *he* is!"

Then they laughed but were soon serious. They were a good-hearted pair, and the beautiful young lady had aroused their compassion.

How did she manage to live through the days that followed? Only, thought Melisande, because of that numbness within her. Only because she thought: I do not care.

She did not hate the woman whose wish seemed to be to hurt and humiliate her; she did not care. When Mrs. Lavender shouted at her: "Martin, you clumsy fool, you're pulling my hair. A lady's maid, you! You're here under false pretences. I don't mind telling you that if you go on like this you'll be out, neck and crop . . ." Melisande did not hear. She was thinking of Fermor, callous in that charmingly furnished hall; she was thinking of Caroline's white and tragic face. "Murderess! Murderess!" were the words she heard.

"Martin, you seem quite stupid. Don't you hear me? Are you dumb, blind *and* silly?"

"Yes, Madam?"

"Do not stand there smiling and looking so pleased with yourself."

I? thought Melisande. Pleased with myself? I hate myself. I do not care what happens to me. Caroline may be dead, and if so . . . I have killed her.

Even in tragedy there was some good, she thought. How do ladies' maids endure serving such women as this unless they feel as I do . . . indifferent . . . not caring?

What a pity, she thought, that I was not the one who walked under the horse. That would have solved our problem.

Fermor? He would have been sad for a while . . . such a little while.

But when she made a flower for Mrs. Lavender's gown, the woman was pleased. She did not say so. She merely had the flower placed on her dress. She looked at it appreciatively. "You can make some more," was all she said. But for the next few days she did not complain so much. She was even communicative. She showed Melisande her jewels, which she kept in a small safe in her boudoir. She unbent when displaying them. She ought to keep them at the bank, she was told, but she could not bear to part with them. She liked to have them with her to try them on, even though she did not wear them all the time.

Melisande thought her appearance was always spoilt by too many jewels which, in conjunction with the red hair, made too startling a show. If the jewels had been worn sparingly with clothes less flamboyant, and her hair was its natural colour, providing Mrs. Lavender could acquire a more pleasant expression, she might suit her name. As it was that name seemed somewhat incongruous.

Melisande had made suggestions about the jewels, but Mrs. Lavender would not heed her. She presumed Melisande was jealous of her possessions.

She showed her the pearl-handled pistol which she kept in a drawer by her bed. "It's loaded," she said, "I always keep it so. I'm ready for any burglars. No one shall get away with my jewels."

Melisande listened in silence. Her apparent indifference goaded her employer to anger; yet her dignity held the woman in check. It was impossible to rave so continually at one who was so calm. Mrs. Lavender could not understand the girl. If she were not so clever at arranging hair and supplying clever little touches to a dress, Mrs. Lavender would have decided to dismiss her; but to her astonishment she found that she was almost growing to like her lady's maid. It was surprising, for Mrs. Lavender liked few people, and she had never before had the slightest regard for a mere servant. She found herself wondering what the meaning was of that strange look on the girl's face. She did not seem by nature meek; she was not like a servant eager above all things to keep a job; it was that blank indifference which was so baffling; it was almost as though she did not care what was said to her; for she never showed the least resentment. It was as though she were living in another world, a world which was invisible to those about her.

Uncanny! thought Mrs. Lavender. But a lady . . . quite a lady—which was an asset really. She was a girl one could be proud to show to one's friends . . . and French into the bargain! So, on the whole, Mrs. Lavender was not displeased with her new maid.

And then Mr. Lavender came home.

Melisande was surprised when she saw him for the first time, although she should not have been, for there had been dark hints from the Gunters, and she already knew that he was considerably younger than his wife.

Sarah, the maid-of-all-work, who sometimes had a cup of coffee with the other members of the staff in the Gunters' basement room, had talked of Mr. Lavender's fondness for the bottle, for handsome waistcoats; she had talked of the scented pomade he used for his hair, of the scrapes he got into with Mrs. Lavender, and how he needed all his blarney to get out of them. It was not that Melisande was unprepared for Mr. Lavender, but for the effect she would have on him.

She was clearing up in the boudoir one afternoon while Mrs. Lavender was taking a nap in her bedroom, when Mr. Lavender came in.

She had heard a step behind her and, thinking it was Sarah who had entered, did not turn round but continued combing the hairs from Mrs. Lavender's brush.

"Oh, Sarah," she said, "is Mrs. Gunter in?"

There was no answer. She turned and there was Mr. Lavender leaning against the door and smiling at her.

There was nothing really alarming about Mr. Lavender's smile. Melisande had encountered many such smiles and she knew that they indicated admiration. She was merely startled.

"G . . . good afternoon," she said.

Mr. Lavender bowed. She noticed how the quiff of yellow hair fell over his brow; she saw the gleam of a diamond tiepin, the ring on his finger, the nattily cut coat and the brilliant waistcoat; she could smell the violet hair pomade.

"This is a pleasure," he said. "You must be my wife's new maid."

"Yes."

To her astonishment, he approached and held out his hand. He took hers and held it, patting it with his other. "I see," he said, "that we are in luck this time."

"It is kind of you to say so." Melisande withdrew her hand.

"My word, you're a pretty girl—if you don't mind the compliment."

"I do not mind. Thank you."

"You're really French, I hear. Why, you and I will get on like a house afire, I can see."

She remembered then Fenella's advice: When she did not know how to respond, to indicate that she did not understand the finer meanings of the English language.

"A house afire? That sounds dangerous."

He laughed, throwing back his quiff as he did so. She saw the flash of his teeth.

"Do you like it here?" he asked solicitously.

"Thank you. It is a kind enquiry."

"You're a charming girl—too pretty to be working for other women."

She was glad that the door leading to the bedroom had opened.

"Archie!" said Mrs. Lavender.

"My love!"

He went to her and embraced her. Melisande, glancing over her shoulder, saw that Mrs. Lavender's face had softened to that expression which Melisande had wished for it.

"You should have said you were coming home," said Mrs. Lavender.

"Thought I'd surprise you. Thought that's what you'd like. You wait till you see what I've brought for you."

"Really, Archie! You're an angel!"

"No, Mrs. L. You're the one who should be sprouting the wings."

Mrs. Lavender said: "You may go, Martin."

"Thank you," said Melisande, in great relief.

She noticed that Archibald Lavender did not give her a single glance as she hurried out.

She went to the small attic room which was hers and shut the door. She felt now as though she were waking out of her daze. What had she done? she asked herself. She had run away from Fenella's, and whatever Fenella was, she had been kind. In Fenella's house, for all its voluptuous mystery, there was a feeling of safety. Here . . . there was no safety. She knew that. She sensed danger . . . "like a house afire."

She had little money. She knew that the notice Mr. Lavender had implied he would bestow on her would annoy Mrs. Lavender more than any incompetence. She was afraid suddenly, for it seemed that the world into which she had escaped was full of a hundred dangers from which Fenella had protected her.

She was only eighteen. It was so very young. Too much had happened in too short a time.

She longed to go back to Mrs. Chubb's, to live for ever in that cosy cottage. But how could she? To become a lodger there she needed money. Moreover Ellen had found this job, and Ellen and Mrs. Chubb would expect her to keep it.

She wanted her bedroom at Fenella's; she wanted the lighthearted chatter of Genevra, the worldly wisdom of Clotilde, the oddly maternal solicitude of Polly and Fenella. She wanted Fermor.

She had run away because she was afraid; and now she was alone in a world full of new dangers.

She went down to Mrs. Gunter for comfort.

"So he's back," said Mrs. Gunter. "Now she'll be sweeter. I reckon he's brought her a lovely piece of jewellery. She'll be so pleased he's thought of her that she won't mind paying the bill when it comes. I bet he's telling her some tale about how he had to stay away on business and how he hated leaving her. Well, it pleases her and she likes to think that one day he's going to be a great business man with money of his own. Did you see him?"

"Yes, I did," said Melisande.

Mrs. Gunter looked at her sharply. "I can see you're a sensible girl," she said.

"I wish he had not come back."

"I daresay he said you were pretty and you and him would get on like a house afire."

"How did you know?"

"He's got his set pieces, and we've had pretty girls here before. I'll tell you something: He's a coward and dead scared of her." Mrs. Gunter pushed Melisande. "Just threaten him with her. That's what you'll have to do if he worries you."

Melisande went to Mrs. Gunter then and laying her head on her shoulder put her arms about her. "It was so pretty-like," said Mrs. Gunter later; "and then I saw she was crying quiet-like. She looked different after that. The quietness seemed to have gone out of her. When she stood back she was like a different person. I never saw her eyes flash so before. Beautiful they looked. And I thought: 'Hello! Here's a side we don't know about yet. I reckon Mr. L. will get slapped if he goes too far!' "

"Martin," said Mrs. Lavender, "do you play whist?"

"A little, Madam."

"Then you shall join us . . . after dinner. Mrs. Greenacre cannot be with us."

"Oh . . ." began Melisande.

"You need not be afraid. We shall not expect you to dress. I shall explain to our guest who you are. Nothing will be expected of you but to play your hand."

"But . . ."

"You'll do as you're asked, of course."

Melisande went to her room to wash. She always locked the door whenever she went in. She had done so since Mr. Lavender had knocked one evening to ask how she was. He had fancied she looked tired, he had said. It had been difficult to keep him on the right side of the door; but she had done so with quiet dignity and great determination.

After that she always turned the key in the lock and, if there should be a knock, asked who was there before opening the door.

She washed thoughtfully and combed her hair.

She had been three weeks with the Lavenders; that meant it was nine weeks since that day when she had walked out of Fenella's house. She wondered whether they had tried to find her. Fenella would have been so hurt; so would Polly. As for her father, he would probably be glad, for now that she had run away she had solved his problem for him. He could not blame himself for what happened to an illegitimate daughter who spurned his care and refused to marry the very respectable young lawyer whom he had provided for her. Genevra? Clotilde? They would not care deeply. She had been but the companion of a few weeks in their eventful lives.

She had to forget what had happened. She had been reading the papers every day since the accident. Surely if Caroline had died she would have seen some notice to this effect. She had never asked Fermor where he and Caroline lived, but it should not be insuperably difficult to find out. But if she did and went to the house to enquire of the servants, she might meet Fermor or Caroline and that was what she must avoid.

She heard a carriage draw up outside the house. This would be to-night's guest. She went to the window and looked down. She could not see very clearly the person who stepped from the carriage, but she did see that it was a man who appeared to be about Mr. Lavender's age.

She was glad that she did not have to join them at dinner. She was indeed not looking forward to the evening at all. Mrs. Lavender would be rude to her, she was sure, and she was beginning to resent such treatment.

Now, when the woman bullied her, retorts rose to her lips. Surely that was a sign that she was growing away from her nightmares and was feeling a stirring of interest in her new life.

She was wearing the black and green dress bought in Paris. It was less fashionable now, and she had worn it scarcely at all while she was at Fenella's. While she was at Mrs. Chubb's she had bought herself two cheap gowns for daily wear—one lilac colour, the other grey.

She combed her hair and parted it in the centre so that it fell in ringlets over her shoulders.

She was feeling nervous when the summons came for her to go to the drawing-room.

"This is my maid, Martin, Mr. Randall. I have sent for her to make a fourth at whist. So tiresome that Mrs. Green-acre could not come."

He rose and, taking Melisande's hand, bowed over it.

He was tall and handsome, with dark hair and dark eyes; Melisande liked him at once because his smile was sympathetic with no hint of patronage in it.

"I am afraid," said Melisande, "that I shall be a poor player. I have played very little."

The young man—who now seemed younger than Mr. Lavender—smiled again. "I am sure Mr. Lavender and I will forgive you if you trump our aces . . . eh, Archibald?"

Archibald mumbled that he was not sure about that. He was very cautious under the eye of Mrs. Lavender; but, when he was sure she was not watching him, he smiled at Melisande in a manner to indicate that he did not mean what he said.

"You may put up the card table, Martin," said Mrs. Lavender.

Mr. Randall helped her to do this.

"There is no need for you to trouble," said Mrs. Lavender. "I am sure Martin can manage."

"It is a pleasure," said Mr. Randall.

They sat round the table and the cards were dealt. Melisande blundered again and again. She had played very little at Trevenning and on those rare occasions when the cards had been brought out at Fenella's it was usually in order to tell fortunes, and when whist was played it was never seriously.

She apologized nervously. "I'm afraid I'm not very good . . ."

Mrs. Lavender said with a short laugh: "You are right there, Martin. I'm glad you're not my partner."

Mr. Randall, whose partner Melisande was, hurried to defend her. "I'm not at all sure that was not finesse, Mrs. Lavender. Not sure at all. You wait and see."

It was very good of him, Melisande thought; she was aware that he was guiding her, seeking all the time to cover up her mistakes.

When Sarah brought in tea and biscuits for refreshment, which, Mrs. Lavender prided herself, was so fashionable, she told Melisande to pour out.

"Why," said Mrs. Lavender, scrutinizing the tray. "Sarah has brought four cups."

Melisande felt suddenly angry. It was because—she realized afterwards—Mr. Randall with his quiet consideration had restored her self-respect. Her spirits were reviving. She would not endure further insults. If necessary she would leave Mrs. Lavender and find someone else who needed a lady's maid.

"You need have no fear, Mrs. Lavender," she said quietly but deliberately, "I did not intend to pour tea for myself. I quite understand that I was ordered to attend merely because a guest failed to appear. I have no more wish to drink tea with you than you have to see me do so."

Mrs. Lavender gasped. Melisande, with trembling hands, poured the tea and handed it round.

Both men were watching her, Mr. Lavender uneasily, Mr. Randall admiringly. In Mrs. Lavender's cheeks two spots of colour burned.

She was unsure how to act. Her first impulse was to tell Melisande to go and pack her bag; but she did not want to lose her. It gave such prestige, to employ a French maid; besides the girl was clever in her way and she would be useful on occasions like this, for she was undoubtedly as well-bred as Mrs. Lavender's guests. There was satisfaction in possessing such a maid.

She said: "Mr. Randall, we must forgive Martin. She is French, you know. That means she does not always understand our English ways."

"I am sure," said Mr. Lavender, "that Martin *means* no harm. I am quite sure of that."

Mr. Randall looked at her with admiration and pity.

"Well," said Mrs. Lavender, "we'll overlook your behaviour, Martin. You may pour yourself tea."

"Thank you, Mrs. Lavender, but I do not wish for it."

Again there was a brief silence. Melisande became aware that she was beginning to relish the situation. She had a feeling of glorious indifference to consequences. I shall be dismissed, she thought; and I do not care. There must be many employers in the world who are no worse than Mrs. Lavender, and surely some who are much better.

"She does not like our English customs," said Mrs. Lavender. "They say the French do not drink tea as we do."

"It is not the customs I do not like," said Melisande. "It is the manners."

"Martin," said Mrs. Lavender, her face now purple. "There is no need for you to remain."

"Then," said Melisande, "I will say good night."

Mr. Randall was at the door to open it for her.

She sailed through. She ran up the stairs to her attic. She locked the door, sat on the bed and laughed. She thought:

How Genevra would have enjoyed that! Then a terrible longing came over her to be with Genevra again, to laugh with
her, to exchange this sparsely furnished little attic for her
luxurious apartments at Fenella's, to wear beautiful clothes,
to chatter in Fenella's salon, and above all to see Fermor
there.

Then she threw herself on to the bed and laughed until she
cried.

But she must pull herself together. She got up and bathed
her face. After the visitor had gone she would be needed to
help her mistress prepare for bed. Mrs. Lavender should not
have the pleasure of seeing that she had shed tears.

She would, of course, be given notice to leave. Very well,
she would have to find herself something this time. And
somehow she would make a new life for herself. She would
live again.

Being alive again meant a return of pride, a return of hope.
She indulged in day-dreams now, as she had when she was
a child at the Convent.

She was Melisande to whom wonderful things must happen. She had been hurt and she had allowed that hurt to crush
her. She remembered the little punishments at the Convent,
which had seemed enormous at the time. She remembered
the first time she had been sent to the sewing-room and kept
there for three hours. It had seemed a lifetime. And in the
same way now, a few weeks seemed a lifetime. But the gloom
always passed and the brightness broke through . . . as it
would now.

She had several happy dreams, but none of them could be
carried to a satisfactory conclusion. None could be complete
in itself. One was that Sir Charles repented of his pride and
came to claim her; he took her back to live in Cornwall. But
how could she go on with that dream? What of Caroline, his
daughter? Was Caroline alive? Was Caroline dead? Then she
dreamed that she was married to Fermor. But where was
Caroline in that dream? Caroline must always be there; Caroline alive made their union impossible. Did Caroline dead
make it equally so? Sometimes she thought of Léon—not the
Léon she remembered, tortured by a terrible tragedy, fur-

tively looking about him as it seemed for the accusing eyes of those who believed him guilty of a callous deed, but a Léon who was a combination of himself, Fermor, and her new acquaintance Thorold Randall. Sometimes she dreamed that Fenella found her and took her back, and that in the salon she met a stranger; he was this new combination of Fermor, Léon and Thorold Randall.

She clung to these dreams. They represented hope. She took new pride in her appearance. She was so pretty, and it became pleasant once more to accept the little attentions which were the natural homage of beauty like hers, and which came from cab drivers, policemen and men in shops to which she went on errands for Mrs. Lavender. All that gave her confidence, new weapons with which to fight the Lavenders.

This was being alive again.

Strangely enough Mrs. Lavender made no reference to the little scene which had taken place in the drawing-room. She had decided to overlook it and put it down to foreign temperament. Melisande knew then that Mrs. Lavender was by no means displeased with her work.

Two days after the whist party, on the occasion of her free afternoon, Melisande came out of the house to find Thorold Randall standing idly outside.

She was pleasantly startled. This was Melisande reborn, eager for excitement. Her green eyes sparkled.

"Why," he said, "it's Miss Martin."

"You want to see Mrs. Lavender? She is resting. But Mr. Lavender is at home."

"I wish to see neither of them. But I was waiting for someone."

"Oh?"

"I should like to offer my condolences for the other night. I was distressed."

"I was not. I was glad."

"Glad to be treated as you were! A young lady like yourself?"

"A lady's maid, Mr. Randall. You forget that."

"I forget nothing. It is distressing to see a young lady like yourself treated in such a way."

''Then that is very good of you. I will thank you and say
goodbye.''

''Please don't say goodbye. May I walk a little way with
you?''

''But you are waiting for someone.''

''For you, of course.''

''But how did you know I should be free?''

''A little careful enquiry.''

She laughed. ''Then it was doubly good. First to wait and
tell me you are sorry. And second for taking so much trouble
to do so.''

As they walked along, he said: ''There were unpleasant
consequences? She er . . .''

''I am still her maid. She has said nothing of the incident.
So you see you should not be so sorry for me. You will make
me sorry for myself, and it is not good to pity oneself. If you
are not pleased with life . . . then you must seek some means
of changing it.''

''It is not always possible to change it.''

''Then one must make it possible.''

''You are a strange young lady. I thought at first how quiet
you were that evening . . . how meek.''

''Crushed!'' she cried. ''Mrs. Lavender had her foot on
my neck. That is what you thought. It was not so. I just did
not care that night. Then suddenly . . . I arise. I throw off
the foot, and there I am, ready to fight for my dignities . . .
my rights to be treated not as a lady's maid but as a person.''

''Why are you doing such work?''

''Why does one work? Perhaps there is a vocation, and
that is one answer. Perhaps one wants to eat, and that is
another. Tell me, Mr. Randall, do you work, and for which
reason?''

''A little of both. I too must eat. My income is too small
for my needs. I am in the Guards. You can call it a vocation.''

''So you are a soldier! I must walk this way. I am going
to visit a friend who lives near the Strand.''

''Then I will walk that way too.''

''So you wish to be a soldier and you wish to earn money.
You are one of the lucky ones. You do the work you like and
by doing it you earn money.''

"I hadn't thought of it like that until now. Thanks for pointing it out, Miss Martin."

"My name is St. Martin. Mrs. Lavender calls me Martin because my Christian name is too long and unsuitable; and no lady's maid could be called 'Saint' by her employer."

"Miss St. Martin. And may I know your Christian name?"

"It is Melisande."

"It's beautiful and it suits you. Melisande St. Martin. We have a St. Martin in the regiment. I wonder if you are related to him. His people have an estate in Berkshire."

"Oh, no, no, no! St. Martin is not the name of my family. I was an orphan . . . left in a convent, you see. I think neither the name of my father nor my mother is St. Martin."

"I see. What a mysterious person you are! May I call you Melisande? Oh, believe me, that is not meant to be impertinent. It is just that St. Martin seems so remote. Melisande—that is entirely yours, and so charming."

"Then do—providing you do not address me so if there should be another whist party, and I am called up to make a fourth."

"I promise, Melisande."

"I turn off here . . . I am going to visit a friend."

"Let me accompany you."

"Her name is Mrs. Chubb, and I had a room in her house. She is so kind. And so is her daughter Ellen who is all-powerful in the world of cooks and ladies' maids. She found me my post with Mrs. Lavender."

"Would you think it impertinent if I asked what you were doing before that?"

"No. I should not think it impertinent, but I might not wish to answer. Here is Mrs. Chubb's house, and I will say goodbye."

"May I wait for you?"

"Oh, but you must not."

"I should like to. Then I could escort you back."

"It is not necessary."

"Please . . . as a pleasure, not as a necessity."

"But I may be a very long time."

Mrs. Chubb, who had been watching through the curtains, opened the door.

"Why, here you are then. I thought I heard footsteps. Oh . . . and not alone!"

"Mrs. Chubb, Mr. Randall. This is Mrs. Chubb, Mr. Randall—my very good friend who has been so kind to me."

Mr. Randall bowed, and Mrs. Chubb summoned her instinct and, obeying its commands, took a liking to him on the spot.

"Well, you'll come in, won't you?" she asked.

Thorold Randall said he would be delighted.

Mrs. Chubb bustled them into her parlour. She glanced quickly at the daguerrotype as though she were asking Mr. Chubb to take note of her visitors.

"It is so kind of you," murmured Mr. Randall. "Such hospitality . . . to a stranger . . ."

Mrs. Chubb went to the kitchen to fetch the refreshments she had prepared.

He was a gentleman. Trust her to know that. A handsome gentleman, too; and he could provide the right ending for her favourite lodger. Mrs. Chubb's instinct had always told her what was what; and right from the beginning it had told her Melisande was not cut out for servitude. Here was the answer; a handsome man who was already half in love with her and would very soon be completely so, who would offer her a devotion rivalled only by that which Mr. Chubb had given *his* wife, and a great deal more in worldly goods besides, Mrs. Chubb was sure.

Mrs. Chubb felt like a fairy godmother. She had done this—she and Ellen between them.

Following that afternoon there were other meetings.

The Gunters knew of them, and they smiled delightedly. Sarah said it was lovely, and that it made her cry every time she thought of it. Mrs. Lavender was unaware of what was happening, because she was aware of little except her own affairs; but Mr. Lavender continued to watch his wife's lady's maid with an ever-increasing attention.

Thorold Randall had become a more frequent caller at the house; it seemed as if he had discovered a bond between himself and the Lavenders. He could compliment Mrs. Lavender as she liked to be complimented, and he was knowledgeable about Mr. Lavender's favourite topic—horses and their chances.

But always he was alert for the appearance of Melisande; and whenever he came to the house he found some means of speaking to her.

Melisande's half-day came round again. She knew that when she left the house she would find Thorold Randall waiting for her. She enjoyed his company; it seemed to her that he was growing more and more like that picture she had built up of that man who was a little like Fermor, a little like Léon, and a little like himself.

For instance, there were times when there seemed to be a certain boldness in him—and that was Fermor. At others he would talk of the lonely life he led, for he was an orphan and had been brought up by an aunt and uncle who had had little time to spare for him, and he would then remind her of Léon. And then he was himself—courteous, almost humble in his desire to please. She was very happy to have him as her friend.

He was waiting for her when she left the house.

"It's a lovely day," she said. "Let us walk in the Park."

She did not often walk there now. She remembered drives with Genevra, Clotilde and Lucie, and she could not enter the Park without fearing to meet them. Moreover young ladies did not walk in the Park alone—that was asking for trouble. But now she was no longer afraid; it was as though she were tempting adventure. If she met anyone from Fenella's house she would feel safe, for she was becoming firmly settled in her new life.

It was pleasant to walk along by the Serpentine chatting with Thorold. He took her arm and led the conversation—as he did so often—away from himself to her.

She said: "You are unusual. Most people wish to talk of their affairs, not to hear about those of other people."

"Perhaps when I am with others, I talk of myself. But you interest me so much . . . far more than myself."

"Nobody is quite as interested in others as in themselves surely."

"Here is one who is so interested in another person that everything else now seems unimportant."

"Ah! You would flatter me. What is it you wish to know of me?"

"I should like to look into your mind and see everything that is there, to know your thoughts. What do you think of me, for instance?"

"I think that you are most kind and courteous to me always, as you were from the beginning."

"Would you like to hear what I think of you?"

"No. It is enough that you give me your company on these half-days."

"It is not enough for me. Tell me why you are here?"

"It is because I like to be here."

"No, no. I mean, why a young lady like yourself is working for a woman like Mrs. Lavender."

"It is so simple. She needs a maid. I need to be a maid. That fits . . . perfectly, you see."

"It does not fit."

Melisande had stood still where she was on the grass. Across the gravel path a woman was wheeling a bath-chair and in the bath-chair was a young woman.

"What is it?" asked Thorold. "Someone you know?"

Melisande did not answer; she stared after the wheel chair. Neither the woman in the chair nor the one who was wheeling it turned her head to look in Melisande's direction.

"What is it?" insisted Thorold Randall. "What has happened?"

"It is . . . someone I know," she said.

"Then . . . don't you want to speak to her? Wouldn't she be glad to see you?"

"Oh no. . . . They would not be glad to see me. Oh, but I am glad to see them."

"Come and sit down. You look shaken."

"Thank you."

They found a seat. He was watching her curiously, but she had forgotten him. She was thinking of Wenna pushing the bath-chair, of Caroline sitting there, wan, pale . . . but alive.

So Caroline had escaped death. There was no more need for Melisande to hear that voice whispering to her: "Murderess! Murderess!" But although Caroline had survived she had to be pushed about in a bath-chair. Why? Was she merely delicate and unable to walk far, or was she crippled?

Still . . . she was not dead, and she had Fermor. As for Melisande, she must cease to think of them. She must banish Fermor from her mind for ever; she must leave him to Caroline.

She lifted her face to the sun and thought that it was a lovely day.

"They upset you . . . those people?" said Thorold.

"No. Oh no! I was glad to see them. I thought she might be dead."

"The one in the chair?"

"Yes. There was an accident. I never heard the outcome."

"Great friends of yours?"

"I knew them well."

"And yet you did not speak to them. You did not enquire?"

"It is all over. It is a part of my life that is finished."

"I see."

"I feel gay. It makes me happy to have seen her and to know that she did not die. I feel that I want to laugh and sing, and that life is not so bad after all . . . even for a lady's maid."

"You are wrapped in mystery. Tell me what you did before you came here."

"I was in a convent."

"You told me that."

"I was in the country for a long time, and then I left and I . . . Well, they wanted me to marry someone and I did not want to. Then . . . I came away. Shall we go from here? I would rather not be in the Park now. I would rather go where I have never been before."

"Just say where you want to go and I'll take you there."

She remembered that Polly had told her how her father and mother had met in a pleasure garden. She had only been to such a place once and she longed to do so again.

"To a pleasure garden," she said.

"Let us go to Cremorne then."

"I have never been there. I should greatly like to go."

"Then that is sufficient reason."

Melisande never forgot those hours she spent with Thorold
Randall. It seemed to her then an enchanted afternoon.
Spring was in the air and she felt happier than she had for a
long time. Perhaps she mistook relief for happiness. She was
gay, wildly, hilariously gay, for Caroline was alive. Caroline
had suffered but she was Fermor's wife, and Melisande could
not be sorry for Caroline now.

Thorold Randall could not keep his eyes from her. She
was more beautiful than ever. Her laughter was merry, her
wit quick. It was as though he found in her another person,
even more delightful than the charming girl he had known
hitherto.

They went into the American Bowling Saloon; they sat
and listened to the Chinese orchestra; they explored the crystal grotto and the hermit's cave.

"This is an enchanted place!" cried Melisande.

"I believe you are enchanted," he answered. "I believe
you are not of this world. None was ever so beautiful, Melisande. I must talk to you. You must talk to me. There is so
much we have to say to one another."

"But there is so much to see here . . . so much to do."

"What has happened to you this afternoon?"

"I have found I like being alive."

"Has that anything to do with me?"

"Yes . . . with you and other things."

"I don't want to share with others."

"But you must. There is the sunshine and this delightful
place, for one thing."

"*I* brought you here."

"But you did not bring the sunshine. You took me to the
Park, but . . ."

"It was the lady in the chair who has made you happy."

She said seriously: "Yes. You see I thought she was dead,
and it made me sad to think it. Now I know she is alive and
is cherished, and I am happy because of that."

"There is so much mystery about you, Melisande. Clear
it away for me."

"What does the past matter? We are here and the sun is
shining, and I have found that I am liking life. I do not care
about Mrs. Lavender any more. She may be rude to me,

throw her hairbrush at me . . . but I do not care. I am finding that life, which I did not think could be good, is good again.'' Her eyes were enormous and brilliant. ''And something else. I believe this: That however bad life became for me, however sad I felt, I should be able to make happiness for myself and those who shared it with me.''

''Melisande,'' he said gripping her arm, ''you are an enchantress, I believe. You are not of this world. You are not human.''

''I should like to think so. What if I could work spells . . . turn men into swine! That was Circe, I believe. Although I would not wish to turn men into swine. Why should I? I do not like swine.''

''But you could turn them into whatever you wished them to be.''

''That would be more sensible.''

''You might have turned the man they wished you to marry into someone more acceptable to you. Who were they, Melisande . . . your guardians? Did you have a guardian?''

''Yes, I had a guardian.''

''I wish you would trust me. Anything you told me would be entirely between ourselves.''

''I do trust you. But I cannot tell you who my father was. I have determined that I shall tell no one. I know now that he is a good man, that he has done much for me and that it is solely because of his position that he cannot acknowledge me.''

He was silent for a while; then he took her hand and said: ''Dear Melisande, you must not think me impertinently curious.''

''No, I do not. I too am curious. I want to know so much about the people I meet. I should like to hear more of you.''

''But your background is so fascinating; mine is so ordinary. There is no mystery about my origins. I told you I was orphaned early, and I lived with an aunt and uncle who had their own family to consider. That is not very exciting . . . neither to live nor to talk about.''

''Life is always exciting,'' she said. ''Everything we do goes on and on and affects what others do. Consider that. My father met my mother in a place like this . . . just by chance, and because of that I sit here in such a place with you. In between, certain people did certain things, and each thing fits into a big picture, and because of each little thing, I am what I am.''

He said: ''Will you marry me, Melisande?''

She was astonished. She had known that she was attractive to him, but she had not wished to consider marriage, and because of that she had shut her mind to the idea.

Now she realized that she was not yet free from her nightmares. The idea of marriage frightened her. To think of it was to bring back memories of those men: Léon who had a guilty secret; Andrew Beddoes who had a mercenary motive, and Fermor who had not offered marriage at all.

She said: ''I do not wish for marriage . . . just yet. It is so hard to explain and seems so ungrateful. It is not that I am not fond of you. I am. I shall always remember your kindness at the whist party. But . . . things have happened. It is not very long since I ran away from marriage. You see, I thought he was in love with me, and it was really the dowry my father was giving me. I could not endure that. It was so mercenary . . . such hypocrisy. I do not wish to think of marriage for a long time.''

''You will forgive my tactlessness?''

''But it is not tactlessness. It is kindness.''

''May I ask you again?''

She smiled. ''Will you?''

''I shall go on asking you until you consent. You will one day, won't you?''

''If I were sure of that, I should consent now. How can we be sure? So much has happened to me in such a short time, I think. There were years at the Convent when one day was very like another . . . and then suddenly he came for me . . . my father . . . and everything was different; and since then, although it is not two years, there has been a lifetime of experience, it seems to me. That is why I am bewildered. Too much in too short a time, you understand?''

''And you want a breathing space. I understand perfectly. Melisande, depend on me, rely on me. When that dreadful old woman bullies you, you can walk straight out if you wish to—straight out to me.''

"It is a comfort. I begin to feel very comfortable. But what is the time?"

He drew out his watch and as she looked at it she exclaimed in horror. "I shall have overstayed my time!"

"What does it matter?"

"I may be sent packing right away."

"That is no longer a tragedy."

"But I am still unsure."

"Come on then. We'll make our way back with all speed. When you agree to marry me I want it to be simply because that is what you wish. I want you to be sure."

"I see how well you understand me," she said, "and I am grateful."

He took her arm and they hurried through the gardens and out to the streets.

Listening to the clop-clop of the horse's hoofs as the hansom carried them to the Lavenders' house, Melisande felt that it had been one of the most important afternoons of her life.

She mounted the steps to the house with trepidation. She was an hour late. There would be recriminations. She must keep her temper; she must not be forced to a decision now. If she were to marry Thorold she must be quite clear that it was what she wanted.

She went to the sitting-room, framing an apology. She knocked.

A voice said: "Come in!" and uneasily she entered, for it was not Mrs. Lavender, but Mr. Lavender who had spoken.

He was sitting in an armchair when she entered, smoking a cigar. His quiff of yellow hair fell over his forehead and he was smiling. She felt a tremor of fear. She would have preferred stern looks.

He said: "Ah, Miss Martin. You are looking for Mrs. Lavender?"

"Yes," she said hesitating at the door.

"Come in," he said. "Come in."

She shut the door behind her and advanced two paces. Then she stood there waiting.

He took the big gold watch from his pocket and looked at it. "Why," he said, "you *are* late."

"I am sorry. I came to say that I was delayed."

"Oh? Delayed? I can understand how such a charming young lady as yourself might be delayed."

"I will go to Mrs. Lavender's bedroom. I expect she will be needing me."

"She's resting. There's no reason why she need know you are late. No need at all . . . unless someone tells her."

"Oh . . . I see."

"I wonder if you do?" he said. "But of course you do. You must have realized that I want to help you, to be your friend."

"That is good of you, but . . ."

"But? You are too modest, Miss Martin. Too retiring. I have been wondering why you keep so aloof from me when you are prepared to be so very friendly with Thorold Randall."

"I have no wish to be other than friendly with anyone."

"Oh come now, deliberately misunderstanding! You're cleverer than that. I wish to be very friendly with you, Miss Martin. Very friendly indeed. That's why I want to help you . . . on occasions like the present one. You ought to be grateful to me, you know."

She hated him. There was something in his demeanour which reminded her of Fermor. The peace of the afternoon was completely wrecked. She felt the colour rise to her cheeks as she said sharply: "You must do as you wish about telling Mrs. Lavender that I am late, Mr. Lavender."

"Does that mean that you are not a bit grateful for my kind suggestion?"

"I merely said that you must do as you please about telling her."

"She might decide to dismiss you."

"As you suggest, that is a matter for her to decide."

"It is very difficult, you know, to find posts without references. If you were wise you would not turn away from . . . friends. . . . "

He had risen and was leering at her. She stepped back.

"Now, my dear," he said, "if you will be pleasant to me I will be pleasant to you."

Her fingers were on the door handle. She turned it and said quickly: "I must go."

And she went out.

In her attic she locked the door and leaned against it.

Her afternoon was spoiled. Mr. Lavender with his leers and insinuations had reminded her of the unpleasantness of the world.

Perhaps Mr. Lavender had something to do with her decision. He had not told Mrs. Lavender of her lateness; often she met his eyes and he would seem conspiratorial, as though there was a secret understanding between them. She was afraid of Mr. Lavender. Sometimes in the night she would awaken with a start. Had she remembered to lock her door? She would get out of bed and with immense relief confirm that she had done so. There was really no need to fear that she had not done so. Never did she enter her room without thinking of him, without making sure that she was safe from him.

His eyes followed her; they would seem to say: "We're going to be friends . . . very special friends."

She was afraid of him as the nuns in the Convent had been afraid. She locked her door; they shut themselves away from the world.

During the day he worried her no more than a wasp would have done. If she kept out of his way, made sure that she was prepared against his stings, what trouble could there be! It was only at night that the uneasiness came, and it came in dreams.

Thorold was a frequent visitor at the house; he spent a good deal of time with Mr. Lavender. They went to the races together; sometimes they watched boxing matches; they were interested in all sport. Thorold said that he came to the house only to see her; it was a good thing, he said, that he knew how to interest Archibald Lavender. He was clever too with Mrs. Lavender, so that she was always ready to welcome him.

A few weeks after he had first asked Melisande to marry him he repeated his proposal.

Melisande realized suddenly how empty her life would be if she lost his friendship. Mrs. Chubb, in whom she had confided, thought it was the best thing that had happened to anyone since she herself met Mr. Chubb. Mr. and Mrs. Gunter who saw 'the way the wind was blowing' were equally sure that it was a good thing.

"The fact is," said Mrs. Gunter, "you're not cut out to work for other people, my dear. You ought to be a lady with a maid of your own. That's my view and Gunter's."

It was folly to hesitate. There was tension now between herself and Mr. Lavender. His smile was less pleasant; there was in it a hint of impatience. He was so arrogant, she guessed, that he could not believe that she really disliked him. Her fears of the man were increasing with each day.

And so, when Thorold again asked her to marry him, she accepted the proposal.

His delight was so intense that it was infectious.

As they walked through the Park she felt gay, certain that the future would be good, sure that she had done the right thing.

"We must marry soon," he said.

Only then was she a little uneasy. "I think we should wait a little while."

"But why?"

"To . . . to make sure that it *is* the right thing."

"I know it is the right thing."

"Yes, of course it is, but . . ."

They seemed to mock her, all the other men whom she had known. How can you be sure? they seemed to ask. Haven't you thought at other times that you were doing the right thing? Fermor seemed to ask: "What do you want? To escape from the Lavenders? Think again, Melisande. *I* may be looking for you. *I* may be waiting for you."

Thorold said: "You don't trust me."

"Oh, but I do."

"It worries me. It alarms me. You don't, you know. You won't even tell me the name of your father."

"I have decided I must never tell that to anyone. You see, he cares so much that it should be kept secret."

"I understand how you feel. But to a man who is to be your husband . . . it seems such a little thing to tell."

She said: "He is so proud. He wanted no one to know about my birth. I shall never forget when he discovered that the servants were talking."

"That was in the country, wasn't it?"

"Yes . . . and it was then that I had to go away. You see, he is a good man, a respectable man, and his one lapse must have caused him so much pain and anxiety."

"Perhaps it caused your mother even greater pain and anxiety?"

"Perhaps. But he looked after her as he looked after me. My future was taken care of."

"It must have cost him a good deal; and then he would have given you a dowry."

"He is a rich man."

"And you won't trust me with his name?"

"Please understand me. I want no one to know it through me. Please, Thorold, don't ask me."

He kissed her hand. "Everything shall be as you wish. Now and for ever."

Mrs. Lavender said: "Mr. Lavender and I are going into the country for a few days, Martin."

"Oh yes, Madam."

"I thought of taking you, but I have decided against it. I shall manage without you for two or three nights." Mrs. Lavender looked sharply at Melisande. "Of course I don't expect you to be idle while I'm away. There is my lace dress which needs mending; there is a tear in the skirt. You'll need to be very careful with that. You might go through all my clothes while I'm away. Make sure that everything is in order. And you can wash those nightgowns and petticoats that need it. Oh . . . and make me a flower of those pieces of velvet . . . mauve and green. It will go with my mauve gown."

"Yes, Madam. But I should like to make a black rose for the mauve dress."

"A black one!"

"I think so, Madam."

"Hideous!" said Mrs. Lavender. "Who ever heard of a black rose?"

"Perhaps it is just because one does not hear of them that they seem attractive. Besides, I was thinking how well the black would look on the mauve."

Mrs. Lavender clicked her tongue; but after a while she said: "Well, make the black flower. We can try it."

Melisande felt happy as she packed Mrs. Lavender's bag.

"No need to pack for Mr. Lavender," said Mrs. Lavender. "He'll do that himself."

"Yes, Madam."

She was so happy, she could have sung, but the only songs which came to her mind were those which she had heard Fermor sing. "Go lovely rose" and "The Banks of Allan Water"—and most poignant of all "O, wert thou in the cauld blast."

A feeling of relief swept through the house when the Lavenders left.

"Two days of peace and quiet," said Mrs. Gunter. "That will be nice. Let's drink to the next two days in a glass of my ginger."

Sarah came down and they were very merry.

And that afternoon Thorold called for Melisande, and they walked in the Park together. He looked a little sad, a little melancholy.

"Is something wrong, Thorold?" she asked.

"No . . . not if you love me."

"But I have said I will marry you."

"You told me about the young man your father wished you to marry, and how hurt you were because you realized your dowry had played a deciding factor. I have wondered whether, if you were in a happy home, your future assured, brothers and sisters and fond parents about you . . . you would marry me?"

"Oh, Thorold," she said impulsively, "I am so sorry."

"Forget I said it. If I can be the means of rescuing you from what is uncongenial, I shall be only too glad to do so."

"But . . . I am fond of you. I am sure of it."

"You don't trust me, Melisande."

"But I do. I do."

"Not completely. You won't even tell me the name of your father."

"Oh, Thorold, so it is that! I understand how you feel. It is a hateful feeling. I will tell you my father's name. Of course I will. There shall be no secrets between us. He is Sir Charles Trevenning of Trevenning in Cornwall. He is a man of importance in his own county, and known in London too. You understand why I did not want to tell. Not because I did not trust you, but because I knew that he so ardently wished our relationship to be kept a secret."

"I understand. Of course I understand. You shouldn't have told me, Melisande. I shouldn't have put it like that. But I am glad, glad because you trust me now. We are going to be happy, my darling. Everything will be all right for us now."

That was the end of peace; the end of her brief dream. And now she could wonder at her own folly, at her own naivety which had led her into the trap. There was no excuse this time. It was not her first glimpse of the world. The world was full of evil and she could not, it seemed, learn her lesson.

They met in the Park next day.

Did she notice the difference in him as soon as they met? Was that tenderness, which had warmed and comforted her, replaced by hardness, cupidity, meanness . . . criminality?

"My dear," he said; and he took her hand and kissed it.

They walked arm in arm. She sensed that he was trying to tell her something.

"Melisande," he said at length, "I have a confession to make."

She was startled. She turned to him; he was smiling and she looked in vain for that gentleness which she had loved.

"I am in debt. Deeply in debt. In fact I'm in a bit of a mess."

"Oh, Thorold . . . money?"

"Money, of course. It's that fool Lavender's fault. He has so many tips to give away . . . so many 'certainties'. *He* is all right. He has a rich wife, and he knows how to get round her. Melisande, I'm afraid that if I don't settle up some of these debts I shall have to resign my commission.''

"But surely it's not as bad as that.''

"It's as bad as it can be.''

"You have never mentioned these debts before.''

"I didn't want to worry you. I was afraid you'd despise me. You see, life in the Brigade of Guards is expensive, and for a man with such a small income as I have . . .'' He shrugged his shoulders.

"I suppose so . . . if you bet on horses.''

"One has to be in the swim, you know.''

"I am sorry, Thorold.''

"I knew you would be. . . . That's why I'm sure you'll help me.''

"I . . . help? But I have no money. If I had, gladly would I help.''

He smiled at her. "Why, my dear, you *can* help. There's your dowry. That'll settle everything and set us up nicely.''

"My dowry! I don't understand.''

"But your father was ready to give you a dowry before. He'll do so now.''

"But . . . I do not see him. I . . . I could not accept. I . . . It is so different.''

"It is not different at all. He chose someone for you to marry, and there was a dowry waiting for you. Now you've made your own choice, but the dowry will still be forthcoming.''

"I do not think so.''

"But why not, Melisande? Be reasonable.''

"So you, too, are eager to marry me because I might have a dowry!''

"My dear girl, how did I know your father was a rich man? You only told me yesterday that he is Sir Charles Trevenning.''

"Oh, what a fool I was to tell you that!''

"Listen to me, please, Melisande. I love you. I wanted to marry you the moment I first set eyes on you. I knew there would be difficulties about money. They worried me considerably, so I put off telling you the position. I didn't want to worry you too. And then . . . you tell me that you have a rich father who was ready to give you a dowry. Don't you see! It's like the answer to a prayer."

"How attractive that dowry is!"

"When I asked you to marry me I had no notion that there would be a dowry. You know that. I would be ready to marry you—as you must realize—if you hadn't a penny in the world. But . . . since it is not the case . . . I am delighted. Who wouldn't be—and say so if he were an honest man?"

"I do not wish to talk of this any more."

"Let us be calm. You do believe that if you were penniless I would marry you just the same?"

"I am penniless."

"You need not be when you have a father whose conscience is crying out to be soothed."

"I feel I have met you for the first time to-day."

"Now listen, Melisande."

"I wish to listen no more."

"You must listen to me. You are going to marry me."

"You are wrong. I am not going to marry you."

"You change your mind quickly."

"You have changed it for me."

"Melisande, I understand how you feel. That man hurt your feelings. You have been disillusioned, I know. I understand. But I love you. I want to take you away from that impossible woman, but for God's sake let us be reasonable. I'm in low water. A little money could put me right. Your father is wealthy. A thousand or so would mean nothing to him. He ought to give you an income. He owes it to you. Why shouldn't he, and why shouldn't we accept it?"

"Goodbye," she said firmly.

Now he was angry. "You are a fool, Melisande. An adorable fool, it's true, but nevertheless a fool. You have such crazy notions. He will be glad . . . glad to do this."

"He will not be glad, and there shall be no question of his doing it. He shall never hear of it."

"My dear girl, don't you understand, he'll be relieved to hear of you. He's wondering what's happened to you."

"I despise you," she cried. "I see right through you. 'You don't trust me!' you said. 'Tell me his name.' And now, because I have been a fool, you know it . . . and you are threatening me . . . and him.''

"I? Threatening! My dear, you're becoming hysterical.''

"I hate you. I hate all men. You are all evil . . . every one of you. I wish I had stayed in the Convent. I wish I had never met any of you.''

"My dear, you are attracting attention. I beg of you, speak more quietly. Now . . . you are not looking at this clearly.''

She allowed him to lead her to a seat and she sat down.

"I *am* looking at it clearly.''

"But he owes it to you. He would, I am sure, be pleased to help you.''

"I will not ask him for money.''

"Think of our future, Melisande.''

"You and I have no future together.''

"You don't mean that. I love you and you love me. Now, listen. Meet me here in the Park to-morrow . . . at this time . . . at this spot. I am sure when you are calmer, when you have thought this out, you will see my point.''

"I never shall. And I never want to see you again.''

"Melisande, I beg of you, be reasonable.''

"I am being reasonable, and my reason tells me to despise you.''

"But you and I are to marry. We are not rich and I have been foolish. You have a rich father . . .''

"You will have to settle your affairs without my rich father.''

"Now, Melisande, please . . .''

"I shall never allow you to ask him for money.''

There was a short silence, then he said slowly: "I could ask *without* your consent, you know.''

She turned to look at him in astonishment. "You think he would give my dowry to a man whom I had decided not to marry!''

"No. But he might give the equivalent of the dowry to a man who knows that he has an illegitimate daughter.''

She had turned pale. She stood up. She wanted to move away quickly, but her trembling legs would not allow her to do so.

"You . . . would never do that!''

"Of course, Melisande, of course I would not.'' He stood up beside her and gripped her arm.

"But . . . that is *blackmail*!"

She wanted to throw him off, to run away, never to see his face again. But he was holding her fast.

She thought of Sir Charles at Trevenning receiving a threatening letter and thinking that she had had a hand in it. And she had! She had been foolish to trust this man with her father's name.

She was bewildered and frightened. She was as terrified of Thorold Randall as she was of Archibald Lavender. Here was another of those monsters to disturb her dreams.

Be calm! she admonished herself. This man is dangerous. He is worse than the hypocrite Andrew Beddoes was; he is more than the philanderer that Archibald Lavender is; he is a blackmailer as well. All men are liars; all men are cheats. Oh God, what have I done?

Thorold was now speaking in the gentle voice she knew so well.

"So you see, my darling, you are wrong to put ugly words to this. It is reasonable. It is natural. All fathers give their daughters dowries if they have the money. And think how useful yours will be to us! You meet me to-morrow and I will have the letter ready then. I will show it to you and you will copy it. Then we will send it. You shall sign it with loving assurances. And then . . . you will see how friendly he will be, how ready to help."

She did not answer him.

He went on to talk of their future, of the little house they would have, of how happy she would be when he had rescued her from servitude with the Lavenders.

He left her at the door of the house.

"Goodbye, my love, until to-morrow. Do not forget . . . the same place in the Park. Our seat, eh? And do not worry. I understand what a forthright soul you are. I know you did not mean all the hard things you said. I understand you . . . and *you* understand now, don't you? Don't you, my love?"

"I understand," said Melisande.

What shall I do now? she asked herself. What *can* I do? Whose advice could she ask? There was Mrs. Chubb. Now how could simple Mrs. Chubb deal with a situation like this? The Gunters? Sarah? How could they help?

There was no one to whom she could go. She must act by herself. Between now and to-morrow she must find some means of preventing Thorold Randall from getting into touch with her father.

Perhaps she could appeal again to his sense of decency? But had he any sense of decency? She did not think so. She could hear the words he had spoken this afternoon; she could not forget them. Perhaps she could reply to this threats with threats of her own. How? What? There *had* been threats this afternoon, and there was one thing which stood out among all others: If she would not write to her father, he would. That would be blackmail . . . simple blackmail. She would not endure it. She must think of a way.

Thoughts chased each other round and round in her head. She was subdued before the Gunters and Sarah. She did not want them to ask questions. She would have to take meals with them in the basement room as they had arranged, while the Lavenders were away. She was wondering whether she could go to Cornwall, see Sir Charles, explain to him what had happened, and beg him to advise her.

Perhaps she would do that if she could not make Thorold see reason to-morrow afternoon.

But to-morrow she would reason with him. There would still be time. He would do nothing until after their meeting. That thought made her feel calmer. There was a short breathing space.

After supper, eaten in the basement room where her lack of appetite gave rise to the Gunters' concern, she went up to Mrs. Lavender's room to make the black velvet flower. She was glad she had something definite to do. She tried to give all her attention to the black velvet petals. It was growing dark, so she lighted the lamp and drew the curtains.

While she was intent on her work the door opened suddenly.

Without looking up, she said: "Oh, Sarah, I lighted the lamp. It was so dark I could scarcely see."

"It is getting dark," said Mr. Lavender.

She stood up in alarm. He was standing by the door, his hat and cane in his hand, and he was smiling at her.

"You look startled, my dear," he said; and he laid the hat and cane on the table.

The throbbing pulse in her throat made it difficult for her to find words. She stammered: "Oh . . . I had no idea that you would be back to-night. Mrs. Lavender . . ."

"Has not come back to-night. I had business in town to attend to."

"Oh . . . I see. I'll move these things."

"There's no need to be in such a hurry."

"You will be wanting . . ."

"To have a little talk with you," he said blandly.

"I'm sorry, Mr. Lavender, but I have not the time. I must be getting . . ."

"Oh now," he said, "you don't want to run away. There's no need, is there, with Mrs. Lavender away."

She felt the waves of hysteria rising. Another time, she thought, I should know how to act. But it is too soon after this other matter. It's too incongruous . . . too bewildering. I am going to laugh . . . or cry.

She heard herself beginning to laugh.

"That's better," he said. "I flatter myself I arranged this very neatly."

"I have no doubt you arranged it neatly," she said on a rising note of laughter. "I must leave you now."

"Oh no. You must not be so stand-offish. You have been stand-offish too long."

"Have I?" she said. "Have I?"

"Yes, far too long. Oh, I understand. You're a nice girl . . . a very nice girl. But everything is safe, you see. Mrs. Lavender is in the country."

"I shall soon be safe in my room . . . and you in yours."

She saw the ugly light in his eyes a second before he turned swiftly and locked the door. He put the key in his pocket.

She said: "Unlock the door, Mr. Lavender."

"I certainly shall not," he said. "Not yet . . . at least."

"If you do not, I shall call for help."

"No one would hear. The Gunters and Sarah never would. They're right down in the basement."

"You must have gone mad, Mr. Lavender."

"Well, you have been somewhat maddening, you know."

"I am also strong," she said. "I can bite and kick as well as scream."

He took a step towards her. "I, too, am strong," he said. "Oh come, don't play at this game of reluctance. I know your sort."

"You do not, Mr. Lavender. But I know yours. I loathe you. I despise you. I shall tell Mrs. Lavender how you have behaved."

"She would never believe you."

"But she must know what you are." She was very frightened. He was coming towards her, slowly, stealthily. "Give me the key!" she cried hysterically. "Give me the key!"

He was no longer smiling. She could see the animal lust in his face. She could also see his determination, and she was afraid as she had never before been in the whole of her life. She took a step backward and gripped the table behind her, and as she did so, her fingers touched the drawer. She remembered the pearl-handled pistol. In half a second she had opened the drawer.

She held the pistol firmly.

"Now," she said, "you will stand back."

He gasped and stood still where he was. "Put that down, you little fool!" he cried. "It's loaded."

"I know it is."

"Put it down. Put it down."

"Give me the key."

"Put that down, I said."

"And I said, 'Give me the key.' If you don't, I will shoot you."

"You wouldn't dare."

"I'll give you three seconds."

"By God," he said, "I believe you would. You look wild enough."

"I am wild enough. I am wild enough to kill men like you at this moment. Give me the key."

He brought it out of his pocket.

"Throw it. Here. I give you three seconds, remember."

He threw it, and she kept the pistol pointed at him while she picked it up.

Still covering him, she went to the door and cautiously opened it.

She ran up to the attic and, turning the key in the lock, leaned against the door, looking at the pistol in her hand.

How did she live through that night? She did not know. Desperately, behind the locked door of the attic, she tried to make plans. She was quite certain that she must not spend another night in this house. She must get away somewhere . . . anywhere.

But first she had to see Thorold. She had to prevent his blackmailing her father. That was the most important thing. He was the greater menace. Archibald Lavender was a lustful brute; she despised him and he terrified her; but Thorold Randall was a criminal, and moreover she had played into his hands. She was involved.

She took out the pearl-handled pistol. It was so small that it looked like a toy. What power! When she thought of how it had saved her, she murmured: "My friend!" And half laughing, half crying: "My dear little friend!"

She knew she could not sleep. She did not even undress. She lay on the bed, watching the door with the pistol in her hand.

She had never before lived through such a night.

But Archibald Lavender did not attempt to come to her room. He was afraid, Melisande knew, afraid of her determination and her dear little friend.

Desperately she planned. She must meet Thorold and do everything in her power to prevent his writing to her father. She believed she could do that. She could not believe that Thorold was, at heart, a wicked man. The man she had agreed to marry was kind and considerate; it was because of those very qualities that she had agreed to marry him. But he was in debt, in difficulties, and because of that he had lost his head.

She would not marry him now. That would be quite impossible; but she would not believe that he was a real criminal. His plans had been made on the spur of the moment.

They were not the result of deliberate scheming. She feared and hated all men. The nuns were right. But she believed that some men were weak rather than wicked.

After she had seen him, after she had made him see reason, made him swear that he would not write to her father, what then?

She thought of Fenella, friendly and kind and, above all, tolerant. Perhaps she would go to Fenella and try to explain why she had run away.

This seemed her only course.

At last morning came. She slipped the pistol into the pocket of her dress and cautiously unlocked the door.

There was no sound in the upper part of the house.

She went down to breakfast in the basement room. She tried to act normally; she was most anxious that the Gunters and Sarah should not know how disturbed she was. She could not talk of her fears, and they would not be able to prevent themselves asking questions if they guessed something was wrong.

"*He* must have come home last night," Mrs. Gunter said, as Melisande sat down at the table. "Come in very quiet, he did. Rang the bell this morning and asked for his breakfast. Sarah said he seemed in a bit of a paddy. Quarrelled with *her*, I reckon, and come home in a huff."

"Oh!" said Melisande.

"She'll be home this evening, so he said. We ought to make the most of to-day, eh?"

"Oh yes," said Melisande.

It was difficult to eat, but she managed to force down some of the food.

After breakfast she returned to her room and got her things together. There was not very much. After she had seen Thorold she would have to come back for them, slip quietly upstairs and out again.

She touched the pistol in her pocket; she would not let that out of her possession until she felt herself to be safe from Archibald Lavender.

He had gone out, the Gunters told her. He said he would not be back until evening.

But he might come back unexpectedly, thought Melisande. She had seen more than desire in his eyes; she had seen vindictiveness, the desire for revenge.

The long morning crept by. There was the midday meal to be endured.

"My word," said Mrs. Gunter, "you've got a poor appetite."

"Yes, I'm afraid so."

"That won't do, you know . . . a growing girl like you. It's the thought of her coming back, is it?"

"It might be."

"Oh, you don't want to worry. You'll be all right. I reckon she's pleased with the work you do. Don't want to take too much notice of what she *says*. She couldn't say she was pleased, to save her life."

Melisande went to Mrs. Gunter and put her arms about her. "Oh, Mrs. Gunter," she said, "I shall always remember how kind you have been to me."

"Here! Here!" said Mrs. Gunter; and she thought: These foreigners! All up in the air—laughing one minute, crying the next. I don't know. You don't know where you are with 'em. She's nice though. I like her.

Melisande kissed Mrs. Gunter solemnly on each cheek.

"Well," said Mrs. Gunter. "Well! Well! You seem a bit upset, dear. Anyone would think you was going on a journey."

"It is just that I wish to say . . . thank you . . . and Mr. Gunter and Sarah who have made me so happy in this little room."

"Well, that is nice! We've liked having you here with us. We hope you'll be happy when you get married, and I'm sure you will, for a nicer gentleman there couldn't be, and you deserve him. That's what I said to Gunter: 'A nicer gentleman I never set eyes on, and Miss Martin deserves every bit of her good fortune!' "

"Perhaps we all deserve whatever we get in this life," said Melisande.

"Oh, I wouldn't say that. There's some of us not so lucky."

"I must go," said Melisande. "I have much to do. I just wished you to know that you have made me happy in your room."

"Well, you're welcome," said Mrs. Gunter. "See you later, dear."

Melisande did not answer that. She went up to her room. Her few possessions were already in the bag which she had bought, ready to be picked up. She pushed the bag under her bed.

She put on her cloak and bonnet and went out of the house to her appointment with Thorold in Hyde Park.

He was there first. She saw him pacing up and down as she approached.

"Melisande . . . how glad I am you've come!"

He seized both her hands; she withdrew them quickly.

"You thought I would break my promise?"

"You were a bit upset yesterday. Ah, I see you are feeling better to-day. You've thought about it, I know. You see the point."

"I see it all very clearly," she said. "Thorold, you are in difficulties and you are worried."

"That's so."

"And because of that you have thought of this thing. You were not serious yesterday. I know it."

"Now, look here, Melisande. You've been foolish. It's only right that your father should provide for you."

"And for you too?"

"Well, we're to be married. I'll be his son-in-law."

"You never shall!"

"I thought you were going to see sense."

"I do see sense. I see that, even after what you said to me yesterday, I am still a fool. I did not believe you could be as bad as you seemed."

"Oh, do stop this nonsense. Who's bad? Who's good? Was your father such an angel when he seduced that poor girl?"

"Stop it. What do you know of such things?"

"Don't be hysterical again, Melisande. Let us sit down. Here is the letter I've drafted. I want you to copy it and send it to your father. Read it. It says you have met a man with whom you have fallen in love. You want to marry, and you are sure that he will help you now as he wished to do before."

She took the letter and without glancing at it tore it into pieces. She threw them over her shoulder and the breeze caught them and played with them. She stood up. She was aware of his face, ugly in anger.

"So that is all you have to say?"

"I shall never write to my father asking him for money," she said. "I shall never see you again after to-day. Good-bye."

He caught her by the arm and pulled her round to face him. His mouth was twitching, his eyes blazing. What a different man this was from the one she had thought she would marry!

"You are . . . offensive to me," she said. "Release me at once."

"Do you think I shall let you go like this?"

"You have no alternative."

"Do you think this is the end of the matter?"

"It shall be the end," she said.

"You're a fool. You and I could live in comfort for the rest of our lives. He is a rich man . . . a very rich man. I have looked into that. He could give us a regular allowance. We need do nothing but enjoy life. And why shouldn't he? He would, you can be sure. He'd pay any amount rather than it should be known that he's not all that people think him."

"So," she said, "you are telling me that you are a black-mailer."

"Why shouldn't he pay for his sins?"

As she studied his face it seemed to her that he was all evil, and that he was symbolic of Man.

She said quietly: "You will never write to my father. You will never blackmail him."

"Don't be silly. If you won't come in . . . well then, stay out. Do I need your help so much? You've told me all I want to know."

"No!" she cried. "Please . . . *please* don't do this. Please do not."

"What! Throw away a chance like this? You're mad. You're crazy."

She felt dizzy. She was aware of the shouts of the children

a long way off. "Oh God," she prayed, "help me. Help me to stop him. He must not do this."

And then she remembered the pistol. Impulsive as she ever had been, she thought of nothing now but the need to save her father from this man's persecution. The pistol had saved her from Archibald Lavender. Could it not save her father from Thorold Randall?

She took it out.

"Swear," she said very quietly and very determinedly, "that you will not attempt to get into touch with my father."

"You idiot!" he cried. "What's that! Don't be a fool, Melisande."

"Swear!" she cried hysterically. "Swear! Swear!"

"Don't be a fool. What is that thing? Do you think to frighten me with a child's toy? Melisande, I love you. We'll be happy together, and we'll live comfortably all our lives. Your father will see to that. And if you won't . . . well, you see, don't you, that I can get along without you. But I'd rather you were with me, darling. I'd rather you were with me and would be sensible."

"Swear," she cried. "Swear."

He had laid his hand on her arm.

"Do you think I'm as muddle-headed as you? I'd never give up a chance like this . . . never!"

She threw off his arm and raised the pistol. It was so easy because he was near.

There was a sharp crack as she pulled the trigger.

Thorold was lying on the ground, bleeding.

She stood there, still holding the pistol in her hand.

She heard voices; people were running towards her. Dazed and bewildered, she waited.

PART FIVE

The Condemned Cell

One

They were watching, these strangers. They had brought her to this place, but they would not let her rest.

She had felt listless as they drove into the cobbled courtyard. There were two men, one on either side of her, watching, ready to seize her if she tried to escape.

They need not have feared. She had no intention of escaping, no desire to do so.

They put her into a room with strange women; some had frightened faces; others had cruel faces. All looked at her curiously, but she did not care.

There was straw on the floor; it was cold and there was a smell of sweat and unwashed bodies. At another time she would have felt nauseated; now she could only think: This is the end. My troubles are over.

She sat on the bench and stared at her hands in her lap.

Someone sidled up to her.

"What you in for, dearie?"

There were others crowding round her.

She said: "I killed a man."

They were astonished. They fell away from her in shocked surprise.

She killed a man. She was a murderess.

They took her away to question her.

"You shot this man. Why?"

"Because I wished to."

"Was he your lover?"

"There had been talk of marriage."

"And he was trying to . . . break away? Was that it?"

"He was not trying to break away."

"But you shot him?"

"I shot him."

"For what reason?"

"Because it was better that he should die."

"Do you know that you have committed a capital offence?"

"Yes."

"Do you not want to say something in your defence?"

"No."

"You must want to make a statement."

"I made my statement. I shot him. It is better that he should die."

"You may not shoot a man just because you think he ought to die."

She was silent.

"Look here, we want to help you. You'll want to put up a defence."

"There is no defence. I shot him. I would do the same again. It was necessary that he should die."

She would say no more than that. She was waiting now . . . waiting for the end and the hangman's rope.

In the cell nobody molested her. 'The Queer One' they called her. She had shot a man in Hyde Park and wouldn't say why, except that she wanted him to die. She was certainly a queer one.

She would sit thinking and sometimes smile to herself.

It seemed such a short while ago that she was at the Convent; she had been alive only a short time. Eighteen years. It was not very long to have lived, to have been deceived, to have grown tired of life and to have committed murder.

Always with her were thoughts of the nun who had haunted her childhood. Now there seemed a significance in that haunting. Hers was a similar case. They would take her out and hang her outside Newgate Jail; men and women would come to see her hanged. They would say: "That is Melisande St. Martin, the girl from the Convent who shot a man." They would laugh perhaps and shout insults.

It was not such a cruel fate as that which had befallen the nun. She would not be walled in to die slowly. The noose would be put about her neck and she would pass on to a new life.

One of the warders came to her. He bent over and shook her by the arm.

"Come this way," he said. "You're wanted."

She rose mechanically. More questions then? It did not matter. She would not tell them why she had killed him. If she did, his death would have been in vain. No one should know that she was Sir Charles Trevenning's daughter and that she had killed to preserve his secret.

She followed the man through corridors, up staircases. She did not care where they took her; she did not care what they asked her. She would be firm in her decision to remain silent.

She was taken into a room and the door was locked behind her. A man rose. Her calm deserted her then. She put her hands to her eyes to brush away a vision which she did not believe to be real.

"Melisande!" Fermor came towards her; he had taken her hands; he was holding her against him.

All the numbness was deserting her now. She was becoming alive again. Life and Death seemed to be in that room—and Life was becoming attractive again.

"Why . . . why did you come?" she stammered.

"Why! Did you think I would not? As soon as I knew . . . as soon as I heard. I have been looking for you . . . searching for you. Why did you run away . . . completely lose yourself?"

She threw back her head and looked at him. Now she could do so without fear. She was lost. Death was already claiming her and Fermor belonged to life.

"I am glad . . . so glad you came," she said.

"Certainly I came." His eyes flashed. She had forgotten the power of him. "We've got to get you out of this mess. We've got to get you out of this place."

"This is prison," she said. "This is where felons are put. How can you get me out of here? I shot a man."

"Why? Why? We must build up a defence. We're going

to have the best possible people working on this. You don't think we're going to let . . . to let . . .''

"To let them hang me? You can't stop them, Fermor. I shot a man. I am a murderess.''

"Why, Melisande? *You!* To kill! It's incredible. I don't believe it. It was self-defence. They cannot hang you for doing it in self-defence. We're going to have the best lawyers in England.''

She smiled slowly. "Then you really love me, Fermor?''

He took her face in his hands and kissed it—not in the way she expected him to kiss, but tenderly as he had done once or twice in the past.

"Melisande . . . Melisande . . . why did this happen? How did this happen? Why did you run away? I searched everywhere. I was frantic. I was still searching . . . all these months. At least through this I have found you.''

"We found each other too late, Fermor. If we had known what would happen, perhaps we should have arranged our lives differently in the beginning. But why talk of that now? I am glad you came. I shall always remember it. When I am on the platform . . . and the people are round me watching me . . . when my last moments are upon me I shall say: 'He came to me in the end. He cared enough for that. . . .' ''

He shook her. "For Heaven's sake, stop! It shall never get to that. You are going to be free.''

"It cannot be. I am guilty. I am a murderess. . . . I thought I was when I saw Caroline carried away, but then I saw her in the Park and I knew that I was not. I did not know then that very soon I should be . . .''

"Don't!'' he commanded. "You're hysterical. Now they won't give us long. I want to know everything. Then I shall send the best possible lawyer to you. I am going to get you out of this.''

"But how can you?''

"Money can do a good deal.''

"But not that . . . not that.''

"I shall spend everything I have on this if need be. And then . . . I shall find means of getting more.''

"Oh Fermor,'' she said, "you were the best one. I didn't

see it. You laughed at goodness, at virtue. You were the wicked one, I thought; but now I am not so sure.''

''There's no time for such talk. Suffice it that I have found you, and now there'll be no more running away. I am going to get you out of this. I will. I swear it. Nothing shall stop me.''

''Fermor, you make me wish . . . you make me want to live . . . and I was reconciled to dying.''

''I won't have you speak such nonsense. You're not going to die. It was in self-defence. That's all you have to say. He was threatening you with the pistol and it went off. That is what you must say.''

''But it was not so, Fermor. It is something of which I cannot tell you. I killed him. Deliberately I raised the pistol which I had taken from my employer's drawer. I lifted it and killed him because . . . because I wanted him to die.''

''He had threatened you. He had threatened to kill you. It was self-defence.''

''No, Fermor. No!''

''Listen, Melisande. There will be a trial. Everything that can be done, shall be done. There are ways—have no doubt of that—and I shall find them.''

''Fermor,'' she said, ''why? It is better that I should be here. What good is there in life?''

''This is madness! What good? You will be with me—that is the good which will come out of this, and I shall not be searching for you ceaselessly.''

''And Caroline . . . your wife?''

''She is grieved. She blames herself in some way.''

''She . . . she blames herself! How does she know? What does she know?''

''She knows what she reads in the papers.''

''It is in the papers then?''

''People are talking about the mysterious shooting in Hyde Park. They are all saying that he was your lover, that he had promised you marriage and jilted you.''

She laughed.

''Was it so? Was it so?''

''I can answer that. It was not so.''

''What was it, Melisande? Tell me, darling. I must know

the truth. We must know everything. We must be prepared for cross-examination. But do not be afraid. We will have the best men on our side. Everything that I can do shall be done, and, believe me, I can do a good deal. I have friends who will move Heaven and Earth. Melisande, do not be afraid. Tell me everything. I tell you, I can get you out of this. I can save you.''

She said: ''There is so much I want to know. I did not think I cared, but I do. Caroline . . . is she very ill?''

''She was badly hurt. She walks with difficulty.''

''Ah . . . I did that.''

''Nonsense! She did it herself.''

''And you, Fermor . . . you and Caroline? How is life between you?''

''How can it be anything than what it is . . . what it always has been.''

''I'm sorry.''

''Don't be sorry for others. Be sorry for yourself. You are in a terrible position, my darling. That is why you must be sensible . . . reasonable. We need all our wits if we are to bring this off. We'll do it, never fear. But it is not easy. We have to work at it with all our might and strength, with every means at our disposal.''

''You are so strong,'' she said.

''And here to defend you . . . to make up for everything . . . to show you that I will always be there whenever you want me. Don't be afraid, Melisande. But you must be sensible . . . reasonable.''

''Reasonable . . . sensible! They are always telling me that. It is because I am so unreasonable . . . so far from sensible that things like this happen to me.''

''Now listen, my darling. You've been through an ordeal. At any moment now that door will open and you will be taken back to your cell. I am arranging that you shall have a cell to yourself. I am arranging everything in future. But now, for Heaven's sake, let us waste no more time. We must have our story ready . . . and it has to be fool-proof.''

She was laughing again with that wild laughter which was near to tears.

''Oh, Fermor,'' she said, ''you are not good, are you. You

would cheat your wife . . . you would cheat justice, and yet . . . I wish I could live . . . if it could be with you.''

"Don't laugh like that. Of course you're going to live. I shall send our man along to you and he will tell you what you must say . . . how to conduct yourself. Melisande, you will need all your calm, all your wits; and when you are being questioned by our enemies, you must remember that I am waiting. I shall be there. I shall be where you can see me, and when you look at me, my darling, you will know that I am waiting.''

"Oh, Fermor!'' she said; and quite suddenly she began to weep, for life had ceased to be intolerable and she did not want to die.

Now she saw what she could have done. She could have left the pistol in the house; she could have gone to Fermor; she could have told him of her fears; and then she would not be here now.

She just lay in his arms, unable to speak, unable to think, unable to do anything but weep for the pity of it; and as she wept, the warder came to tell Fermor that he must go.

Andrew Beddoes came to see her.

She was surprised that he should come. He looked neat and just as she remembered him; and yet that anxious expression was something she had never seen before.

He had married, he told her; he had made an excellent match; but he did not forget her. He had come to tell her that he was ready to take on her defence.

"But why?'' she asked. "Why should you do that?''

"Because I wish to do something for you. I have thought of you continually since I last saw you. And now that this has happened, I want to offer you my services.''

She held out her hand to him.

"I misjudged you,'' she said. "I have made so many mistakes. But you must not make one now. You can do nothing for me. I am guilty. I killed this man and I shall have to take the consequences of my act.''

"If you did it in self-defence there would be a term of imprisonment, but your youth . . . your beauty, would, I am sure, make a good impression on the judge and jury. Nobody could believe you guilty of a wanton crime. Believe me, we can hope for leniency. We can have the public with us. You'll be surprised what public support can do. Don't be afraid. We'll work this out together.''

"I shall never forget that you came. I hope you will forgive the harsh things I said to you.''

"There is nothing to forgive. Your ideals were higher than mine.''

"I was so ignorant. I thought men and women were divided into sheep and wolves. I can see now that they are not. What a pity I had to learn such a little thing in such a violent way. But perhaps not. I shall pay for my knowledge with my life. But there will be no more trials, no more lessons of life to learn.''

"Please don't talk like this. You must not be despondent. Your case is far from hopeless. Believe me, a young girl like you has a chance. I have made enquiries. Randall was something of an adventurer, it seems. We can bring in a good case against him, I am sure.''

"Thank you. But I killed him, you know.''

"Tell me the truth. Tell me everything, and we will decide what our case must be.''

"Listen, Mr. Beddoes. I thank you for coming to see me. I shall never forget that you came to see me. There is nothing you can do. I had my own reasons for killing that man. I did it deliberately. I shall tell no one why I did it.''

"If we are going to make a case . . .''

"We are not. I shall go into the dock, and when they ask me if I am guilty or not guilty, I shall say guilty. I shall say I killed Thorold Randall, and my reasons were my own.''

"You must not do that.''

"It is the truth and it is what I shall say.''

"There must have been a good reason. Just tell me the reason. He threatened you? You were jilted by him?''

"No. It is not as simple as that. Goodbye, Mr. Beddoes. I know why you came. It is because you have a feeling, deep in your heart, that you are responsible for the position in which I now find myself. You offered me marriage, and it was because I was to have a dowry . . .''

"It was not only that. I was fond of you. I was delighted at the prospect of marrying you. . . ."

"I believe you, Mr. Beddoes. And you have an uncomfortable feeling that, because of what you did, you may in some measure have contributed to what has happened to me. Please don't feel like that. It has nothing to do with you, believe me. You are exonerated. And one of my most cherished memories will be that you came here and offered your help. You have taught me a little more . . . something that I have taken a long time to learn, I am afraid. Thank you for coming, Mr. Beddoes, and do believe me when I say there is nothing you can do for me."

Reluctant and bewildered Andrew Beddoes went away.

There was yet another visitor.

It was no use trying to hide from the world now. All London . . . all England knew that Melisande St. Martin was a prisoner and that she was to face her trial for the murder of Thorold Randall.

So . . . was it surprising that Léon should find her?

He came to tell her that he had never forgotten her, that he had begged Sir Charles and others at Trevenning to tell him where she was. He had put notices in papers begging her to let him know where she was.

"At first I was hurt by your desertion," he said, "and I felt that, since you did not trust me, we were better apart, for I could never convince you of the truth. But after a while I wanted above all things to make you understand."

"The truth, Léon?"

"It was an accident, Melisande. I swear it was an accident. He was wilful; he would go out on that day. I warned him not to venture on to the jetty. But you know how headstrong he was. He never could forget that he was in a way the master; I was the paid companion. I shall always remember that moment of horror, the realization that I was powerless, that if I plunged in I could do nothing. All I could do was run for help . . . and that I did. After that I knew there would be no rest for me until I learned to swim. I wanted to be ready in case I should be in a similar position. I used to think that if I could *save* a person from drowning I would rid myself of the terrible feeling of guilt which obsessed me. That was why I had to learn . . . immediately. I could not bring myself to ask someone to teach me, so I went to the quietest cove and threw myself into the sea. I was determined to swim and . . . I found it easy enough. Every day I did that. Someone saw me, I suppose, told someone else . . . and soon many had seen me. They talked of me; they suspected me. . . . How they love a dramatic story, even if it is not true!''

"Léon, Léon, I misjudged you so. How you must despise me!''

"It was natural to distrust. And then . . . you did not love me, did you, Melisande? Perhaps it would have been different if you had.''

"I do not know. It is so hard to know. Léon, what tragic people we are, you and I!''

"And I talk of my troubles now! Do you know why I have come to see you? It is for this: I am going to save you. It must be possible. I am going to engage the best lawyers and we will fight this. And I will wait, Melisande, however long. You will know that I shall be waiting for you.'' He took her hands and kissed them. "Who knows, this may be a blessing in disguise, for through it I have found you.''

"Léon, I shall not forget what you have said. I shall remember it on the morning I die.''

"Don't speak of death like that.''

"How did I speak of it?''

"Finally. As though it were settled.''

"Léon, I believe it is settled.''

"No, no! Anyone looking at you can see that you are no murderess.''

"But I am. I shot him, Léon. I killed him.''

"He had treated you badly. I have already been talking to a lawyer. We can appeal to the pity of the judge, of the jury and the public. He ill-treated you.''

She was silent.

"I know it,'' he said. "He deserved to die. Your case must be presented to the jury with all the sympathy you deserve. You are so young and beautiful, and anyone, by looking at you, can see that there is no evil in you. This man deserved to die. Melisande, you only have to tell why, and you will be saved. Oh, my dearest, how wonderful it is to find you again! There may be a wait of . . . perhaps some years . . . but I shall be waiting. I shall make your stay in . . . wherever they send you . . . as comfortable as possible. I shall come to see you, write to you, make our plans. You remember we were going to New Orleans? That is where we will go, Melisande. The time will pass; then we'll marry and we'll go away to a new life.''

"You must go without me, Léon."

"Without you! How could I! I had always planned to take you with me."

"You believe in me! You believe in me though I did not believe in you!"

"I love you, remember. Meeting you changed my life. I had forgotten how happy I could be, until I met you; and when you went away, distrusting me . . . I knew that I had never been miserable before, such was the depth of my suffering.''

"And I was to blame! I am to blame for everything. I have been foolish and I do not deserve kindness. Léon, go away and forget me.''

"Now that I have found you! I shall never go away from you again!''

"Go to New Orleans. Build a new life for yourself there. I cannot help you, Léon, because I have killed a man. I must pay the penalty for that.''

"No, no! You despair too easily. Tell me the truth. Tell me what he did to deserve what you did to him. You only have to tell me and, I know, you will be safe.''

Was it true? she wondered. Would people understand if she said to them: "He was about to blackmail my father, and I could not endure it because it was through me that he was in a position to do so?''

They would be sorry for her if he had jilted her. What if they knew she had killed him to save her father's good name?

They would be sorry still. They would punish her, but mildly, because Léon and Fermor would have the best men to defend her.

But how could she say this without divulging her father's

name! And if she did that it would seem that she had killed
Thorold Randall in vain.

"Melisande," Léon was saying, "you must not despair.
We will fight this together, and I shall be waiting for you . . .
no matter how long."

She wanted to live, how desperately she wanted to live;
yet she was firm in her determination. She would not tell the
truth. She would not mention her father's name. And how
could they—all the best lawyers in the land—work for her if
she would not help them? How could they arouse the public's
pity, how could they plead with the jury, how could they
influence the judge, when she would not tell them why she
had killed Thorold Randall?

She lay in her cell—her own cell. Fermor had arranged that.
Léon had wanted to, but Fermor had forestalled him.

There were letters from Fermor and Léon. There were
more visits. They were right when they said that money could
do most things. It bought them many interviews with her.

They pleaded with her; they stormed at her; they cajoled
and they grew exasperated.

"This silence is madness!" cried Fermor.

He came with his lawyer, the best he could find.

"We must have a sympathetic case," said the lawyer. "If
you plead guilty and offer no defence, the verdict is a fore-
gone conclusion."

"Don't be an idiot!" stormed Fermor. "Speak . . . speak
. . . you little fool! What did he do to you? Why did you
shoot him?"

She often thought of those little scraps of paper which had
fluttered away on the breeze. If someone could have found
them and pieced them together, they would have the answer
to the mystery.

She would never give it.

There came that day which she had dreaded and for which
she yet longed. It was the beginning of the end.

She saw them in the court—Fermor, Léon; and there was
Genevra with Clotilde and Polly—and yes, Fenella herself!

They all seemed so remote; she was scarcely aware of

them. They belonged to another life, it seemed—the life before she had known Thorold Randall.

She looked indifferently at the judge and the jury. She listened to the procedure. It was short. It had to be short, for there was no defence.

She was addressed: "Prisoner at the Bar, you stand accused of the murder of Thorold Randall. Are you Guilty or Not Guilty?"

And she answered as clearly as she had intended: "Guilty."

She did not hear the words which were spoken. Her memories were passing before her eyes in a succession of rapid pictures: Sir Charles outside the *auberge*; their meeting in the Convent; Paris and the dress shop; Trevenning: Fermor and Léon there; Fenella's salon; Fermor in the little house which he had provided for her; Fermor loving, Fermor tender, Fermor fierce, Fermor mocking. She saw Mr. Lavender, leering at her, and she remembered the moment when her fingers had first closed over the pearl-handled pistol—her friend which had saved her from Mr. Lavender, which had saved her for death. She was in the Park facing Thorold. "You shall not . . . you *shall* not. . . . Swear to me . . . Swear. . . ." And that was the end, the end of the story which had begun in Vauxhall Gardens.

At times it had seemed as though it were a comedy, but it was the last act that decided.

The judge was putting on the black cap. Vaguely she heard those dreadful words: "This Court doth ordain you to be taken from hence to the place from whence you came, and from thence to the place of execution, and that you be there hanged by the neck until you are dead. . . . And may the Lord have mercy on your soul."

There was silence in court. She looked at Fermor. His face was blank at first; then suddenly it was angry and determined. He was determined that she should not die. She knew it and exulted in that.

Léon had buried his face in his hands.

And then a wardress was at her side, leading her away.

Two

Fenella was lying on her *chaise longue*. Polly sat beside her. Neither of them spoke. Polly's eyes were red; Fenella had no words to say for she felt that if she attempted to speak her emotions would choke her.

She would never feel completely happy again. This should have been a triumphant time, for Genevra was about to marry her lord; and that was a matter for rejoicing, congratulation and amusement; but how could she feel triumph when one of her girls was to be hanged for murder?

And I, in my way, am to blame, thought Fenella. I did not know her. I did not understand her. So many of us are to blame, and that beautiful child will suffer. There can never be real peace for me again.

Polly buried her head in the shawl which she had placed over Fenella's legs and began to weep again. Fenella touched her head. She said: "Don't, Polly. It's unnerving. Why has she let this happen? Why couldn't she defend herself? They could at least have saved her life. Why, Polly, why?"

Polly looked up. "There was a reason, Madam dear. There must have been a reason why."

"Yes, there was a reason. Fermor could not make her talk . . . even Fermor. Polly, she will haunt me all my days. I shall never forget her. I have been careless with her."

"It wasn't your fault, Madam dear. No one could have been kinder. She ran away from you, but that was because of the young man and his wife. You never did anything you have to feel reproaches for."

"But, Polly, we let her go."

"We tried to find her," said Polly quickly.

"We didn't try hard enough, Polly. We shrugged our

shoulders, didn't we? We said, 'Well, she won't marry Beddoes and there's nothing we can do.' And Polly, we knew, didn't we, that she was meeting Fermor? We ought not to have allowed it. But we liked him. . . . He was charming and we thought it amusing to watch what happened. We were like two children putting spiders in a basin to see what happened. Well, we've seen now. One of them is married to a crippled wife; the other will hang by the neck.''

"No, Madam, don't say it. It can't be. Somebody's got to do something.''

There was a knock on the door. It was Genevra, her eyes swollen.

She said: "There's a gentleman to see you. He won't wait. He's got to see you right away.''

"But I can't see anybody.''

"He says you must. He says it's urgent. It's about her . . . about Melisande.''

He was already in the room; he looked so haggard and old that Fenella scarcely recognized him.

Then she rose and said: "All right. All right, Polly . . . Genevra, leave us together.''

And when the door closed she said: "So, Charles, you have come.''

"I heard the result,'' he said.

"Well?''

"Fenella, we can't let this happen. Something has to be done.''

"Several of those who love her have tried.''

"But . . . it can't happen. How *did* it happen?''

"You have been a long time coming. I thought you would have come before.''

"I never thought that . . . this would happen. I thought . . . as she is so young . . .''

Fenella turned slightly away from him and said: "I take some blame to myself, but I should not like to be in your shoes.''

"She is my daughter,'' he said, "my own child.''

"Your own child . . . and to die on the gallows!''

"Why did she do this! Why did she do such a thing?''

"We don't know and she won't say. But depend upon

it, we all have driven her to it in some way. I with my carelessness . . . I did not look after her as I should. I, with my salon, which is half fashionable drawing-room, half brothel . . . I, who am half mother, half procuress . . . I have had my share in this. Fermor with his desire for her . . . that fool Beddoes . . . that Frenchman who has been here talking until I feel I shall go mad . . . they have all played a part in this. But you . . . you are the chief mourner. On you rests the chief blame.''

"It began by my meeting Millie there in Vauxhall Gardens. It was wrong. It was wicked. This is my punishment.''

"Your punishment! Meeting Millie! What nonsense! Why, you might have had a happy daughter. Poor little Melisande! At first she was the orphan; then she found she had a father who thought so highly of his reputation and his standing that he must send her to a woman like me, because he could think of no other way of ridding himself of her.''

"Stop! Stop! I tried to do what I could for her. I tried to arrange a marriage for her . . .''

"Yes, yes. And she discovered that a young man was being bribed to take her. That turned her to Fermor. No wonder she was tired of the world. No wonder she will not speak. Oh, Charles, I saw her in the dock. She did not seem to be listening to the judge. She was standing calm and quiet, as though her thoughts were far away and she was waiting almost eagerly for death. It was so pitiable. She . . . so young . . . only eighteen! Oh Charles, so young to die . . . and so tragically to want to die.''

"Fenella, there must be something we can do.''

"Charles, you go to her. It will comfort her. You are her father. You go to her. I believe she would wish to see you.''

He shrank from her and she laughed suddenly in mocking anger.

"That would be tragic, wouldn't it? You might be seen. Why is Sir Charles Trevenning visiting a young girl who has been found guilty of murder and sentenced to death? Oh no, you must not be seen. There must be no rumours concerning you. Your daughter can hang by the neck until she is dead, but that is of small account as long as no one knows she is your child.''

"Fenella, I beg of you, be silent. I will go. Of course I will go."

She stood up and stared at him.

He took a few steps towards her, holding out his arms. She ran to him and threw herself against him. She was crying.

He said: "Melisande . . . Melisande . . . my daughter . . . my little girl."

She looked at him, smiling. "We are as we were in Paris. Do you remember? Then I had to pretend . . . that you were my father. You were bringing me from my finishing school, and we pretended, so that people should not talk."

"It was no pretence," he said.

"No," she said, "it was no pretence."

"I did what I thought would be best for us . . . for us both."

She nodded. "Yes. You wanted me to have a husband . . . and a dowry."

"You are trembling."

She answered: "It would have been so much better if you had not talked of a dowry."

She saw how old he had become. Anxiety had put those lines about his face and the shadows under his eyes.

"You should not have come," she said. "So much leaks out. They write in the papers about me."

"It does not matter. It does not matter now."

"But they will wonder why you . . . a man in your position . . . should come here."

"Then they must wonder."

"You must not come again."

"I wish I could stay with you all the time."

"Oh, no, no. It would do no good. I am happy because you came. I always wanted to have a parent. Mother . . . father . . . it did not matter which. All the children in the Convent were like that. Home! They wanted homes. The nuns were good to us . . . but homes . . . fathers . . . mothers, sisters and brothers . . . they were like water in the desert, warmth in the snow, water to the thirsty, food to the hungry. Do you understand?"

"I understand. And I am sorry . . . deeply sorry."

"Why? You must not be sorry. I was one of the lucky ones. There was a little girl, Anne-Marie. Her rich aunt came for her. But you came for me . . . my own father. That was better than a rich aunt. Yet I did not want you to come here."

"Why not? Why not, Melisande?"

"Because people may say: 'Why did he visit her? What is the relationship between them?' And then everything would have been in vain."

"What do you mean . . . in vain?"

"That people must not know. There would be scandal. Think of your life at Trevenning. There you are so respected. Think of your friends . . . your position . . . your relations . . . all those things which mean so much to you. It was because of that that I am here now. It was because of that that I killed him."

"You killed him for that . . . for me . . . ? I don't understand, Melisande."

"It does not matter now, does it? All is over and done. I know now what you have done for me . . . how much. . . . I know what it must have cost you to come to the Convent, to sit outside the *auberge* . . . you, who thought so highly of your position. Yet you came to see me, you ran risks for me. I never forget it. I was hurt when you sent me away from Trevenning. I was hurt because the opinion of the servants meant more to you than my presence there. But now I understand. I understand so much. I have had nothing but kindness from you. I was only your illegitimate daughter, wasn't I? I was not the same as Caroline. And you did so much for me. You were so concerned. You tried to find me a husband and would have given me a dowry. And now you come here and see me, and you risk so much. It grieves me that you should risk so much. It was for you that I killed him. For you . . . and perhaps for myself . . . for my self-respect, I think. Yes, I think that was the main reason. I had betrayed you. I had told him your name and what you were to me . . . and he threatened that he would demand money . . . money from you for the rest of your life."

He was silent, staring at her.

She went on gently: "You must not be upset. It is all over.

I do not think I shall mind dying. It is all over very quickly, they say. And I think they will be gentle with me. Oh, don't, I beg of you . . . I cannot bear to see you weep. You, who are proud and so full of dignity. Please . . . please . . . do not, I beg of you."

But he could not restrain his tears. He put his arms about her and murmured brokenly: "Melisande . . . Melisande . . . my daughter."

It was she who had to comfort him.

They sat round Fenella's table—Fermor, Charles, Léon and Andrew Beddoes.

Fenella looked from one to another, her eyes alert. Charles had come to her from his interview with Melisande, and Fenella had lost no time in summoning the others.

"Now," she cried, "we know the reason. We know why she killed him. Mr. Beddoes, you are a lawyer. What next?"

Andrew said: "If we had known before. . . . If she had spoken. . . . But she has been sentenced to death. . . ."

"It is no use going over what has happened," said Fermor roughly. "What can we do next?"

"If we can save her from death . . ." began Léon.

"*If* we can save her!" cried Fermor. "Of course we can save her. We must save her. If necessary . . ."

Fenella laid a hand on his arm. "Fermor, be calm, my dear. You are thinking of storming the prison, riding away with her. These are modern times and you cannot do such things. But what we can do is consider this quietly, logically, and with all speed. We must approach this in the modern way. We must not think of breaking into her prison, but breaking through rules and regulations. Our means will not be ladders and ropes, but influence in the right quarters. That is how things are done in the modern world. So let us be calm and think clearly."

"He was a blackmailer," said Andrew. "Blackmailers are despised by all decent people. There is little sympathy for them, and leniency is often shown to those who attack them. And in her case it was not even to save herself that she killed this man. She was thinking of her father. If she had said so . . . oh, if only she had told this in the court . . . most certainly it would not have been the death sentence.''

''It is no use saying *If*!'' cried Fermor. ''She has! And what now? What do we do? We sit here saying if . . . if . . . if! How does that help her? We've got to get her out.''

Andrew said: ''She would, of course, be sentenced to a term of imprisonment . . . no matter what motive she had. No one can kill and escape altogether.''

''How long would she . . . ?'' said Léon. ''How long?''

''Ten years perhaps. Who knows?''

''Ten years!'' cried Léon and Fermor together.

Fenella said: ''Now this is not getting us far. Let us deal with the first thing first. She must be reprieved. I have made many friends over the last twenty or thirty years. I have always believed that a word in the right quarter . . . a little discreet suggestion by someone in a high place . . .''

They were all looking at her eagerly.

''Please do not hope for too much,'' she went on. ''I cannot say whether I shall succeed. I can only try. I shall go now . . . at once . . . to see an old friend of mine . . . someone who, I know, will help me if he can. I am going to plead with him . . . beg him . . . go down on my knees to him. I am going to show him how I consider myself involved in this. I am going to tell him the whole story. I am going to make him do all that can be done . . . if I am able to. Charles, I want you to come with me. I want you to wait in the carriage while I see him. I shall not ask you to come in with me at first, but perhaps later I may need you. He will have to know whose daughter she is. I must hold nothing back from him.''

Charles rose and Fenella, standing beside him, laid her hand on his arm.

She said: ''Everybody in this room is fond of her. There is not one of us, I know, who would not do everything in his power to save her.''

''Everything I have . . .'' said Charles.

She looked at him and thought: Your fortune, your name . . . everything. . . . That is how it is with all of us. We are so shallow in our ordinary lives, but when tragedy comes, when there is need to show the best in ourselves, we find that we are, perhaps, a little better than we thought we were.

"If it is a question of money . . ." said Fermor.

Léon put in: "I inherited a fortune. I can . . ."

She waved them back.

"We have money," she said, looking at Fermor and Léon. "We have skill." She looked at Andrew. "And we have the will of a father to save his daughter at all cost to himself. And in addition we have my little bit . . . my friendships . . . my influence. Oh, I have had many friends; too many friends, some say. But can one have too many friends? Come along, Charles."

She turned in her gracious way and looked at the three men who were watching her and Charles. She said: "Wait here. We will come back and tell you the result."

They waited—Fermor, Léon and Andrew. They stood at the window and watched the carriage drive away.

Then they sat down or paced the room while the time passed with maddening sloth.

The news was spreading through London and the country.

She shot him because he was threatening to blackmail her father. The tragic story was exposed, the whole country was indignantly demanding fair play for the young girl who had killed a man to save her father's name.

There were deputations to the Home Secretary. Many men of influence asked him to show leniency. Fenella's friends were with her; and Sir Charles was sparing no effort to save his daughter.

The rich and the influential, the poor and the sentimental, were demanding that the death sentence should not be carried out.

And so at length came the news. There was a reprieve for Melisande St. Martin. Her case must be considered in a new light. She had killed, but in extenuating circumstances; and she was no ordinary murderess.

The news was brought to Melisande.

She was not to die. She was to go to prison for some years, for no one could take a life and go free. Human life was sacred—even the life of the blackmailer.

So she was to live.

"The time will pass," said the woman in uniform. "You'll get used to it. And for good conduct you get a remission of sentence. And with friends outside working for you, you'll be out in six or seven years . . . perhaps less."

Six or seven years! At eighteen, it seemed a lifetime. Five years ago she had been at the Convent, and one day passing the *auberge* she had dropped her *sabot* at the feet of an Englishman; she had thought of that as the beginning.

Now they would take her away to her cell and she would wear the prison clothes, eat the prison food for what would seem a lifetime.

"It will pass," they told her. "You're lucky. Don't you see how lucky? A little while ago they would have sent you to a transport ship. Besides, you've got friends outside to make your lot easy while you're inside . . . and friends who'll be waiting for you when you go out."

There were years in which to think about the future.

Sir Charles had said to her: "You mustn't be afraid any more. I'll do everything I can to make your stay . . . there . . . as comfortable as possible. And when it's over, I'll be there . . . waiting for you . . . waiting to make up . . . waiting with a home for you to come to. . . ."

So she had a father waiting for her; she was indeed one of the lucky ones.

Léon had said: "I will wait for you. The time will soon pass. We'll be married. We'll go to America as we always said we would. I shall be there at the end . . . waiting. . . ."

There were not many who were so loved, who had a home and a husband waiting for them.

Fermor had said: "Don't think I shall let this rest. I shall do everything I can to get you freed. And you know . . . when it's over . . . I'll be waiting. . . ."

It was comforting to think of them.

To be shut away from the world for many years! In a way it would be like being buried alive . . . but not in a granite coffin. She would breathe and eat and think during those years. During them she would leave her girlhood behind and become a woman. Years to live through, to try to understand all those people who had had such an effect on her life.

"Come along," said the woman in uniform.

And they went, their footsteps echoing hollowly in the stone corridor.

It would be like passing through a dark tunnel and it would take her many years to pass through it. But at the end would be waiting those who loved her.

She could not know what would happen to her during those years, but when she was free, one of three ways of life would be open to her. Which would she take?

She felt vaguely comforted. There was no need for impulsive action now. Was there good in everything then? Because of the years she must spend in prison, she would have time to think of the future and the people who loved her.

She seemed to hear their voices echoing in the stone corridor, those who loved her, those who, in their way, had played their parts in putting her where she was—and in saving her life.

Charles, the father who offered his daughter a home; Léon who would be her husband; Fermor who would be her lover.

A wardress opened a cell door.

This was her new home. Here she would sit and dream and think of the past, the present and the future.

The door clanged behind her; the key was turned in the lock.

She closed her eyes and seemed to hear their voices all about her: "Melisande! We are waiting, Melisande."

What do

Philippa Carr

and

Jean Plaidy

have in common?

They are both pseudonyms for bestselling novelist

VICTORIA HOLT!

Discover these historical novels by
JEAN PLAIDY,
who is also VICTORIA HOLT.

Look for these exciting

historical romances by PHILIPPA CARR,

who is also VICTORIA HOLT.

These bestselling novels by
VICTORIA HOLT
are available in your local bookstore.

SEVEN FOR A SECRET

by
Victoria Holt

Her mother's severe illness brings Frederica
Hammond to live with her aunt where she
shares a governess with Tamarisk St. Aubyn,
whose family owns the local estate, and
Rachel Grey, an orphan. The three girls are
inseparable as they grow to womanhood
until seduction, scandal, and murder threaten to tear them apart.

Coming in paperback this fall
from Fawcett Books.